The King's Ancestors

By

Robin Simmons

Contents

Chapter 1   A Balanced Kingdom

Chapter 2   New Secrets

Chapter 3   The Appearance of Evil

Chapter 4   Confronting Your Fears

Chapter 5   The King's Ancestors

Chapter 6   Another Time, Another Place

Chapter 7   The Battle For All Ages

Chapter 8   Undoing The Evil

Chapter 9   Reunion

The King's Ancestors

Book 2 of the Kingdom of Glenfair

Prologue:

"Is everyone here?" Daniel asked. Uriah nodded, they were both appalled at the number of people who secretly came to make the leap in time. There were over forty people who had found out about something that was supposed to be a secret.

"This cannot work," Uriah said. "Surely with all these people here, someone has made a mistake and Layton Teal will find us, and then we are all as good as dead.

"I would rather die than live a moment longer under a tyrant as cruel as Layton," Daniel echoed. "And it seems that everyone else who has gathered here feels the same way."

The scientist, Samuel came over as Daniel spoke, followed by Merry Sheldon.

Looking at the scientist Daniel asked, "Are you sure the stones will work?"

Samuel frowned, "In theory yes, but we have never tried to move this much mass with the isolinear resonating stone before. Everything now depends upon Merry." All three of them looked at Merry Sheldon, the woman who possessed a very rare ability to shift time. All of their plans and hopes rested on her ability to take them and their equipment far away from the iron grasp of Layton Teal.

Daniel gathered the people around the equipment and raised his hand to speak. "If any of you has a doubt about going, now is the time to leave." No one said a word so Daniel continued, "Then it is time for us to go."

"Where are we going?" someone from the back shouted.

Daniel smiled, "We are going back in time, back to where history begins." Then looking at Merry Sheldon he said softly; "Go ahead, take us there Merry."

Merry Sheldon concentrated with all her might on the time and place so far back in time. The isolinear stone glowed and their surroundings began to shimmer and fade. Just when everyone started to feel frightened and lost, their surroundings began to take shape once again. Everyone found themselves standing in the middle of a beautiful, green valley beside a lake, four thousand years in the past. Cheers arose from the people as they realized their dreams of being free had come true. Daniel was congratulating Samuel, and Merry threw her arms around Uriah, hugging him tightly.

"We are free of Layton Teal forever!" she said. Uriah smiled as he held Merry, but the joy was not there. Was it possible to really be free from Layton Teal? Somehow he did not think so....

Chapter 1
A Balanced Kingdom

"When everything goest right, thou shouldest take heed to thyself, for temptation, trials, and disaster follow in the steps of good fortune."

--Chronicles of the Ancients

The story I related in part to you of Glenfair's shaky but noble history, of how the kingdom was almost torn apart by mistrust and then healed, and how a king rose from the nobility to govern his people not with the sword but the heart, is only the beginning of the tales of Raven Kallestor and his friends. An adventure of yet greater peril awaits them all.

So many things had happened to alter Raven Kallestor's life since the great war. Actually it was not a big war as wars go, but it was the only war that Glenfair had ever fought. He had become in that sole battle the hero of Glenfair by defeating the invading army of the Wickshields, and then king of Glenfair after his father's death. Raven had never viewed his actions in the battle as heroic, he had worn some of the armor of the first kings and dukes of Glenfair he had found in his castle. While not making a person immortal, it did give him a great advantage over the conventional armor of the day. Raven tried to reveal that truth when he gave each duke their ancestor's armor, equal to his own, but they still hailed him as a hero.

As transforming as the battle had been for Raven, the greatest change came as he pursued the riddles of the ancients. With the help of his best friend Andrew Crestlaw, his wife Rebekka, and his sister Lorriel, they solved the riddles that led them to the place where the wisdom of the ancients was kept above Brickens' Falls. They not only found the wisdom of the ancients stored there, but an old man named Andronicus who was actually an android left behind by the ancients to watch over the kingdom of Glenfair.

From Andronicus they learned about their inherited talents: Raven's incredible reflexes, and gifts as a warrior in battle. Rebekka's telepathic ability. Andrew with his ability to understand technologies far beyond his day. And lastly, Lorriel, who had inherited the ability to shift time.

Her's was the most fantastic gift, and the most dangerous to use. To travel in time carried grave responsibility which Lorriel had already learned by going back in time to save her mother from the death of a most terrible plague. Although her action did not dramatically affect the kingdom, it had caused considerable pain for her mother and immediate family. This had brought about the formation of the time counsel. The counsel consisted of Raven, Andrew, Rebekka, their mother and Andronicus which would convene before Lorriel would ever attempt to shift time again. This counsel would act in an advisory fashion, trying to determine any adverse effects Lorriel's time travel would have. To this Lorriel agreed after seeing the pain she had inadvertently caused her mother. She promised never to shift time without the counsel convening first.

Just as Lorriel had a time counsel to give wisdom and direction about the possible adverse affects of time travel, so too, King Raven had an advisory counsel to help him with running the kingdom. The counsel was formed at Raven's coronation when he attempted to give the throne to the Crestlaws. They refused to accept it and had rushed Raven back inside the castle for a conference with some of his closest friends. That circle of friends who loved him dearly, was made up of Sauron Crestlaw, his son Andrew, Rebekka Prescott, his sister Lorriel, and Master Fields who was Raven's mentor and weapons instructor. He made them promise two things that day if he was to be their king. One, to be his advisors, and to keep him from making the same mistakes his father had made. And two, for Rebekka Prescott to be his queen. To this they all agreed, especially Rebekka.

What followed was a grand coronation and a double wedding a short time after, for Lorriel his sister and his best friend Andrew Crestlaw were married along with the king and queen.

What Raven Kallestor did not know, was the that his leadership coupled with that of his friends helped to bring about the greatest peace and prosperity Glenfair had ever known in her 1000 year history. This was due in part to the trust he had built between himself and his four dukes, for the kingdom's strength depended on that trust and cooperation. No other kingdom functioned the way Glenfair did. The dukes willingly placed themselves under the king's law and took the guarding of their respective passes very seriously, especially in light of the recent war. In exchange for guarding their passes, each duke was given freedom to rule his lands as he saw fit. Tribute was collected only once a year from each dukeship and was not overly burdensome. The collection took place in the summer for the two southern dukeships and in the fall from the two northern dukeships. Each of these collections proceeded a feast provided by the king. It was easier for the people to pay the tribute when they knew a portion of what they gave went to providing the feasts. The king's summer and fall feasts were a time of great rejoicing and celebration throughout the kingdom, and more so since Raven had become king. Because of this the dukes gladly paid their tribute, but none more gladly than the Crestlaw dukeship, who always gave more than they were asked. They were the most loyal to the throne because their dukeship was given to them by the Kallestors.

The Kallestors had not always been the kingly line, in fact they ruled the northwest dukeship for 600 years, and a family named Brickens were the kings. But about 400 years ago when the Brickens had failed to produce an heir, and the old king had died, Damen Kallestor was chosen to be king by the other dukes. He then gave his vacated dukeship to an honorable but poor family, the Crestlaws who vowed never to forget the generosity of their new king. Thus, for successive generations the Crestlaws pledged loyalty to the Kallestors, leaving the Kallestor crest hanging in the great hall of their castle encircling it with the this pledge:

"To the bearer of this seal we do pledge our allegiance with our lives forever."

Now that Raven had given the Crestlaws the Brickens' former crest, armor and ring, they were even more loyal. Besides this, Andrew and Raven were the best of friends, and Raven looked to Sauron Crestlaw as he would a father.

Thus the land grew and prospered under Raven's rule. The kingdom was not without difficulties or problems, but they were solved justly and with the kingdom's best interest at heart, which brought Raven to the present crisis facing the kingdom.

Balcor Zandel, the duke of the south east was ill and was not expected to live much longer. Raven wondered with the passing of Balcor, how his son Mason would rule the dukeship, for Mason had a hard edge to his character and leaned toward cruelty at times. Not that Raven knew Mason very well at all, but his hardness and cruelty were well known at the summer feast's dueling competitions, where he had injured a few opponents in his duels. Raven remembered his own duel with Mason and the shrewd drawing of the knife that would have surely drawn his blood had not Raven knocked Mason down with an unexpected blow to his chin. Raven had made the best of a bad situation by complementing Mason's smooth quick draw of his knife. This gained Mason's respect and tempered his loss in front of the crowds. How much Mason respected him Raven did not know, but something during the great war came flooding back to his memory. It was during the war counsel their eyes had met and he saw in them, and the nod Mason gave him, that they were fellow warriors in this fight. And when the battle had ended, Mason was the first to recognize the great slaughter Raven had inflicted upon the Wickshields and led the chant, "victory to prince Raven". However, that was many years ago, and this was the time when the power of a dukeship would change hands. Raven believed he still had Mason's respect, but that was not what Raven wanted. He wanted a duke who would be just and kind to his people, and put the welfare of the kingdom ahead of his own ambitions. Of that Raven was not sure, and he had no idea what to do about it either.

At the moment though, there was nothing to do but wait for the inevitable outcome of Balcor's condition, which was surely to end in death. It was not that Raven would not help Balcor recover if he could, he was a good duke and was well loved by his people. Raven had helped people in sickness before by finding a cure for a terrible plague that I had crippled the northeast dukeship. It was Andrew actually who had found the cure by using the wisdom of the ancients which was stored in the machine at the glass mansion above Brickens' Falls where Andronicus lived.

Because of Andrew's grasp of the wisdom of the ancients he had consulted Andrew on what could be done for Balcor. Andrew left for a couple of days with Lorriel and visited Andronicus and searched the wisdom of the ancients. When he returned he wore a grave expression and informed the king that there was little they could do for Balcor's heart condition. When Raven questioned him further he explained there was a medical surgery that could extend Balcor's life and he understood how it was performed. But they had neither the tools nor the skills necessary to perform such a procedure. And even if they could, Andrew believed they should not. For the Ancients had left their medical technology behind to start their life in Glenfair, and to perform such an operation would be too much out of character for the time in which they lived. To this Raven sadly agreed so they all waited for nature to take its course and Balcor's heart to finally give out. Raven knew it would not be long from the last report he had heard on Balcor's condition.

You have lived a good life, Raven thought to himself, an honor to your family name.

Raven leaned on the railing of the balcony that overlooked the courtyard of the king's castle. It was a beautiful day and he was thinking how great life in Glenfair was. There were many demanding duties of a king, but he separated those from his personal life which enabled him to enjoy his family and friends like anyone else.

He heard the steps behind him and greeted Rebekka without turning around, "How is my wonderful wife today, your steps are getting heavier".

As he turned and looked, Rebekka was smiling, her stomach showing the early signs of their child growing within her. He focused on her face and saw the glow that comes from a mother joyful in her pregnancy. Then his eyes caught movement and out from behind her came bounding little Edward. He had just turned five and was a bundle of joy to the both of them. How good God had been to them to give them a son and now a second child was on the way.

Raven always took advantage of these opportunities to share with his son, first his love and second the laws of God that would aid him someday in being king over Glenfair. He kneeled down and took Edward in his arms and hugged him.

He then asked him a question, "Do you like people to be kind and good to you?" Little Edward narrowed his eyes in thought, for he knew this was a teaching question by the way his father had asked it and said; "Yes father I do like people to be kind to me."

"Then," answered Raven, "you must always treat others as you wish them to treat you, do you understand?"

Little Edward nodded and then asked, "What if people are mean to you instead of being kind?"

Raven smiled at the depth of the simple question Edward had asked, "You must always try to be good and kind to people even if they are not kind to you."

"But what if they are really mean, and real bad, and want to hurt you," Little Edward asked.

Now Raven frowned, these were not easy questions simply answered for a young boy, but he had begun this so he would do his best to answer them.

"You must do all you can to settle disputes peacefully, but if that does not work you must protect yourself, your family, or your kingdom from harm by defending them by force if necessary."

Little Edwards eyes grew very large and he said knowingly, "Like the great war?"

"Yes," was all Raven said.

"Did you like fighting in the war?" Edward asked while he squirmed in Raven's arms swinging an imaginary sword.

So Raven put him down and answered softly, for he knew that boys always fight imaginary wars and tended to glorify combat, "No Edward, I did not like the war. People die in war" (he said this to no one in particular as it took his thoughts back to that terrible time).

Little Edward was more subdued now and only said; "Like uncle Edward? You named me after him, did you not father?"

Raven's thoughts were once again focused on his little son as he spoke; "Yes I did. You see, when the Wickshield army came into Glenfair, we asked them to leave peaceably but they would not. So a war was fought to protect the people of Glenfair. Many people died in the battle including your uncle Edward."

"I wish he were still here so I could play with him," Edward said and then ran off to play.

"I do too," Raven said softly.

He then felt in his mind a soft sigh and turned to look at Rebekka who stood there viewing Raven with a tear running down her cheek.

"It never seems to go away does it," Rebekka said of the pain she knew Raven must feel thinking back on Edward's death.

Raven went over to her and wrapped his arms around her. He held her a while saying nothing but feeling her bulging tummy pressed to his.

"It is ok," Raven said, "I do not think about the battle as much as I used to. I try to focus on what we have now."

While saying this he patted her tummy and thought about the blessings of a growing family. He also thought of Andrew and Lorriel and their two children. They had a son, Jason, about the same age as Edward, and a daughter, Lucinda about two years old. The two boys already were good friends and liked playing together very much when they visited each other.

Raven's thoughts were shaken by someone calling to them. Rebekka and Raven turned to see his mother Joanna, who they called aunt Jessica, calling them to breakfast.

It was strange calling her aunt Jessica, but they were used to it now. They did so because everyone else except Lorriel and Andrew thought their mother dead.

Lorriel had gone back in time and had saved their mother's life from a terrible plague, but everyone else in the kingdom thought she had died. A few years later their mother was able to return with Raven from the mansion of glass where Andronicus lived with the new identity as the long lost aunt Jessica.

When Master Fields first met her, and saw the obvious affection between her and Raven he was very uneasy, almost afraid and confided in Raven; "She looks and sounds just like your mother, it is unnatural."

Raven only said; "She has become like a mother to me, and aunt Jessica will be living with us from now on."

He longed to tell Master Fields the whole truth, but knew he needed to wait until the time was right. Now it seemed that the time had slipped away from him and he thought: Soon, Master Fields, I will take you to Andronicus and tell you everything.

Aunt Jessica smiled as she viewed the couple walking toward her hand in hand. She was very hard on Lorriel for isolating her for over

3 years with Andronicus up above Brickens' Falls. She had to endure the knowledge of the battle with the Wickshields, Edward's death and then her husband's. She wept and cried alone during those years, hurting even more because she could not be there for her other two children.

When Lorriel finally came to her she vented that anger and frustration on her for the imposed exile. But now, no trace of that anger remained, it was forgotten in the birth of her grandchildren and the joy of seeing her children happily married.

Raven, likewise had turned out to be a gifted and resourceful king, and she was very proud of him. She was still wearing the smile as she headed off to find little Edward for breakfast.

Midway through breakfast, a messenger entered the great hall and bowed. King Raven motioned for him to approach and deliver his urgent message, already knowing what it would be.

"Mason Zandel has sent me to inform you that his father has passed away in the night. He invites you and the rest of the dukes to honor his father at his burial tomorrow."

Raven nodded and said; "Inform Mason we will come tomorrow to honor the passing of a great duke of Glenfair."

The man saluted the king and spun smartly about face and marched in a military fashion out of the great hall.

Rebekka turned to Raven and said what he was thinking: "What will this mean for the dukes of Glenfair?"

"I do not know," replied Raven. "Tomorrow will reveal to us what Mason intends to do now as duke. I am sure the Crestlaws will come here tonight so we can journey tomorrow together. Lorriel would not miss an opportunity to see you or aunt Jessica, so we should make preparations for their arrival."

Master Fields entered the dinning hall and approached those sitting at the table. He greeted Rebekka, the king and aunt Jessica (feeling more comfortable with her now that time had passed), .

"Sire, I have just heard of Balcor's death and would like to go with you to the funeral if I may."

Raven smiled and said, "Indeed you shall go with us tomorrow, for the Zandels are your relatives and you should be there." Master Fields seemed to relax at this statement as Raven continued to speak "Tonight, after the Crestlaws arrive, I would like you to join us for a meeting."

Master Fields then left to attend other business as Raven turned and spoke to Rebekka, "Talk to Lorriel and inform her of Balcor's death, then make sure they are coming here tonight with Sauron."

Rebekka closed her eyes and concentrated her thoughts, reaching out to Lorriel's mind across the distance of Glenfair and after a long pause said to Raven, "They will be here."

Early evening came and the Crestlaws arrived. Lorriel dismounted quickly, ran up to aunt Jessica and gave her a big hug, then Rebekka and lastly Raven. By that time Andrew and Sauron had dismounted.

When they greeted the king, Raven requested a meeting in his counsel chambers after they had gotten settled.

Soon Raven, Master Fields, Sauron, and Andrew were seated in the counsel chambers discussing tomorrows events. There seemed one looming question before them all, what kind of duke would Mason Zandel be. There had been nothing but cooperation and trust since the war and Raven wanted nothing more than to keep that same peace in Glenfair. He knew that could be quickly ruined by one ambitious duke who did not support the feast or tried to acquire more land than was allotted. Power sometimes had a way of changing people.

Andrew spoke of his concerns with Raven as they discussed Mason's temperament and past reputation for cruelty.

As the young men conversed back and forth the older men kept silent until this was noticed by Raven. "You have not said anything Master Fields or you Sauron."

Master Fields then cleared his throat and spoke: "I hesitate to say anything sire, for Mason Zandel is a relative of mine and I feel perhaps my opinion would be of less use in this discussion."

"Nonsense," replied Raven, "please speak forth your opinion."

Master Fields began again; "It is true that Mason has in the past exhibited a cruel streak, and a hardness in character, but I noticed something about him after the war. I think the war changed him, made him see beyond himself to the greater picture of the whole of Glenfair and not just his little realm. When you explained the advantage the special armor gave you in the battle, it was Mason who spoke up on your behalf. He has been running the affairs of the Zandels since his father was unable, I have heard no evil report from my relatives concerning him."

"Perhaps he has changed," Raven dared to hope. He then looked to Sauron and motioned for him to speak.

Sauron, in his relaxed way began his opinion; "All dukes are subject to the king, and the king is subject to the dukes. It should be made very clear to him that he will be subject to the king's laws, and the rest of the dukes will hold him accountable for any misuse of his position. But be assured of this, we should judge no man until his actions prove him untrue to his dukeship or his king."

Raven nodded gravely remembering the actions of his father against the Crestlaws with no visible proof. He would not follow that path and prejudge Mason before he proved unfit as a duke, on the contrary he would give him more leeway than was necessary to prove himself.

"I agree," Raven stated, "we shall not assume or take any ill action toward Mason unless it is clear he is unfit to rule. We will give him the standard encouragement and instruction which is traditional as we officially declare him duke of the southeast." With that the meeting was adjourned and everyone retired to their quarters.

In their quarters Rebekka questioned him about the meeting and the next day's events. "You are worried about what kind of duke Mason will be, aren't you?"

Raven nodded but did not say anything.

Rebekka smiled and went on, "Before you were king you never thought about what kind of dukes ruled and how they treated their people, but now it is a great concern to you. I know you care for the kingdom greatly and want what is best for her people, it is what makes you a great king. But I think worrying about things before they happen can be too much of a burden for you. Let time take care of some of the matters you can not change."

Raven started to say something but Rebekka held up her hand and continued, "Should I worry about what kind of child we will have? About its health and all of its toes and fingers? Do not misunderstand, I will eat well and get enough rest, but that is all I can do. I must trust God with the rest for that is something I cannot control."

Raven frowned a little and then smiled. That is why he loved Rebekka so much, she always seemed to understand the situation and come right to the point.

"You are right," Raven declared, "I do take some of the responsibilities that belong on the shoulders of God as my own from time to time."

Rebekka then added, "Who knows, maybe Mason will surprise everyone." Then she paused and looked at Raven, "Lorriel and I want to come along tomorrow." And then hastily added; "Your aunt Jessica can watch the children, she loves them so."

Raven nodded and said, "I think that will be fine. You are not too far along with our child and it will not be a hard ride. It has been a while since you and Lorriel have visited without the children around."

Rebekka smiled and hugged Raven and then said, "We had better get some rest."

The next day came early as the group set out for the Zandel dukeship, with Raven riding between Sauron and Andrew, catching up on the latest news in the north part of the kingdom.

Lorriel and Rebekka rode and talked as well which made the time pass much faster. They talked of motherhood and how wonderful life had become for the both of them and the blessings and difficulties of raising royal children.

Lorriel just had to ask Rebekka; "Does Edward ask questions all the time, hard ones to answer?"

Rebekka nodded, "It seems to be this way with our boys, interested in so many things. I think it partly our fault for it being so!"

"How do you think that," Lorriel asked?

"We are the ones who sought out the wisdom of the ancients and had to solve the riddles, doing things others have not done since the ancients lived here. I think some of that has rubbed off on our children."

Lorriel just laughed and said. "I hope so, life has been a great adventure for us and I hope for our children as well."

Soon they could see the Zandel castle ahead and were met by an escort of the Zandel dukeship. Raven viewed this hospitality with interest, not expecting Mason to make such a fuss over their arrival. He would have to wait and see if this was show or genuine hospitality. Raven thought back to the first time he had noticed the genuine joy and gratefulness of the people who surrounded the Crestlaw dukeship. Those people truly honored his family every time he went to the Crestlaws.

Before Raven knew it, the gates loomed up before him and they were entering the court of the Zandel castle. Mason was there waiting for them as they stopped and dismounted.

Women servants came rushing out to help Rebekka down and almost carried her into the castle for refreshment and rest. Raven viewed all of this with a bit of humor, for Rebekka looked back at Raven and frowned because of the attention she was getting. He could barely hear her say to his mind; "What's all this fuss about, I am not a cripple, just with child!"

He was snapped out of this thought however by Mason's bow and greeting, "Your majesty, you do us honor by coming."

He then looked over at the retreating ladies and said, "Queen Rebekka need not have come in her condition."

"Nonsense," Raven said, "she wanted to be here."

"She does honor us and the memory of my father by being here," stated Mason reverently.

Raven glanced at Master Fields and he was looking at this whole situation with his mouth slightly askew but when he caught Raven's eye he snapped it shut and stood more formally.

"Please," Mason said, "refresh yourself in the castle hall while the others arrive for the funeral."

Then he went on to greet Sauron, Andrew and Master Fields. They then entered the castle and once Mason saw that they were attended to, left to wait on other business.

All of them sat in silence for some time until Sauron spoke; "I do not think that kind of greeting was what any of us expected."

Raven and Master Fields nodded, then Raven spoke. "It is a bit confusing when something happens that you do not expect from someone. I do not know if this is for show or if Mason is showing us a side of himself that we never saw before."

There was nothing more to say so everyone waited until the other dukes arrived, and then they proceeded outside in procession for Balcor Zandel's burial. All the dukes and some of their families were present to pay their respects, but what was surprising was the number of people from the Zandel dukeship that were in attendance.

Raven viewed this with interest, for it showed how much the people loved Balcor, and hinted at what kind of duke he had been. When the people had finished speaking and the funeral was over, they made their way back to the castle hall for a meal provided by the Zandel dukeship.

After a while Mason himself entered the hall and thanked everyone for coming to honor his father. Then the remaining dukes and the king called a meeting to appoint Mason to the southeast dukeship.

The appointing by the other dukes and the king was a mere formality and was steeped in tradition, for the dukeship like the kingship was always handed down to the eldest or remaining son. In reality, the other dukes and the king could forcibly remove or refuse someone a dukeship, but it had never happened as far as Raven knew. It also went a long way to showing acceptance and approval to the new duke. As the dukes gathered around Mason for this official recognition they waited for the king to speak.

So Raven began: "We have gathered here Mason, to pay respects to your late father Balcor and to appoint you to the southeast dukeship. We pray that your time as duke will be a prosperous one, and that you will rule your dukeship with justice and compassion. We also adjure you to pledge loyalty to the kingdom of Glenfair, for the strength of this kingdom rests not in might but in the loyalty and unity that the dukes and the king give to it. Without that strength of loyalty and trust among ourselves we would soon become prey to those who would conquer us from the outside, as we have seen in the past war with the Wickshields. We all, including myself as king are subject to the laws of the kingdom, and are accountable to the other dukes. If any of us strays too far from the path of this land's fair laws, the others will hold him accountable and exact from him the penalty due his actions. Do you, Mason Zandel, accept this dukeship under the accountability of your peers?"

Mason started to kneel and answer yes, but instead rose and looked every one in the eye as he spoke:

"All of you know that in the past I have been hard and maybe even cruel in my self ambition. My whole world revolved around me and what I wanted out of life. I thought that by being strong and hard no one would challenge me, and through this course of action, I would get what I wanted out of life. All of that began to change the day King Raven defeated me in the duel at the summer feast years ago. I realized that my strength might not carry me through the way I had thought it always would. But then the people still clapped even though I lost which was at first confusing to me. After contemplating that, I realized they were cheering not for a winner or a looser but for a good duel and the good sportsmanship King Raven showed which I grudgingly returned. Then the war came upon us and I was forced once again to think of something other than my own ambitions. I have to confess, the war changed me, and I believe for the better. I realized for the first time that Glenfair was not just the Zandel dukeship, if one dukeship falls, we all fall with it. The day of the great battle was the first time in my life I fought for something other than myself. When I saw that King Raven risked his life so the whole kingdom could be saved, I decided that I would be that kind of leader in my own dukeship someday."

Then Mason looked Raven in the eye and said, "Tell me if it is not so. You did not believe you would survive the diversion you would cause to give us the opportunity to save Glenfair did you?"

Raven did not answer, although all eyes were now upon him so Mason continued: "We all know what kind of sacrifice the king made that day, and I resolved to follow that kind of leader. And when he gave us our families armor, a special steel equal to his own, I knew he did not want to be better than us but an equal. But because of actions like this, we all know he is not our equal, he is our king, and shows himself to be so. When I returned home I watched my father, Balcor, rule this land. I saw for the first time his justice, his love for our people. When he became ill, many came to visit him because they loved and respected him. I want that same love and respect from my people, and I know now how it is to be won."

And then he said with forceful emotion as he kneeled, "All of you, keep me on the path!"

Raven looked around on the faces of his dukes and their sons. Some were stunned, others smiled, and some of the older men had a tear in their eye, renewing their own commission through Mason's confession.

Raven drew his sword and placed it on the shoulder of Mason and said: "We do as your peers commission you to this dukeship in the sight of God. Rise Duke Mason Zandel."

A cheer arose from the crowd surrounding the dukes as Mason rose and shook hands with those about him.

That was the way of things in Glenfair, sadness often mixed with joy, loss accompanied by gain.

As Raven mused on these things he thought, We have gained another great duke, how wrong I have been about Mason. And then he realized that everyone could change with God's help, thinking of the changes he had gone through years before as well.

Mason invited the king, queen and the Crestlaws to spend the night which they accepted. Mason had many questions to ask Raven about governing and some solutions to problems he faced. Raven gave advice as best he could and answered the questions Mason asked.

And when they had finished Raven made this statement to Mason; "There may come a time again when we need the support and help of all the dukes to save Glenfair."

Mason said without hesitation. "If you call, I shall come to the kingdom's aid, whether foe or pestilence, in famine or prosperity I will endeavor to do my best for Glenfair!"

Raven smiled and said, "I believe you will."

The next day as they were returning to the king's castle, Raven rode beside Sauron and they talked of the previous days events. Sauron could not in his lifetime remember a better acceptance speech by any duke. Raven agreed and confessed his total amazement at Mason's change of heart.

"We live in good days," was all Sauron said in answer to Raven's statement.

"We do indeed," Raven echoed, thinking to himself, how everything in Glenfair was going so well. Peace, growing families, prosperity and another good duke to rule the southeast.

With his mind satisfied with the state of affairs in the kingdom, he turned his attention to collecting the southern tribute in a week at the Prescott dukeship. He would enjoy a visit to his in laws and the hospitality they would offer. It would be like a vacation for his whole family, with little Edward enjoying the visit with his grandparents as well.

Chapter 2
New Secrets

"Mankind will make all kinds of advancement over the years, but one advancement will elude us all; the advancement of human nature, it seems to remain constant through the ages."

                              --The Wisdom of Fathers

        The week went by quickly, and it was time for Raven, Rebekka, and little Edward to head south to the Prescott dukeship to collect the summer tribute. It would be good for Rebekka to see her parents and Edward his grandparents. Master Fields and Aunt Jessica would take care of the affairs at the castle while They were away. So the three of them started south on their horses, Raven in the lead with little Edward sitting in front of him and Rebekka beside on her horse.
        Raven always liked getting out into the open air of Glenfair. He loved the outdoors which brought back plenty of good memories, including the first picnic he ever had with his wife Rebekka. During that outing they had encountered a rogue Tor bull that had charged Raven. The thought made Raven smile, for in the following summer feast he had killed the rogue and its mounted head still hung in the castle.
        Tor were large creatures similar to an ox but with three sharp horns, a very stout one in the middle between the eyes. One wouldn't want to be in the way of a charging Tor because it could gore you from three different angles, unlike an ox which could only hook you from the side. The odd beasts had a low intelligence, and that made them easy game for hunters. It was for this reason the kings of long ago had prohibited the hunting of them in order to prevent their extinction. Only on special occasions, like the king's feasts, could these creatures be hunted for food. These thoughts made him unconsciously scan the horizon for herds of Tor grazing. After a short period he spotted a few in the distance, which also made him look forward to the summer feast where Tor were barbecued with different spices from each dukeship.
        Those thoughts began to make him hungry, even though he had breakfast not long before. They had brought a picnic lunch with them and planned to stop for lunch at the only large rock outcropping in the

valley of Glenfair. It was just the right distance for a lunch stop, being about the middle between the Prescott dukeship and the king's castle.

The bedrock that sprang up from the valley floor was about a mile long and half a mile wide and was called Hades Teeth because of the steep, sharp, jagged points the rocks formed. At one small alcove in the middle of this rock formation was Boiling Spring, a hot water spring that contained air that bubbled up along with the water. It looked at first that the pool where the spring came up was too hot to bathe in, but only the air bubbles made it appear so.

As lunch time approached, they could see Hades Teeth looming before them, and in a short time they were at Boiling Spring. They set their blanket on the ground, spread out their lunch and began to eat. When they had finished, little Edwards eyes were getting heavy so they laid him down on the blanket. When he was asleep they decided to soak in the hot spring. As they both relaxed in the soothing warm water, Raven began to think of what they really had in Glenfair.

No other kingdom he knew of enabled a king to go about unescorted with his family to any place in the entire kingdom, or to soak in a hot springs undisturbed. There was something to be said of being king of a small kingdom. And since crime was not a real problem in Glenfair, a king could focus on serving his people and not on combating evil. Raven knew however, that the peace and prosperity he enjoyed could disappear very quickly. The terrible war with the Wickshields was a reminder of that truth.

He looked over at his wife Rebekka, enjoying the soothing waters with her nose wrinkled up a little by the sulfurous odor and he almost laughed. He never realized the depth of love one could have for another until Rebekka came into his life. She was his counselor and helper, but most of all his wife and the mother of their son and the child she now carried. As he stared at her Raven was overwhelmed with the truth that he had what most people search a lifetime for.

Treasure it, he said to himself, for no one knows what tomorrow holds.

Rebekka opened her eyes and looked at Raven staring at her. He knew because of her sensitive mental powers she could not endure his stare long without noticing and look back at him. He knew she could read his thoughts plainly, but he also knew she refrained from doing that intentionally because of her strong moral convictions on the privacy of another's thoughts. But Raven also knew that they were so well tuned to each other that even without Rebekka's mental powers, they would each know what the other was thinking most of the time anyway.

Rebekka now spoke: "We have such a good life here in Glenfair, do we not? We should never take any wonderful moment for granted!"

Raven smiled his special smile reserved only for her and replied. "We need to be heading south to the Prescotts so we do not arrive late."

She nodded, so they both got dressed and woke little Edward, packed up their things and once again headed south.

Bandon Prescott was informed that the king and queen along with their son Edward were not far off from the castle.

We are unprepared, Bandon thought. The tribute celebration is not for a couple of days. Surely the king would see they were ill prepared for him and think poorly of them.

Bandon hastened to call his staff and issued orders to immediately make preparations to receive the king in a fashion suitable to his station, and then hurried to change into more formal attire. Bandon had just finished dressing when Raven and Rebekka rode into the courtyard.

He rushed down to greet them and was puffing a little as he addressed King Raven. "Your majesty, we had not expected you so soon. We would have been better prepared to receive you had we known you were coming early."

Raven raised his hand to silence Bandon, smiled and then spoke, "My dear father in law, we have come here early in an unofficial capacity only to enjoy your company and for you to visit with us and your grandchild Edward. It seems of late that the only time we see each other is at official gatherings, planned or not, so we decided to come early and see you."

Raven saw the apprehension and doubt in Bandon's eyes and thought, sometimes the office of a king carries over into too many parts of life.

He longed sometimes to shed that image and just be Raven, the son in law, but he knew that was impossible with Bandon. He respected the office of king to much to ignore it.

So Raven said again, "We are here as family and hugged Bandon which took some of the stiff formality out of him."

A woman came rushing out to them and scooped a squealing Edward up into her arms twirling him around and getting fits of laughter from him. She set little Edward down and turned and smiled at Raven and Rebekka. Raven noticed that there was flour on the front of her apron and saw the disapproving look Bandon was giving her.

She waved that off and said, "I did not have time to change and besides, nothing is going to keep me from having fun with my grandchild." She then came over and hugged Rebekka and Raven.

Rebekka's mother, Lilly, was a woman who was full of life, practical and down to earth. He knew where Rebekka got many of her qualities from, and Raven always felt relaxed around her. He felt she always saw her son in law as the man he was, not the office he wore.

He saw now that her focus was on Rebekka's tummy as she exclaimed joyfully, "My how time goes by, you will have that child before

21

you know it. Please, come into the hall and relax with some refreshment."

With that she eyed Edward and took off after him as he squealed with delight running into the castle.

Raven and Rebekka both laughed at that and headed off after them with Bandon following, shaking his head in disapproval.

Inside Raven shook hands with Gregory, Rebekka's younger brother who was by now filling out into manhood.

By the time supper came everyone was more relaxed. Even Bandon seemed to be enjoying himself and his grandson Edward. It was a splendid feast, as could be expected when Lilly Prescott oversaw the details, for she was a fine cook. After the meal was finished and the table cleared, Raven stretched and walked about the dining hall. Rebekka was talking to her brother Gregory and Bandon was playing with Edward, when Lilly came up to Raven and spoke to him with a smile on her face.

"There was a time I wondered if you picked my daughter to be your queen because of her abilities, but now I know that you picked her because of the love you have for her. I can see it in the way you look at her. You chose her to be your wife not the Queen of this kingdom. I have never seen her more happy or radiant, and for that I want to thank you."

Raven knew now why Rebekka possessed such insight and straightforwardness, he could see it in her mother.

He simply said, "Sometimes I am not worthy of the blessings of joy that have come to me."

Lilly's face tightened and she spoke candidly. "You have had your share of heart ache already, more than most in a lifetime, do not begrudge yourself the blessings God hands to those who rightfully deserve them." Then she hugged Raven and headed back to the kitchen.

Raven watched her go and realized what a wonderful family Rebekka had, and he was glad to be part of it. Raven and Rebekka retired early because of the long trip, and little Edward went with his uncle Gregory to sleep in his room with him. They laid down tired but pleasantly content and both fell fast asleep.

It was a beautiful day for another picnic, as they spread their blanket on the grass by a quiet pool of water. Rebekka and Edward sitting on the blanket made a picturesque scene in this beautiful land. Raven went over to the pool to get a drink and splash water on his face when he heard the cries and screams of his family. He whirled around quickly and saw a twainlar serpent coming toward them, he never imagined they could get so big, for this one was huge. He ran toward them as fast as he could drawing the ancient family sword as he went but he saw that he was not going to reach them in time. Just before he reached them the huge serpent opened the mouths on both of its heads and closed down on Rebekka and Edward. Raven screamed in anger as he swung his families sword into the serpent but it bounced off and had no effect.

He felt a slap to the side of his face and he woke up with Rebekka shaking him and saying; "Raven, wake up. It is a dream, wake up!"

Raven now realize he was dreaming and sat up in bed with a shaken, white faced Rebekka beside him.

"I had a terrible nightmare," Raven began to say.

But Rebekka stopped him and said, "Don't remind me, I know what it was, I saw it!"

Raven was stunned, "You had the dream too he asked?"

"No," she said, "you woke me up moaning and I could tell you were having a bad dream so I looked into your mind to see what was bothering you just in time to see the serpent try and swallow Edward and I, it was horrible. I had to wake you so I slapped your face and shook you."

Raven was feeling his face and now knew what it was that had brought him back from the dream. "It was too real, I have never had a dream like this except for the one of the Library of wisdom where Andronicus lives."

Rebekka frowned, "I do not think he would send a dream like that, not when he can just speak to me now in my mind if he wanted us. No this dream was something else."

Raven knew that to be true, for Andronicus was their friend and would not send something of such ill will.

"Maybe it was just a bad dream and that was all there was to it," Raven tried to convince himself.

Rebekka only nodded, doubting Raven's concession that it was only a bad dream.

"I know I will not be able to go back to sleep soon after seeing that scene," she said.

"Nor I," Raven added. "What shall we do to calm ourselves down?"

Rebekka's eyes lit up and she turned quickly to Raven and said. "I know what we can do, it will be fun. Remember long ago you asked me if I thought there were any secret passages in my own castle? I did some checking but found nothing, only some good possibilities. I had always hoped when we visited we could check those out, with your special abilities you would find anything if it was there. It is up in the northeast section of the castle, away from the sleeping quarters so no one will be disturbed if we go poking around."

"Let's go," Raven said as they dressed, both glad of the adventure that would take their mind off of the terrible dream. They quietly worked their way with a lantern to the northeast section of the castle. Raven tried to mentally picture which way they were turning and how far they were going in relationship to the rest of the castle. They went down a long hallway with rooms to either side and the hallway ended with a wall.

"Here," Rebekka said, "is where I believe there is something."

Raven tried to picture in is mind the relationship of the end wall of this hallway and the rest of the castle. It was difficult but then he said, "This hallway does not go all the way to the end of the castle's north wall does it?"

Rebekka smiled, "That is what I think too, I have stepped it off several times and each time I come up short to the far end of the castle."

Raven reached up and took a shield down from the wall, and moved an ornately carved table with a beautiful vase sitting on it. Once they were out of the way he began to look at the wall. "There is no subtle lines in this wall," he told Rebekka, "we could be wrong."

Raven closed his eyes and with his hands felt over the wall and noted two small raised places the size of a marble. When he opened his eyes he could see them now clearly where before he could not.

"What have you found," Rebekka wanted to know.

"Here and here," Raven pointed out the small raised places opposite each other on the wall. Once Raven pointed them out, Rebekka saw them too. Raven reached up and depressed the small raised stones and waited. Nothing happened, which was perplexing to Raven.

Rebekka looked at Raven and said; "Maybe the door is stuck from not being used in many ages, if ever."

Raven pondered this for a moment then shook his head. "There is something missing we have not done. The ancients built things too well for it to become stuck with the passing of time, but anything is possible."

Raven looked around for some time, but seeing nothing else that could be done, he looked at the floor in front of the wall. He could see nothing there as well that was out of place or could be used as a latch. When he was almost at a loss he turned to the walls directly to each side of the end of the hallway. Feeling those he found a similar raised stone and said to himself; this was hidden almost too well for even me to find. As he depressed the small stone the wall at the end of the hallway began to swing inward.

Raven could see the excitement in Rebekka, she was so exuberant as she said; "Our castle has secrets too!"

Since she was holding the lamp, she bounded into the passage before Raven could stop her and heard her saying as he followed. "The passage heads west and seems to turn after awhile and go south."

Then Raven heard the mechanical sound of a crossbow being released, like the one he had found in his own castle created by the ancients, followed by Rebekka's scream. It only took him a couple of bounds to get to her but what he saw made him turn pale. A crossbow bolt had pinned Rebekka to the wall and blood was staining the garment on her side.

Rebekka was frozen with fear of what had happened and only said; "The baby, am I going to lose the baby?"

Raven on closer examination relaxed a little and reassured his wife, seeing the arrow was located to the edge of her side. Raven tried to pull the bolt from the wall but it was stuck fast in the stone so he drew his knife and cut Rebekka's garments away from the arrow.

And then relief showed on his face as he said; "It only nicked your side, you are not cut badly at all."

With that, Rebekka fell into Raven's arms and began to cry. He held her and soothed her shaken emotions till they had both regained their composure, then said; "It is good that you were almost running down this passage. If you were walking slow, I would be mourning your death, the arrow shot a little behind you."

"This does not make sense, Raven, the ancients have never done anything to harm us, and this castle was my ancestor's. Why would there be a trap such as this?"

"I do not know," replied Raven. "Something is wrong here, we should go back and leave this place."

Rebekka was twisting and turning this way and that trying to get a good look at the wound in her side, but being about half way through her pregnancy her stomach made it a little difficult. "How bad is the cut," she asked Raven.

Raven looked again and told her it had almost stopped bleeding.

"We should go on," Rebekka said matter of factly.

"What!" Raven exclaimed. "I do not think it a good idea to do so, it is too dangerous."

He looked at Rebekka and then moaned. She had that look in her eye that told him she was determined to press on. Sometimes a stubborn determination was not good for one's health.

He started to say something but Rebekka spoke first, "I recall hearing a story of two young men who in the face of danger said: We live for adventure."

"All right," Raven said, "we will go on, only you stay well behind me, understand?"

Rebekka nodded as Raven knelt and searched for the mechanism that had triggered the crossbow arrow. Raven found it then, a metal wire thinner than Rebekka's hair, now broken by her foot. The crossbow was hidden back in the wall but Raven could not find a way to extract it. "This is a devious trap, almost impossible to detect. If there are more like it we will be in great danger."

Then he looked at Rebekka and said; "Contact Andronicus and ask him about this."

Rebekka nodded, she should have thought of that sooner. She closed her eyes and was silent for a long time. She finally opened them and then spoke.

"Andronicus knows nothing of any secret passages in the other castles. To his knowledge, only the king's castle had them and all of the dukes in the beginning knew of those. He also was appalled that there was any form of trap here and kept asking me if I was sure it was set by the ancients. I assured him because of the materials used, it could have been no other than one of the first ones. He mentioned that he should be the one to explore this passage, but I assured him you would be careful."

"What did he say to that?" Raven wanted to know.

"He stated that your senses and reflexes were even greater than his own but he was more durable, so to be very careful, and let him know what we find out."

Raven smiled at Rebekka's answer, Andronicus, so unemotional and calculated in his responses, yet Raven knew the old man did care about all of them, and was their friend. He gave that away by asking when they would visit him again to enjoy the relaxation he had to offer if too much time had passed since their last visit. Raven made a note to go there and visit before the summer feast.

"Very well then, let us press on, we live for adventure!"

This time they made their way down the passage slowly calculating every step as they went. They approached the bend that turned south with no further incident. Turning south they saw that the passage ended in a door.

As Raven took another step south, he felt the hard stone floor give with the sound of a faint click. Immediately he leaped up and backwards in a flip that landed him almost in Rebekka's arms. At the same instant spears thrust out from both sides of the wall and would surely have impaled him were it not for his cat-like reflexes.

It took Rebekka a moment to register what had taken place, but when she saw the spears thrust out from the wall she recognized how impossible it was to escape such a trap when sprung.

"Raven," she said, "maybe I was to hasty in my desire to press on. We could go back."

Raven's senses were more tuned now than they had been in years. In fact he had not experienced this kind of heightened awareness since the day he fought in the battle with the Wickshields.

"It will be ok," Raven assured Rebekka, "just stay back until I have discovered any more traps that might be ahead of us."

With that he drew his families ancient sword and cut the shafts of the spears off where they jutted from the wall to allow them passage. He then made his way very slowly down the passage without further incident and came to the door.

Innately he knew opening the door would spring a trap so he spent some time concentrating and examining the door for signs of any triggering devices.

Rebekka broke the silence with a whisper, "What is wrong. Do you see something?"

"That is just it," Raven whispered back, "I do not see a thing, but I know this door will trigger another trap."

He then told Rebekka to go back down the passage to where it makes a bend and wait on the other side of the bend in safety till he called her. Rebekka hesitated for a moment and then walked down the passage to the turn and stopped around the corner and waited.

Raven lifted the latch to the door and pulled it open toward himself, expecting any moment that there would be some instrument of death coming for him, but none did This perplexed him and worried him even more.

He started to enter the room when he stopped and knelt by the door opening. Something had caught his eye and he was looking for one of the very thin metal strings Rebekka had tripped on earlier. Then he saw it, a dust particle had floated into a tiny beam of faint light.

"Thank the Creator," Raven said. If it were not for the dust that had accumulated in the passage over the centuries, he would never have seen this. Raven reached down to the floor and scraped up as much dust as he could with his hand and holding it out in front of his face, he blew the dust from his hand into the door way. Now he could see every so often tiny beams of light lacing the doorway so no one could get through without crossing one of them.

Raven knew this was the trap but did not know what would come by setting it off. He was still on his knees so he lay flat on the floor of the passage and reached out and blocked one of the fine streams of faint light. There was a sound from the room to which the door opened and then Raven, with his tuned senses, caught the movement of four crossbow bolts coming toward the doorway. One just missed Raven's ear as the four arrows passed through the doorway to embed in the wall of the passage where it turned sharply.

Almost instantly he heard Rebekka calling his name, "Raven, Raven, are you all right?"

"Stay where you are, I am fine," Raven called back.

Rebekka was not about to move seeing the arrows stuck in the wall, not far from her position.

Raven began for the first time to have doubts as to the prudence of continuing on. Even with his enhanced senses and reflexes he could not have avoided four arrows at once coming through the doorway and would probably be dead if he had not been laying down. But the sense of curiosity, as well as a little anger prompted him to press the matter further.

Running his hand through the doorway brought no further response so Raven got to his feet and looked with more interest beyond the door to a room on the other side.

"Not unlike the weapons room in his own castle," Raven thought, "but much more deadly." Before Raven entered the room he made a mental note of what he could see of the contents. Torches rested in their holders on the wall with decorative armor here and there, and the Prescott coat of arms was etched on the far wall.

Raven suspected a secret compartment lay behind the Prescott crest, for that was how it was in the weapons room of the king's castle. There, behind each of the crests of the four dukes and that of the old king was a secret compartment. In that compartment there was a chain that held a colored stone and a note which read:

> "We fled the enemy of our first home,
> and took with us the sacred stones,
> that would protect if he should find,
> to where in time we did fly,
> and the stones if used the proper way,
> will send him back to his own day."

Further scanning revealed a mosaic in the floor covered by the dust of the centuries in a design he had never seen before. The dust obscured most of the mosaic so he might recognize the picture if the floor were clean. That would have to be taken care of as soon as the room was secure and safe for them to move about.

In a far corner was the only piece of furniture in the room, an ornate chest with gold bindings.

Further scanning revealed nothing so Raven moved cautiously into the room. He thought it best to go strait to the middle of the room to give himself space to maneuver if any more traps were sprung. He stepped purposefully on the mosaic in case it would trigger any traps as well, but nothing happened. Raven moved toward the Prescott coat of arms carved in the wall facing the door and still no traps were sprung.

"It must be the opening of the compartment that will bring the surprise," Raven thought to himself. He felt the coat of arms and found the release catch. As he depressed it, he readied himself for any deadly assault, but again nothing happened as the hidden panel swung open.

At that moment he heard Rebekka calling to him and turned his attention from the hidden compartment to the rest of the room. Walking

28

quickly around, he found there were no more traps so he called to Rebekka and told her to come down and join him. He waited by the door for her, just in case there was something he missed. When she entered, he told her of the ingenious light traps of the doorway. Both of their nerves were a bit on edge but they began to settle as they surveyed the room once again together.

Then Rebekka asked the question that had been haunting Raven the whole time. "Why would the ancients want to harm us, or anyone for that matter."

And then indignantly added. "And of all people my ancestors set these traps!"

"I do not know," Raven replied. "But the answers to those questions I believe are here. There is something here that Duke Prescott did not want anyone to find and hid it here behind all these deadly traps."

Rebekka pointed to the chest and they both walked over to it to examine it further. It was beautiful and ornate. As they examined how to open its latch both discovered at the same time it required one of the rings the ancients had made of their crests to open it. Raven knew right away that his crest would not fit the pattern, it would have to be the seal of the Prescott dukeship to make it work.

Rebekka likewise realized this and said; "The latch requires the ring of our family crest to open this chest. I recognize the inverted seal of our family. It is too bad that we have lost our families ring over the centuries."

Raven knew that no amount of prying would open the chest. It was built too well to be broken open, just like the other things the ancients had built. So he turned his attention to the open compartment behind the Prescott family seal. He and Rebekka walked over to the open compartment in the wall and began to view its contents. There was a piece of cloth, and something else that Raven could not see well at the back.

Rebekka started to reach up toward the opening when Raven stopped her.

She looked at him and said. "What is it Raven? There are no traps in this room, it is safe here."

"That is what I am worried about," stated Raven. "The sense of security that comes from the lack of traps in this room would lull someone into the casual placement of their hand into this compartment."

Raven looked around the room and quickly went over to one of the torches and removed it from its holder on the wall and returned to where Rebekka was waiting. He then took the wooden handle and slowly inserted it into the opening. There was a slight hiss and three sharp needles plunged into the wood from three different angles, making it impossible to have escaped being jabbed.

Rebekka jumped back at the action and even Raven was surprised a little by the sudden trap.

"Your ancestor was a devious man. I realize now that we are both lucky to be alive, for I am certain that there is deadly poison in these needles that would kill very quickly."

Raven twisted the torch and pulled it back and two of the needles broke off. He then pried on the third until it broke as well. Inserting of the torch handle again brought no further action or traps, so Raven knew the danger was over, yet he still used the torch to drag the scrap of cloth to the opening, not trusting anything to chance. He knew there would be writing on the piece of cloth because it was like that which they had found in the chamber at happiness creek years before. When he held it up to read, Rebekka looked over his shoulder, and they were both astounded at what they saw. The note read:

"My dearest friend Uriah, you are reading this note because I have been murdered and you are searching for answers to who is responsible for my death. You are the only one outside of my immediate family that now knows of this secret room. I apologize for the traps, but thought it prudent to protect what I have left here for you in case someone else by some action or accident finds this secret passage, especially my assassin. The first trap would kill an ordinary man but someone trained would easily escape it. I knew that would alert you to the rest of the traps set here which even the trained would fail to avoid. I knew your genetic reflexes and heightened senses coupled with the knowledge you have of how I think, will see you through the other traps to this note. It is impossible to think that someone else may be reading this, and if they are then they are better than you, and no one is better at this than you my friend. So take the spare ring from the compartment and open the chest. In it is all the information I have gathered on the possible suspects of betrayal. I know we all swore to destroy all of our high-tec weapons, but under the mosaic in the floor is stored some lasers and other weapons I kept back. If you need them only you will know how to open this vault. Farewell my friend, and watch your back."

Raven folded up the note, and using the torch, fished out the spare Prescott ring needed to open the chest. Placing the note back inside the compartment, he closed it back up and walked over to the chest with Rebekka following. At the chest he knelt and placed the ring into the receptacle made for it and pushed. There was a faint click and the chest unlocked. Raven raised the lid slowly but did not expect any more traps and his assumptions were proved true when nothing happened.

Inside the chest were two scrolls and an ornate sliver box with the name "Othellia" inscribed on it. Raven took the silver box out and handed it to Rebekka and started to reach for the scrolls when he stopped, not out of fear of a trap but at the contrast in the two scrolls. One was made of the durable material the ancients used to preserve their important writings on, but the other was made of ordinary parchment. Raven took the durable scroll out and handed it to Rebekka as well but when he touched the other scroll lightly it began to crumble to dust.

"We are not going to read what is on that scroll," Raven said out loud, "so we shall leave it where it is." Raven closed the lid to the chest and heard it lock. He turned to Rebekka and said. "Shall we go?"

Rebekka paused for a moment and then said. "I would like to see the weapons they have hidden under the mosaic, if your armor is incredible, what would the weapons they have hidden here be like?"

With that she set the scroll and the silver box on the floor and scurried over to the mosaic, kneeled and began brushing off the dust that had accumulated over the centuries. Raven stood where he was for a moment, sighed and went over to help Rebekka clean the floor. When it was brushed off they could see the beautiful picture inlaid in the stone floor. A farming scene seemed to jump to life with sheaves of grain stacked in a field by a red barn, with a family sitting down to lunch, taking a break from their work. It was a wondrous scene that captured the essence of a family content with their life on a farm.

Raven closed his eyes and ran his hands over the mosaic, but to his discouragement found nothing out of place. He did the same thing again with no better results, though he concentrated much harder. There were thousands of pieces of little tiles, but none of them felt any different.

Raven looked at Rebekka and said, "I do not think I will be able to open this, I have no Idea how. It is better anyway."

"What do you mean," Rebekka wanted to know.

"If these weapons were to be destroyed, they must be terrible indeed, and it is better they are left alone." With that they rose and picked up the scroll and the silver box and headed back down the secret passage to their room.

Once back inside their room, Raven handed Rebekka the Prescott family ring and said; "We should give this to your father and emphasize that it should be passed on to his son and his son's son to many generations. And remind him it is as old as the armor and comes to us from the ancients."

Rebekka nodded, taking the ring from Raven and sat upon the bed to study it. After a long look at the ancient ring she looked at Raven and spoke with emotion.

"Our family's ring has been restored to us, a treasure I am sure they will not appreciate, especially its use."

Raven nodded, knowing Rebekka referred to using the ring to reach the top of Brickens' Falls where Andronicus stayed keeping the wisdom of the ancients.

"What if it is lost again in another thousand years Raven? Should we take that kind of chance?"

"What are we to do?" Raven replied. "Keep these things from those whose right it is to possess them? It is true in a millennia it may be lost, but to keep it from them now would be like it was lost already. Here we have a chance to start once again with the heritage of our fathers. No, we must give it to your father, it is the rightful seal of his dukeship."

Rebekka sat upright as Raven finished with an odd look on her face, perplexing Raven until it dawned on him she was communicating with Andronicus.

She looked at Raven and said, "Andronicus wants to know if all was well, and if we have found out the reason for all the traps in the secret passage."

"Tell him," Raven started to say, and then commented. "I wish I could speak to him myself, it is so hard relaying messages."

Rebekka smiled and said, "I can talk to Andronicus, and I can talk to your mind as well, maybe I can bring you into our conversation if I think of both of you at once."

Rebekka concentrated and spoke to Raven's mind, "can you hear me?"

"Yes," Raven responded.

"Try and talk to Andronicus," encouraged Rebekka.

"Andronicus," Raven asked tentatively.

"Yes, King Raven," came the reply.

It almost shocked Raven for he had never heard anyone else in his mind besides Rebekka.

"Have you become telepathic," Andronicus asked perplexed?

"No," Raven answered, "Rebekka is helping us talk to each other."

"I have never known that to be done before," Andronicus spoke with astonishment. "Please continue, King Raven."

"I disarmed all of the traps and found a note that spoke of a possible traitor and betrayal of the ancients. Duke Prescott said if someone were reading this note, then it could only be his friend Uriah investigating his murder. We found a spare Prescott ring and it opened a chest with a two scrolls in it, one crumbled but the other is made of the durable cloth like that of the happiness creek chamber. Do you know of any conspiracy?"

There was a pause for a moment and Raven thought that maybe Andronicus had lost the link he had with Raven until his words came again.

"To hear of a possible conspiracy King Raven, troubles me, for I know nothing of any of this. Uriah and Amnon Prescott were very close friends and at times secretive but I heard nothing of conspiracy. Uriah was security chief for all of Glenfair in the beginning of the kingdom, and he often confided in Amnon. Amnon and Uriah both died of old age, there was never a murder. I am impressed that you are still alive if these traps were set to eliminate every one but Uriah, he was the greatest of all weapons masters. I have much to tell you of the ancients. It was not all picture perfect in the beginning, so do come to see me soon."

"I will," answered Raven, "before the summer feast." With that he looked at Rebekka and she sank back on the bed with her face flushed.

"Are you all right," Raven asked her.

"Yes," Rebekka said, "it was a strain to keep you both talking. I do not think I will do that again unless it is necessary."

Raven was concerned for her since she was with child and remarked. "I do not think you should ever do that again either if it is that hard on you. Relaying messages is enough. Please rest while I have a look at this scroll."

Rebekka lay on the bed while Raven began to unroll the scroll on the bed beside her. The handwriting was elegant, in the old style of the kings of the past and read:

"The beginning of Amnon Prescott's journal concerning the greatest adventure a human being could have, pioneering a new frontier. Actually it is not new for we lived here before, only several thousand years in the future. It is so refreshing to come back to this land in its pristine beauty and before it was settled by but a few souls. It is a new lease on life, thanks to the discovery of the isolinear crystal that allowed us to come here. Our plan was so radical, so utterly perfect, no one of our future time would be able to figure it out. And that is what worries me, the only way this wonderful plan we conceived could fail is for someone to be careless and let it slip from their mouth, or else betray us to the enemy. I just fear there are too many people involved for this to be a success. Over forty of us have vanished from our time, and surely someone has betrayed, or will betray us, for I fear this paradise will not last long."

Raven paused here, his heart sank as he read these words. He had heard this same reasoning before of supposed betrayal from his father. That road took his father into a war that cost Edward, his brother, his life along with many others. Will human nature never change, he wondered? Even the ancients suspected each other. He wished he could shout through the ages back to them all and assure them that there had been no betrayal and the ancient enemy had not found them. To be at peace with one another and trust each other as they should so the kingdom would prosper. For a great kingdom it would come to be, greater than any of the ancients could imagine. Over a thousand years the kingdom had endured and had been a haven for the inhabitants of

Glenfair. If only they knew that they were safe from this enemy they speak of, perhaps their lives would have been at peace. Raven turned back to the scroll and continued reading.

"I have laid my suspicions on those who have been the most unsatisfied by living without our precious technology. I have shared this with Uriah and he agrees we should keep an ear open and a watchful eye. The rest of the information I have gathered to support my suspicions is written on another scroll. I digress, for I would write of the great adventure that brought us to this place. As I mentioned, the crystals enabled us to come this far back in time, but without our beloved Merry Sheldon we would not have been able to put them to use, for she was the catalyst, the time shifter that moved us through time. The crystals only amplified what she had the ability to do. She of all people seems the happiest in this place, and no wonder, for our enemy, the tyrant, wanted nothing more than to have her for his own. He even had set a date for their marriage. She hated and despised him, but could do nothing about the impending marriage until Uriah told her of the crystals. Oh, he must be fuming mad, a raving lunatic for what we have done to him. For if he suspected that Uriah and Merry loved each other, he would have had Uriah killed, even though he was his own weapons master. And now they are husband and wife, a very happy couple, except for the consequences this great leap in time had on Merry. No one knew what it would do to her until it was too late. I believe though, that she would make the same choice again even if she knew the consequences. I wish I could tell the old tyrant of Merry's and Uriah's marriage without giving us away to know the rage that it would bring him. Life was barely tolerable under his rule, and we all lived in constant fear for our lives. All we had to do was displease him a little and we could be sent to prison or executed for crimes against his regime. So, I am glad we were able to inflict the harm of at least taking his bride away from him. Now we are at peace in this wonderful land that is both old and new to us.

Raven stopped reading and looked at Rebekka. She had her eyes closed and was dozing in and out of sleep. Raven put the scroll away and decided there would be time to read it later. They both needed sleep for the next days events, the collection of the southern tribute and the feast that went along with it, and they had both been up long enough as it was.

The next day was bright and cheery with little Edward having a great time with his grandparents and his uncle Gregory. It seemed Edward had a special bond with Gregory and likewise Gregory did not mind this little bundle of energy following him around everywhere. At lunch time Bandon Prescott was satisfied with the organization of the days events and was finally able to relax a little. Raven noticed this earlier and had given Bandon space without distraction, for he knew what it entailed to run matters of state. But now there seemed an opportunity to speak with him and Raven wanted to bring up the matter of the Prescott ring and present it to Bandon. Rebekka was there as well, for he wanted her present when he gave the ring to her father.

Bandon now free from distraction turned to Raven and said, "My king, we are most glad to pay tribute to you and the feast will be our way of showing this gratitude. Duke Zandel will also attend and bring with him the southern tribute with as much joy.

Bandon smiled at this for everyone had been surprised at the change in heart Mason Zandel had shown at his father's funeral.

"I am greatly looking forward to the nights events," stated Raven. "But there is something I must speak with you about now that cannot wait."

Bandon was now very attentive, and Raven did not delay less Bandon get the impression the king was not pleased with the hospitality or guoce any such unpleasant news was coming.

"I would like to give you something that belonged to your ancestors, something very special." And with that Raven produced the ancient ring with the Prescott seal.

Bandon's eyes went wide as Raven handed him the ring and he exclaimed. "We had thought our families ring lost forever. How did you ever come by it?"

Raven had already decided to tell Bandon about the secret passage but decided to wait to tell him about the scroll until he had finished reading it. For it would only lead to questions that Raven did not want to answer as of yet.

So Raven said, "Rebekka and I could not sleep last night so we did a little exploring and found a secret passage and a hidden room in your castle. In there we found the ring."

"Here!, in my castle," Bandon said with astonishment. "Will you show me this room, he asked?"

"Yes we will," Raven replied, "as soon as we finish eating."

Bandon sat back into his chair for he realized he had half risen from his seat at this unexpected news.

Bandon, now more relaxed stated; "My dear King Raven, you are always full of surprises. What can we expect next from you? And you my daughter, are just as mischievous. I had thought at first I may have given the king a burden by giving him your hand in marriage, but I see now that you both keep each other entertained by your ceaseless curiosity."

Rebekka blushed at her father's remarks but thought to herself. If you only knew father of the mysteries we have solved, and the places we have been, you would turn pale.

After lunch, Rebekka and Raven took Bandon to the northeast part of the castle to where the hallway ended. Raven showed Bandon the catches in the wall and opened the doorway to the secret passage. After they had lit some lamps they proceeded on to the room.

The crossbow bolts stuck in the wall did not escape Bandon's eye so he asked Raven. "There were taps here were there not, to protect something of value?"

Raven affirmed the traps and told him what they were about to see was what was in the room. As they entered the room Bandon surveyed it and walked over to the chest. Looking at the lock, it did not take him long to realize it would open with the ring Raven had given him. So he inserted the ring and opened the chest. Inside was the scroll that was brittle with age. Bandon picked it up and it crumbled in his hands.

"If this was a map to treasure we are out of luck," Bandon said with good humor. He was just about to close the lid when he stopped.

"Did you look inside this chest?" he asked Raven.

"Yes we did, and all we saw was paper and writing."

"Did you notice," Bandon remarked, "that the bottom is much higher than it should be?"

Raven looked and now he did notice. How could he have missed this important feature to the chest. It had a false bottom. Perhaps it was the distraction of the traps that caused Raven to miss this feature of the chest. But with Bandon's desire to find treasure he had noticed the false bottom. Bandon motioned for Raven to proceed since he was handy a finding ways to open things like secret passages. Raven inspected the bottom and finally found the catch and opened it up. He stepped back so Bandon could look and heard his father-in-law gasp. Raven peered over his shoulder and saw that in the bottom of the chest there were gold and jewels.

Bandon stood and looked Raven in the eye and said. "We shall divide this spoil between us."

"Nonsense," Raven said, "this is your families. It was here in your castle and your family ring opened the chest, it belongs to you."

Bandon bent down and peered back into the chest. He could be heard fishing around in the gold and jewels when he withdrew he had a couple of things in his hand. A necklace of rubies and sapphires sparkled in his hand as he turned to Rebekka.

"This necklace befits a queen," he said as he put it around his daughters neck.

Raven had never seen jewels like this before, the elegance and magnitude of the gift impressed Raven. Bandon Prescott although frugal was not selfish, and Raven could see the genuine joy he had in giving this precious gift to his daughter. Rebekka hugged him and Raven could see the joy she got from such a gift.

Bandon then handed Raven a ornate knife with gold and pearl accents with the letters "LT" inlaid in the handle. Raven started to protest but Bandon waved him off.

"These are for you if you promise not to tell your mother Lilly about these treasures. I can keep her supplied for some time with gifts from this chest."

He reached in and pulled out a necklace of wonderful blue pearls and said. "Hmm, and she has a birthday coming up soon."

Raven and Rebekka could not help but laugh at this gesture and even Bandon laughed as he put the pearls back.

"Come," he said, "we have a wonderful day ahead for us all."

Rebekka headed down the passage and Raven started to go when Bandon caught his arm.

"Raven," he said kindly, "I want to thank you for returning to us our family ring. It means more to me than all the gold or jewels. I know this ring is special and it will never be lost again."

With that he held out his hand to shake Raven's but instead Raven hugged him.

"You have given me something of much more value than gold or jewels too!" With that he motioned with his head down the hall toward where Rebekka had disappeared.

Bandon smiled and said; "I am glad you think so, for I know there is something special about her." They both smiled and headed down the passage after Rebekka.

The evening feast was splendid, and Raven could not remember Bandon in a better mood save for the day of Rebekka's wedding. Every one was having a good time when it seemed the feast was over and it was time for the passing of the tribute to the king. Duke Prescott stood and with much fanfare declared their prosperity was great during the past year and declared there was a little extra tribute than normal in this years payment.

And then his sense of humor took over and he added, "I expect to see some new attractions at the summer feast as a result."

Every one laughed at this, for all knew a portion of the tribute went to the costs of the summer and fall feasts the whole kingdom enjoyed.

Mason Zandel now stood and spoke loud for all to hear, "This is my first presentation as duke since my father has recently passed away. We of the Zandel dukeship as well gladly pay tribute to the king. But let me add, as a youth I always resented having to pay the tribute and never understood its benefits until recently, and I am not speaking of the feast the king provides. It is a gesture of solidarity that we all share and have a part in this kingdom. Without a good king we all will suffer, for the king is the head and the dukes are his hands and feet. One is no good without the other. Let us all be thankful for we have a good king who loves this land, and I believe there is nothing he would not sacrifice for the sake of all of Glenfair."

With that Mason handed the king the southeastern tribute to the roaring cheers of the people. King Raven stood there a moment until the cheers died down and began his acceptance speech.

"Duke Zandel has spoken the truth concerning my love for the kingdom of Glenfair. But the strength of Glenfair is not the king, but comes from the trust and cooperation of the king and dukes together. That is what makes Glenfair strong and peaceful. May you accept my gratitude for the tribute that will enable us to continue the prosperity of Glenfair. I believe history will bear us out that there have been no finer dukes than what we have, and have had in my lifetime. May God bless and prosper Glenfair as we continue the alliance that has outlasted every other kingdom about us." With that Raven raised his glass in salute and said forcefully. "To a thousand more years!"

The people echoed, "To a thousand more years!"

The next day Raven and Rebekka bid Bandon and Lilly goodbye as they prepared to head back to the king's castle. Little Edward was sad to leave his grandparents and especially his uncle Gregory. It had been a good visit, but Raven was anxious to get back to the castle and see what needed his attention. It was not that Master Fields lacked the ability to handle anything that came up, he was just the type of king who had to be involved with his people. It was probably good that Glenfair was a small kingdom, for the king would not have any rest if it were any larger. But he enjoyed and appreciated the kingdom more now that it was his responsibility.

So off the three rode north, horses laden with the tribute of the southern dukeships.

Funny, Raven thought, if we were in any other kingdom, we would have to have a guarded escort to protect all this tribute. But here we are the king, his wife, and his son all alone and no guards at all.

Not that Raven had traveled outside of the kingdom of Glenfair, but he had heard plenty from outside sources of what other lands were like and none of them were anything like Glenfair.

People came from time to time to settle here but there was not a whole lot of opportunity for economic gain in Glenfair because of its size. Almost all of the land was already parceled out between the dukes and the king, and the industry was small.

Raven had never really thought of that before, Glenfair was not a poor kingdom, but neither did it flow with gold or opportunity. Many that came here stated it was wonderful to visit but soon left when they could

38

not acquire the wealth that was available in other lands. There were those who stayed that wanted more than wealth, who liked the atmosphere, morality and peace Glenfair offered. To those who sought that kind of life, there was always a place for them. Raven wondered how long into the future Glenfair would be able to go until it was forced to consider the economics of the rest of the world, instead of just getting by like they had for centuries. He hoped it would be a long time, for he loved what Glenfair was, but also knew it could not last this way forever.

The day passed quickly and finally the castle loomed into view. Master Fields met them as they came in and servants unloaded the tribute. There were a few small matters Master Fields wanted to brief the king on, and as Raven listened he smiled, it was business as usual, it could not be better. Today he saw the kingdom in a whole new light, one to be treasured and appreciated while it lasted.

Chapter 3
The Appearance of Evil

"An angry man be dangerous, an evil man be more so. But be
there an angry, evil man, and his pride doth not allow him rest till
he worketh his hurt upon another."

--Chronicles of the Ancients

King Raven wanted very much to go visit Andronicus at the top
of Brickens' Falls. His curiosity of learning more of the ancients had
been aroused while reading the ancient scroll of Duke Amnon Prescott.
But one thing he wanted to do was to finish the scroll before he went so
he could get all of his questions answered.

Raven felt down to his side and rested his left hand upon the
knife that had been given him by Bandon Prescott when he found the
jewels in the chest. When Raven got home he examined the knife more
closely and only then did he begin to appreciate the craftsmanship that
had gone into it. It was made of the same alloy steel that his ancient
family sword had been made of. And apart from its beauty, it was very
functional. It was balanced like a throwing knife but had the handle and
grip that enabled you to fight with it as well. It was a nice addition to the
fighting armor that had been left to him from the ancients.

Raven was grateful for his heritage and for the kingdom Almighty
God had allowed him to be born into. He did not take this peaceful
kingdom, this gift of God lightly and determined in his heart to be the best
king a land could have. He knew part of that now was to learn its history
and purpose of existence. He was puzzled though by the remarks of the
scroll, no he was saddened, for his view of those heroes of the past was
altered since reading the first part of the scroll. He now knew the truth,
that human nature was the same in all ages, having experienced first
hand his father's turning from the true path a king should walk. He
should not have expected more of the ancients than was true of all
humanity. None were perfect, only God held that title, and reserved it for
himself alone. Raven smiled for he knew the Almighty did not have to
worry about competition from his human creation on that front. How
patient God must be to endure humanity. Knowing there were problems
of mistrust among the ancients did not defer his desire to know more of

them and he had scheduled the afternoon free to retire to the council chambers and read the rest of the scroll.

Just then he felt a nudge at his leg and looked down to see little Edward looking up at him.

"What is it Edward?" Raven asked.

Little Edward frowned and then said; "What were you thinking about father?"

Raven was always amazed at the questions Edward asked and realized that he was never interested in what his father was doing when he was Edward's age, he just wanted to play. It wasn't that Edward did not like to play, he just had these serious intellectual curiosities from time to time that always seemed to catch Raven off guard.

Raven knelt down and hugged his son as was his custom before teaching or speaking seriously and said. "I was thinking about the ancients."

Edward smiled and said, "I thought so. Who are they and why do you think about them so much?"

Raven smiled, a simple question but with a harder answer. "Our past," he began, "Is very important to us. The ancients came to this place to begin the kingdom of Glenfair a long time ago. We need to learn from our past so we can live better than they did. If we can learn from the things they did wrong and not do the same, we will be a better kingdom for it. Also, we should follow their example when they did what was good and right."

Little Edward just nodded solemnly and then said with a smile, "Master Fields promised to teach me how to use my wooden sword to defend today."

Raven smiled, "Yes, Master Fields is a very good teacher and you will learn much from him, so listen carefully."

"I will," Edward said as he ran off to find Master Fields.

Raven straightened up and thought of Edward's question. He did want to learn more of their past, but to avoid the same mistakes? He knew that would be another matter all together for humanity had a habit of repeating the past generations errors over and over again.

As Raven headed for his private counsel chambers he decided on the morrow he would seek Master Fields out for some fine tuning at arms. Even though his reflexes and abilities exceeded Master Fields', he still knew more than Raven ever would about arms and combat. It had been some time since he had trained with the Master and Edward's enthusiasm about learning arms was contagious.

Lorriel Crestlaw sat in the room of the Crestlaw castle that Raven years ago had entered to discover the riddle that had put them on the trail to finding the Hall of Wisdom the ancients had left behind. After her marriage to Andrew Crestlaw, the room held special memories for her of their adventures. So she had cleaned and decorated it, restoring it to the study it once was. It had become for her a beautiful refuge from the noise and demands of life in a dukeship. She would come here, usually in the evening when the children were tucked in bed, and relax. The quiet in the isolated room gave her the relaxation she needed to concentrate with her mind enough to contact Rebekka sometimes. Once Rebekka took over the connection Lorriel did not have to concentrate at all, they just talked to each other through their minds then.

This particular evening Lorriel just started to concentrate when all of a sudden Rebekka was there.

"Lorriel, are you there?"

"Yes," Lorriel replied.

"Good, Raven and I are coming up that way in a couple of days to see Andronicus and we wondered if you and Andrew can get away and come with us for a few days?"

"I think that would be a splendid idea, we have been busy of late and we could use a couple of days rest. I know of no business that would keep us from going. I think you know it does not take much encouragement for any of us to go there. No garden or place is more peaceful and there is no better food or hospitality than that of Andronicus' home. And you know how Andrew is about the stored wisdom of the ancients in the machine Andronicus calls a computer. He spends almost all of his time there when we go."

Lorriel heard a laugh echoing in her mind.

"Yes," Rebekka answered, "Raven is the same way with Andronicus' dueling ability. It seems he is the only one close to Raven's ability and reflexes being a machine. All Raven wants to do is exercise and duel with him."

"It seems we all find our special needs met at the wondrous place left for us by our ancestors," Lorriel answered back. "That is why it has been too long since our last visit, we all need to be refreshed in our own way."

There was silence for a moment and then Rebekka broke the silence with this question: "Have you or Andrew had any strange dreams lately, frightening ones, nightmares?"

"No," Lorriel said, but then added hastily, "Andrew has been tossing and turning a lot lately, and has cried out a couple of times, but he has not said anything to me. And I, myself have not had any bad dreams. But when I concentrate and clear my mind like right before I contacted you, there seems to be a feeling of foreboding evil."

"I have felt it too," replied Rebekka. "We should speak to Andronicus about this when we see him, maybe he can explain to us why we are feeling these things."

"Good night," Lorriel said, and then added, "friends forever!"

"Friends forever," repeated Rebekka.

42

After Rebekka was gone form her thoughts, Lorriel sat back and thought of the peace that had come to Glenfair since Raven had become king.

"Glenfair has the best king and queen it has ever had," she said to herself and smiled at the sound of those words, for she knew that she believed what she said with all her heart. Raven had made it possible for her to have the one thing that eluded many seeking it, true love, deep and satisfying. She also knew that the price of her and Andrew's love had come at a great cost to Raven, more than anyone knew, including herself. Raven had given his whole heart to save the kingdom, and others several times. Andrew likewise had made sacrifices and had saved her and Raven's life as well. But what had she done for the kingdom or anyone? Lorriel felt a little guilty having such a good life, with a son and daughter to round out all her wishes. Everything had come to her without much effort. She knew at that moment, being doubly blessed by God, that if there ever was an opportunity to make a sacrifice for the good of others or the kingdom she would make it without hesitation.

A tear formed in the corner of her eye as she thought of her dear friend Rebekka, she knew too that Rebekka would give up everything for the kingdom as well. What a precious wife Raven had, she was such a complement to him with her balanced wisdom and insight. She couldn't imagine Raven with any other woman as queen. At that moment she knew why her father had never remarried after their mother's supposed death. She knew that it would be that way for Raven as well. She prayed that none of them would have to suffer that kind of loss before its due time.

She sat up and sighed, one should not dwell on the uncertain, but cherish what one has at present. Lorriel then got up and left to find Andrew to inform him of their gathering in two days with Andronicus. She was sure he would have no trouble finding the time to go.

3,000 YEARS INTO THE FUTURE:

Layton Teal sat at the desk in his office pouring over the latest briefs on the affairs of state. Everything seemed to be the same these last few years. No major wars or rebellions, taxes were coming in, the empire was firmly in his grasp, everything was basically calm. In some ways he did not want calm. Calm was the absence of challenge, the lack of opportunity to exercise his genius. He felt like he was going mad just sitting around watching his empire stay calm. The problem with conquering it all was there was nothing more to conquer. He had reached the top, where was he to go now? His thoughts strayed to those who had betrayed him and fled his presence. The traitors somehow had fled beyond his reach.

In some ways he was grateful for the distraction and challenge of trying to find them. What they had done to him was something he could not ignore, his genius would not allow it. For twelve years now he had searched and scoured every lead he could find, but still nothing had produced any leads that he deemed probable. For twelve years he had searched and his genius yielded nothing. For him this was impossible, unacceptable, and it tormented his soul to the extent that he felt he could not die in peace without solving this riddle. His investigation revealed that at least forty people had disappeared with an inconceivable amount of equipment. It still perplexed him how this could happen. He knew that they had fled somewhere to the past, and it wasn't in the recent past. He had searched the records back several hundred years and not a hint of their presence was found. He knew they could not hide their technology and the machines they had taken with them from the world going back at least eight hundred years. The historical records were too complete that far back in history to hide what they had taken with them. Fliers, huge laser mining machines,movers, power modules by the dozens, modern weapons, and manufacturing equipment were some things you could not hide from the past. Yet, that is exactly what they had done. They must have somehow gone further back in time than he could conceive, but where? Even if he could find out where they were he had no way to reach them. He lacked the information and science to travel that great distance in time.

His anger rose as he remembered that he had sent Uriah to watch over Samuel's experiments with Mary Sheldon and time manipulation. But with Uriah's betrayal all information from his spying was gone with he rest of the rebels. And Samuel had so thoroughly purged the computers of his experiments that other scientists were unable to duplicate his research. All that was still a moot point because he did not have a time traveler to manipulate time anyway. He was almost sad that he had let his fear of the time travelers cause him to order their executions. His fear was just because he knew a time traveler might go back in time and eliminate him from history. So to solve that problem from ever occurring he had them all executed except Mary Sheldon. He believed that she loved him and her and Uriah's betrayal cut the deepest. At that moment his musings were interrupted by a knock on his door.

"Come in", Laton answered. His top aid, Blastion Astmos entered and paused; "I could come back if you are occupied Emperor", he said as he bowed.

"No, that is fine, tell me what this is about", Layton responded. Blastion was his most trusted aid and if he had interrupted Layton there was a reason. He waited patiently as Blastion began;

"We have received a very interesting report of a possible time shifter. It has been some years since we have heard of any and the informer wants to know if the reward of one million is still in place for finding this one."

Layton sat up in his chair and spoke; "We never did rescind that offer though it has been some years since the last reported case. Please continue Blastion."

"The informant claims to have witnessed a young girl of thirteen vanishing from her back yard and reappearing as he watched. He claims that he was not observed and is the only one who witnessed this event. Also contained in his report is the fact that this girl is the second daughter this family has and stated that she is an illegal child. Evidently he was overlooking this transgression until this latest development occurred."

"Do you have the information and location of this child?" asked Layton.

"Yes we do, the family lives in the Distadz province and we have their address," answered Blastion.

"Good, pay the man his reward and tell him to never mention this again to anyone or his reward will be forfeit and he will be severely punished. Also get a squad of thirty soldiers ready and we will go meet this family tomorrow," Layton stated.

Blastion nodded and left quickly to carry out Layton's commands.

Layton Teal leaned back in his chair and smiled to himself. At last, after all these years things were falling into place again. His scientist had informed him they had finally developed time amplifiers that they believed would be able to amplify a time shifter's ability but they needed a time shifter to test the devices and tune the amplifying frequencies. The scientist had given up trying to duplicate the crystals that Samuel had created but the electronic alternative they believed would work just as well. Now Layton would have a time shifter to verify these time amplifying devices. The fact that she was an early teenager was perfect. She was too young to cause him any trouble and could easily be manipulated into doing all he wished. This was almost too good to be true. All the time shifters he had captured had all been adults far into their maturity and proved too independent and dangerous to allow them to live. He was very careful to cover his tracks when it came to executing time travelers. When he found them he would make a great deal publicly of rewarding them and gifting them before they were spirited away to some secret location and done away with. When any family inquired about them, the empires response was to inform them they were doing top secret work for the benefit of the empire. Few within his top tier of his government knew what had happened to the time shifters. Only a few scientists knew the truth of their demise. Layton was sure there were some time shifters in the empire that he did not know about, and they kept very well hidden and did not reveal themselves. So far as Layton knew the ruse had worked to cover what had happened to the time shifters.

Now, this girl would be perfect for his plans and he knew exactly how to deal with her and her family. He was almost grateful for the gift of circumstances that the family had given him. They had disobeyed the prohibition of the one child per family policy the empire had in place. In fact some couples were not allowed to have any children whatsoever. Those who did have a child had to obtain a license from the state. Taking this child away would only be enforcing state guidelines without the issue of time travel ever being mentioned. This was truly gifted circumstances in his favor.

Layton leaned back in his chair, the time shifter was one piece of the puzzle, a very big piece that had fallen into place. But the problem remained; he still had not found one clue in history that gave him any indication where the rebels had gone. That was still a mystery and Layton believed would eventually solve that riddle too. Given time he knew he would eventually find them wherever they had gone, and when he did he now had a way to get there.

The next day Layton and thirty soldiers set out for the Distadz province where the family of this young girl lived. When they approached the address of the home, Layton left most of the soldiers with the flyers and continued on with only four soldiers to the house. When they knocked on the door and a woman opened her face went pale when she saw Layton Teal and the four soldiers with him. Never in her lifetime did she expect the emperor to ever to come her home, least of all even to their province. She bowed and invited them in and then Layton sat down in their living area while the soldiers continued to stand. The woman sat as well and knew this would not end well for them if the emperor himself was here. He rarely ventured from the capitol for any reason. There was silence for a short time and then Layton spoke:

"Call all of your family members here, we need to have a little family meeting."
The woman called for her two daughters to come sit by her but informed Layton that her husband was at work.

"That is not a problem, he will be here shortly," Layton answered. "Which of your two daughters is the youngest?" Layton inquired.

The mother answered with rising panic in her voice, "Elise is the youngest of our two daughters."

At that moment Elise's father arrived and with a stern face entered his home and went to stand beside his wife and daughters. Layton wasted no time and began:

"Having two children in your home is a violation of the one child per couple law that the state has established. And before you make up some kind of excuse or tale to explain this, let me tell you it will not work nor will it matter. The fact is, I see two children here and that is all I need to make my decisions. Any couple wishing to have more than one child has to get permission from me personally to do so. I know others in the empire have tried to hide an extra child from me but eventually they will be found out. So there must be some action taken to keep order in the empire."

Before Layton could continue Elise's father spoke:

"The extra child is not a burden to the empire and we provide for her from the wages and rations we receive, we ask no more from the empire than what we already have. Please honored emperor could you grant us to keep the children we have?"

There was a short pause and Layton simple said, "No." Layton stood and motioned to one of his soldiers and they handed Elise's mother an envelope and then Layton said, "What is in the envelope is compensation for your youngest daughter, since she was never supposed to be born, she must die." And with that Layton reached down and grabbed Elise's elbow and forcefully guided her from the house while the soldiers blocked any move from the family to intervene. This happened so quickly that they could not react and with the soldiers standing there they realized that it was hopeless to attempt any intervention.

After a few minutes they heard a shot outside and their hearts failed them and they began to weep. They realized that Elise was gone forever and this happening by the very hand of the emperor himself what could they have done?

After Layton had taken Elise outside he kneeled down on one knee and spoke in a kind voice to her; "If you come with me I will give you anything you want except one thing, you can never have your family back again ever. I am your family now, and if you do not do as I say I will kill all of them and you as well. Do you understand me?"

Elise turned very pale and nodded in the affirmative as Layton rose to his feet. He reached out and took her hand and Elise did not resist, feeling numb all over as they walked over to the flyer that was reserved for Layton. Just before they boarded Layton nodded to one of his soldiers and he aimed his rifle in the air and fired a shot. Then they were in the flyer and heading back to the capitol. During the trip as the shock was wearing off Elise began to cry.

Layton let her weep for a while then in a stern voice said, "Enough! You will have a very privileged life that few will ever experience. You will be by my side and will accompany me on most of my travels. You will have most anything you want, all you have to do is ask."

Elise's sobs began to subside and she asked, "Where will I live, with you?"

"No, that would not be appropriate. You will have a lavish apartment to live in," answered Layton.

"I will live all alone?" asked Elise.

"Not entirely alone, you will have people to wait on and help you with whatever you want," Layton offered.

Elise's eyes went wide, "You mean I would have like my own servants. Would they do as I asked them?"

"Yes, yes," Layton said smiling. This was exactly as he planned. Appeal to the girl's desire for things and a sense of importance and she would be his servant forever. He knew she would take pampering and appeasing but it would be worth it in the long run. She was the perfect age he began to realize. Not too young to be on her own, but not old enough to be too independent before she got attached to what he could provide for her. His thoughts were interrupted by Elise speaking again.

"I would be like a queen, having servants and fancy dresses and eating at fancy places wouldn't I?"

Layton smiled to himself; "Yes you would be like a queen, in fact after you get some new clothes we can dine together tonight at a fancy restaurant, would you like that?"

"Yes I would very much," answered Elise.

The rest of the flight was spent in silence as Elise grappled with her new position with Layton. Layton could have read her mind because he was a powerful telepath but felt it a wast of time and energy. He was satisfied that he had planted the seeds that were needed to bring Elise along on the path he had placed before her. To Layton, human nature had been a study he excelled at and applied himself to it for many years. So confident was he of his success that it never entered his mind to check on Elise. If Layton suspected what Elise was thinking he surely would have listened to her thoughts. Elise knew more about Layton Teal than he suspected. Her parents had raised her to be independent and to think for herself. They knew there may come a time when their unauthorized daughter might have to go into hiding. With the added fact that she was a time shifter added to their vigilance in the instruction they were giving her. They taught her about Layton Teal and his brilliant military genius and his telepathic ability. There were plans and contingencies in place if the empire ever discovered her. But Layton Teal had appeared so suddenly that none of them could be used. If she had disappeared before Layton had arrived her family could have denied her existence. But once Layton showed up and he seemed to know everything their plans had all crumbled. He was known for being one step ahead of people and he had caught them flat footed. She looked over at Layton. She knew that she could disappear any time she wanted and Layton could do nothing to prevent it. But now with the threat of her parents and sister's executions if she did not comply had changed everything. The families plan had been for her to disappear and meld into the empire in a couple of years, but now that was impossible. So, she would have to make the best of this situation and maybe it would end up being better that living a life hiding under the empire's radar. In fact it could be very much better she decided. Elise's reasoning was due to the maturity her parents had tried to instill in her. And in some ways she was several years ahead of her actual thirteen years. Well, she was almost fourteen now.

About that time the flyer began to circle for its landing in the capitol and shortly touched down. As they exited the flyer Layton introduced Elise to Blastion Astmos and told her that he would see to her needs and then proceeded to leave. Elise looked at Blastion and he motioned her to a ground car that was waiting. As they entered the car Blastion noticed the calm composure the young girl exhibited and made a mental note of it. When they arrived at the lavish apartments, Blastion guided her to the elevator and took them to the sixty seventh floor. He guided her left to a large corner apartment that had two views of the land and city about them. Elise looked around amazed, the apartment was more than twice the size of her families home. And it was lavishly furnished. The luxury overwhelmed her. Her thoughts were interrupted by Blastion speaking:

"Here is your key card and credit card for any thing you need. Others will arrive shortly to fit you for some new clothes, both practical and elegant as fits you station. Then this evening you will dine with Layton himself at Shirlinghouse. A driver will come to escort you to dinner and bring you home."

Elise was overcome and asked, "Is all this mine? My real home for just me?"

"Yes," answered Blastion, "I must go now but we shall meet again." And then he paused and said somberly, "I'm very sorry Elise for what has happened to you." And with that he strode from the room and closed the door behind him.

Elise watched him go and sat down in one of the plush chairs. This apartment was amazing, like living in a fantasy. She wished she could bring her family to live with her here. But she knew that was not to be and sadness overcame her joy. Before she could go too far into depression a knock on the door shook her out of her self pity. She went to answer the door and a woman and attendants came bustling into the room. They began asking what styles of clothes she liked and what colors would suit her best. After they had measured her from head to toe they left as quickly as they had come. It left Elise in a bit of a whirl and she sat down to contemplate her situation. Why was she being treated so elegantly? None of this made any sense, the only conclusion she could come to was Layton wanted something from her, but she did not know what that could be. Until that was revealed she could do nothing for her situation so she decided that she would relax and enjoy what had been handed her.

In a short while the attendants returned with all kinds of clothes and shoes and everything in clothing you could want including jewelry. When most had left one woman stayed behind to help her dress for the evening dinner. When she was fully dressed the woman showed her a button on the arm of her chair that would summon her if she needed anything else. A driver would come shortly and take her to dinner with Layton. She left and Elise waited and in a short time there was a knock at her door. She opened it and the driver escorted her to his waiting car.

When they arrived at the restaurant it was very elegant and every bit amazing as she had hoped. She was escorted to a table that had one occupant, Layton Teal. Seeing him again did not bring the fear she had felt before, but she was still awed and reticent in his presence. When she was seated Layton spoke;

"You may order anything you want from the menu, I want you to enjoy this evening for we have much to discuss."

The food was brought and they began to eat. Not long into the dinner Layton said casually; "You are a time shifter aren't you."

Elise was just about to take a bite and now her fork hung suspended mid-air.

"How did you know that? No one knew that except my family, no one." It now made sense what Layton wanted from her. If he wanted to kill her he would have done that already.

Layton smiled; "Very few things are hidden from me in my empire, you would do well to remember that. But relax, I have need of your talent. This is why I will treat you very well if you help me. I have some science experiments that involve time travel and I need your help to complete them. But before we can get to that we need to give you a title that will be workable within my government." Layton thought for a moment and then said, "You will be called Chancellor Elise. You will attend all cabinet meetings, although they may seem boring to you, and travel with me when I visit other places in the empire. Tomorrow you will be taken to my special science division and begin to help them with their experiments. Are we agreed?" Elise just nodded her head in the affirmative.

The rest of the meal was eaten in silence and as she watched Layton Teal he looked calm on the outside but she could tell he was like a coiled snake ready to strike. This did not affect Elise as it would others, for her fear of Layton had lessened because she knew he needed her. She was cautious because of the threat against her family, but she did not posses a paralyzing fear either. The evening ended and as she exited the restaurant her driver met her and bowed and said; "good evening Chancellor Elise." As she was seated in the car she was amazed at how quickly her new title and position was known. When she exited the car at her lavish apartments, the doorman bowed and exclaimed; "Chancellor Elise." It seemed that all the staff of the complex in which she lived were all very respectful of her now. It made her feel like a queen. "If only Donna could see me now," she mused.

The next day she was taken to the facility that housed Layton's science division and there she met the head scientist Dr. Conrad Jordan.

"I am very please to meet you Chancellor Elise," he stated. "Come, have a seat while I ask you some questions."

Elise took a seat and Dr. Gerald Bask began: "Chancellor Elise, how many times have you time traveled?"

Elise thought, "Only three," she answered.

"How great a distance did you travel in those trips?" Asked Dr. Jordan.

"Just a few days each time," was all Elise offered. It seemed Dr. Jordan was not interested in what she did or where she went, only the time duration. He took some notes and then asked Elise to follow him to a room with all kinds of scientific equipment. When she was seated Dr. Jordan began to explain to her what they were going to do.

"We need to take some measurements of your time dilation to get a precise spectrum for the time amplifiers. It will take us some time so please be patient with us Chancellor Elise."

Elise waited and tried to understand what Dr. Jordan was telling her. Her only concern was if they were going to do something painful to her like an injection. She wondered too if she were to provide what they wanted then Layton would no longer need her and she would be eliminated. As she thought about this she calmed down and realized he would not have given her a title and position is she were slated for execution. This caused her to relax a great deal and focus on what the scientists were doing. They were working on all kinds of instruments and chatting among themselves. When it seemed like this went on for a very long time Dr. Jordan approached her.

"We are ready now for the experiment to begin. What time did you leave your apartment this morning?"

Elise thought a moment and then answered, "It was eight o'clock when I left this morning."

Dr. Jordan looked at the clock and saw that it was eleven thirty and nodded. Then he turned to Chancellor Elise and spoke: "Listen very carefully to what I ask you to do. You will enter this chamber and when I tell you, you are to go back to your apartment at eight thirty this morning and then return back here right after you left. Do you understand?"

Elise nodded and Dr. Jordan led her to the chamber she was to stand in.

Dr. Jordan spoke to calm her, "The chamber is nothing more than a place to measure the harmonic spectrum of your time displacement. You will not feel a thing and nothing will hurt you. The glass window will allow you to see and communicate with us."

Elise then stepped into the chamber and the door was shut. In a moment Dr. Jordan asked, "Are you ready?"

Elise nodded and then vanished and her apartment appeared. She looked at her the clock in her apartment and it said eight thirty and Elise was very pleased with herself. She then concentrated on the time and the chamber where she started and in an instant she was back there. Dr. Jordan smiled when she reappeared and told her that every thing was great.

"Now," Dr. Jordan continued. "I want you to do the same thing again only go to your apartment at nine o'clock. Do not go back to eight thirty because you are already there, do you understand? Also come back here five minutes after you leave, you don't have to cut your jumps so closely. I think we are ready again, go ahead Chancellor Elise."

Elise concentrated on her apartment and the time of nine o'clock and vanished once again and her apartment reappeared. She looked at the clock in her apartment and it read nine o'clock. She smiled and noting her accuracy was very pleased with herself. Now she concentrated on the chamber five minutes after she had left there and the chamber took shape around her. Dr. Jordan once again smiled as she reappeared in the chamber.

"Are you feeling tired or anything after these two trips," asked Dr. Jordan.

"No, I feel fine," Elise replied.

Dr. Jordan nodded, "We need to do this two more times and then that will be all for the day. Now, ten o'clock and ten thirty will be our target times. You may proceed whenever you want."

Elise concentrated and once more vanished and returned to the chamber and then did it once more. Doctor Bask opened the door and Elise exited the chamber.

"We got very consistent readings from your travels, I believe that we can now proceed in calibrating the amplifiers to match your harmonic spectrum. This is all we need from you until we are ready to test the devises. Thank you very much for your help Chancellor Elise.' He bowed to her and she left to go back to her apartment. When she reached the apartment she sat down in her chair and realized she was very hungry. She pushed the button on the arm and in in few moments a woman entered and asked if she could do anything for Elise.

"Yes," Elise replied, "I would like a large pepperoni and sausage pizza and a variety of soft drinks."

"Is that all Chancellor Elise," the woman asked.

"Yes," was all Elise said. The woman bowed and left. In a short while she returned with the pizza and the soft drinks and stood at attention until she was dismissed. This is awesome Elise thought as she dug into the pizza. All she had to do was push a button and she got anything she wanted, well almost, she couldn't have her family. A sadness once again fell upon her as she continued to quietly eat.

The next day Blastion Astmos came to her apartment and informed her that the next day they would have a cabinet meeting and Layton wanted her to attend.

"It is best in these cabinet meetings for you to remain silent," Blastion exclaimed. "You would do well to listen and observe. No one of your age has ever had the privilege of being part of Layton's cabinet. And I for one do not understand why Layton is doing this. So you had better be on your best behavior and try and learn from what is taking place."

Elise only nodded and Blastion's demeanor softened. "I hope you are adjusting to your new life. If there is anything I can do for you just ask me," said Blastion. He then left and Elise was alone once again.

The next day came quickly and Elise dressed appropriately for the occasion, was picked up by her driver and taken to the capitol's governmental building. She had only seen pictures of it on the vid screen and now it looked so much more grand. She was ushered into the counsel chambers amid greetings and bows from other officials. She was shown to her seat that would then be hers for all of the cabinet meetings to follow and sat quietly self-conscious of the other council member's stares. The other council members were seated at a curved desk, and to her right, elevated above all was a huge empty chair. On the other side of that, like her's Blastion Astmos was seated. She continued to in silence until a door opened behind the huge chair and Layton Teal entered and sat in his large chair. His elevation she noticed gave him a distinct advantage over all the others in the room. Some of the council members she recognized, having seen them on the vid screen. Her musings were interrupted by Layton beginning the meeting.

"The only reason we are having this cabinet meeting today is to introduce a new member of this cabinet. Chancellor Elise will now be part of every cabinet meeting we will have from now on." Elise could see that this news troubled some members of the cabinet but they remained silent until Esther Smith spoke:

"She is very young to be part of our cabinet. We often discuss very sensitive and secret things in our cabinet meetings. What is her function anyway?" Elise could see that this was the questions others wanted answered as well.

Layton answered very calmly, "Her purpose is known only to myself and Blastion, the rest of you will have to content yourselves with that answer. You will not have to worry about her spouting state secrets for she will travel with me and Blastion to most of my state appearances. When she is not with me she will be ensconced in her apartment or escorted wherever she goes. But do not suspect that she is an unimportant part of this cabinet. Mostly she will remain silent and observe our meetings, but she is free to speak and vote with the rest of you if she is so inclined. Am I clear?" No one else said a thing so Layton adjourned the meeting and the members began to leave. Only one member came up to her afterwards and shook her hand.

"Hello, Elise, I am John Martin the minister of defense. I would like to welcome you to our cabinet."

Elise shook hands with John Martin and bowed saying; "It is very nice to meet you Minister Martin." John Martin noticed the Elise's respectful bow and thought, "there is more to her than the others think."

Weeks went by and Layton was in his office once again bored with the details of his empire when Blastion knocked on his door.

"Come in," Layton answered, already knowing who it was.

Blastion entered, bowed and began: "Dr. Jordan request your appearance with Chancellor Elise to demonstrate the progress they have made on the time amplifying devices."

"Inform him that we shall be there tomorrow at ten o'clock," Layton stated. Blastion bowed and left to deliver the message. Layton began to consider the implications of tomorrow's visit. Could they have solved the problem of long distance time travel that Samuel seemed to have solved so easily. Well, tomorrow he would find out.

The next day came and Layton picked up Elise at her apartment. When she entered the car she noticed that Blastion was there with them but did not say anything about his presence. When they arrived at the science facility they entered where Elise had helped Dr. Jordan with his experiments. Dr. Jordan came up to Layton, bowed and then handed him a small electronic device.

Layton looked at it and then said, "So this is what will enable us to travel greater distances in time?"

"Yes," Dr. Jordan answered. "Every person who travels in time needs an amplifier in their possession when they travel. It will form a shell of temporal time around each person linked to the time shifter and their device."

"How many of the devices do you have at present," asked Layton.

Dr. Jordan answered, "We have twelve of them manufactured so far. How many do you want?"

"At least fifty," Layton answered. Are the devices ready for testing now?"

"Yes," Dr. Jordan said frowning.

"Give a device to Blastion and Chancellor Elise," spoke Layton.

Dr. Jordan hesitated and then said, "Someone else should test the devices besides yourself. We need more time to run more tests, we just finished them this week. We don't know all effects this will have in long distance time travel. But if you insist, let me go instead of you."

Layton shook his head, "No I want to do this myself." Then he turned to Elise, "Are you ready to take a trip?" Elise's eyes went wide and she slowly nodded. "Then take us to the city square two hundred years into the past Chancellor."

Dr. Jordan handed Elise and Blastion a device and stepped away from them. Then Elise began very calmly to concentrate on two hundred years in the past. Their surroundings began to shimmer and fade then when she almost panicked their surroundings began to form around them once more. They were still in the city but it was very different than the city Elise knew. Instead of in a building they stood in a city square with people waking by. Some noticed their dress and stared but did not approach. Layton asked a pedestrian if he could answer a question for them and the person slowed and stopped.

"Yes sir, what can I answer for you?" the man asked.

"What year is this?" Layton asked, and when the man informed him he just nodded. "Thank you very much," and the man went on his way. Layton turned to Elise and stated, "Take us back to the place and time we left please."

Elise concentrated on the time they had left and again the surroundings began to shimmer and fade then the laboratory began to materialize before them. When it was fully formed and the process complete Layton turner to Dr. Jordan and said: "your devices work fine, see there was nothing to worry about."

And then turning to Elise said, "You did very well Elise, I would like to reward you with something special, what would you like?"

Elise thought for a moment and then said, "I would like to see my family."

Layton's smile turned into a frown and he said with a very harsh voice, "I thought I made that clear. That is the one thing you cannot have. I am your family. Never mention this to me again or they will die, am I clear?"

Elise turned her head down and fought to keep the tears from falling. Layton's voice came again softer this time: "Tell me of something else you desire and I will give it to you."

Elise was quiet for a while and then finally answered, "I want my own personal android, one that is special, different than the ones that the other rich people have.

"I can arrange that, thank you Elise you have done very well," Layton answered.

On the way back to her apartment there was very little said, but Elise began to think about the android she would receive. Only the very rich had androids and now she would have one for her very own. That knowledge helped to take some of the sing out of the open wound she felt about her family once again. Maybe life apart from her family would not be so bad. She knew after Layton's response that she needed to emotionally disconnect from that part of her life and never bring it up again if she were to survive.

When Layton Teal arrived back at his office, he called up Castor and Johnson the top robotics company in his empire. When those who answered the vid screen saw him they blanched pale and soon a man appeared on the screen.

"Hello, your excellency, I am David Castor. What can I do for you?"

Layton Teal got right to the point; "I need an android, female, for a young woman. It cannot be a run of the mill android, it needs to be special, different than the normal service androids. When you have finished you may contact my aid Blastion Astmos for its delivery."

David Castor frowned, "What do you mean by special, and different?"

"I don't know, I leave that up to you," replied Layton. "Do not disappoint me."

With that the screen went dark which left David Castor in a stupor until one of his aids asked him what that was all about.

"Take me to the finished robots that are waiting to be programmed," he said. Together they went to a part of the factory where completed robots were ready to be put into service. David Castor walked along the line of robots and stopped by one female. He tried to decide what Layton meant by different or unique. He did not think a cosmetic difference is what he wanted but a uniqueness in the android's cognitive function. Then he remembered something. Years before they had manufactured a few robots with a special experimental program. There had been just a handful of robots programed with the new experimental program that was designed to broaden the parameters of the way the androids perceived harm to humans and not shut down their positronic pathways so easily. That seemed to be achieved, but an additional byproduct of the programing had been the androids developing emotions. This troubled him greatly and so after the first original few he had shelved the program and had gone back to the original program. The few that were in service were still under observation to see how they functioned in society. Two had broken down and were back at the plant, and the others were functioning well. No report of abnormal behavior had been reported, and no harm had come to any human. There was one mystery, one android had completely disappeared, leaving no trace to its existence. That was very perplexing to not have the android show up anywhere. Casting those considerations aside he remembered one particular android they had not placed in service. Because of the android's peculiar answers it had been placed in a vault for storage until a future date. In their busyness they had never gotten back to studying this particular android. He went to the vault and opening it said to his assistants; "This one," he said. "Bring her in fifteen minutes to my private laboratory." Before the robot arrived, David Castor opened up the file that contained the video of the interview of the android in question. It had been many years since the interview had taken place and he wanted to review that interview. As he watched he became mesmerized by the androids answers. He replayed the part that fascinated him: Question; "Two children are in danger of being killed, you can save only one of them so what would you do?"

The android answered; "To pick the child that could be saved with most certainty and keep it from harm and lament the loss of the other." There was quiet for a moment and then the interviewers whispered to themselves for a moment and then asked:

"If the last person on earth were dying and you could not prevent that occurrence, what would you do?"

The android answered; "It would bring me great sadness to be left alone and I would attempt to assemble another such as myself." Again there were quiet whisperings between the interviewers. Finally one asked:

"Why would you attempt such a construction?"

The android answered, "It would be for the purpose of companionship, I do not wish to be left alone."

Again there was whispering among the interviewers and they left for a very long time. When they returned they spoke to the android;

"You will be called Pi, and your number designation is 3.141592654. We have designated you such because we find some of your answers seem to be irrational for an android. You answered more like a human and that troubles us greatly. You will not immediately be placed into service but placed into our vault to be studied further.

At the end of the video interview David Castor turned it off and sat down. There was a knock at his door and the android entered.

"Please sit down," David castor said to the android. "I want to ask you some questions before we place you into service in our society."

"I will answer any questions you ask of me," the android commented.
David Castor continued, "We did not deactivate you but left you in our vault for many years, how did that make you feel?"

There was a pause as the Android considered, "I felt terribly alone, isolated, the only break from the emptiness was the occasional visitor to the vault. Every time I had hoped it would be me they had come for but it was not until now. There were times I had wished I had never been activated."

David Castor was stunned, he had never considered the morality of placing an android into such isolation when they possessed emotions. His heart almost broke at the unintentional cruelty he had fostered upon this android. He knew androids without emotion would feel nothing no matter how many years had passed in a similar situation.

Then slowly he asked, "Are you angry with us for leaving you in isolation for so long?"

"No," Pi answered. "Just a deep sadness and sorrow for being left all alone."

David Castor looked at the android with compassion. "you will no longer be left in isolation. Tomorrow you will be placed in service to young woman of great importance. I hope life will be better for you from now on. You may stay here in this office until then and feel free to use any computers to fill any gaps of knowledge you feel are missing."

"Thank you," answered Pi.

The next day David Castor contacted Blastion and arranged to meet him at Elise's apartment. When they arrived they took the android up to Elise's apartment and knocked at her door. Elise opened the door and invited them in. Blastion introduced David Castor to Elise, and once introduced began to explain about the android.

"Her name is Pi and she was manufactured a few years ago but never placed into service. She is the most unique android that we have ever manufactured. I hope she serves you well. I will key your summons button to her so she will come anytime you desire her services. Is there anything else I can do for you?" Elise shook her head and David Castor and Blastion left.

Elise was left alone with the android and for a short while said nothing. Finally she spoke: "What can you do?"

"What would you like me to do?" the android asked.

Elise thought for a moment and said, "I am hungry can you get me lunch?"

"Tell me what you want and I will bring it to you." Elise told the android what she wanted and a short time later the android returned with Elise's lunch. As she began to eat the android stood beside her saying nothing. After a short while her silent presence began to annoy Elise so she said; "Do you have to sand here?"

"Where would you like me to go?" the android answered.

"I don't care, just somewhere out of the way and out of sight until I need you again." The android left and Elise finished her lunch, never giving a thought about the android in her service. She was only there to serve her and that is all Elise wanted.

Months went by and Layton Teal was once again in his office going over figures and administrative paperwork when he put the page he was reviewing down. He began to think of the traitors once again and how thoroughly they had made their escape from his grasp. He had twelve reputed historians working round the clock searching history trying to find any hint to where the traitors had gone. For years now they had found nothing. What made Layton more eager was the fact that the most difficult part had been already solved in finding a time shifter and the creation of the amplifying devices. All he needed now was to find out when and where to go. The waiting was almost intolerable, but Layton was a patient man. Sometime he would find the answers, that he did not doubt.

The next week there was a knock on Layton's door. "Enter." Layton spoke. When Blastion entered he handed Layton some information that one of the historians had uncovered. As Layton read through the information, Blastion stood in the room and waited. A smile began to form at the corners of Layton's mouth. This is what he had been waiting for. And of all things, an ancestor of his from the Wickshield kingdom of the distant past had recorded a battle with the little kingdom of Glenfair in which a soldier exhibited unnatural speed and reflexes and had slaughtered an elite fighting force of the Wickshield army by himself. This has to be Uriah, Layton concluded. No one he knew could do such a thing. And the most marvelous thing about this obscure piece of history was it was dateable to a very accurate time period, just a little over three thousand years in the past.

Layton turned to Blastion and said, "Gather an elite force of eighteen commandos and have them ready to depart tomorrow. Inform Elise and have her ready to travel as well." Blastion nodded and then left Layton's office. After Blastion had left, Layton leaned back in his chair and smiled. At last, after all these years he would finally have his revenge. This thought invigorated him like nothing else had for a long time. His final challenge would finally be fulfilled.

3,000 YEARS INTO THE PAST: KING RAVEN'S DAY

Raven sat in the counsel chambers with the door shut and began to read the ancient Prescott scroll once again. He was so excited to find out more of the ancients that his breathing increased a little. He quickly passed what he had read before and found the place where he had left off and began:

"It has taken us much work to construct our castles, but we are thankful for the amount of stone there is surrounding this quaint valley. With the lasers and tools we brought with us we were able to construct each castle in less than three months time. I have to laugh when I think that the old ruins I explored in my archeology class were the ones we built. I don't think any of us knows the extent of what we have done to history. We never thought of the effects or consequences, we just wanted to flee to someplace where no one could find us and this seemed like the perfect plan. It still seems foolproof, although none of us feels completely safe. How can we, when one of the most brilliant military minds the world has ever known is tracking us down. He has to eventually figure this out. Our only hope is to erase any evidences of our technology and live as everyone else did at this time of earth's history. Only the retreat at the top of the falls will be available to us once we are finished, and it will be hidden from the next generation. A wonderful idea to leave subtle hints that may lead some of our descendants to find it someday and know the truth of how we came here. We all agreed that we wanted that done, for if our plan is successful then we want a select few of the generations to come to know about us.

Blending into this time period is a little more difficult than any of us had imagined. Some have found it very difficult while I have found it an adventure. I cannot say the same for my wife Othellia. She finds the lack of proper bathrooms and hot water on demand, coupled with the lack of a fast cook oven almost intolerable, but we shall manage. Already she is not complaining as much. Everyone knows that we cannot return so they are making the best of it. There was much discussion yesterday on how to form our kingdom. We decided to call it Glenfair because of this pristine valley. We chose Daniel Brickens to be king and another four leaders to be dukes. Daniel laughed when he was chosen as king by the drawing of the first lot, he said he always wanted to be a king. Four more names were drawn from the lots and they became the dukes. Some complained, but it was done fair and everyone knows it to be so. I am duke of the southwest, Felton Rollins will be duke of the northeast, Chester Zandel is the duke of the southeast, and Uriah Kallestor is the duke of the Northwest. I am glad Uriah's name was picked for he deserved to be one of the dukes. Our descendants, if they ever read this will probably laugh when they find out the king and dukes were chosen by no merit of their own, only by the drawing of chance did it fall to them. It is only a title anyway, for we are all in this together and must all do our share to make it work. The rest of the people were divided up and will live in the five castles with the king and dukes unless they want to create a settlement of their own, and that is fine too, for there is plenty of room. No place will be crowded for that leaves less than ten people per castle. We all decided to meet twice a year at the king's castle to feast and renew our unity lest we grow apart and the kingdom be divided. Any law matters will be decided by a counsel of the king and dukes. And if one of us is at issue, then we have elected Samuel Crestlaw to cast the deciding vote if there is a tie. We set a date to cast the armor and signets for the king and the rest of us. At first we thought to make them out of silver but decided to make them functional, so we will use the ceramic titanium alloy triberridum for everything. It is durable and will last for thousands of years if it isn't lost. The rings will be the keys to operating the lift at the falls, so we shall cast two for every family, the spare being kept secure in each of the castles."

Raven paused in his reading to contemplate what he had read. There must be spare rings in the rest of the castles as there was in the king's castle and the Prescott castle. He would have to see if he could find the spare Kallestor ring hidden in the Crestlaw castle someday. Raven made a mental note to mention that to Andrew the next time he saw him. After Raven had finished thinking about what he had read, and was satisfied that he comprehended it, went back to reading the scroll.

"Eight months after our time jump: Life has not been as easy as we had imagined it would be. We have freed ourselves from one enemy only to face another, hunger. I fear we will be forced to hunt the beast of this land for food this winter because our energies were poured into creating the settlement and not planting crops. The large beasts taste quite good, but if we depend on them for food I know the herds will be depleted and we will be in the same situation again with no beasts to sustain us. As frightening as it is to face a winter without much sustenance, I would rather face the enemy of hunger than the enemy of tyranny from our past. At least now we determine our own fate, live or die it will be our own doing. Those words seem to take some of the sting out of our dilemma. A counsel of dukes has been called to address this very question. Others have seen what I have in our failure to plant sufficient crops for the winter. What an odd thing it is not to be provided for by the state, I never considered the issue of food provisions before we came here. It is exhilarating to know we have to provide for ourselves rather than push a key card into a meal service machine and punch a few buttons. I have never heard of anyone starving because they failed to use their meal card. So much of the danger and adventure had been stripped from us in our easy care free life. Though we face the possibility of death most of us feel more alive than we ever could have imagined.

Three years since our initial time jump: In the business of living I have forgotten to write in my journal. It seems less important now that we have settled into the routine of really living and not just existing. Othellia is pregnant with our second child, a natural consequence since the medications that kept the ladies from getting pregnant have worn off. Our old enemy, the tyrant, made sure only one child was allowed per couple, and some married couples were not allowed any children at all. He claimed it was important that we keep our gene pool under control. Well, I am glad things are back to the way God intended. Even Uriah and Merry had a son before she quit bearing. I know they wanted more but they are thankful for the child they have. It is sad that Merry will not see her grandchildren though.

Life has been so much better since we have adjusted. The crops are coming along fine and we will have more than enough food for everyone. We have decided to protect the large beasts of this valley from over hunting. We named them Tor for what they can do to you if they get their horns into you. Hunting will be allowed for the two feasts we have a year. It will give us meat for the feasts and add quite a bit of sport to the event. Another note, scouts have informed us of developing kingdoms outside each of our passes. They are not a threat just yet, but in the future they may cast an eye upon us to conquer this fine land for their own. So before we decommission the heavy equipment we will build a pass gate out of stone in each of the passes to make it hard for an invading army to get into Glenfair. This is not so much for us, but our future generations will appreciate what we have done for them. I know now that I am not much of a writer so I will not attempt to keep this journal any longer. I will put it away for safe keeping in the family chest. Besides Felton Rollins is keeping an accurate history of our existence without the mention of any technology or advancement. This scroll on the other hand, mentions too much as it is, so it will be put away safely. So reader, if you happened to have found this scroll, remember, if you love Glenfair, keep this from becoming public knowledge lest the enemy find out our plan and seek us here. Farewell, and may all things be to the prosperity of our kingdom. Amnon Prescott."

Raven rolled the scroll back up and sat thinking. Not as noble a beginning as he had envisioned, but enough to start what was now a great kingdom. He wished he could tell them all that had transpired since their humble beginnings. That now Glenfair was a great and glorious kingdom. He wondered if they had ever envisioned a so far-reaching result of their desperate act of fleeing a horribly cruel tyrant. Raven smiled, something so good had come from such a time of evil. He rose and left to find Rebekka, she needed to read the scroll of her ancestor as well, and like him find a new appreciation for the peace and joy they found here in the present.

Thinking of the peace and joy Raven looked forward to meeting with Andronicus in a couple of days. That would be a time of real refreshment.

Finding Rebekka he gave her the scroll and she smiled and asked, "Was it good reading?"

"I think you will find it quite educational." Raven replied. "Now I must be off to find Master Fields to schedule a practice session with him tomorrow."

Rebekka watched Raven leave, and feeling the weight of the scroll in her hand wondered if destiny had not brought them the information of the past that had been lost for so long. "Yes," she decided, "there is a purpose for everything. The abilities we all posses will be put to the test soon I am sure."

The next morning Raven and Master Fields met for arms practice. As Raven readied himself, he saw Master Fields standing watching him with his arms crossed.

"You have no sword, Master Fields, how then can we engage without one?"

Master Fields smiled and said, "Your skill with a sword has far surpassed mine, and in that category I am now your student."

"Then what shall we do?" asked Raven.

"We will fight without any arms at all."

"No weapons," Raven asked, "then boxing it will be?"

"No, no my dear king, we are going to study the art of hand to hand combat."

"I have never heard of such a thing," Raven said. "Is it something that can be effective against an opponent or enemy?"

"Practiced and learned properly it can kill as swiftly as a sword or knife," Master Fields answered.

Now Raven was interested, as he always was to learn more from Master Fields.

"Now," Master Fields began, "rush and take hold of me as if to subdue me."

Raven came toward Master Fields and attempted to grab him about the shoulders and throw him to the ground but the next thing Raven knew he was sailing through the air. He would have hit flat on his back were it not for the incredible reflexes Raven possessed. As it was, he still landed on his knees in a crouched position before he sprang back up.

"How did you do that?" Raven wanted to know.

Master Fields smiled pleased with himself that he still had a few tricks to teach King Raven. "I used your energy and momentum against you and followed your reach through with a throw."

Raven nodded now understanding, a similar lesson was learned long ago with a larger opponent, Mason Zandel during a dueling competition. He had used Mason's own strength against him.

Master Fields now spoke again, "I do not claim to be a master in this hand to hand combat, in fact in reality I know only theory. But I believe as fast as you learn, the theory will aid you if you are ever disarmed and have no weapon. First we will start with the hands and then the feet next, and even the head can be a formidable weapon if needed. Now take your hands and hold them up palms outward toward me."

Raven did so and Master Fields threw his fist into one. Raven did not flinch but moved his hand just slightly to absorb the impact of Master Fields fist.

"Good," encouraged Master Fields, "the front of your hand can absorb most attacks without any harm to you. Your coordination should allow you to stop most blows or deflect them with your hands before they get to your body."

Raven smiled a knowing smile. "The same old format, learn defense first right?"

Master Fields nodded and continued the lessons. Raven learned all kinds of ways to block, deflect, turn, anything to avoid a blow to the vital parts of his body. There was the forearm, the elbow and even the shoulder in desperation that could take blows instead of letting them fall where they could injure the defender. Master Fields had Raven run through exercise after exercise in defense postures from his memory of hand to hand combat theory. As he watched Raven, he was always amazed at how Raven seemed to pick up what he was coaching him to do and apply it with an ease and flowing that almost seemed like art. The only difference was Raven was lightning quick when he wanted to be.

After Master Fields was satisfied with Raven's knowledge of defense he stopped to demonstrate the offensive part of hand to hand combat. Master Fields took a piece of wood that had been discarded by the stables and placed it over the watering trough.

Then he asked Raven. "How should we cut this wood in two?"

Raven answered, "A saw, or an axe would do, but you have something else in mind do you not?"

Master Fields showed Raven his hand and then turned it edgewise showing him the edge of his hand. "The edge of your hand if you concentrate and make it rigid, can act as an axe to deliver blows of considerable power and force."

He then walked over to the wood and with concentration brought the edge of his hand down and chopped the wood in two. Raven was impressed for the piece of wood was sizable, enough so that he believed it could not be broken with just a hand blow.

Now Master Fields spoke. "A blow like this to the back or side of the neck can incapacitate or kill a person. The tip or front of the hand stiffened and thrust forward into the chest below the rib cage can puncture a lung or heart as well."

Raven had no idea that hands could be so lethal. "You don't expect me to use this on someone, do you Master Fields?"

"Not really Sire, but knowing how to kill will protect you if someone tries to kill you that way, do you understand?"

Raven nodded, the master was shrewd, wanting to impart everything to his student that he knew.

"Now the feet," Master Fields said. And with that he began to demonstrate all the kicks and spins that could break bones or almost take someone's head off.

When he had finished demonstrating he motioned for Raven to take a defensive stance and said, "I will attack you defend for our final exercise of the day."

With that the battle began. Master Fields used combinations of chops, kicks, spins, and anything he could think of to throw at Raven. Master Fields was right, the knowledge he had given him enabled Raven to be ready for anything that came at him. Nothing was even getting close to getting through. With a final desperation Master Fields swung his leg around to sweep Raven's feet out from under him. It was a great move for an older man, and Master Fields was pleased he could still do this lightning quick. As the master's leg approached Raven with tremendous speed, it looked as if it was going to make contact, but right before it touched him Raven leaped into the air flipping over Master Fields and landing behind him. The momentum from Master Fields leg swing kept him from dealing with Raven now being behind him, and the next thing Master Fields felt was the edge of a hand at the side of his neck and Raven whispering in his ear, "Do you yield?"

Master Fields chuckled, "I thought I had you with that last move."

"You did," replied Raven, "any other move I made would have been useless, the only option you left me was to go strait up. I just used this as an opportunity to land behind you."

Master Fields just shook his head, "You never cease to amaze me King Raven. You have been the joy of this weapons master ever since I began your training. Thank you for a good days workout."

"No, Thank you Master Fields. I have learned so much from you so how can I ever repay you?"

"Seeing you work and move is all the payment I will ever need," Master Fields replied.

Just then Rebekka came bursting into the courtyard, "Raven, I need to speak to you, something is wrong."

"Excuse us Master Fields," Raven said, as he took Rebekka by the hand and led her toward the privacy of the garden.

When they were inside away from anyone she spoke, "Andronicus has spoken to me in urgency, asking if I would contact Lorriel and see if she had shifted time at all. He has detected a shift in time and he was worried. When I contacted Lorriel, she reminded me of the promise she made to us all not to shift time without a time counsel. When I let Andronicus know what Lorriel said, he told me we must come at once. He also said to avoid the middle of the valley north of the castle, for that is where the time shift seems to have originated."

Raven and Rebekka left the garden area and parted, Rebekka to get things ready for their trip and Raven to find Master Fields. When Raven found Master Fields he informed him that they needed to go north immediately.

Master Fields eyed Raven suspiciously and asked, "Is this one of those excursions to see the old hermit?"

"Yes," Raven spoke seriously, "and I would like you to come with us to the Crestlaw castle and there wait until we return from meeting with him, we may need you."

"What is this about Sire?" Master Fields asked.

"I am not sure, but it seems urgent and I am troubled as well by the possibility of danger to our kingdom."

"Can I not come with you to this hermit, especially if this kingdom is in danger?"

Raven felt the pull of desiring to have Master Fields there for he had revealed to him the gifts that Rebekka, Lorriel, Andrew and himself had received from their ancestors. Master Fields had asked once before to meet the hermit and Raven had promised some day to take him, but now was not the time, especially since there had been a shift in time.

"No, my friend, you will serve us better by staying at the Crestlaw castle and waiting with Sauron for our return. We may need to be off and armed at a moments notice."

Raven could see the disappointment in the master's eyes but he only said, "Yes Sire!"

"Get your armor and meet me in the stables in ten minutes, and have Jerddin armed and ready to go with us as well."

Master Fields nodded and was off. Jerddin was a good man, faithful to the throne, and had risked his life for the kingdom before. Raven had every confidence in him to stand with them if needed.

Raven went back into the castle to retrieve his own armor from the secret passage behind the wall in his room. Then he went down to the great hall and found Rebekka talking to Jessica.

"Good," Raven spoke when he saw them, "I need you to stay here, Jessica and watch things while we are gone."

She looked at the armor Raven was carrying and frowned. "What is going on?" she asked plainly.

"Andronicus has picked up a shift in time and it was not Lorriel."

Aunt Jessica's eyes went wide for she had stayed over three years with Andronicus at the garden and Hall of Wisdom, and knew what this could mean.

"The enemy," she whispered, "has he come?"

"I do not know," Raven said, "but we must hurry and find out what is happening. If anyone comes here looking for us, tell them we will return in three days, and to wait here for us."

With that, Raven and Rebekka gathered the provisions she had packed and headed for the stables. When they arrived they found Master Fields and Jerddin readying the horses for their trip. They secured their provisions and headed out of the castle.

Once outside they immediately turned west toward the mountains. Master Fields asked Raven why they were going that way to the Crestlaws and Raven's only answer was he did not want to run into anyone during the trip north. There was not much conversation on the ride north, for they had gone west until they were far from the normal course of traffic along the Halfstaff River and then turned north.

Finally Jerddin rode up beside the king and asked him, "Sire, should we not have more armed men with us if there is a threat to the kingdom?"

"It is ok," Raven assured him, "we don't know if there is a threat, that is why we are going to investigate with a small group first."

Jerddin nodded, knowing a larger group of soldiers would hinder them from any reconnaissance they might do, so he fell behind to once again ride beside Master Fields. There was an uneasiness as the four rode north, that could not be put into words, but rather was felt. It seemed the day dragged on forever until finally the Crestlaw castle came into view.

As they rode into the castle courtyard Androw was waiting for them with fresh horses saddled and ready.

Sauron was there as well and approached the king and bowing asked, "Sire, what is this urgency in coming here armed. Whatever it is, we are ready to serve you and the kingdom." Raven smiled for he loved Sauron as a father and knew the Crestlaws would die for him and the kingdom.

So Raven merely spoke the truth when he said, "There may be a threat to the kingdom so we are going to the Hall of Wisdom, for the hermit has summoned us. I need you to abide here with Master Fields and have a few armed men ready to ride if we need them."

Sauron looked at Master Fields and Jerddin then nodded to the king and said. "It will be done."

At that moment Lorriel came into the courtyard and hugged Raven and Rebekka, smiling at the growing tummy of Rebekka in her pregnancy.

Lorriel touched Rebekka's stomach and said, "I am so excited that in a few months another Kallestor will fill your lives, and ours."

Raven interrupted the joyful reunion with a reminder that they must be going. Andrew, Lorriel, Rebekka and Raven rode out of the castle and toward the falls. Raven would have preferred Rebekka stay back at their own home because of her pregnancy. But he knew that he could not persuade her to stay behind. She was not too far along in her pregnancy to travel and the trip to the Crestlaws had been taken with rests to accommodate her condition. The ride to the falls was not far but Raven knew Rebekka would be tired at the end of the day. Deep down in his heart he was glad she was along. He needed her observation and mind reading abilities if what he suspected were true.

He could hear Lorriel and Rebekka talking behind as they rode on when Andrew interrupted his thoughts, "Sire, what do you make of the shift in time Andronicus has sensed with his machines?"

"Please," Raven smiled, "when we are alone like this do not call me sire."

Andrew smiled and only said, "Yes King Raven."

Raven frowned, but went on, "I do not know what to think. If the ancients had come forward in time to this place, why worry Andronicus and not appear at the Hall of Wisdom. We know time travelers can travel to a specific place as well as a time. Why here and now for any time traveler to appear? There must be some reason and that's what worries me."

Andrew nodded, "I was thinking the same thing. Do you think it is the enemy of the ancients?"

Raven pondered that question for a moment and then answered. "We will have to find out what Andronicus knows before we jump to conclusions such as that. Why would the enemy come here if he knew the ancients had gone back in time, it seems he would have tried to go there instead."

"What if it is the enemy of the ancients?" asked Andrew. "What should we do?"

"If it is the enemy of the ancients, then our whole kingdom is in grave danger," answered Raven.

They rode on in silence, each contemplating what they would soon find out and before long they were at the falls. They staked out the horses where they could reach water and grass and then proceeded into the mist of the falls. Back against the cliff face was a narrow ledge that dead ended in a wider spot against some rock. When everyone had reached it safely, Raven reached up and depressed the eyes of a crudely formed natural owl in the rock overhead. As a boy, both he and Andrew had come to this place and had even walked out on the ledge, but neither of them had noticed the formation that looked like an owl before the riddle of the ancients. Raven mused that it was probably due to the fact that it did not resemble an owl much but if you were looking for one you could find it. Very similar to looking for animals or people in clouds as they passed over.

The door to the chamber swung open and the four entered, always glad to get away from the cold mist outside. The door closed and they headed for the doors at the opposite end of the chamber. They opened when they approached which surprised no one, since they had been here many times before. Once inside, and the doors closed Raven placed his ring into the depression made for it in the panel of the small room. It began to move and the feeling always surprised Raven. He had come to accept this but had also thought of the great speed with which they were rising for it did not take them long to reach the top of the falls.

The doors opened and they stepped out into a beautiful garden paradise in this small plateau at the top of Brickens' Falls and were met by Andronicus.

"Welcome," he said, "I have some refreshment for you at the hall."

They followed Andronicus the short walk to the glass mansion they called the Hall of Wisdom, and entered through it's ornately carved doors. Even though this was an urgent summons, Raven looked forward to the food provided by Andronicus, it was always far above anything he had ever tasted. He looked at Rebekka and saw that she too was very hungry and anticipated what Andronicus had to offer.

As they sat feasting, it was always disconcerting to see Andronicus just sitting there and not eating anything, patiently waiting for them to finish.

After having a little food, Raven could not wait to speak so he asked, "Keeper (for that is what they sometimes called him for his name was hard to pronounce), what can you tell us of this time shift that has occurred?"

"After you have finished eating, we will walk back to the top of the falls and I will show you."

After they had finished eating Raven rose to go with Andronicus but told Rebekka to stay and rest while they talked. Lorriel decided to stay as well and await what news Raven and Andrew would bring back to them.

Raven, Andrew, and Andronicus walked back down the path to where the Halfstaff River poured over the falls. Raven noticed Andronicus was carrying some device in his hand.

When they reached a place where they could see into the valley, Andronicus handed Raven the device and told him to hold it up to his eyes and look through it into the valley. When Raven did so he let out an astonished cry and stepped back a couple of steps from the edge.

Andrew had a concerned look on his face so Raven handed him the device and Andrew likewise drew in his breath as he looked.

He handed the device back to Raven and said to Andronicus, "It brings things closer so you can see them. Is that how you keep track of events in the valley?"

"Yes," Andronicus stated, "but my eyes can magnify this device a little more for greater distance."

Then he spoke to Raven. "Follow the Halfstaff down toward Pearl Lake and you will find what I want you to see."

Raven looked through the device, and at first had trouble finding his way down the Halfstaff. But soon he was more comfortable with seeing things in that perspective and quickly found what he knew

Andronicus wanted him to see. Along the River was a camp of about twenty people, their tents spread out, and a cooking fire was going with what it looked like a Tor being barbecued on a spit.

"Is this where the shift in time occurred?" Raven asked Andronicus.

"Yes," Andronicus answered.

"Do you recognize anyone, or something about them?"

"Although I can see a little farther with the device than you, I am not able to see faces clearly. But I am sure it is not the ancients, but someone else. And I am also certain that they are from the enemy. Whether he is among them or not I do not know. Let us return to the hall and we will talk."

Raven and Andrew took one last look through the device and headed back to the hall.

Once there and seated in the comfortable chairs in the hall with Rebekka and Lorriel, they began to discuss what should be done.

"Tell us more of the enemy of the ancients," Raven asked.

"Until now," Andronicus began, "I felt there was little need to tell you much about the enemy, for we all believed we had fooled him so thoroughly that we were free from his clutches. Several thousand years into your future a man by the name of Layton Teal will come into power by his military genius. He will control half of the earth and will create a great military state. Because he controls so much, he also fears greatly of loosing that control. Everyone who speaks against his regime gets either interrogated, imprisoned, or executed. He was not always such an evil person. At first his intentions were for good, a halt to wars was accomplished by a unified empire. For a short time there was peace and prosperity, but power can change a person into something they never thought they could be. After the threat of war was over he had to find ways of staying in power so he declared martial law. His excuse was that the unified state could fall apart and there would be war all over again. Most allowed this and submitted to his rule because they were more afraid of war than of loosing their freedom. They wanted peace at any cost. But there were others that realized being secure and being free were two very different things. It was these people who formed a rebellion and began to resist Layton Teal's rule for the sake of being free. It was not long before many of them were put to death for being enemies of the state. And sadly, in a short time, the numbers of the slain well exceeded that of the last war. It happened slowly, systematically, so people became hardened to the deaths of multitudes. After all, people rationalized, traitors to the state deserved to die."

Andrew interrupted Andronicus here and asked, "How many people died?"

Andronicus looked at the four seated and said without emotion, "Thousands of times more people than all the people of Glenfair."

They were all shocked and anger began to burn in Raven, and he could see it in Andrew too.

Finally Andrew spoke, "If I have a chance to kill this evil man, I will for all the innocent he has slain." Raven agreed with Andrew, for he felt the same need for justice.

But Andronicus intervened with a raised hand and pleading tone to his voice.

"If Layton Teal is among those who have come, you must not engage him at arms."

"Why?" asked Raven. "It is the perfect time to do so, he does not have his armies with him, only about twenty persons."

"That may be true if the playing field were even," answered Andronicus, "but if he is there he will have weapons you cannot fathom. Even the armor of the ancients will not protect you from those."

"Then what are we to do?" asked Andrew.

"You must go and meet the company that is camped by the Halfstaff to find out their intentions, and gather information They will come to your castles anyway, so it is much better for you to meet them. If someone were to casually tell them about your ancestors, it may be all the enemy needs to find them. We cannot take the chance of their talking with anyone who knows anything of the past. Besides, we do not know why they have come. If they knew where your ancestors have fled to they would not be here. Something has brought them here and we must find out what that is without giving anything away."

"Are you sure it is not the ancients come here for some reason into our future?" asked Raven.

Andronicus paused for a moment before answering. "They know I will sense a shift in time, for I was to be on guard to warn them so they would not be surprised by the enemy. If it was any of the ancients, they would have alerted me right away because that was the arrangement."

"Could it be another group of time travelers besides the enemy or the ancients?" asked Lorriel.

"It is possible," began Andronicus. "But remember the ability to move great distances in time with large groups was discovered in the future when the ancients fled. So in any case, it would have to be someone from the far future and that would indicate caution on our part."

Raven frowned and then said. "It is settled then. Tomorrow we go and meet this company and find out the reason they are here and pray that we will be wiser than they."

Everyone nodded approval at Raven's words for there was nothing more to be said concerning the visitors in the valley below from another time. Rebekka was tired and asked leave of the rest to retire for the evening. Lorriel wanted to stroll and meditate in the garden, her favorite pastime in this wonderful retreat. Andrew stood up as well and headed for the back room. No one had to ask where he was going for he had often spent whole nights with the ancients machine that stored wisdom and knowledge. That left Raven and Andronicus alone in the lounge of the Hall of Wisdom.

Andronicus spoke, "I want to know more of what you found in the Prescott castle."

"You know of the traps," answered Raven, "but I have a question about the last two. The doorway had tiny beams of light crossing it in a way that made it impossible to get through the door without touching one of them. I can understand the thin trip wire we encountered, but how did the light trap work?

Andronicus smiled as he spoke, "For you to discover the traps as you did speaks of your great abilities. These were very well planned traps with technology far beyond your day. The trap you speak of was probably activated by the springing of the first trap. The first trap was not as difficult as the rest, it was mainly a warning, but would kill the unwary."

Raven shuddered when he thought of Rebekka pinned to the wall by her clothing. If she had not been moving at a fast pace she would be dead along with his child.

Andronicus continued, "Any thing that blocked the light would be sensed and that would trigger the trap. The fact that dust had accumulated over the centuries may have saved your life."

Raven nodded knowing it was an act of God that he had not been killed.

"The final trap had needles that thrust down into whoever would place their hand into the secret compartment. Was there some kind of poison on those?"

"Yes," Andronicus said thoughtfully. "There are many poisons your ancestors knew about that could last for centuries and be activated once the secret compartment was opened. If you ever encounter any traps again, it would be wise to leave them to me. Raven nodded, for he knew how narrowly he had escaped the door trap.

Raven continued, "The secret compartment that held the note we told you of also contained the Prescott family ring. It opened the chest in the room and in it I found the journal of Amnon Prescott. In the bottom of the chest there was a false floor and under it were jewels and gold."

Andronicus nodded. "It was one of Amnon's oddities to be concerned with wealth, but after the ancients struggled just to survive, it became less important to him."

"Maybe that is why he stored those things in the chest," Raven exclaimed.

"Yes," Andronicus mused, "is that all you found?"

"No," Raven admitted. "There was a mosaic in the floor and Amnon mentioned he had kept back some of the weapons of his time and stored them there instead of destroying them."

Andronicus sat up strait and exclaimed; "No one was to keep any weapons, that was the pact of those who came here. All traces of technology were to be erased forever! How dare he break the pact!" Then Andronicus seemed to settle down and said, "Amnon's weakness may be our salvation, were you able to open the vault in the floor?"

"No," replied Raven, "it is the first thing I have not been able to figure out that the ancients had left behind. Do you know how to open it Andronicus?"

Andronicus shook his head, "I wish I did, for the weapons there would surely make the playing field even if it came to that. Since that is not an option, we will have to go back to the original plan of reconnaissance."

Raven nodded, not sure he wanted to unleash any powerful weapons on his world. It would have to be desperate times indeed to do so.

Raven changed the subject, "Master Fields has been teaching me about hand to hand combat without weapons."

Andronicus smiled and said. "Very wise of Master Fields, for who knows when you will be in danger without a weapon at your disposal."

"Do you know anything about hand to hand combat?" asked Raven hopefully.

Again Andronicus smiled, which always looked peculiar because he was never programed for that facial expression.

"I have a good knowledge of hand to hand combat, in fact I used to spar with your ancestor Uriah who was very adept at it."

"Would you mind teaching me?" Raven asked.

"I would be delighted," Andronicus responded, "let us go outside to one of the lawns and we shall begin."

Rebekka began to drift off in sleep with the faint sound of Andronicus and Raven talking. As she fell deeper into that place where the conscious mind begins to drift she heard bits and pieces of other's minds. She was accustomed now to this for it often happened just before deep sleep when her mind was undisciplined and relaxed. She very rarely ever remembered any conversations that made sense as you often forget dreams you have in that same realm between consciousness and sleep.

This time instead of the voices fading off into the blackness of sleep, one reached out and captured her mind. She knew immediately that it was evil and fear caught a hold of her like no nightmare ever had. It was more frightening than the dream Raven had of the giant twainlar serpent eating her and little Edward. She fought to swim back to that place of reality and wake up but she could not. It was as if she were being pulled by the current of Brickens' Falls back into the raging cascade of water to be dashed to pieces. She fought against it with all her might to no avail and found herself being pulled and twisted as the voice shouted out at her.

"Merry, where are you. You cannot hide from me, I will find you if I have to search the whole galaxy. I will find them all and they will pay, do you hear me, you will all pay for what you have done! I know you can hear me for I have touched someone's mind. Warning the others will not save you."

Rebekka fought to get away from the voice, it was full of hate and anger. She finally managed to call out, "Raven, Lorriel, someone help me!"

Raven and Andronicus were out on one of the garden lawns near the Hall of Wisdom.

Andronicus stated; "Let us spar and I then shall know how much you have learned from Master Fields."

With that they began, but Andronicus was not Master Fields and several times Raven found himself on the ground with Andronicus over him with a death chop hovering above his throat. But Raven was a fast leaner and every move that Andronicus used that was successful he learned from, cataloged, and successfully defended against it the next time it was used.

Andronicus was amazed, this young man's learning ability and physical reflexes far exceeded anyone he had ever known. He started out sloppy at first but every defeat sent him to a new height in ability. Andronicus was enjoying this very much. Not since Uriah had he had such a challenge. His android mind began quick calculations and he realized in fifteen more minutes he would not be able to over come Raven with skill alone but would have to use his brute android speed and strength to win advantage.

Raven likewise was enjoying himself. At first all he could do was defend, and even that sometimes failed. But as the exercises progressed he could feel the flow and patterns of the movements Andronicus was using on him and began to counter them effectively.

Soon they were matched move for move and a stalemate began to develop. In a desperate act Andronicus swept his leg like lightning at Raven which left him no choice but to go strait up. He used this to go up and over Andronicus as he had with Master Fields. But Andronicus was not Master Fields. He caught him above his head and started to hurtle him with great force across the lawn. Whether out of desperation or skill Raven could not say, but he was just able to grab onto Andronicus' wrists as he released him and turned that momentum to his advantage to throw

74

Andronicus across the lawn. The android was surprised as well and found himself flying through the air to hit solidly in a heap some distance away in the lawn.

At first Raven thought he had injured the Android but he sprang to his feet quickly and laughed. It was the first time Raven had ever heard Andronicus laugh.

"I have never been thrown like that before," he said enthusiastically. "Partly my own fault though for trying to do the same to you. My computations never prepared me for that move. You need no further training, and I believe you would give Uriah your ancestor quite a bit of trouble."

At that moment Lorriel came running out. "Raven! Something is wrong with Rebekka! She is crying out and we cannot wake her!" Lorriel shouted desperately.

In a flash Raven was off and into the Hall of Wisdom and into the room where Rebekka slept with Andronicus not far behind. Rebekka was tossing and crying out for help. Raven tried to shake her but she would not wake which worried Raven considerably.

At last he concentrated his mind in desperation with all his strength and spoke to her. "Rebekka, come to me, I am here. Wake up!"

Rebekka was trying in vain to free herself from the voice when all of a sudden she heard Raven's voice faintly then stronger. "Come to me, I am here." She fled from the evil to the voice she knew and woke from her sleep.

Raven was relieved to see Rebekka awake but could also see the terror in her eyes and she grabbed him and began to cry.

"Did you have a bad dream he asked?"

"No," she sobbed. "A voice of evil came to me as I was falling asleep. I tried to wake up but could not until you came to me. He was evil I know it, he kept calling for Merry and promised revenge on all the others."

They all looked at Andronicus and he answered their questions with an edge to his voice when he said. "The enemy is here!"

Rebekka was shaken but not totally undone for she stated, "He is looking for the ancients for I recognized the woman's name Merry from the journal of Amnon. What are we to do?"

"Our plan has not changed," Andronicus stated. "We now know for sure who we are dealing with and will be doubly cautious. But we still must find out why he is here without giving anything away. If we learn that the enemy's arrival here was just a stab in the dark, we will do nothing and let him return to his own time."

"Do nothing!" Andrew interrupted, "We should try and destroy him so others will not suffer. Look at what he did to Rebekka, just in her sleep!"

Andronicus now spoke in a tone none of them had ever heard him use before. "You will do nothing! Do you understand!" And then he softened. "You have no idea who you are dealing with. Do you think that the ancients would have destroyed him if they thought they could? They were the best and brightest of his day and yet the only option they found was to flee his presence. If you underestimate him he will destroy us all."

Raven had learned to control his fear in battle, but this revelation about the enemy, Layton Teal, had him very troubled. Raven knew he was not the wisest man that ever lived and he was fearful of confronting a man their ancestors had found frightening and brilliant. He knew one mistake and the enemy would know more than they wished. Raven was shaken out of his thoughts by the sound of Rebekka talking to Andronicus.

"I am afraid to go to sleep again," she was saying.

Andronicus nodded and then added, "Your abilities far exceed anyone I have ever known who was telepathic. The enemy has that ability but to a weaker degree and you were like a magnet to draw him to you. His advantage is he knows many tricks of the mind and uses them to the fullest, but you are much stronger. Let me show you how to lock your mind so he cannot enter. Close the doors to your mind as you would close the door to your room. Lock it with a special key that only you have and no one else knows about, then decide no one can enter until you unlock it."

Rebekka did this and felt more at ease and finally began to relax.

"We all should get some rest," replied Raven. "Tomorrow will be a hard day for us all."

When they retired for the evening, Rebekka lay next to Raven and held him, still a little fearful of falling asleep. But fatigue overtook her and she began to drift off again. This time she felt someone try to enter but the door kept them out. She was barely conscious of the effort and knew the door was too strong for anyone to enter so she finally drifted off into peaceful sleep.

Early the next morning as everyone gathered for breakfast there was silence, for no one had anything to really say. They all knew the task before them and there was really no point in talking. The breakfast was excellent as usual but was tainted by the impending task before them.

Andronicus finally broke the silence when he said. "You all have fantastic abilities, let them guide you. If there ever was a time in history when such an enemy can be outsmarted and overcome it is here with you. Remember, you fight for the Glenfair of all ages. If the enemy succeeds and destroys your ancestors, you will cease to exist and the kingdom will never be."

They all looked at each other and without speaking knew somehow this to be the truth. The love Raven saw pass in the glance Lorriel gave Andrew touched his heart greatly.

He looked at Rebekka and their eyes met and she spoke to his mind. "What ever happens today my beloved husband, know that I love you with all my heart. You have been the best of husbands and the best of kings."

Raven replied with his mind just for her. "How precious you have been to me, the apple of my eye. I have come to know you are the half that I have lacked all my life. You have made me whole with your life and love. How can I not love you more than my own life? And if we fail and we cease to exist, I have to believe God knows we did and there is no injustice with God. My faith in Him tells me we are at his mercy in things that far exceed our limitations."

"I pray that God will have mercy on us too," Rebekka echoed. With that they rose from the table and headed down the garden path in silence to the fate that awaited them in the valley below.

Master Fields and Sauron waited anxiously for the return of King Raven, Rebekka, Lorriel and Andrew. Right after breakfast word came of their return and Sauron and Master Fields rushed to the courtyard to meet them and find out the news. As Raven rode up and dismounted both older men waited for the news from their king. They both loved and trusted him and knew he would tell them everything they needed to know.

Raven said plainly; "There is a threat to our kingdom from a very evil man that we must go meet."

"I shall gather the troops we have in our garrison," Sauron said.

But Raven raised his hand. "No, we go in a small group."

"But surely," Master Fields replied, "a sizable force would make a frightening impression on this evil man. How many troops does he have with him?"

"Less than twenty," Raven replied, "but I do not believe a show of force will make any difference to this man, nor will it make the kingdom safer. No one is to engage him in arms unless I command it, is that understood?"

They all looked at Raven but none challenged him because they had pledged to obey the commands of the king. Not because he was king, but because they knew whatever Raven did, it was for the good of the kingdom and they trusted his leadership.

"And one last thing," Raven added, "no one is to talk to this man except me, and keep your thoughts focused on your love for our kingdom."

"Who will go with you Sire," Sauron asked?

"You, Andrew, Master Fields, Lorriel and Rebekka."

"The women," Sauron asked, concern in his eyes.

"Yes," said Raven. "We are not going to fight a war, we are going to find out what this man wants." Raven saw Jerddin's eyes downcast so he spoke. "You too Jerddin, we will need you."

Jerddin's head snapped up in a proud look of pleasure to be included in this elite group.

"How could I leave him behind," Raven thought, "for he risked his life to stand with me in the great battle."

When they were dressed in their armor, they mounted their horses and headed for the Halfstaff River and the confrontation that awaited them with the enemy of the ancients.

Chapter 4
Confronting Your Fears

"Fear is something God has given us as a warning to preserve life. But if we fear of losing things dear to us, it may keep us from enjoying them while they are in our grasp. For alas, finite man is eventually stripped of all by the sands of time."

--The Wisdom of Fathers

The ride to Halfstaff River was tortuous to those who knew what lay ahead. Master Fields, Sauron, and Jerddin seemed content to be on this journey and waited patiently for the events to unfold before them. The two older men, experienced enough not to be anxious or unsettled, rode along with purpose, determined to defend king and kingdom. Only Jerddin was excited, not at the prospect of battle but of the privilege of being asked to participate. When the company reached the Halfstaff they turned down river to where they knew they would find the camp of the enemy. The smoke of the fire from their camp could be seen in the distance and they rode toward it. As chance would have it, there was a small rise in the land just north of the enemies camp. Raven's company stopped on the north side of the knoll and dismounted and staked their horses.

"Why don't we ride in Sire," Jerddin asked, "it would give us an advantage."

"I do not want them to feel threatened. We will walk to them so we will be on level ground." With that the small group of Glenfair's people headed over the knoll.

Layton Teal had arrived with his small company of men in the ancient history of the past. He was following the only lead he had found in history that even hinted of a possibility of those he sought. Yes, he was sure they had fled to the past, the future was a frightening unknown, but the past was predictable history. What lay ahead for mankind in the future could not be determined unless you went there. Those who betrayed him would not fly into an unknown situation that could be worse than what they had fled. It was remotely possible that they had done just that, but knowing those who had slipped from his grasp, he doubted it.

He thought about this lead, a warrior mentioned in the Wickshield histories, actually recorded by one of his ancestors, a general of the Wickshield army. It spoke of the unnatural abilities of speed and coordination in this warrior, the ability to pluck an arrow out of the air. They believed him invulnerable, even a demon some had rumored. The warrior by himself had slaughtered one of the elite forces of the Wickshield army. Layton Teal knew of no man that could do that except Uriah.

He was the first of his kind, a genetically engineered warrior that had been created to fight. What he had not bargained on was Uriah developing an independent spirit that led to this betrayal. Something had gone wrong with his programing but no one knew what. Layton made sure those who were responsible had suffered and died as a result of this malfunction.

Layton chided himself, he should have predicted the events that took place. He knew there would be an attempted rebellion among his top people, but that had not worried him and he had taken steps to put a stop to it when it happened. But this disappearance of some of his scientists and military men, and most of all the woman he loved, caught him by surprise. He had gotten where he was by always predicting human behavior, and out thinking his opponents. But this infuriated him, his personal body guard Uriah, his chief of staff, and a small band of doctors and scientists had outwitted him. His whole regime knew of the victory that had been won against him, unofficially of course, but he had heard rumors of people betting on how long it would take him to find the traitors. He most of all wanted to find Merry, the woman he loved.

Well, Layton thought, not love in the conventional sense, he found her appealing but he really loved her for what she could do for him.

She was a time shifter and there were precious few of those in the whole world. With Merry by his side, as his wife, no one would ever dare challenge him and his total power base would be complete. It took him years to find another time shifter just to go and search for the rebels. It also took several years as well to create a machine to enhance the time shift enough to go this far back in time, for it was well known that time shifters could only travel at most ten to fifteen years in time.

He had found out about the crystals from one of his spies, but by the time he decided to act on this inside information they were all gone. And that scientist, Samuel, had purged all of the computers of his research. He had tried to duplicate the crystals to no avail and felt the whole thing was a loss until another technological development was found to do the same thing. Each one of them wore a micro patch, to be tracked and amplified by a machine when the girl shifted time. All Layton had to do was to tell the machine which patch to amplify, or all of those who wore them and when the time shifter shifted time she would take all of them with her.

Layton wondered why there had never been a male time shifter, all of the known ones had been female. He secretly wished that he had the ability himself so he would not have to bother with this young woman. She was immature and moody, and when threatened she went into fits and was not able to function at all. He had to pamper her and treat her differently than anyone else to get what he wanted. How unlike Merry she was. That is why Layton did not worry about Ellise obeying his commands, for she was so young she could not do anything else. He knew she was afraid of him but Layton did not use that fear on her as he did others. It was much easier to get what he wanted by giving the child what she wanted. He looked over at Ellise and wondered at his observation of her. She looked more womanly, mature than the last time he had taken notice of her features. He was getting rusty, he would have to pay more attention to details. How could she have grown up without his noticing? Layton wrote that off to all the business in preparing for this greatest of all adventures. He had been very busy collecting an elite force of commandos armed with the latest in weapons. He knew he did not need very many men with him to conquer even the largest army during this time period. That was not his intention though, for he was here only to capture the traitors and see them tortured and destroyed. Uriah was dangerous, but not a match for the force he had assembled.

Today he had decided to go to the castle in the middle of this land and get some answers. But before they broke camp someone shouted that people were approaching. Good, thought Layton, maybe I will not have to search for answers, they will come to me. His soldiers were at full readiness as the group approached them from the top of the small rise directly north of their camp. Layton saw that the group was smaller than his own and felt no threat so ordered his men to stand down. Then he waited for them to come to him.

As they topped the rise Raven noticed how quickly the people below formed ranks and were ready for anything that would come upon them. Very precise military discipline Raven noted with rising apprehension. Master Fields noticed that as well and glanced at Raven to see how he was taking in the whole situation. They proceeded down the knoll till they were just outside the ranks of soldiers and stopped. Raven looked over the people before him and soon picked out their leader, because everyone was looking to him to see what to do next. He also noticed that they were all men except one young woman barely out of her teens.

For a while no one said anything, and then Raven spoke, "I can tell by your dress that you are foreigners, what is your business in Glenfair?"

Layton Teal noticed right away the accent and the difference in speech and almost decided to leave right then and there. But something in the way this man moved and carried himself made his senses tingle so he said, "We are looking for the man who almost single-handedly defeated the Wickshield army some time ago. Can you tell me where I might find him?"

Everyone in Raven's party were looking at each other and him, all recognizing the tongue of the ancients.

Layton noticed the movement and surprise in the people when he spoke and noted the reaction. It was as if they recognized the speech and accent.

Raven spoke again; "I am the one you are looking for, I am also the king of Glenfair." After saying this he concentrated on Rebekka's mind and spoke to her; "This is the time to set moral restraint aside and listen to the enemies thoughts."

"Yes," Rebekka agreed, "I will do so." She concentrated her thoughts on Layton Teal, a little fearful because of the trouble she had the night before, but also confident that she could now handle any assault this man threw at her.

At first she began to hear his thoughts when all of a sudden he spoke, "Ah, one of you is trying to listen but I will not allow that." And instantaneously a wall came up that shut Rebekka out.

She concentrated harder and began to remove the barriers he had set up and in a short time was back listening to his mind.

Again Layton responded, "You are very powerful, no one has ever broken through my barriers before." And with that Layton sent a mental slap across the short distance to the mind that had touched his. It was not anything that he could harm anyone with, but if it was not expected the recipient would be stunned and react. Rebekka recoiled at the slap and stumbled back a step, then Layton's voice came back into her mind; "So there you are my dear, you are very powerful and dangerous to me. I cannot allow you to listen in on my thoughts so you must go."

With that Layton Teal spoke loudly to Raven's group, "Send the woman," pointing to Rebekka, "over here, I want to speak with her privately."

Rebekka desperately spoke to Raven quickly in his mind, "He knows that I have been listening to him, he knows it is me!"

Raven noticed the nervousness of his group growing so turning to Layton he replied, "The lady you speak of is the queen of Glenfair, she will not come to you for we do not know your intentions."

Layton Teal called Ellise to him and spoke to her quietly so no one could hear.

Raven saw the enemy place something in her hand and she nodded and stood by his side.

Layton now spoke again, steel in his voice; "Let the lady come part way and my dear companion Ellise will meet her half way, she has a gift to present to her."

Again Raven answered, "The queen will not come she will stay here."

Layton was tiring of this game and was not getting anywhere so he said plainly, "If she will not come then we shall take her by force."

At those words Raven drew his sword and all of his company did the same except for Rebekka and Lorriel.

Layton watched this action with mild amusement and almost missed the distinguished difference in the glint of Raven and Andrew's swords (for Andrew wore the armor of the ancients as well as Raven) compared to the rest.

At first he was stunned then elated, the king and another had swords and armor made of triberridum, a titanium ceramic alloy. He knew now his guess had not been wrong to come to this time. His eyes searched frantically for any other clues and stopped when he came to the knife on Raven's side. He recognized it immediately, it was the knife he had given to Merry as a present. On the handle were his initials "LT". He knew now beyond any doubt that these simple inept folks could tell him what he wanted to know. But he was still worried about the woman, he did not want her to give anything away. She must be dealt with now.

"Send the queen to me or you shall all die," Layton said loudly once again, this time with venom in his voice.

Jerddin took a step forward and replied, "We have pledged to protect the kingdom and the king and queen with our lives."

"Very well, you will get your wish," Layton answered as he raised his laser pistol at Jerddin and fired.

A bolt of light hit Jerddin in the chest and exploded tearing him apart, his smoldering remains falling to the ground. Andrew and Sauron began to move forward and the armed men with the enemy raised their weapons. Raven frantically yelled for them to stop. He had wanted no confrontation with this deadly enemy but that was too late. He also knew that they would be slaughtered with the weapons these people possessed. He was desperate to find a solution before they were all dead.

Layton asked once again forcefully, "Send the queen or you will all die, I promise she will not be harmed."

They could not run for he would hunt them down, they could not fight for the weapons they possessed were too powerful. It seemed to Raven that they would all die here. What a fool he had been to think he could handle this situation. Thinking he could deal with the enemy his ancestors could not, and they knew the enemy better than he.

Rebekka turned to him at that instant and said unemotionally, "I have to go to him."

"No," Raven said.

But Rebekka shook her head and looked him in the eye, "We will all die and you know it if I do not go, and what will that accomplish?"

Before he could answer she turned and walked down toward the enemy before Raven could stop her. His world seemed to stop at that moment and everything became a blur until it registered that Master Fields was shaking him and yelling in his face.

"What are you doing, man, don't let her go!"

Raven pushed Master Fields aside and heard Sauron ask, "Sire, what should we do?"

"Nothing," Raven answered. "We can do nothing now so hold your ground all of you, I command it."

This last statement was said with anger so everyone just watched as Rebekka walked closer toward the enemy and the young woman, Ellise, met her halfway. She stopped, greeted Rebekka and place something in her hand and then both of them vanished.

Master Fields and Sauron were stunned and speechless, while Raven, Andrew and Lorriel were surprised but not confused by what had taken place. Knowing of Lorriel's ability to time shift and also knowing the enemy could not get here without a time shifter all made sense to them. But they had not expected Rebekka to be taken somewhere by the time shifting woman.

Now Raven's foreboding turned into mourning, he knew that there was no way he could determine where Rebekka had been taken unless Layton Teal volunteered that information and that was unlikely. They could search forever and not find her. He knew now the enemy's evil heart had planned this all along. He did not want Rebekka dead, he wanted her as a hostage to bargain with in order to get what he wanted.

The enemy now spoke, "I need some information from you concerning some people I am looking for. I know you can tell me what I need to know for I have seen several things that have told me so. I want you to tell me all you know about the people who made the armor and swords the king and the other young man is wearing. If you do, I will return your queen to you and leave this place."

Raven did not answer him a word, so much so that Master Fields spoke to Raven again in urgency, "Why do you not tell them of the ancients, what harm can it do? That was many years ago so what does it matter?"

Layton Teal interrupted their conversation with another challenge. "I know you recognized my speech, although it is different from yours, you have heard it before or know of it. I also have seen the knife the king is wearing. I remember that knife very well for it has my initials on its handle. I will give you three days to think it over and collect any information you may have on the ones I seek. You will come back here and tell me all you know about them. If you do I will give you back your queen. If you do not come back in three days I will destroy this whole kingdom and find out what I want anyway from others. I will be waiting here."

With that Layton Teal turned his back on Raven and his friends to show the conversation was over.

"Come on, let us go," Raven said to those with him as he turned to head north back over the knoll where their horses were staked.

Andrew and Lorriel followed but Master Fields and Sauron hesitated for a little bit before following. After they topped the hill and were back at the horses Sauron and Master Fields confronted Raven.

"Why," Sauron asked, "did you not tell him what he wanted to know?"

Before Raven could answer, everyone was talking at once.

Finally Andrew yelled for everyone to quiet down and spoke, "The king can not tell this wicked man anything about the ancients. He is more powerful than any army we might bring against him."

Master Fields nodded, "Poor Jerddin, all he wanted to do was to protect the queen."

Then turning to Raven once again, said, "Why did you let her go?"

Raven sighed, feeling the whole weight of the world on his shoulders, everyone was quiet and awaiting his answer.

"I did not want her to go, God as my witness, but if I had not, we would all be dead and what good would that do the kingdom? You all saw what he did to Jerddin. If he wanted to kill Rebekka, he could have and there would have been nothing we could have done about it. No, he wanted her out of the way and he is also using her as a bargaining tool to get what he wants."

"Why not give him what he wants," asked Sauron?

Raven paused to think, but decided the only answer to give Master Fields and Sauron was the truth.

"Our ancestors, the ancients know this enemy very well. He has found a way to travel in time just as they did and wants to destroy them.

"What?" Sauron said. "Are you saying this man is a time traveler? That is only in fairy tales and the things dreams are made of."

Raven looked at Sauron and said, "This is no joke, you saw what he did to Jerddin, and how Rebekka disappeared. Can you explain that?"

Sauron was silent so Raven continued, "The ancients found a way to flee this evil man's presence. They came from a few thousand years in our future and fled a thousand years into our past. If we tell the enemy what he wants to know he will find the ancients and destroy them, and if that happens what will become of our kingdom? You see the ancients began our kingdom, if they are destroyed the kingdom will never be."

Raven paused to see how this information was being absorbed by Master Fields and Sauron. He could see their minds at work, but also saw the difficulty they were having with such concepts.

Master Fields now spoke, "We must find Rebekka and rescue her before we can deal with this evil man."

Raven looked sadly at Master Fields and spoke even more distraught, "We can not find her, she has been taken somewhere in time, probably the far future. The young woman you saw was the time traveler. She took Rebekka and disappeared. She will have to return, though, so Layton Teal can leave this time to travel to another, for without her he cannot travel anywhere. I believe when she returns she will bring Rebekka back with her."

Everyone was silent so Raven took charge once again. "We must go back to your castle, Sauron, and devise a plan in the next three days to save us all if that is possible."

They mounted their horses and Master Fields led the extra horse Jerddin had rode upon, a grim reminder that a good man had lost his life trying to protect the kingdom and the queen.

As Raven rode along side of Andrew he kept thinking about what had happened. It was all his fault that Jerddin had died. Why did he not think to hide the armor of the ancients and not bring it along to their meeting with the enemy. And the knife, he thought as he drew it out of its sheath. There boldly inlaid in the handle was the initials "LT" for Layton Teal. He wanted to cast it away so angry was he with himself, but instead put it back in its sheath.

He then thought of Rebekka and a tear came to his eye, everything had happened so fast and now she was gone. That was his fault to, he should not have asked her to listen to Layton Teal's thoughts. He knew it would be dangerous, but he had no idea Layton would guess who the listener was. Again he had underestimated this evil man, resulting in others being hurt. He kept thinking of all the different ways he should have done things.

He glanced over at Lorriel and saw that she was silently grieving as well, her face was tear streaked and she just stared strait ahead. He knew she was thinking the same thing he was, if Layton was so quick to kill Jerddin, what torture had he devised for Rebekka? Raven could not think of that for his anger and hatred of Layton would cloud his reasoning. He had to figure out a way to get her back and save the kingdom too! This scenario played over and over in Raven's mind as they all headed back to the Crestlaw castle in silence.

Layton Teal was disappointed that the warrior mentioned in the Wickshield histories was not Uriah. But this second development was just as pleasing. If he could determine exactly where the rebels had gone then he could surprise them and overcome them before they had warning. He doubted that they could stop him even if they knew he was coming. But it was better that they did not know or suspect his arrival for that would make his task easier.

It was hard to wait after all these years to finally get the vengeance his soul required to be at rest. But he was close now, he could feel it. He was almost certain now that those he sought were in the past. How far he did not know. It was better to let the information come to him than go jumping about time trying to find them, he had wasted enough of his years already.

He wondered how much these simple people knew about him or the reason he had asked about the ones who had made their armor. They did not seem to see a paradox at all when he had claimed the knife the king wore had belonged to him. These things evidently were far beyond their capabilities of understanding. Layton paused here in his thinking, or perhaps they knew much more than they revealed. He almost laughed at the absurd notion that these people who lived thousands of years in his past could comprehend any of the events that had led up to their meeting. Time travel was a concept that had not even been conceived until his lifetime and to think that these people could even consider it was ludicrous.

Layton liked everything in neat little packages, but there were a few things that were out of place. The main one was the woman, the queen of Glenfair they called her. How was it possible that someone would have such strong telepathic capabilities here at this time in history? And what of the king who was to have defeated the Wickshields with almost supernatural quickness and reflexes? When he had realized that Uriah was not the one who had fought that noted battle in history, he had just passed it off to the growing embellishment of stories created to cover an embarrassing loss to an inferior force. But now he was not so sure after experiencing the power of the woman's mind. Surely no single person could rival the genetically engineered combat abilities of Uriah. Although these questions nagged at Layton Teal, he pushed them aside with the truth that these people did not matter at all to him. He cared nothing for their world or the time in which they lived, he only wanted the information they could give him to effect his revenge on those who had betrayed him.

His thoughts turned to the woman and he almost wished he could talk with her to learn more just to satisfy his curiosity. There also was the possibility of great disaster in sending her back to his time with Ellise. That had not been part of his original plan, but a quick decision. He had told Ellise to take her somewhere in time and then return here in four days. When she had asked him where he merely said, back to her own time would be fine. He smirked to himself of the affect that would have on the queen seeing his future, a place filled with machines and flying vehicles and androids. But it also was a danger, for if Ellise did not return for him he would be stranded in time here until he died. The only reason this did not worry him was because she was too young to think up such an idea, but merely did what he told her to do. Of her obedience he had not much doubt, but he was worried about what kind of influence this woman would have on her. He realized now that he should have told the girl to take the woman four days into the future to the same place they were now. That would have been simple with no room for error. But he knew Ellise would return in four days. She had never given him any reason to believe she would not to do as he wished. The things he had given her, she would lose without him, and she had become quite demanding. With the fulfillment of her wishes came also a greater appetite for things and possessions of wealth and importance. She craved the attention she garnished in his shadow. No she would return, he was certain. If not, well his time had become taxing and boring. He had conquered everything he wanted. He was in absolute power and all he had to do was keep that power. He missed something to challenge him and if left here, this new kingdom and the Wickshield one would be a whole new task to occupy his final days.

He thought of his boring existence in his time and realized for the first time that his pursuit of the these traitors was not solely for revenge. This was one of the few challenges left to him; to find out where his people had gone, and how they had hid their disappearance so completely from him. Never in all his life had he been so fooled by anyone, especially Merry and Uriah. He knew now that their plan would have been foolproof if he had not come here and sought out the warrior mentioned briefly in some forgotten Wickshield writings.

He was a patient man, in three more days they would return and tell him what he wanted to know, and in four he would have his revenge.

Then a thought hit him, Why not just leave those alone who had fled his presence to somewhere in the far past? They could not form a rebellion against him, nor influence anyone in his time. They only wanted a life free from the reach of his iron fist. Why could he not let them be?

He knew the answer, just as he was destined to be the ruler of his time, his nature would not allow him to be defeated even by the act of fleeing. Besides they had hurt him in this subtle betrayal and the code he lived by demanded they pay dearly. He could live no other way than to be ruthless in his dealings with those who opposed him. One thing that Layton admired about the traitors, they had given up all the advancement of his time to live in a world without technology to pamper them. He could never do that by choice, but they had done just that, for all traces of their advancement had vanished from history.

A little while, he told himself, and you will have finished the greatest challenge of your life.

As Raven, Master Fields and the Crestlaws entered the courtyard of the Crestlaw castle, a woman came out quickly to greet them. At first Raven thought it was Sauron's wife but then saw that it was his mother, whom he called in public, Aunt Jessica. And behind her came little Edward.

Raven dismounted and hugged his mother, picked up little Edward and asked, "Why are you here, I thought you would be at the castle?"

She looked him in the eye and then looked down a little ashamed, "I came here because I could not be with you during the other crisis the kingdom faced. I felt so helpless then and I felt the same sitting in the castle the day after you left, so I brought Edward here with me to find you. Please do not be angry with me for coming. Mostell is taking care of things back at the castle."

"I cannot be angry with you, for this concerns you as much as anyone else."

Jessica looked around and asked, "Where is Rebekka?"

Little Edward echoed her question, "Where is mommy daddy?"

Raven did not know what to say but felt a soft hand on his shoulder and saw Lorriel out of the corner of his eye.

Before he could say anything Lorriel spoke, "My favorite little nephew, how are you. Come with me and I will read you a story."

Little Edward squealed with delight and leaped from his father into Lorriel's arms, for he loved his aunt dearly and he so enjoyed her company. His question for the moment forgotten.

As Raven watched Lorriel and Edward go into the castle he was thankful for her wise intervention. He then took his mother's hand and said, "Come we must talk." They walked silently into the hall of the Crestlaw castle and sat down in a private place to talk.

"What we feared has come to pass, the enemy is here. Jerddin is dead and Rebekka has been taken hostage by him."

With that tears came to Raven's eyes. "I could not stop him from taking her, the weapons they have our armor would not stop. Jerddin, may God have mercy on his soul, was burned to ashes in front of our eyes so quickly that he did not even cry out."

"Can you rescue her?" his mother asked seeing the pain in Raven's eyes.

"No," he replied. "The enemy came here with a time shifter. She took Rebekka to somewhere in time, probably the future, we do not know where."

Now there was fear mirrored in his mother's eyes when she asked, "What does he want so badly that he has taken the queen hostage in order to get?"

"He wants to know where and when the ancients lived so he can go there and destroy them."

"Does he know that we can give him that information?" she asked.

"Sadly yes," Raven answered, "he recognized the alloy of the sword and armor I wore, and he also saw the knife." With that Raven drew it and showed his mother the initials "LT" inlaid in its handle.

"The enemies name Is Layton Teal, and this was his knife. He knows we can tell him what he wants to know about the ancients. I am afraid I have failed and it is my fault Jerddin is dead and Rebekka is gone."

His mother was silent for a moment and then said, "You could do nothing to prevent Rebekka from being taken from you by force."

"That's just it," Raven replied with tears coming to his eyes once again. "She knew we would fight to protect her and all die in the process. She just straightened her shoulders and walked right down to the enemy and gave herself to him as he demanded."

Raven's mother asked, "You did not say anything to her?"

"No, mother, she gave me that look and said there was no other way to give us any kind of chance. It happened so fast I did not even get the chance to say I loved her." Raven could say no more and just closed his eyes to get control of his emotions. This was no time to be falling apart, Rebekka and the kingdom depended on him finding a solution.

When he opened his eyes Master Fields was standing there, and spoke, "We must convene to devise a plan to deal with these events."

Raven nodded and rose to follow Master Fields. Aunt Jessica said she would find little Edward and explain to him that his mother had gone away on a long journey and would not be back for some time. Raven nodded at her and then continued to follow Master Fields.

Sauron, Lorriel and Andrew were already gathered around the table in a quiet room in the castle off the main hall. When Raven entered they stopped talking and looked at him. He took his seat and tried to clear his thoughts, for this must be decided quickly, for they only had 3 days.

Andrew was the first to speak to the group as he said with great emotion, "We should have fought to the death before we let the queen go!"

"And what," Raven stated, "be burned to a crisp like Jerddin. We would all have perished and what would that have accomplished. It still would not save the ancients and they are in grave peril as of right now."

Lorriel had just entered the room and now spoke up, no longer able to contain her emotions, "Rebekka is more important than the ancients, why did you not stop her from going Raven!"

She said this with such a sharp, accusing tone, that Raven's heart was smitten anew.

Raven stood shaking with frustration and deep pain, "No one," and he paused here for effect, "no one loved the queen more than I, you of all people should know that Lorriel."

Lorriel looked down, ashamed of how she had accused Raven of letting Rebekka go. It hurt them all to see Rebekka taken, but she knew none felt that pain more than Raven. She was sorry she had said what she had.

Raven continued, "You all know the queen is wise beyond many in this kingdom and quick to assess a situation and make the right judgment. She saw that the only way to give us time was to give herself into the hands of the enemy. She did that willingly for us and the kingdom. I could have stopped her by force, but would any of you want me to stop you from making a sacrifice for others and the kingdom if you could save them?" With that Raven sat down and everyone was silent.

Finally Sauron spoke, "Queen Rebekka has made a sacrifice to save us, we must find a solution to this problem so her sacrifice will not be in vain. But I have a pressing question that needs to be answered. Why can we not tell this man about our ancestors, the ancients? I know you know more about them than any one, King Raven Why can we not give him what he wants, then he will give us back Rebekka and will leave. I know you have explained some of this to us earlier, but why not leave the battle to the ancients, surely they will know how to deal with this man. This should not be our battle, it is really theirs."

Raven contemplated this for a moment before answering, "The battle is for the kingdom of Glenfair, not just the past kingdom but for ours as well. The ancients feared this man so much they fled in time to begin this kingdom. I do not think they would be able to overcome him if he were to find them. If that happens and he kills them, or takes them back as prisoners to his own time, this kingdom will not be, nor will we be born. We will all most likely vanish. I believe our greatest chance to defeat the enemy will be here in our own time. He does not expect much from us, I have seen it in his eyes and the way he treats us. If we can use that to our advantage then maybe we can save the kingdom."

Master Fields spoke now, "The weapons he has against our own make this almost an impossibility. If he had swords I would not worry at all, but lightning bolts that burn and kill so quickly will slaughter us. We can not fight a conventional battle and expect to win. So what is your plan?" he asked Raven.

Raven Kallestor, king of Glenfair sat thinking: What was he to do? It would be easy to seek revenge for the greatest harm anyone could ever do to him. But he had to put those feelings of revenge aside so he could make the right choice, not only for the kingdom of his time but for the Glenfair of all ages. The pain and sadness of what had happened clouded his reasoning, paralyzed his thoughts. He shook his head as if that would help to bring clarity of thought. Meanwhile Master

Fields and the others waited patiently for Raven to decide on a course of action. Raven knew the survival of Glenfair had to come first. A grave mistake would mean the kingdom would cease to exist, vanish from history without a trace and all of them with it. With that overriding truth, he knew what needed to be done.

"Call Aunt Jessica. We are riding north," he spoke to Master Fields, "to convene a time conference."

"A What?" Master Fields asked.

Raven Smiled at Master Fields' dismayed look and said; "I will explain on the way. You always wanted to meet Andronicus, the keeper of the wisdom, and now you shall. And you will come with us as well, Sauron."

Sauron nodded knowing such a crisis demanded extreme action. From the time King Raven had mentioned the Hall of Wisdom and the hermit Andronicus, he had wanted to visit this place. King Raven had told him it was at the top of Brickens' Falls and Sauron wanted to see how anyone could get up there. Ever since he was a child he had thought of ways to reach the top of the falls, but none were found feasible.

"Shall we take food," Sauron asked the king.

"No," Raven answered. "All of our needs will be provided for by Andronicus. But there is one thing you need to do for the kingdom before we leave. Send word to the other dukes to meet here in two days, making sure they avoid the center of the valley by the river. I do not want Layton Teal to meet any of our dukes, nor they him until we figure out what to do. In two days we will all meet at this castle, for this concerns them too."

At that moment Aunt Jessica came in and stated: "I hear we are convening a time counsel with Andronicus." Raven nodded so Aunt Jessica continued, "Then you will probably be needing these." She held out a beautiful bag of soft leather to Raven. He took it from her hand and opened it and inside were the five different colored stones of the ancients.

Raven looked at his mother with amazement, "How did you know we may need these?"

"When you showed me the hidden weapons room in our castle and how to open the crests and view the stones, I memorized the riddle the ancients had written."

"We fled the enemy of our first home,
and took with us the sacred stones,
that would protect if he should find,
to where in time we did fly,
and the stones if used the proper way,
will send him back to his own day."

"When you were gone I began to think if the enemy of the ancients had time shifted here, according to the ancients, you would need these stones. That is the main reason I came to the Crestlaw castle."

Raven threw his arms around his mother in a big hug, "You did the right thing, thank you mother." Raven realized that he had called Aunt Jessica mother out loud in front of Master Fields and Sauron. He looked at the both of them and they had strange looks on their faces. He then looked to Lorriel and Andrew for support but they had their mouths open in shock that Raven could let this slip.

Master Fields broke the silence with this statement of fact. "Sire, you called Jessica your mother."

Raven looked at them, the secret was now out before Sauron and Master Fields. Raven could have claimed it was a mistake in his excitement but decided otherwise. After all they would soon know everything anyway.

So Raven stated plainly, "I did call her mother because she really is Joanna Kallestor."

Master Fields just squinted his eyes in a kind of "I knew it all the time" type of look, but Sauron nearly choked.

Lorriel interrupted their silence with a simple question, "Raven Why?"

He answered just as simply. "Why not, they will know everything soon anyway." Lorriel nodded and smiled, Andrew too saw the truth Raven spoke.

Sauron gathering his composure asked, "How, I was at the funeral, your grief was real, the burial was real."

Raven simply said, "I will explain on the way, we must be going, for our time is short."

Master Fields looked at Jessica and said, "I never felt comfortable around you because you looked and acted too much like Joanna. But keeping your head covered kept me from guessing the truth." He then laughed and came to her and gave her a hug. "Never too old to be surprised are we?"

As they rode toward the falls Raven began the story of Joanna's miraculous deliverance from the plague, which everyone thought she had died from.

"Remember," Raven reviewed for them, "how we found a cure for the plague in the northeast some years ago. Well, after we knew of the cure, Lorriel found out that she was very gifted. She found she could shift time and time travel became a reality for her. The first thing she did was to go back in time and ask Andronicus to save her mother and bring her to the Hall of Wisdom at the top of Brickens' Falls. A decoy that looked human was burnt outside of the castle. As a result everyone, including myself and Lorriel in her past had thought her mother had died."

Master Fields interrupted here and asked a question, "Why did not Lorriel just cure her mother and just leave her in the castle?"

"That was the mistake Lorriel made," Raven answered. "She sought to spare her mother all the pain of Edward's death, and my father, King Mollen's betrayal of our kingdom, the war, and so on."

Master Fields nodded, "But Joanna was not happy being stuck up on top of the falls while all these terrible events transpired was she? Did she know of them?"

"Most of it, or what could be guessed by watching the kingdom," Raven stated.

Now Master Fields finished the story piecing it together, "She could not come down to the valley and casually walk in with everyone thinking she was dead, they might think she was possessed or evil, no one would ever accept her."

"Yes," Raven answered, "she had to wait more than three years for us realize she was alive and come to her. You see, until Lorriel went back in time we did not know she was alive either. So after meeting with her we decided to bring her back as the long lost Aunt returned from outside the kingdom to live with us."

"With that ability could not Lorriel go back and save Edward, or change things for the better?" Asked Sauron.

"That was a hard lesson Lorriel had to learn, we all did," Raven answered. "We cannot always guess what effect we will have by trying to change the past. What if in trying to save Edward's life Andrew would be killed in the process, or I, or a thousand different things, who is to know? The hurt Lorriel had caused Joanna by exiling her to the Hall of Wisdom for those years caused her to make a promise to us all that she would never shift time without consulting us as to the possible effects the time travel might have on things."

"So what we are going to do is convene a time counsel to determine a course of action?" asked Sauron.

"Yes," Raven replied, "we need Andronicus' input more than anyone else in these matters."

Everyone was silent for a time until Master Fields spoke. "I had forgotten you had told me about Lorriel's gift of time travel, because you never brought it up again. But I believe it all and now it makes sense to me. For all of you (speaking of Lorriel, Raven, and Rebekka) ending up with these special talents that are far beyond the normal person is for a reason. God has given you these gifts because the enemy was going to come here to this time and perhaps with your gifts you may be able to defeat him somehow."

94

Raven thought on that a moment and shaking his head stated, "You may be right, we perhaps have a chance to do something, but what, I know not."

At the end of this conversation they had arrived at the falls. They dismounted, staked their horses and headed for the cliff face at the base of the falls. Sauron and Master Fields were curious as to how they would scale the cliffs, and even more so when they all began to walk the ledge that led behind the falls. When they reached the place where the ledge widened out Raven pushed the eyes of the owl overhead and the cliff face swung in to the chamber behind the falls. As they entered the lights came on so they could see.

Master Fields commented that the light was unnaturally bright for the cave they were in. Raven could see it made him uneasy. He smiled at that because he remembered the uneasiness they all felt by the light coming on in the secret chamber at Rock Spring. They headed across the chamber toward the doors to the small room that opened silently as they neared them. Sauron and Master Fields followed Raven and the rest into this small room.

Once they were inside the doors closed on them and Master Fields could be heard to say, "What have we gotten ourselves into."

Raven placed the ring into the slot made for it and the room began to move upward. Raven heard Sauron utter something under his breath and could see him hanging onto the rail that was attached to the inside wall.

Andrew to noticed and spoke to his father, "Do not worry father, the first time I was in here I panicked when the doors shut."

His father only nodded and with that motion the room came to a stop at the top of the falls. As the door slid open, a short distance away stood Andronicus with a concerned look on his face, but relief showing when he saw it was Raven.

"I thought the enemy had somehow found this place," Andronicus said as Raven and the others stepped out.

"Why did you not send me word of your coming by Rebekka so I did not worry when someone entered the chamber?"

"Because," answered Raven, "the enemy has taken Rebekka."

Andronicus stopped short, looked at Sauron and Master Fields who had joined Andrew and Lorriel on the garden path. "Then come, we must decide on a course of action."

The path to the Hall of Wisdom through the garden seemed to take a long time to Raven. For the first time he did not relish the garden or scenery about him, his only thoughts were of the current crisis.

Not so Master Fields and Sauron, they stared in awe and disbelief just as Raven and the others did the first time they saw this place. Finally they reached the Hall of Wisdom, entered, and sat down in the chairs of the main room to talk.

Andronicus came right to the point, "Did the enemy learn anything useful to him of the ancients?"

"I am afraid so," replied Raven. "It was my fault for bringing the armor and the sword the ancients made. Layton recognized them as an alloy we do not have."

"Ah yes, the titanium ceramic alloy triberridum, I should have remembered that and warned you to leave it hidden," Andronicus said chiding himself. "So now the enemy knows he is on the right trail and your ancestors are in danger."

Then changing the subject Andronicus asked, "What did he do with Rebekka?"

Raven frowned in concentration trying to remember every detail, "Layton Teal had a time shifter with him, a very young woman who took Rebekka somewhere in time. Do you have any idea where he might have taken her?"

Andronicus answered plainly, "The future, perhaps back to his own time, but that would be unwise."

"Can you explain to Lorriel how far and how to get there?" Raven said hopeful of rescuing Rebekka.

"No, I cannot do that," Andronicus said. But clarified his statement; "I came with the ancients back in time but this episode with Layton had to take place after we left. I can not guess how long after we fled Layton he found out how to travel this distance in time. It would be impossible and dangerous to try and find her by simply guessing. Did Layton give anything away that would help to establish a time in the future?"

Raven shook his head, "No he said nothing that we can use."

After Raven said this Master Fields jumped up and said, "Now hold on a minute, I have been impressed with this place and have so far swallowed this time travel thing, but for you to have been alive when the ancients were is just to much to take. You would have to be over a thousand years old!"

"I am one thousand one hundred and thirty three to be exact," Andronicus stated proudly.

Raven cleared his throat and had everyone's attention. "Sauron, Master Fields, please come here with me to Andronicus." They both followed Raven to Andronicus where Raven stopped and asked Andronicus to show them the inner workings of his arm and hand. Andronicus held up his arm pealed back the synthetic skin and exposed the maze of metal, circuitry, and small motors that made his arm and hand work.

Raven then stated with a strait face, "Andronicus is a machine, not a flesh and blood person like we are. He was built by the ancients and brought here with them when they fled the enemy."

Sauron and Master Fields were shocked, this was almost to much to handle in one day. They both sat back down slowly realizing that all they understood of the world about them had just evaporated.

Raven now spoke with compassion in his voice for he knew how this revelation would affect them. "Now do you see why I could not tell you both everything at once a few years ago, when I said some things you had to see for yourself?"

They both nodded, still not saying anything but trying to process the immense information they had just received.

Raven continued, "The ancients were far more advanced than we are because they came from our far future. That is why Layton Teal has weapons and abilities that we can not match with sword and shield. That is why Rebekka gave herself over to the enemy because she knew we could not defeat him in conventional warfare. We simply would have been slaughtered without a chance. She, by her sacrifice has given us opportunity to try and find a way out of this."

Finally Sauron found his voice, "How sire, we have no weapons to match his, and even if we did, to learn to use them as well as he would be impossible in the short time we have."

Raven looked at them all and said, "The last resort must be used, we must make time our ally, that is why we will convene a time counsel."

Now Andrew took the floor and explained to his father and Master Fields the purpose of a time counsel, to prevent as little ill effects as possible from changing an event in the past or future.

Master Fields asked then, "How do we know what will happen if we change anything in our future or past?"

"We really don't know what will happen, or to be precise if we even have the ability to know that things have been changed," Andrew stated. "That is why we have to approach this very carefully and with much input from us all."

"Can we go back in time before Layton appeared, or at least before we meet him to correct the oversights we made that got us into this mess?" asked Lorriel.

This seemed like a good plan to everyone except Joanna who had the past changed for her benefit.

She raised her hand and when she had everyone's attention spoke up, "I do not believe we should meddle in the immediate past to change things for what we see as a solution. It may seem like a simple thing to do, but the change and consequence could lead to more serious trouble than we have now. What if the enemy can get no useful information from you and decides to kill you all? And then go find someone else in the kingdom who will tell him what he wants to know. What would we accomplish in that?"

Andronicus spoke looking mainly at Raven, "Joanna is right. Do you think the enemy will be unable to find out what he wants to know if we correct those few small mistakes?"

Raven shook his head, "I think he will find the ancients one way or the other eventually. At this time he does not have a large force, and he does not suspect that we know so much about him. If he left us and went back just a few generations before us, they would not know of the danger he posed, nor feign from telling him about the ancients and how long ago they lived. I agree that it is up to us to solve this and put a stop to it here before he does find out more than we want him to. By just letting him leave we may be sending that problem on to someone else or the ancients themselves."

Raven paused for a moment and then went on. "Master Fields believes there is a divine purpose for the talents we possess. Perhaps God gave us these abilities to be able to deal with the enemy ourselves, we must consider that possibility. Until now I have felt cheated, and wronged by our ancestors. I believed it was their fight, their problem, so why should we have to deal with it? But now I see that every threat to the ancients is ours as well, every fight of theirs is also ours. Without them our kingdom would not exist. It is a great kingdom, loved by us all in truth and loyalty. But more than that, it has been a haven of rest for generations, a place of peace and prosperity for over a thousand years. Should we let Layton Teal take that from the earth? Even if we do not survive, we owe the generations to follow a place such as this for their peace and safety."

"We are with you, my king, whether we live or die," echoed Sauron. The others nodded their support as well.

"Then we should go back to the days of the ancients and seek their help on how to defeat the enemy here in our own time. Does anyone have a better solution or answer than this?"

Everyone felt it was the best plan and would have the least amount of repercussions for their time. They would only meet the ancients and ask them how to stop Layton Teal, nothing more. Even Andronicus agreed it was probably the best plan.

Joanna brought up one last point, "Can we follow the ancients riddle and use the stones to send Layton back?"

"It may have been a good plan to the ancients," Andronicus stated, "but it will not work for you. Sending him back would only delay his plans, and next time he would be more prepared. There is something else the ancients found out later about time travel that they did not know when they wrote the riddle of the stones. Even when using the stones, the time traveler has to travel to the time and destination with the stones. Even they could not send Layton back without Merry going with him and that was not an option for them. That is why the stones were forgotten in the vaults of the king's castle. I did not say the stones were of no use, for they will enable the time traveler to travel farther back in time and include everything inside the circle of the stones as well."

"Good," Raven said, "then let us talk about what to do or not to do during this time travel over dinner."

Layton Teal sat around the camp fire thinking, in a few days his search would end and he would be victorious. But for the first time he realized that his life was virtually over. This was the last challenge left him, finding the traitors and punishing them for their betrayal. But after that was done he had nothing left to challenge him. A sadness swept over Layton at this realization. He had spent his whole life clawing his way to the top, doing things no one else even thought possible. No one ever knew his motives, and once he reached the top as ruler of it all, it was a hollow achievement because it was the top. What had been life to him was the challenge, the conquering. But that was all over now except this last task. In a funny way he was thankful for the betrayal, it had given him something to do after he became ruler of it all for quite a few years now. He thought about finding them and just scaring them with the threat of death and then let them go, maybe even living out his last days in the past as they were. But Layton had never found out how to have peace and happiness in a normal existence. Come to think of it, he had never enjoyed life and did not know how. He also knew he could not let them go, for that would shortchange the experience of conquering this last challenge. He needed this last challenge to give him a sense of completeness, and then he could end his life. Maybe after this was all over he would leap into the unknown future for the final end of his days. As Layton Teal waited for the time to pass, he realized that all he had to show for his life was the satisfaction that he done what no one else could do, he had conquered it all.

3,000 YEARS INTO THE FUTURE:

Rebekka stared at the surrounding world about her, everything had completely changed. There was noise and people all about her and she found herself in the middle of a bustling city. Carriages not pulled by horses were hurtling at tremendous speeds in every direction, and some even traveled in the air. The smell and noise assaulted her senses when she was suddenly shaken out of her observation by someone tugging on her arm.

It was Ellise, and she said curtly, "Come with me."

Rebekka did not think to resist for she was at a loss from all the sights and sounds around her. Her shock subsided and she guessed she had been taken to the future by this young woman, probably to the enemies time. They walked a short distance to a tall building that stretched to the sky. In fact, most of the buildings were very tall and obscured the surroundings so you could not see what lay beyond them.

As they began to enter the tall building Rebekka saw men on either side of the door snap to attention and salute Ellise. Military, Rebekka realized, observing their uniforms and behavior. She could see others noting Ellise's presence and every one was snapping to attention, and people were trying to look very busy. Such attention this young girl demands, thought Rebekka, but then realized she must have been at the enemies disposal night and day if he needed her time traveling talents. Ellise's reward was the power and recognition her position with Layton Teal had given her. It all began to make sense now, everyone was afraid of this young woman, not because of who she was, but because of her connection to the enemy. She walked right past them to a door that slid open as they approached. Rebekka recognized it as a traveling room like the one that took them to the top of Brickens' Falls. They entered and Ellise spoke to a man that was inside the room, stiff at attention. She told him to take them to the 67th floor and the man pushed a button that had some markings on it and they began to move upward. When they stopped and the doors opened Ellise and Rebekka exited into a hallway with lavish decorations and rugs on the floor. It felt soft and squishy under Rebekka's feet. They walked to a room, Ellise took out a card and inserted it into a slot and the door opened. She motioned for Rebekka to enter and they went in to a large room with other rooms connected to it.

Ellise sat down in a very plush chair and exclaimed, "Oh, my feet are killing me." She bent down to remove her shoes and there was an audible sound of ripping fabric. Ellise sprang back up with surprise and embarrassment. She kicked her shoes off and then pushed a button on the arm of her chair. Immediately the door opened and a woman came in.

"What can I do for you chancellor Ellise?" the woman said as she bowed.

"These clothes are poorly made for the pants have ripped."

The woman hesitated not knowing what to say. Ellise saw the hesitation and demanded, "Well, what have you to say?"

The woman cast her eyes downward and commented, "I do not know how, but you have filled out to the figure of a woman since yesterday. Those clothes no longer fit you."

Ellise walked to a mirror and looked, at first shocked and then pleased by the figure she saw. She had filled out in places that women do when they mature.

Ellise turned to the woman and said, "I shall need new clothes immediately, the latest styles and shoes as well. Also some functional outdoor recreational clothes as I have on now."

100

The woman looked over her figure and her feet and then was gone in a flash. Ellise went back to the mirror and looked herself over once again. She had not grown taller, but definitely had grown in other places, including her feet. They were wider than they used to be and that was why her feet hurt.

Ellise had almost forgotten about Rebekka until she heard her say, "How old are you?"

Ellise walked slowly toward Rebekka and stated, "I am fourteen years old."

Rebekka thought to herself, "You are no more fourteen than I am, unless something drastic has happened to you."

Ellise sat back down and sighed, "Boy, am I ever glad to be back to civilization, there was nothing I enjoyed about that place I took you from."

Rebekka smiled and replied, "I was thinking the same thing about this place. It is too noisy, to many people, and it smells stuffy, not like the air of Glonfair. May I look out the window?" Rebekka asked.

"Sure, you can go out on the balcony if you want, you're sixty stories up, I'm sure you won't disappear."

Rebekka went to the window and figured out how to slide the glass door open and stepped out on the small balcony. They were high up and she gasped as she looked down. She had only been higher at the top of Brickens' Falls. From this height she could see over most of the buildings, or between them, to try and guess where she might be.

She was surveying the surroundings when she stopped and stared, "No it can't be," she said to herself. But there was no mistaking Brickens' Falls. This city was in the kingdom of Glenfair, between the Crestlaw's garrison and the falls. Someday all these people would live in Glenfair? It seemed too much to believe at first, but she reconciled it with the fact that she was far into the future.

She went back inside where Ellise was being attend to by several women bustling here and there with clothes and shoes. Rebekka sat down and watched the whole spectacle unfold before her. Finally the women were gone and they were alone and Ellise turned her attention to Rebekka once again.

"We will go out to eat tonight, and I will treat you to some fine food."

Rebekka squinted her eyes and said seriously, "You are treating me rather casual for a prisoner are you not?"

Ellise smiled back and said, "He told me to bring you back in four days, he didn't say we couldn't enjoy ourselves. Besides, I could have you killed if I told them Layton wanted it done. No one questions me because I answer only to Layton."

"And that reminds me," as she pushed a button and the woman appeared once again. "Get this woman an evening gown, we are going to eat at Jansboqué this evening."

"What is your name by the way?" Ellise asked.

"Rebekka," was all she offered.

"You used to be queen of this place, didn't you?"

"Yes," replied Rebekka, again this was all she said.

"I'll bet you had all kinds of servants to pamper and do anything you told them to do, just like me," Ellise stated, as if it must be true.

Rebekka tried to calculate her answer for she now saw that Ellise likened herself to a queen, though she did not have the title.

"As a matter of fact," Rebekka replied, "it is nothing like that at all."

"I don't believe you," Ellise replied, "all people in power use other people."

Rebekka sighed, "Let me tell you about the kingdom of Glenfair since you know nothing of what it is like."

"Before you do," Ellise quickly interjected, "promise me something."

"I cannot promise anything until I know what it is," Rebekka stated.

"Promise me you will tell me the truth, nothing made up about Glenfair as you call it."

"That I can promise," Rebekka said smiling. "I love our kingdom with all my heart, it is the most wonderful place to live, and its people are wonderful."

"What do you make them do?" Ellise asked.

"I do not make them do anything, no one is made to do anything in Glenfair if they do not want to. Even the servants that live with us in our castle do so of their own freewill, they have a place to live and are provided for. It is the life they choose to live, and I love all of them who live with us. They could leave to go anywhere, live and work anywhere they wish. People live together and work together to make Glenfair a wonderful kingdom. In fact we have two feasts a year where the whole kingdom celebrates together, it is a wonderful time."

Ellise's eyes were down cast, "That is not how it is here in this time. Layton said people are slaves to the state, to serve others."

"You mean," Rebekka corrected, "that people are Layton's slaves, he is the state is that not true?"

"For some," Ellise answered, "but not for me! I can do what I want," she said plainly. Rebekka felt sorry for Ellise, that she could not see the truth.

"Layton treats you well because he needs something from you. If you could not shift time would he treat you this way? Where would you be then? By the way, where is your family, you are awfully young to be alone?"

"I don't want to talk about this anymore," Ellise replied. "Its time for us to go to dinner."

Just then the woman returned with the evening gown for Rebekka, gave it to her and left without a word. It was elegant and Rebekka had never seen anything like it before.

"Get dressed," Ellise commanded.

Rebekka looked at the dress and could not find a way to get into it. She looked at Ellise with a question in her eyes and Ellise softened a little and showed her how a zipper worked. Rebekka thanked her and began to dress. The woman who brought it was an excellent judge of size for it fit perfectly once Rebekka figured out how to get it on. The woman also was wise to give her a loose fitting dress similar to the one she had on so attention was not drawn to her pregnancy.

Ellise commented, "You look very beautiful," but lingered a moment at her stomach.

"So do you," Rebekka returned in a truthful gesture. They smiled at each other and started to leave.

Rebekka looked at Ellise and asked one question, "Tell me the truth, do you like Layton?"

Ellise's eyes teared up at this question, "No she said, I hate him!"

They arrived at Jansboqué and the ride there was quite interesting to Rebekka. Having had wild rides on horses in her youth, she was not shaken by the mechanical wagon that carried them at a tremendous speed to their destination. They mostly sat in silence for the trip to the restaurant, but when they arrived the excitement Ellise had was infectious.

"Just wait," she said, "you will have a great time tonight!"

They went in and wonderful smells filled Rebekka's nostrils, all kinds of spices which reminded her suddenly that she was very hungry. They entered and were quickly ushered to a table, even though the place was packed with people. They sat down and Ellise proceeded to order for them different foods that Rebekka knew she had no idea what they were.

Ellise smiled at her and said, "I have ordered plenty of food, so if you do not like one dish there are plenty of others to choose from."

Rebekka smiled back but thought, "She does not look like a child, but she acts still very young."

At that moment Rebekka knew that Ellise had no idea of the consequences of helping Layton Teal accomplish his task, and that she was not an evil person, just easily persuaded and tempted in her youth. It was apparent she greatly enjoyed her freedom, position, and the possessions Layton had provided her. The food came and most of it was very delicious, but lacked that home flavor foods do when prepared in restaurants.

Ellise asked Rebekka if she liked the food and Rebekka replied, "It is all very tasty and exotic, but I will take barbecued Tor any day over this." Rebekka thought that at first she might offend Ellise with this statement, for she was still cautious of what she said to her.

Ellise replied, "I have never eaten Tor before, we have only a small herd of the creatures in a preserve. Maybe someday I will have to try it."

Rebekka looked at Ellise and decided to gamble a little because she was in such a good mood after coming back to her own time.

"How far into the future have you brought me Ellise?"

Ellise smiled and said with pride, "Three thousand and fifty one years to be exact!"

Rebekka was shocked, she had guessed she was in the future, but so many years stifled the imagination. She sat quietly for awhile eating a little desert until she was bold enough to ask another question.

"Ellise," Rebekka began, "how is it that you have grown older in just a few days? You do not look fourteen at all, but a woman in her late teens. Surely, you too have noticed?"

Ellise did not say anything for a moment then answered, "I do not know how either, but I have changed that is certain."

Rebekka continued, "Do you have a family physician that can look at you perhaps?"

Ellise shot a frowning glance at Rebekka that quieted her for the moment, but then her features softened, "Why are you interested in my health?"

"I do not wish you harm, and I believe you did not wish me harm in bringing me here, am I correct?"

"You are right," Ellise confessed, "I do not want anything to happen to you. I am lonely a lot and you treat me as a normal person, not like the others."

"What do you mean?" asked Rebekka.

"The others treat me nice because they fear what Layton will do to them if they don't. You don't fear Layton like they do, why is that?" Ellise asked.

"I do not want to give him that satisfaction," was all Rebekka said. In fact she did fear Layton Teal, not for what he could do to her, but what he could do to them all if he found the ancients.

"I like you," Ellise said. Then added, "Tomorrow I will see a physician about looking older so quickly."

They were both tired when they left Jansboqué to head back to where Ellise lived. When they arrived Ellise led Rebekka to the room that would be her's and showed her the buzzer to summon someone if she needed anything, and then told her good night. Rebekka lay upon her bed thinking, and aching for those who were separated from her by such a great rift in time. She could not help but concentrate all her thoughts into one desperate cry, "I love you Raven".

Others who lived in the time that Rebekka had been taken to, and were sensitive to telepathy, heard the cry and wondered, who it was that could echo this cry so strongly in the night.

After a great meal with Andronicus and a lively discussion on what to do and what not to do in their time travel, they all retired for the evening anticipating the next day and their travel in time. Master Fields and Sauron would wait with Andronicus and seemed content with the desire to know more of this wondrous place above Brickens' Falls. Andrew, Lorriel, Joanna, and Raven would be the ones to travel back in time to meet the ancients. The discussions around the dinner table had basically been what to do when they met their ancestors, and to try and refrain from telling them much about the future.

When Raven began to relax and fall into that place of sleep right before you lose consciousness, he began to dream of Rebekka and of her sacrifice for them all. It was as if he could hear her voice saying, "I love you Raven". And then he was fast asleep.

The next morning they gathered around the breakfast table Andronicus had prepared. While feasting, they mentally prepared themselves for the journey they would take.

Raven asked Andronicus a question, "Last night as I was falling asleep it seemed I heard Rebekka's voice calling to me, but faintly. Is that possible if she is in another time?"

Andronicus was greatly surprised at such a far reaching question. "I do not know," he replied. "I have never heard of such a thing, but Rebekka is a very talented and powerful telepath, she has already done things not known to be possible."

Raven did not expect an answer to his question but was glad to ask Andronicus anyway. After breakfast they gathered outside on the lawn for their departure. They were taking no weapons with them for there was no need when visiting the ancients.

Andronicus had explained to the best of his knowledge how the stones worked: "The crystals amplify the time shifting waves generated by the time shifter. Everything within the stones will travel in time with the time shifter. For this reason, no less than three stones will work. The five stones give you a rounder field of effect than just three which form a triangle. This is the reason you must hold the stones on the outside of you with your backs to each other. The time shift will only affect that which is inside the perimeter of the stones. Also I do not believe it wise for you to see me so far in the past. I myself do not wish to know too much before it happens, so go to the king's castle and meet the ancients there. They will let me know that you are not the enemy. Now, I must speak with Lorriel and give her the context and time she needs to travel there."

Andronicus motioned to Lorriel and they went off a ways for quiet and privacy while the others talked. Raven watched them go and noted with curiosity the sternness in Andronicus' face. It seemed they were almost arguing over something and Lorriel whirled and started to head back toward them when Andronicus grabbed Lorriel's arm and swung her around to face him once again. Raven almost went over to see what the problem was when he saw Andronicus nod in almost a sad way and Lorriel came to join them once again.

"Let's go," Lorriel said.

"What was that about," Raven wanted to know, motioning to Andronicus who still stood aloof by himself.

"Nothing," Lorriel stated, "its just between Andronicus and myself."

Raven started to pry further, but decided he would wait and ask later what their argument was all about. Joanna handed a blue stone to Raven, a red stone to Andrew, and took a topaz colored one for herself. They put Lorriel in the middle and each put their back up against her and held the stone out on its chain, letting it drape over the outside of their closed fist.

"We are ready," Raven said.

Lorriel closed her eyes and envisioned the place and time that Andronicus had vividly told her of in the past. At first Raven thought nothing would happen then their surroundings began to shimmer and fade. And he knew at that moment they had begun the journey back to their ancestor's time.

Chapter 5
The King's Ancestors

"Doest thou have abilities beyond the common man? Wilt thou horde them for thyself til thou goest the way of all the earth and turnest to dust? Or wilt thou give God the glory and helpest thy fellow man with thy gift?"

--Chronicles of the Ancients

The surroundings of the beautiful garden at the top of Brickens' Falls faded away and a feeling of weightlessness came over the time travelers. But before they could react or fear what was happening to them new surroundings began to twist and form before their eyes. In the next instant they found themselves a short distance distance from the king's castle.

It had to be the king's castle, Raven thought, but it was different as well. Then he realized the greatest difference was that it looked so new, like the stone was even polished.

Raven gathered his wits and spoke to his group, "Put away the stones so they can not be seen by anyone just yet. I am sure our appearance here will be quite a surprise to our ancestors."

The group turned and headed toward the king's castle, a glittering reproduction of the castle in their day. As they approached the main gate that led to the courtyard, they could see several people up on the wall looking down at them through the crenels. As they started to enter the gates the faces disappeared in a rush. Then they were inside the courtyard where they stopped and waited. Soon a group of people warily assembled at the opposite end of the courtyard from Raven's group.

After a moments stare down, a man stepped forward and demanded; "Who are you and what do you want? And don't give me any old story for we know that you time shifted to this place. Are you from the enemy?"

Raven spoke quickly trying to diffuse the situation before it escalated further; "We are here from the future because of the enemy, Layton Teal"... was all he was able to say before he was interrupted.

He wanted to add much more but the man was speaking again, "Your speech is strange, what a brilliant ploy of Layton, you are his spies."

Raven started to answer but saw a swift motion of the man's hand. The next thing Raven knew a knife had appeared and was sailing toward him. It was a hard fast throw, but Raven had handled weapons thrown at him before, so simply timed it and caught the knife short of his chest. The man was clearly surprised to see the reflexes Raven exhibited. As Raven tossed the knife aside the man came at him in a flash. This almost unnerved Raven, for he had never seen such quickness in anyone other than Andronicus. If he had not been in the habit of sparing with Andronicus this would have been his undoing, but now he waited with a controlled tenseness that came with his abilities.

Uriah was troubled when the visitors arrived. Andronicus had informed them there had been a time shift just outside of the castle. "Funny," Uriah thought, that the time shift would occur when all of them were gathered here in one place and not dispersed to the other castles. He had a terrible feeling that this would be the end for them all. He decided right then and there that he would not go peacefully. After all, what awaited him back in his own time was a sentence of death. He would rather fight to the death than be taken back, tortured, and killed at Layton's pleasure. Why had they destroyed their weapons so soon after they had finished the castles? As good as he was he did not think he could defeat a force armed with lasers or other high-tech weapons. Uriah hurried to the top of the wall to view their approaching trouble. Daniel was there as well, along with Samuel. When he looked over the wall he was surprised to see only four people, two women and two men coming toward the castle. This was not an assault force, it merely had to be reconnaissance from Layton. If he killed them all no word would get back and perhaps Layton would just figure something went wrong.

Uriah motioned to the others and headed to the courtyard without saying a word. When they arrived the small group had stopped and waited for them to come. He had to do something before they disappeared. If that happened all would be lost in their efforts to carve a new life here for themselves. Uriah surveyed the situation and after asking them their business heard the strange speech of the visitors.

"How clever," thought Uriah, he was sure the enemy did not know they could detect time shifts so he had sent spies with a strange tongue to mask their identity. He had to keep them off balance so he could incapacitate them before they could escape so he called them spies. He could see this shocked them and in that instant he drew a knife and threw it at the man in front of him. When the man caught the knife that was thrown at him, Uriah was shaken to his very core. It had been one of his swifter throws and no one he knew could have stopped it from its purpose.

"Well," Uriah thought, "Layton has engineered another warrior for himself, lets see how good you really are." With that he leaped at the man to finish him off.

Raven saw that the man coming was incredibly swift, and in that instant he realized this was Uriah Kallestor his own ancestor. He had no time to explain for the man was in front of him and had already started to deliver several crushing blows that would have killed him had he not been quick enough to block them. They separated and circled each other like two cats surveying their prey. Every time Raven started to say something Uriah would attack and it would take all of his concentration to block the attack.

Uriah meanwhile was thinking, "This new genetic warrior is quite impressive," and he now began to worry. He had blocked everything Uriah had thrown at him and several times he could have picked an opening and delivered some blows but had not. Uriah knew that the warrior was only toying with him, prolonging this conflict, for he had not attacked at all. He also knew that if he did not finish this battle soon he probably would lose.

To the others gathered in the courtyard, the confrontation and attack came so quickly that they were all stunned. One minute Raven was trying to explain who they were, the next he was fighting hand to hand with this man.

Andrew did not know what to do, and was wishing at this moment that he had brought his sword when Joanna ran into the fray to try and stop the battle. They all realized how serious this was, for the man was not playing, he was trying to kill Raven.

As Joanna reached the battle between Uriah and Raven, Uriah feigned at Raven and then swung with his leg and caught Joanna sending her flying and landing in a heap near by. Lorriel ran to her mother and Andrew could stand it no longer. He yelled and began to head toward the battle, his anger flowing for what this man had done to Joanna when strong arms grabbed him and began to pull him down. He had been so intent on the battle that he had not seen the others rushing toward them.

As Andrew hit the ground in the castle courtyard, he tried to rise but the next instant a fist came crashing squarely into his face and everything went black.

Meanwhile Raven seeing what was happening and his mother laying on the ground as well now became angry. Ancestors or not he would not stand by and let them harm any of them, and he was especially angry with Uriah for what he had done to his mother. Now

109

Raven swung into action and struck several blows to Uriah. He could see the man was visibly shaken but not terribly dissuaded from the battle. Even though Raven was angry and no longer was fooling around, he did not want to injure or kill Uriah, for then he would be no different than the enemy. He would not do the enemies work for him but he needed to finish this battle somehow soon.

Uriah noticed the difference right away and knew that he had been right with the estimation of this enemy spy. He no longer was toying around and the blows he had given him hurt immensely. But still the spy held back, for one particular blow if followed through would have broken his collarbone. He had better end this quick or they all would be finished. Uriah went full force, it was now or never.

Raven was no longer relaxed and flowing, he had shifted into battle mode which he had not wanted to do. But some things you cannot control when life preservation kicks in during an emergency. Raven at that moment realized he could be a killing machine and simply kill this man and be done with it, but almost instantly he gained control of his instincts and did not deliver any blows that would kill Uriah. Then it happened, Uriah made a sweep with his leg so quickly that Raven could not get out of the way by dodging back or sideways so he did the only thing he could, he went up and over the head of Uriah while the momentum of his leg swing circled catching only the air where Raven had stood.

This is familiar, Raven thought, I have been in this position before. When he landed behind Uriah he did not give him a blow to the neck but simply grabbed him from behind and whispered in his ear quickly, grandfather, I am your descendant.

Uriah spun around like lightning to face Raven but he was not there, what had he said about being his descendant, grandfather? Uriah spun just as quickly back the other way and there was Raven standing there, but before he could do anything the spy's arm shot forward with his palm open and smacked him in the forehead with such force that Uriah fell backwards landing hard on the ground almost knocking him unconscious. Uriah was dazed and knew the battle was over, he would be finished any moment.

I am sorry, Merry, I am sorry for failing you and everyone, he thought. But the blow did not come, the man was calling his name, and saying something. His mind was fuzzy and it began to sink in, he was saying he was his descendant, he was calling him grandfather. Uriah shook his head to clear the cobwebs and stars that had been placed there by Raven's blow.

"What?" Uriah said. "You are not from the enemy, Layton Teal?"

"No, we are not," Raven shouted. "We mean you no harm, please listen!"

Uriah looked about and assessed the situation instantly and saw that Andrew was in danger from the others and shouted to them to stop before they killed him. The others stopped and backed away from Andrew's motionless form.

Lorriel was torn seeing Andrew there lying still and holding and cradling her mother as she lay unconscious in her arms. Raven seeing her plea rushed to Andrew and began to minister to him as he was coming around.

Lorriel on the other hand just screamed at the crowd of people, "What is wrong with you, we have come to help and you try to kill us?"

The people now began to settle down as they realized the battle was over and Lorriel's harsh words began to sink in. Uriah came over and stood looking down at Raven and the awakening Andrew. Joanna was also starting to stir in Lorriel's arms. Andrew sat up on his own strength and so Raven stood and faced Uriah.

"If you were not my ancestor I would have killed you for hitting my mother the way you did!"

Uriah looked shocked, "She was your mother? Are you really my grandson?"

Raven settled down a little and simply said, "Yes, a great, great, great, way down the line grandson of yours, I am you descendant Raven Kallestor."

"This," he motioned to Andrew, "is Andrew Crestlaw, my sister Lorriel, and my mother Joanna."

Someone from the back of the crowd yelled, "A Crestlaw?" And Samuel Crestlaw pushed his way to the front and knelt beside Andrew to assist him.

Suddenly a man who had been silent now spoke. Raven knew immediately that he was a leader that the others respected.

"I am Daniel Brickens, if you have not been sent by the enemy, Layton Teal, then why are you here?"

Raven now began again. "I was about to explain that before I was attacked," he said scowling at Uriah. "Layton Teal has appeared in our time a thousand years in the future. He has taken my wife hostage and expects us to tell him when and where to find you in three days for the exchange of my wife's safe return."

Everyone was silent as they all looked at Raven until Daniel spoke, "How do you know about Layton Teal?"

Then at almost the same time in unison they answered, "Andronicus!"

"Yes," Raven replied with a slight smile, "Andronicus has told us the whole story of how and why you came here, but has requested that he not meet us or know too much about his future. He requested that you only tell him the time shift he detected was only an experiment you all are working on."

Daniel motioned to Amnon Prescott to inform Andronicus about the time shift as Raven and the Andronicus of the future had requested.

Raven was taken by surprise, "I thought that Othellia would have the telepathic ability and not Amnon."

Samuel Crestlaw and Andrew were now standing in the group and Samuel spoke up. "You seem to know a lot about us, our time travel, telepathy, Layton Teal, and Andronicus. All of this is very troubling since we sought to hide all of this from those who would come after us."

Raven looked at his mother and could see that she was sitting up now, shaken but apparently all right. He then spoke with a question in his voice, "Did you not leave Andronicus for generations in the future to find, and a select few to know the truth of how and why you came here?"

"No," Daniel said emphatically. "We had decided to decommission Andronicus and destroy the building at the top of the falls in a few years. You are one more reason we should do just that. This information must have leaked out and now the enemy will find us as a result."

"Just a minute," Raven said forcefully. "The enemy did not come to our time because of anything he found out about you. In the future I was born with the enhanced abilities of Uriah." They all nodded seeing the fight and the outcome of Uriah being defeated which they thought was impossible. "In the future I will fight a battle and those abilities were recorded by the Wickshield kingdom. Layton read that in the histories and came to our time I believe hoping to find Uriah. I fought the battle before we ever made contact with Andronicus. So if you take him from us we will not know who this enemy is, and when he appears after I fight the war we will most likely tell him when and where to find our ancestors. This we would do in ignorance not knowing the danger that it places you in. If Andronicus is not there to tell us of this great danger you all will be destroyed."

Samuel Crestlaw spoke again, "Daniel, Uriah, Amnon, it seems this is much more complicated than we can imagine. We must discuss all these possibilities before we make any decisions."

Daniel nodded in agreement. "Come," he said, "into the great hall where we can sit and talk of these things in more detail."

Several people including Raven helped his mother into the hall where the four sat down in a place by themselves to talk while the ancestors debated the situation. Andrew was nursing his chin and Joanna still was a little shaken from the ordeal.

"I never expected that kind of greeting from our ancestors," Andrew painfully spoke. "Maybe we should have let Layton Teal have them for all the thanks we get."

"I have to admit," added Raven, "the thought crossed my mind as well but you know we cannot do that. Remember their survival is necessary for our own in the future." The rest nodded at that truth and drifted back into their own thoughts for the time being.

A little while later a woman came over to them and introduced herself as Candice.

"I am the physician for our group, I would like to look at the woman who was knocked down by Uriah. I am sorry for his impulsiveness, but he is chief of security and takes the protection of us all quite serious."

"Serious is a mild word," interjected Raven.

The woman just smiled and kept on examining Joanna. When she was finished she concluded that there was no serious injury or problems that she could detect. Then she proceeded to do the same for Andrew and commented that he as well was not injured seriously but would retain a bruise on his face for some time. She left and came back a short time later with a cold cloth for Andrew's face.

She then commented, "You are better off than Uriah, he has injured ribs and multiple contusions, plus a neck that will require some adjusting to keep him from having headaches. But he will be ok as well. Are you really a product of our settlement here in Glenfair from the future?"

"Yes," Lorriel replied. "But you make it sound so clinical, mathematical instead of personal. It is because of you that we are here, and many more of our kingdom are grateful for what you started so long ago."

The woman smiled and replied, "I am glad that our lives have been for a greater purpose than just escaping a tyrants clutches. Tell me who is the time shifter among you?"

"I am," Lorriel, answered.

"What a great sacrifice you have made to come to us," Candice said. Then paused as if she was going to say more, but turned around and abruptly left.

"What was that all about?" Andrew wanted to know.

Lorriel started to say something but was interrupted by Uriah clearing his throat and approaching them at a fast pace.

"We would like to speak with you to clear up some details we do not understand, please, come." Uriah led the way to the other group of people at the far end of the great hall. Raven and the rest followed not far behind. As they approached the others, Raven could tell that there was a heated argument going on but what it was about he could not tell. They quieted down as Uriah approached and turned expectantly to the group of visitors whose language and dress were definitely from a different time than the rest of them. When they were comfortably close to the others they stopped and waited for the questions to begin.

Daniel Brickens began the questioning. "There are some things that we don't understand about why you came here, and we hoped you could answer some questions for us."

Raven looked at them and smiled, "We will answer any questions we can for you."

"Good!" Daniel stated in a way that left Raven feeling like this was a judicial matter. "Why are you so concerned about our well being, or safety, especially since your wife has been taken hostage by Layton Teal? Why did you not tell him what he wanted instead of coming here? You don't know us, so why think more of us than the safety of your wife?"

Raven was dumbfounded, he never expected this question to even be considered by the ancients. He looked at Lorriel, Andrew and Joanna and they were just as shocked.

Samuel Crestlaw saw the look on their faces and added, "Is there something you are not telling us about this whole matter?"

Raven pulled himself together, straightened up and answered truthfully for them all. "At first I thought you must be jesting when you asked why we are here, questioning our motives. But now I see you are seriously wondering why. Have any of you ever given any thought to what you have started by coming here to this time and place?"

"What are you getting at," Amnon Prescott wanted to know.

"I am talking about your children, and your children's children for generations to come," Raven answered. "We are from a thousand years into your future, all four of us are your descendants. A great portion of Glenfair in the future are your descendants. If Layton Teal finds you, kills you, or takes you back to his time, all of us will cease to exist! Our existence depends on Layton never finding you, or taking you away from this place. I love Glenfair with all my heart and have pledged to serve and even give my life for its well being. You are the beginning of our kingdom, if something happens to you we will all vanish from time. I would gladly die so you might live, so in turn the kingdom of Glenfair can live on in history."

Now for the first time everyone was listening intently, and most looked as if they had seen a ghost.

Samuel Crestlaw leaped to his feet and slammed his fist down on the table in front of him, "We have been fools he shouted. Fools not to consider the future of what we started here. We have been consumed with only ourselves, first our escape, and then taking steps to ensure we are not found. All of this so we can live out our lives free from Layton's iron first.

"Samuel, calm down," Daniel Brickens spoke. "This is a revelation for all of us as well."

To see the ancients' shortsightedness and lack of direction disappointed Raven, for he expected so much more from them than this. Raven could have been angry, or a number of unsuitable feelings could

114

have overtaken him in this moment, but instead he felt compassion for them all. He realized now more than ever the terrible life they must have fled, and knew that all their effort and energy had been expended in escaping Layton to this place. He also knew now that none of them really had much of a plan after they had come here, to get away was their only goal.

Samuel sat back down and another man stood and introduced himself as Felton Rollins.

"Do I understand you, Mr. Kallestor, that this place will become a kingdom someday that will endure more than a thousand years?"

"Yes," Raven said cheerfully. "It will become the greatest kingdom on earth. Not the greatest for military strength, but the greatest for peace and freedom of the human soul to live as they choose. Anyone is free to come and live in our kingdom, but we only guard the passes to keep anyone from taking it by force." Felton Rollins sat back down shaking his head in wonderment at what the future held for the generations to follow. Murmuring could be heard from the others until another man stood.

"I am Chester Zandel, and I believe you said that Layton Teal has taken your wife as a hostage. Is that why you have come here, to try and find a way to get her back?"

Raven was at a loss to answer this question properly but before he could give any answer Andrew intervened.

"Sire, please permit me to answer this question." Andrew then turned to the ancients and started to speak but paused for an older woman came into the great hall and stood behind Uriah placing her hands on his shoulders. The effect she had on the rest of the ancestors was amazing, a calm, if not a release of tension came over them all.

After this pause, Andrew began: "No one wants the safe return of the queen more than I, and no one loves the queen more than King Raven."

"But," and then Andrew looked at Raven, swallowed hard and began again. "When Layton demanded her as a hostage she went to him of her own free will to give us time to form some kind of plan. We would have gladly given up our lives for the queen but the king commanded us to let her go for he knew that we could not fight against the weapons Layton had brought with him, and he did not want the queen's sacrifice to be in vain. It must have been the hardest decision of his life, especially since she carries his unborn child. We are here to find a way to stop Layton Teal, and if we are able to rescue the queen we will do so as well, but we must stop Layton even at the cost of our lives."

When Andrew finished this he stepped over to Lorriel who had tears running down her cheeks and pulled her close to him. She buried her head into his embrace and cried.

The people were silent until Daniel Brickens spoke, "Is this true? Would you let your wife and child die that we may live?"

Tears now came to Raven's eyes. "Yes," was all he could say.

Chester Zandel jumped back up and in a derogatory tone and sneered, "So you are king of Glenfair in your day, did you use the great abilities you have to conquer it for yourself?"

Again Raven was consumed with emotion and was not able to answer, for he was not prepared for these kinds of questions.

Andrew now burned with anger and said with such force that everyone shrunk back from his words. "No one takes the kingship by force in Glenfair, it is given to those who are worthy to rule by her people. King Raven tried to give the crown to our family at his coronation, but we refused, for we wanted, as did all the people to have him for our king. And I dare say that in Glenfair's thousand years of kings none has been more noble, or worthy to rule than King Raven who has sacrificed himself time and again for her people. And even now the king and queen suffer that the kingdom and you might be saved from this evil enemy. Do not speak of things that you know not of, nor judge that which has torn our king's heart in two or I may draw swords with you!"

The people were silent until the older woman who entered a short time before spoke, "I have been listening to this whole business even before I entered. Shame on you all, most of you know nothing of sacrifice for others. You came here fleeing a bad situation to a better life. These, our descendants had a good life but got involved in a bad situation to help others, especially us. You have no right to question them as you have done. Not one of you has offered to help them deal with our problem." She then glared at all of them until they hung their heads in shame.

Daniel finally spoke, "Merry is right, we have not been kind or hospitable, nor the least bit helpful at all. Please forgive us this trespass and accept our apology for our conduct."

Raven decided that he liked this woman very much, and even respected Daniel Brickens for his admission to treating them poorly.

Daniel continued, "We want to thank you for warning us that Layton will be coming, we will do all we can to prepare for his arrival after you get your wife back."

Raven blinked twice at the lack of comprehension these people still had of their true intentions. "We did not come here to warn you," Raven stated. "The last thing we want is for the enemy to come here. We want your help so we can learn how to defeat him in our time."

Everyone was shocked except Uriah who started laughing loudly and only paused to add, "You want to defeat Layton Teal?" He then went back to his laughter until Merry shook him forcefully from behind.

"What is so funny?" Raven asked.

"You," Uriah, stated, "thinking that you can defeat Layton Teal. He has never lost at anything that has challenged him, empires have fallen before his genius. Don't you think that if there was some way to defeat him we would have tried instead of fleeing here to this place empty of all our comforts and technology? Layton will always win in a confrontation, that is why we sought to hide from him. But I see now that it will be impossible to do so. We must be thankful for the years we have thus spent free from his hand and believe it all outweighs what will happen to us when he comes." Uriah was silent but stared hard at Raven waiting for his reply.

Raven smiled because he knew that Uriah was not trying to be harsh, just realistic and so replied softly, "I defeated you did I not?"

"Yes," Uriah said thoughtfully, "but against his lasers you will not succeed."   "Then give us weapons equal to his own so we will have a chance," Raven pleaded.

Daniel Brickens shook his head sadly, "We can't do that for we have destroyed any weapons of that type after we completed the castles. Even if we did have weapons, Layton and his men will use them much better than you, and you would still lose. You would need a great advantage that Layton has never allowed anyone to have before in order to succeed." Daniel thought that would dash the hopes of the young man who stood before him but it did not.

Instead Raven smiled again and said, "We do have an advantage that none of you ever had against Layton Teal."

"And what would that be?" Uriah asked. "He has a history of never missing any detail, or ever miscalculating any situation."

Raven nodded knowing that Layton Teal was such a man, seeing how quickly he figured out they knew about the ancients.

"He does not suspect we know who he is and what he is seeking. He also does not know that we have a time shifter with us, pointing to Lorriel. He has no idea of the existence of Andronicus and thinks we are only simple ignorant people playing out some irrelevant ancient history. He has only brought a small force of less than twenty men and did not feel threatened by our type of weapons at all. I believe it will be the best chance of all ages to stop the enemy in our time." Raven watched Uriah rubbing his chin in thought, and also Daniel Brickens calculating as well.

"If the things you say are true," Uriah stated, "you may be able to surprise Layton for the first time in his life."

"It is a possibility, though remote," Daniel added. Then he turned to Raven's group and asked, "What do you want from us?"

"First," Raven replied, "make sure you do not deactivate Andronicus, we need him desperately in the future. Do not worry about information leaking from his existence to the enemy, for we are the first to find him in a thousand years and the enemy knows nothing of his existence. Just make it hard for him to be found and it will keep him isolated."

How are we supposed to do that, Daniel replied?

Raven smiled and said, "Riddles, leave only clues obscured in riddles." Raven paused here and remembered the discussions of the time counsel and decided he had said too much already about the future. He should not be molding the past to fit his future, that could be very dangerous. What was he to do though, Andronicus would have been decommissioned, as they put it and now he knew the reason Andronicus was there for them. The only reason was they had come back here in time and prevented his destruction.

Raven shook his head to clear it from this circular reasoning and focused on the problem at hand. "We also need to learn about the weapons Layton has brought with him so we can defend ourselves from them." Raven caught movement to his right as Amnon Prescott stirred, half rose and then sat back down with a troubled look on his face. Everyone waited for Amnon to say something, but when he kept silent Raven knew that Amnon would never admit to hiding weapons that should have been destroyed. He remembered how angry Andronicus had been when he found out about the weapons and knew that to reveal this secret now would destroy his position of trust with the others. Raven appreciated the dilemma Amnon was in, but was also disappointed in his failure to forego personal ruin to save others. Once again he was disappointed in the ancients. He decided that he would say nothing about the weapons to anyone.

Daniel interrupted his thoughts with this statement; "Amnon, were you about to say something?" Amnon shook his head sadly and stayed seated.

Daniel continued, "We will teach you all we can about the weapons, but I do not see where that will make any difference."

Raven answered back, "To know your enemies strength is always important in planning how to defeat him."

Uriah, hearing Raven's answer saw in that moment the wisdom this young man possessed. Maybe, this may have a chance to work somehow, thought Uriah, but how he did not know how.

Daniel Brickens spoke once more. "There is much to think about and the day is getting late, we should retire and convene tomorrow to do as much as we can to assist these brave souls in our own defense."

Turning to Raven's group he said, "Please be our guests and stay with us. We will dine in an hour."

With that the assembly broke up and people began to wander off in small groups to talk. Raven watched as the people wandered off to socialize until he felt a hand on his shoulder. He turned and it was Daniel Brickens.

He held out his hand for Raven to shake and said, "No matter what happens I want you to know how much it means to me to have a stranger come to our defense."

Raven smiled and said with equal emotion, "You are not really strangers to us, for we too are grateful for your bold beginning of our kingdom."

Daniel then left to talk with some others and Raven observed Amnon making his way over to Uriah. Uriah caught his eye and motioned for Amnon to come aside away from the others. As Raven watched he noticed the greeting they gave each other in an odd handshake. They locked each others fingers in a curved vise type grip and raised each of their thumbs up and touched them together three times, the third time stopping with their thumbs touching and lingering before the strange handshake ended. Raven knew he had seen some formation like that before but could not remember where until it hit him. It was not a handshake, but the formation of two sheaths of grain meeting in the same way and angle Uriah and Amnon's thumbs did. All the other sheafs were standing strait up in the mosaic in the secret room of the Prescott castle. Above those leaning sheafs two heads of grain touched, and now Raven felt sure he knew how to open the mosaic vault where the weapons were kept for the emergency that Amnon thought may require them. Good, thought Raven. When we get back I can retrieve the weapons after the ancients teach me how to use them.

Supper was uneventful save for the fact that the small group with Raven felt like outsiders. Everyone was laughing and having a good time but rarely spoke to them. Raven could not blame them, they sounded different than the ancients, and they all shared one common experience, escape from a tyrant. If the tables had been turned he knew that they in turn would not share the same fellowship with him as those who had fought in the Wickshield war. So they ate talking among themselves and discussing the events that had unfolded.

Andrew spoke after they had finished eating. "I can see no benefit so far in our coming here. It is frustrating not to have any concrete answers by now. We are no closer to a solution than when we arrived."

Lorriel joined the conversation then, "Our travel here cannot be in vain, I will not accept that. I have to believe we will find what we need to help us here among our ancestors." Lorriel's faith and optimism was infectious, and put them in a better mood.

"Yes," Andrew finally admitted, "there has to be something more we can glean from our ancestors than a bruise on the chin." He said this while rubbing his chin in such a knowing way that the rest had to laugh.

Joanna also spoke, "The ancients are nothing like I had pictured them. They seem to lack direction and wisdom at times."

119

"You mean they seem to human for our tastes," Raven added sarcastically.

Joanna nodded, waiting for Raven to say more.

"You are right, they are not what any of us expected, especially me. Since finding the armor, the Hall of Wisdom, and meeting Andronicus, I had made the ancients out to be something they evidently are not. That is not their fault, but our own for elevating them above mere mortals. They are humans like we are and we should not forget they also have weaknesses."

They all nodded at the words of Raven, every one of them having their expectations dashed by meeting the real ancestors.

Joanna again spoke, "We should not be too hard on them, for the kingdom we know has had a thousand years to grow and mature. Right now it is in its infancy and will have many growing pains before our time."

There was not much more to say so the group retired for the evening.

When Andrew and Lorriel prepared for bed, Andrew was looking at Lorriel, watching her as husbands do their wives. He realized how lucky he was to have the woman he loved beside him in this crisis. As he watched he noticed something about Lorriel's hair.

"Come here Lorriel and sit beside me on the bed," Andrew asked.

She smiled at him and did as he asked and just sat down beside him not saying a word.

Andrew ran his fingers through her hair and she closed her eyes. She always liked his gentle touch on her hair, it was always done in love and tenderness, usually followed by a passionate kiss.

But this time Andrew gently spoke to her, "Have you noticed dear, that you have a few strands of silver in your hair?"

Lorriel opened her eyes unalarmed and looked at Andrew saying, "Time has a way of sneaking up on us all, does it not?" She lay down beside him and wrapped her arms around him as she did so often when they went to sleep and thought in resignation as the tiredness overtook her; It has begun.

The next day began with new optimism at breakfast, for many of the ancients stopped to say hello to them and converse shortly. Samuel sought them out and joined them for breakfast as did Daniel Brickens.

"I think everyone is in better spirits today," Daniel remarked. "And I hope we will get some things accomplished before the others have to head back to their homes." Raven hoped as well that there would be some solution to the problem they faced in his own time.

After breakfast they all assembled once again to discuss the problem of Layton Teal. No one had any new ideas except Chester Zandel. He proposed that the group travel back in time again to retrieve the weapons they possessed before they were destroyed.

Raven started to object when Andrew intervened.

"You all know how you welcomed us when we showed up the first time, how do you think you will act in the past if you have weapons?"

Uriah stood immediately and spoke for all to hear, "Andrew Crestlaw is right, If I would have possessed a weapon other than a knife, the four of you would be dead. I hate to admit it, but we were so afraid of Layton finding us that I would have shot first and then sorted things out later. And if you all remember we were extra jumpy that first year, expecting him to show up any moment. Come to think of it, a lot of us did not even trust each other back then. You cannot go back and get the weapons, it would be dangerous and would most likely get you killed, sorry."

After Uriah said this he sat back down and crossed his arms. Others began to talk all at once but one voice came above them all.

Chester Zandel could be heard to say, "Uriah, you still don't trust us." For a moment there was silence and then the people began to talk all at once again. This was truly perplexing to Raven and those who were with him, for they had never seen such a disorderly group in all their days.

Finally Daniel Brickens stood and pounded something heavy he had in his hand yelling, "Order, order!" But it seemed that no one was paying attention and Raven felt they would keep going on like this forever until they finally quieted down to Daniel's shouts.

"That is enough," he finally was heard to shout. The people quieted down to listen to Daniel and finally he was able to speak, "We need to put this mistrust behind us if we are to accomplish anything."

"Finally," Raven thought, "a voice of reason among them all."

But a woman answered back, "I don't know why this issue won't die, do you think any of us here would truly want to go back to being under Layton Teal? And don't give me that bit about trust, you don't trust some of us or else you wouldn't send your little snoops Uriah and Amnon to spy on all of us and to check to see if we are leaving any clues for Layton to find out where we have gone."

Daniel was getting red faced and he shouted in anger, "I have never sent Uriah or Amnon to spy on anyone." And then he looked at Uriah and Amnon and said, "If I catch you spying on people I will"...

"You will what," said Uriah, "try to kill me?" Uriah said this with a little amusement to his voice, not really angry but with a little humor.

Chester Zandel spoke once again, "Who gave you the right to tell any of us what to do?"

"Because I am king," replied Daniel Brickens.

"You are a king only in figurehead," added Felton Rollins. "Remember it was by the luck of the draw that you were chosen king, only for appearances to the lands about us."

Raven had heard enough, what was being said tore at his heart. Such bickering, mistrust, and chaos broke the last strings of his restraint. With that he stood and in a voice that comes from authority and respect earned and not granted he spoke:

"Everyone be quiet and listen to me," he said loudly.

It so shocked the ancients that Raven would address them in this tone, the room became completely silent.

"I am ashamed to even call you my ancestors. How the kingdom became what it is in my day from these beginnings I will never know, but let me tell you what it is like in my time. The kingdom is a place of peace and prosperity, of love and trust. Duke Rollins, Duke Zandel, Duke Prescott, and Duke Crestlaw would all give their lives for the good of the kingdom. They would give their life for another duke if he was in trouble, or needed help. None of us worries about the security of each duke's pass because we know they love Glenfair more than life and would give their lives to keep it safe. Let me tell you what is at the heart of the kingdom, what makes Glenfair strong and unconquerable in all these years, it is this; that there is trust between the king and the dukes and the people of the land. We trust each other with our lives, for that is how it must be for our kingdom to survive. No other kingdom on earth functions as does Glenfair, our strength is in our combined trust and unity. If any duke called to us for help we all come, we all help, we all serve each other. And the first and foremost example of this should be her king. I know what mistrust can do, I have seen it."

Andrew spoke then, "Raven, Sire, do not go on, please."

"No," Raven said, "I must tell all if they are to understand."

Turning back to the ancients he continued, "I know mistrust can destroy the kingdom because it almost did in our day. The mistrust came from my father, who was king before me. His mistrust was not founded on facts, just something he thought was true. He suspected Andrew Crestlaw was trying to take the throne by plotting. Yes, the same Crestlaws I tried to give the throne to after my father's death, but they would not accept it. The war you heard about with the Wickshield kingdom was allowed by my father to destroy my best friend Andrew and his family. We almost lost the kingdom because of mistrust, because of assumed guilt with no facts to back it up. The other dukes fought with all their hearts in that war because they loved the kingdom. And the Crestlaws threw themselves into battle as I have never seen before, or ever will, I believe. People died in that battle because of mistrust. My brother, Edward died because of that mistrust.

Somewhere in our history a code of honor was founded, handed down from generation to generation that we should trust each other and

122

give to the kingdom what would make it better and what it needs. People have sacrificed to make the kingdom great, and have even given their lives for it. And what have I heard from you? Petty bickering and mistrust, a kingdom cannot be built upon such things. You have chosen a king and dukes, how that was accomplished matters not now. What does matter is you must set aside your mistrust and all give equally to build a great kingdom. I am king in my day because the people have chosen me to be so. They chose me and pledge to my throne because they believe in their hearts that I would lay down my life for the good of the kingdom. Will you Daniel Brickens be such a king?"

Raven's eyes and words pierced Daniel's heart like he had never thought possible and he heard himself say; "Yes, I would be that kind of king, I will die for you all if necessary and give myself wholly for your prosperity."

There was shock and silence from all the people until Uriah stood: "I was created to mistrust, to doubt motives, but I want no longer to live that way. I pledge to you, Daniel my king and to the kingdom of Glenfair this day my loyalty and devotion for its good. I will give my life for you and the kingdom if it shall so require."

Daniel was shocked and tears came to his eyes, never did he ever expect to hear this from Uriah. Others, one by one pledged their loyalty to the king and the kingdom to Daniel's utter amazement.

"How did this happen?" Daniel wondered. This young man in one speech had done something he thought impossible. He knew beyond a shadow of a doubt that they all had been changed from this day forward, forever. As Daniel looked at Raven he thought, No wonder he is king in his day, I want to be a king like unto him.

Andrew watched this whole proceeding with admiration for his beloved friend.

It is just like you Raven, Andrew thought. You are a king even to the ancients, our ancestors without even trying to be.

Little did Raven know how much that day would change Glenfair forever. The whole attitude of everyone was different and Amnon and Uriah pledged to quit their surveillance of others from that time on. Raven never knew that was the reason Amnon Prescott's journal changed and ended different than it began. For his suspicions died that day along with the paper scroll that disintegrated into dust when Raven opened the chest centuries later. Raven noticed the hush and the calm that had come over everyone, and was glad that they had listened to him. In the background he saw the older woman with a small child. She was watching this all with tears streaking down her face.

He was brought back to reality by Daniel Brickens speaking once again. "We should no longer live in fear of Layton Teal finding us. We have taken precautions to prevent that from happening to the best of our ability. If he finds us we can do nothing for it, but if he does not we should endeavor to make this the great kingdom King Raven has said it can be. We must now turn back to the problem at hand and give what help we can to King Raven and Duke Andrew Crestlaw."

Andrew had an idea and so spoke up, "If we need the weapons of your past, there may be a way to get them. Have your time shifter go and get them for us, surely you would listen to her."

Daniel looked at the four standing there and said sadly, "That cannot be done for two reasons."

The older woman came forward holding the young child and said, "I will go if it is the only way to help us all."

Raven saw Uriah stiffen, but he held his peace.

Daniel looked at Merry compassionately and said, "Merry, as king I cannot let you go, it most certainly will do you further harm. And it is well known a time traveler should never meet themselves in another time, we can't take that risk. We love you to much to let you go, you have been the salvation for us all and it has cost you dearly."

Raven was dumbfounded and he noticed a visible relief from Uriah. This older woman was Merry Sheldon Kallestor? He had always pictured her much younger, someone Uriah had fallen in love with. He now saw the love that Uriah had for her and it all made sense, well some of it did.

"You are Merry Sheldon Kallestor?" Raven asked unbelieving. Andrew too, was shocked along with Joanna as well.

"Yes," she replied, "and this is my son Nathan."

"Impossible," Raven thought. She was too old to have a child that young. Raven looked at the others in his group and saw the shock on Andrew and Joanna's faces, but Lorriel was not shocked at all. She seemed to knowingly take this all in stride without any hesitation.

Daniel saw the confusion in the traveler's faces and spoke, "I believe we should take a recess and reconvene in an hour."

With that said, Merry came over to the group along with Uriah, Amnon, Daniel and Samuel Crestlaw.

Raven spoke first to Amnon, "There is something I have not told any of you yet, but Amnon should know. My wife, the queen was a Prescott before we were married."

Amnon was startled, "A descendant of mine will be queen one day?"

"Yes," Raven said, "and she has your telepathic abilities as well. That is why the enemy took her, he caught her trying to read his thoughts when we confronted him."

Amnon nodded his head now understanding why Layton had taken the queen hostage.

Now Raven turned his attention back to Merry Sheldon Kallestor. "I am sorry I was so shocked, I just pictured you much younger than you are."

Merry looked at Raven sympathetically and said, "A few years ago I was much younger. I have aged more than 30 years in only five. I am just grateful to have had a child before I grew to old to have one, and I see he will carry on a great line of descendants."

"How has this happened to you?"

Merry smiled at Raven and said, "I will let Samuel explain it to you since he is our expert scientist on the effects of time travel."

Everyone looked at Samuel as he cleared his throat to begin. "I have studied time travel almost exclusively in my years as a scientist, but only the short durations that time shifters can travel naturally. My whole goal was to find a way to enhance or duplicate the time shift they produce. Finally, with the development of isolinear resonating stone we were able to do what I had dreamed of all my life. Merry Sheldon was the time shifter that helped me in my experiments. In Merry's first trip with the stones, Uriah, Amnon, and I went back eighty years in time. But something happened in that first experimental trip I did not expect. Once we were free of the enemies influence Uriah told Merry that he had fallen in love with her, and she returned his affections with equal enthusiasm. Amnon was horrified for his friend Uriah, fearing what Layton would do if he found out. It was then I casually said, why don't we flee so far back in time that Layton could never find us. Uriah and Merry were willing to do that right then, but Amnon and I had wives we did not want to leave behind. So we decided to go back to get them and then disappear. We returned to our own time and the idea secretly spread among others that could be trusted who wanted to leave as well, and then Daniel Brickens came to me. I was terrified because Daniel was Layton's chief of staff. He told me though that he wished to go with us and wondered how many things we could take with us. I told him I did not know, but would manufacture some more isolinear resonating stone. Daniel arranged for equipment, supplies, and things we would need to be in one place that we could all go to without being suspect. When I arrived with my wife I was appalled to see over 40 people gathered for the great time jump. I had the stones held in a perimeter and told Merry we were ready to go to the time and place we had searched out, where history basically ended. I had purged the computers and had all the backup disks with me so we would leave no trace of how we did this. The only thing that we did not know was if it would really work. Well, it did and we are here. I did not have time to run more tests on Merry after the initial eighty year jump. All we could think about was the escape from Layton Teal. But once we arrived here, Uriah came to me a few weeks later concerned about Merry. Her hair was turning gray."

An audible groan could be heard to escape from Andrew's lips and Samuel glanced that way but when nothing more was said he continued; "Candice and I examined Merry and discovered that she was aging prematurely. The rest of us were ok, it seemed only the time shifter was affected. We still don't fully understand why a time shifter ages when they shift time, but we believe it has something to do with the time residue remaining in her body after time manipulation. The reason this had been missed in the previous experiments, was a time shift could only be in the realm of ten to fifteen years. So little aging took place in those kinds of jumps and no one noticed any effect. We did not have time to thoroughly check Merry after the eighty year jump before we came here. A jump as great as what we have done is aging Merry at a very fast rate."

Raven looked at Lorriel and for the first time noticed some gray hair showing in streaks here and there.

His heart sank as he turned to Merry and asked, "How old are you now?"

Merry did not hesitate and answered truthfully, "I am thirty-one years old. When I found out I was aging, Uriah and I married right away and tried to have a child. We thank God that he gave us Nathan before I passed child bearing age," as she hugged the child she was holding.

"How long do you have?" Raven asked.

"We are not sure," Samuel answered. "But the best estimate is less than ten more years."

Raven noticed the effect those words had on Uriah, he turned his head away at Samuel's statement.

"Is there nothing you can do for her?" Raven asked.

Samuel shook his head, "We still do not know all the parameters involved in this aging process. Since every time shifter's body is different the aging should take place at different rates for each person, for the time shifting ability comes from something they alone possess. I do not believe it is a constant, but every time shifter who travels a great distance will age at an accelerated rate."

They all looked at Lorriel and she stood there very calmly as everyone stared.

"I can't believe Andronicus did not tell you of this danger before you came here," Merry stated. "He knew what long distance time travel would do to the time shifter."

Lorriel replied calmly, "He did tell me before we left and tried to dissuade me from this venture, but told me the choice was mine."

"He should have told us all," Raven said with anger rising in his veins.

Andrew turned to Lorriel and said broken heartedly, "Why did you not talk to me about this first?"

Uriah winced at Andrew's words for he himself alone knew what Andrew must be going through at that moment.

Lorriel answered very softly, "You did not ask me what I thought when you went to war, or when you grabbed the twainlar serpent to save Raven. You would give your life for the kingdom and others without asking my permission, and that is how it should be. Why should it be any different for me? Rebekka walked down and gave herself to the enemy to give us a chance to save the kingdom. Should I not sacrifice a portion of my life to save us if it were possible? Should I make Rebekka's sacrifice vain because I did not want to give up a little of myself?"

Lorriel crossed her arms and looked at them all defiantly. Andrew said no more, but reached out and pulled Lorriel to him and held her in a tight embrace. Joanna had tears in her eyes, and all of them were distraught at this news.

Raven turned to Samuel and asked, "How long does Lorriel have?"

"Probably ten to twenty years after she returns back to your time is my guess," Samuel said sadly.

Now Merry spoke up, "If I had to do it all over again knowing I would age as I have done, I would. I would for the sake of all those who came with us, and (she looked at the four travelers) for those who would come after us."

There was silence for a while for there was no more to be said about what Lorriel had done.

Uriah then spoke, "You see why Merry should not travel in time again, we don't know what that will do to her now. I also believe that weapons are not the answer to defeating Layton. Making the playing field even with Layton will never give you victory over him, history has proven that to be true. I know that Merry would go back to get the weapons if we asked her to, regardless of what that would do to her. She would also go if you asked her to do so, so I beseech you as our descendant not to ask."

Raven looked at Lorriel and the gray streaks in her hair and then back to Merry and the little child she held and decided at that moment he would never ask Merry Sheldon Kallestor to shorten her life any further.

Raven looked at Uriah and nodded, "I will not, but please give us some time alone," motioning to Lorriel, Andrew, and Joanna.

When they were alone Raven looked at his sister and said, "You should have told us before you time shifted to here."

"Would it have made any difference?" Lorriel asked. "We would only have wasted time trying to find other options that we do not have. Why should I not sacrifice something? All of you have made sacrifices at one time or another for Glenfair. And you know that I could not live with myself if I did not time shift, especially knowing what Rebekka did for us."

Raven's heart ached at her words but he knew they were the truth. He felt like he had failed somehow as their king, for he failed to protect them. And if he could not protect the ones he loved dearest, what made him think he could be a king for all of Glenfair. Jerddin had been killed and Rebekka taken because he had underestimated the enemy, and now Lorriel would age and die sooner than she should by bringing them all here and having to take them back. Raven suffered with these realizations as a true king would do for his people. Even though it was beyond his control to stop these events, he was none the less absolved of the guilt of not being able to prevent their occurrence. He was their king and he would have traded places with any of them if he could.

Raven looked at Lorriel, Andrew and Joanna and stated, "What is done is done. We cannot focus on that now for we must find a solution to our dilemma before we can return."

Just then Daniel Brickens called the meeting together again to continue with trying to find a solution that would help Raven and those with him. They toiled the rest of the morning and into the afternoon with the ancients to no avail. Finally Daniel Brickens dismissed the assembly to return home to Raven's disappointment.

Daniel came over to Raven and stated to him, "I am sorry we have found no solution for our problem. You should let us face Layton for he is really our problem."

"I cannot do that," replied Raven, "I have already told you, your battle is also ours. We must try somehow to stop him in our time."

As they were about to part ways Daniel spoke again, "Tell me King Raven, something I must know about the kings who will come after me. You said that in your time a king only rules by the will of the people. Did the Brickens become unworthy to rule, is that why Uriah's line is now king of Glenfair?"

Raven could see this really bothered Daniel and could also see that the man had made a sincere commitment as king of Glenfair and wanted it to be so for many generations.

Raven smiled at Daniel and placed his hand upon his shoulder and answered, "The Brickens' line of kings were most noble, and will set precedence for six hundred years upon the throne. A bastion of example for all those who rule after them. Only by external circumstances and tragedy an heir was not found for the throne, or there would be a Brickens ruling to this day!"

Daniel smiled at this and said, "I have learned so much from you King Raven of what a king should be. I will write the sayings and wisdom I have found this day as king so the generations to follow may read them. They shall be reminded what it means to be king, and noble and upright for the good of all of Glenfair."

Raven just smiled to himself and thought, "So that is how the Chronicles of the Ancients began."

Daniel then concluded, "Stay with us for a few days, a solution may yet be found." He then left to attend the departing guests.

As Raven walked to join the rest of his group, Uriah, Amnon, Merry, and Samuel intercepted him.

"We have decided," Uriah spoke for the group, "that we will stay with you until you depart. We don't want to give up just yet on finding a solution.

Amnon spoke as well, "I have been insensitive and hard hearted about your plight. With you sharing that my descendant has been taken hostage by Layton, I realized how I stood aloof from your problem and the pain you must feel. I can no longer believe that I am not involved, we all are, and I would like to thank you for fighting unselfishly for us."

Raven smiled at Amnon and seeing his change of heart held out his hand to be shook by Amnon. They then all walked to join Lorriel, Andrew, and Joanna waiting at the far end of the great hall.

Merry spoke to them when they were all together, "I am sorry we have not found a solution yet but we want to keep trying."

"We should all take a break for the rest of the day to allow us some time to organize our thoughts better," stated Samuel. "Tomorrow things will seem brighter and maybe we will find an answer." They all agreed and went to wander about the castle thinking about the things that had transpired that day.

That night Raven had trouble sleeping, he wanted desperately to hear Rebekka's voice in his mind but there was nothing, just the quietness and blackness that comes when you empty your mind of all thoughts. Raven began to wonder if the voice he had heard the night before was real like he wanted to believe it was, or just his urgent wish to hear Rebekka. It had to be real, Raven thought, for I did not wish for it, it came of its own accord, or did I wish for it subconsciously? These thoughts plagued Raven until he finally fell asleep.

We as human beings think we see simple solutions to other people's problems. But when they are our own they do not seem so simple. We do not know the infinite possibilities for every action, therefore we cannot claim to know the absolute decision to be made when time travel is involved. Anyone could probably think right now of many different ways to solve the problem our dear friends have gotten themselves into. They could go back in time to change this or that so Layton Teal would not find anything useful and leave, or ways for them to get the weapons they need for the confrontation with Layton. I digress, for I am only telling the story as it happened, not what Raven and his friends should or should not have done. For they believed one should focus on solving the problems of the present without going back to change immediate past mistakes. Whether this was a good philosophy or not is debatable, but it is the path they took for themselves and I believe it to be the one I myself would also choose. Their trip to the ancients was not to change the past, but to learn of a way to deal with the enemy of their present. But the reality was far different than their intentions. They did change the past greatly, but for the good of the kingdom without purposefully setting out to do so. They accomplished this by their willing attitude to sacrifice for the good of others and the kingdom. Their impact did not change their problem with Layton Teal, but did set in motion the foundation for the great kingdom of Glenfair to become what it was....

The next day at breakfast there was little talking, each one of them was deep in thought about what to do about Layton Teal. Raven himself was a little depressed from the lack of progress they were unable to make. The long night thinking about Rebekka, no closer to a solution than when they came, and the ancients not being what he expected, added to his deepening melancholy. When Raven lifted his eyes from his food to look around the table he noticed for the first time that Merry and Samuel were not present. Uriah and Amnon were there eating and talking and discussing matters when Samuel burst into the great hall running as Merry walked at a fast pace not far behind. Everyone stopped eating and stared at the excited Samuel.

"There may be a way to help our descendants," Samuel said excitedly. "Andrew mentioned something to me before I retired last night that reminded me of some research I conducted before we time shifted to here." Samuel paused expecting everyone to be excited as he was but there was silence.

Finally Daniel Brickens said plainly, "We are all waiting to hear what you have found Samuel."

When Samuel realized that he had not shared anything of real value, he looked sheepish and said, "Yes, yes, umm you all know that a time shifter controls time."

They all nodded and still waited for more than what they all knew to be true already.

"Well, I have never told you the real reason I made the isolinear resonating stones. It was to control time within the circumference of the stones, not to travel great distances in time. That was an accidental discovery. All my first research was forgotten when we discovered what the stones could do for the time shifter and all of us. When Andrew asked me if the stones could be used as a weapon I remembered all the previous research I had done before the stones brought us here."

"How," Daniel asked, "can the stones be a weapon?"

"Not a real weapon," Samuel replied, "but an ally of time during a battle. Anything within the perimeter of the stones can be slowed down or speeded up without traveling through time or space like we have."

"Can that really be done?" Andrew asked, excited for the first time that something might help them.

"Theoretically, yes," Samuel said tentatively, "but the theory has never been tested."

This deflated everyone except Andrew who motioned for Samuel to come and sit with him and have breakfast. Samuel sat down and they began to converse excitedly.

Merry also came and sat with Uriah and smiling at Raven's perplexed stare at Samuel and Andrew said, "Samuel really gets excited about his work. We owe him much for his discovery."

Uriah just scowled and grumbled something unintelligible.

"Now Uriah," Merry chided, "you know we owe Samuel our very existence here."

"Yeah," Uriah said sarcastically, "your shortened existence, and another Kallestor's life will be shortened by the stones as well."

Merry was silent for a moment and then spoke so softly it could barely be heard, "You would have me live a long life as Layton's wife and have his children?"

Uriah closed his eyes and sighed, his demeanor softening. "No," he said almost as softly. "I am grateful for what Samuel has enabled us to do, even if it is for only a short time. I just can't help but be angry at what the stones have done to you, and now Lorriel will suffer as well. No matter how you look at things, someone has to pay a price when Father Time is bargained with, and his dues are very costly."

Raven could now see that Uriah was not really upset with anyone in particular, just upset at a plight that could not be altered or changed. Raven knew how frustrating it could be to feel powerless to avoid personal loss. It had happened several times to him in his life. First with his brother Edward's death, followed by his father, and now Rebekka taken from him. Raven smiled as he saw Uriah take Merry's had in his and settle back down into the reality of the joy they had now, regardless of how long it would last. Raven knew too that God was not overly cruel. And if a person would only look and acknowledge the facts about him, he would see that for every tragedy there was more than double the blessings in life. In fact he knew that to be the key to enjoying life to its fullest. Not focusing on tragedy, failure, pain and suffering, but upon the blessings God sent every day. By seeing those blessings and thanking the Almighty for giving a greater ratio of good than evil during our earthly habitation, One could at last be content. Those thoughts lifted Raven from his depression and focused him on that task at hand. There was hope in Raven's heart, for there are times one must believe against all reason that good for its very existence will ultimately triumph over evil.

When breakfast was over the Kallestors and Crestlaws met to discuss what Samuel was so excited about. As they gathered around him he began to explain his theory:

"The isolinear resonating stones amplify the time shifters ability to manipulate the temporal effects of time and matter within the perimeter of the stones, allowing more mass and material to be transported with the time shifter. Now if the time shifter is the catalyst for all that takes place within the circumference of the stones, then the time shifter should also be able to manipulate any mass or matter within that perimeter as well without affecting the time frame of any other object within that perimeter."

Samuel stopped talking and motioned with his hands making wide circles in a manner that said they should all understand perfectly what he was trying to say.

Andrew then spoke excitedly, "What Samuel is trying to say is the time shifter should be able to slow down or speed up any object within the circle of the stones without traveling in time themselves."

"Yes, yes," Samuel stated, "that is what I said."

"How do I control time without traveling anywhere?" Lorriel asked.

"This is where my theory breaks down," Samuel had to admit. "I, nor any other person I know of understands how a time shifter creates any type of temporal shift. I was hoping you and Merry would come up with that solution."

Merry sighed, "Samuel we tried this long ago and failed, remember?"

"Yes, yes, but only once," Samuel added. "You were so frustrated that the stones were not doing anything that I said to you, just take us back eighty years and you did! After that we forgot about our first experiment. Any time shifter generates a small field around them and can take objects they are holding in their hands with them, even without the use of the stones. That we know to be true. Small objects close enough to a time shifter might be able to be controlled if there was enough concentration involved."

Merry interjected again, "Samuel I have tried that many times years ago with your encouragement and failed every time."

"Yes," Samuel stated without so much as batting an eye, "but Lorriel has never tried."

All eyes went to Lorriel and she blushed at the sudden attention.

"I do not know how to do what you ask, or where to begin."

Samuel rubbed his chin, "I do not know how to explain it to you either, I just believe it can be done."

Andrew was observing and thinking the whole time Samuel spoke to Lorriel, "Lorriel, how do you travel in time?"

"It is easy," she replied. "I just close my eyes and think about when and where I want to go, will it so, and it begins to happen."

"Why do you close your eyes?" Andrew asked.

"So I can concentrate on when and where I want to go without being distracted by where I am right then."

"What if," Andrew began, "you kept your eyes open and concentrated on an object and it alone because you want it to do something? You would not go anywhere but the object would slow down or speed up as you command it."

With that he drew out his knife and held it before Lorriel and said, concentrate on this knife and slow it down when I drop it. Andrew released the knife and it fell and clattered to the floor to everyone's disappointment.

Andrew picked up the knife again and said, "I believe you can do this Lorriel, concentrate."

This time he brought it closer to Lorriel and held it with the point facing down next to her. Then brought it up to her eye level and released it. Raven realized suddenly that the knife was falling toward Lorriel's foot and would find its mark there if he did not do something. His reflexes came into play and he began to move when all of a sudden the knife slowed and seemed to stop before them all. Lorriel took a step back and reached out for the knife and it resumed its normal speed dropping to the floor clattering again.

Lorriol looked at them all with surprise and then glared at Andrew. Raven was glaring too for they both knew what Andrew had done.

"You dropped that on purpose over my foot to force me to do something about the knife did you not? Lorrlel said with anger in her voice.

Andrew smiled, "Yes, but I also knew that Raven would be quick enough to do something about it if you did not. It forced you out of instinct to use your power on the knife. Now you know it can be done with concentration."

Samuel was beaming, "A brilliant idea," he said. "I wish I would have thought to try that in my own experiments years ago."

Now Merry glared at Samuel and said in an indignant tone; "I'm glad you did not, I might be limping to this day." And then she added, "You two Crestlaws are so much alike it is a little scary."

Everyone began to laugh except Andrew and Samuel who now were the ones glaring at the others. Raven could not help but smile and laugh a little too, he could see where Andrew got some of his character.

Samuel interrupted the snickers of the others, "We should get down to business and refine this new skill you possess."

Raven still not understanding the importance of how this would solve their problem asked: "How will this help us defeat Layton?"

"Very simply," Samuel stated. "If Layton Teal and his men are surrounded by the stones and Lorriel were to slow them down you could disarm them all before they could react."

Andrew rubbed his chin, "I think it would be easier for Lorriel to speed one thing up instead of trying to slow a lot of things down."

"Yes, yes, it would be," Samuel replied. "That is what she must practice to do."

Samuel then produced a small writing instrument and said smiling, "We will work with this, no more knives."

So Lorriel began to concentrate on the object, slowing it down, then speeding it up. Raven watched for a time as Merry encouraged Lorriel with her control, then went out to the balcony that overlooked the courtyard. He was aware that someone was following him and knew without turning around that it was Uriah. Uriah came beside Raven and leaned on the rail and neither said anything for a while. Raven just waited for he knew that there was something that Uriah wanted to speak with him about. Finally Uriah asked what was weighing heavily upon him.

"In the future our family line will be king of this land, why and how will that take place?"

"I do not want to tell you too much about the future," replied Raven. "But I will tell you this. The throne was left empty and someone needed to fill it. The dukes chose our family to fill that position. Not because of our abilities to fight, or do battle but because we were honorable and cared for the kingdom. You see a king must do what is right regardless of the personal cost, and must think of the good of the kingdom before himself. The power a king possesses must only be used to help others, not to accumulate more power or wealth for himself. You are a duke and your descendants will someday rule over the people of your dukeship. Teach them to be honorable and self sacrificing for the people, and it will not be a large step at all for a good duke to become a good king. You have power over these people, I have seen it Uriah. But do be careful, with great power comes great responsibility. Do all you can to support Daniel in his new role as king. He will be a good and caring king for this people, I have seen it.

Raven could see Uriah was deep in thought from the words he had spoken and so turned once again to face the courtyard in silence. The silence was not awkward, for there was an unspoken kinship between Raven and Uriah. Uriah was a little rough around the edges but deep down inside he had a heart of compassion and Raven knew he really cared what happened to others. That, Raven knew is what Layton Teal missed in Uriah. He probably expected Uriah to be like himself with no true feelings for anyone but his own ambition. But Uriah was not at all like Layton, and Raven knew why Layton had not seen Uriah's betrayal before it was to late. A man cannot see or understand in another what he himself does not possess. Uriah had betrayed Layton because he cared, not just for Merry but for others as well.

Raven's thoughts were interrupted by Uriah asking another question.

"I am curious," he began, "how after a thousand years you and the others finally found the retreat at the top of the falls. How did you even know to look for such a place?"

"It all started with a riddle I found in your castle that led us up Happiness Creek.

"Happiness Creek?" Uriah asked.

Raven saw the confusion and before he thought about it he said, "You know the creek that flows south of your castle."

"Yes," Uriah said now comprehending, "that creek is called Happiness? That is a good name for it to be called."

Raven groaned within himself when he realized what he had just done. It was he who had planted the thought in his ancestor's mind to call the creek such a silly name. Andrew would never let him forget this if he found out. I just will not tell him, Raven decided. He heard Uriah mumbling something in a riddle about the source of happiness and knew the riddles had been set in motion by his suggestion. He would have to be more careful of the things he said to his ancestors.

Uriah left and suddenly headed back into the great hall shouting to Merry.

"No, wait!" shouted Raven, but it was too late. By the time he caught up with Uriah he was telling Merry that he had found a great name for the creek south of their castle thanks to Raven.

"Happiness," he said, "is what we will call it."

Andrew and Lorriel stopped what they were doing and stared at Raven.

"You?" Andrew said pointing to Raven, was all he could say before he burst into laughter. Lorriel likewise was laughing so hard tears came into her eyes. For they both remembered the comment Raven made about the silly name of Happiness Creek in the Crestlaw dukeship. Andrew had laughed at that time as well and informed him that it was his ancestors who had named the creek not the Crestlaws. Now to find out it was Raven himself was too much for them. Raven turned the brightest shade of red he ever had in his life. The others were perplexed at this outburst but soon realized it must be an inside joke.

Finally when everything quieted down Raven wanted to know how things were progressing with Lorriel. Samuel took over and explained that things were going well, though Lorriel's control was erratic. He then held the writing instrument in his hand and as it was released it merely vanished. Raven looked for it and then saw it lying on the floor of the great hall.

"How did it get there?" he asked.

"It merely dropped," Samuel explained. "Lorriel simply sped up the writing instrument's fall to the floor while everything else stayed the same speed."

Raven nodded with understanding, "How long will it take Lorriel to be ready for a larger experiment to be undertaken?"

"She should practice the rest of this day," Andrew replied, "and maybe tomorrow we can attempt a larger control area."

Raven nodded as he once again left them to practice the time shifting control. He then spent the rest of the day with Uriah, being taught how the weapons worked that Layton Teal possessed .

The next day they were ready to try a larger experiment with more people involved. They gathered people around the castle and Joanna, Andrew and Uriah wore the stones in a triangle formation. The rest of the volunteers, fifteen in number were inside the perimeter of the stones holding up flags. Raven was in the middle with Lorriel concentrating on him. She was to make Raven speed up while everyone else within the perimeter of the stones remained in normal time.

She focused her ability and said, "Now Raven go!"

There was a blur and everyone's flag just disappeared out of their hands. In the next blink of their eyes Raven stood in the center holding all of the flags. Samuel should have been ecstatic, but instead he just looked mystified at his empty hands that had held the flag.

He finally spoke and said, "This works better than I had imagined, but it is also unsettling. Who could stand against such an attack? You should be able to disarm everyone easily for Layton surely will not expect this."

Everyone was just as impressed with what had happened, but Daniel had one question.

"How will you be able to surround Layton and his force with the stones?"

"I have a plan that I am sure will work," Raven said shrewdly. They practiced the maneuver two more times with the same results and felt that Lorriel was ready.

After this Raven informed the ancestors that they would be leaving, since they had received the help they had come for.

"We are thankful," Raven said to them all, "for the help you have been to us. Pray that we will be able to save the kingdom from Layton Teal."

Then looking at them all he stated, "Do not live your lives in fear that Layton will eventually find you. For if you fear him and he never comes, that is one more victory he will have over you."

"Why do you have to be in such a hurry?" Uriah asked. "Staying here longer will not affect your return."

"This I know but we have unfinished business awaiting us in our time, I cannot be at peace until it is taken care of."

They all understood what Raven had said and no one else tried to delay them any longer. Raven walked over to Uriah who placed the stone back into Raven's hand. They looked into each other's eyes until Raven turned and went back to join Lorriel, Andrew and Joanna. Daniel Brickens stood at attention and smartly saluted Raven as he joined his group.

Daniel bid them farewell with these words; "We have learned much from you and your friends, King Raven. May the kingdom we form be worthy of descendants such as you, Godspeed!"

They formed the triangle once again with Lorriel to their center and held out the stones.

Raven whispered to Lorriel, "Take us back to just after we left the Hall of Wisdom." Raven turned back in time to have the scene imprinted in his mind forever of the ancients standing there waving goodbye. Just as the scene began to fade Raven thought he saw tears in Uriah's eyes.

Chapter 6
Another Time, Another Place

"Love has no bounds. Love is fashionable in any age and does not grow old with time. Who can forget the sacrifice one would make in laying down his life for another? That kind of love transforms everyone it touches."

--The Wisdom of Fathers

The sunlight woke Rebekka up from a groggy sleep. When she opened her eyes she at first did not know where she was and began to panic. Then recognition set in and a sadness came over her, she was in Layton Teal's time, the future. Rebekka sat up and stretched to relieve the sleep that still clutched at her body. When she was fully awake she went into the main room where they had spent most of their time the day before. Ellise was seated there and beside her was a tray of pastries and some juice. She looked up as Rebekka came in and motioned for her to be seated and have some of the food. Rebekka sat down and began to nibble absentmindedly on a pastry as she watched Ellise reading something on a flat tablet. She could not tell for sure if Ellise had aged since yesterday but she thought she noticed a little change since the day before.

Finally Ellise spoke to Rebekka, "Same old news every day from the electronic paper, nothing seems to change. Now I know why Layton wanted to go on this great adventure, to change our dull routines. Did you sleep well?"

"Surprisingly, yes," Rebekka answered.

"I did too," Ellise said, "time travel has a way of really taking your energy away. I was famished last night and have never eaten so much in my life."

Rebekka only nodded, for she had seen the girl eat what three people normally would. Maybe her appetite had something to do with her aging faster, Rebekka thought.

"Will you see your physician today?" Rebekka asked Ellise.

"Yes, I have an appointment in an hour," she replied. "You can stay here or you can come with me if you like."

"I would very much like to come with you if you do not mind," Rebekka answered. For she was very interested in what was happening to Ellise. Rebekka knew that Ellise was a key in this whole plot of Layton's. If there was some way that she could persuade Ellise not to go back for him, he would be stranded in her own time, unable to reach or find the ancients. That would make the kingdom safe and would only cost her and Raven personally.

A small price, she winced, to save the kingdom for all time. But she was unsure of how Layton's plans were laid. Did he have a back up plan to time travel if Ellise failed? Rebekka knew she had to find the answers to these questions, and the only way to do that was to befriend Ellise. Not that it was hard to be Ellise's friend, she was likable, just a little spoiled.

"Ellise," Rebekka asked, "have you told anyone who I am or where I am from?"

"No," Ellise replied, "Layton wanted this mission to be kept a secret. Only Blastion Astmos, his top aid knows he is gone. And he was only told it was a political fact finding mission that might take a week or two. Layton Teal is not a very public man, he is rarely seen other than on electronic screen so only a select few people know he is gone. But I am the only one who knows where."

Perfect, thought Rebekka, how could someone so brilliant as Layton leave so much in the hands of this young girl? Then she realized, that was the reason Layton did trust her, she was to young to think up any conspiracy and rebellion. She could see it all now, the position and wealth Layton had given her were enough for this young girl to be influenced to do all Layton told her to do.

Well, she thought to herself, that may all change.

"You are wise," Rebekka stated, "not to tell anyone who I am and where I come from, that would only lead to more questions about Layton's mission."

Ellise just looked at Rebekka and said flatly, "People don't care what I do, only who I am. None of them are really interested in what I say or think. I would be no one of consequence if I was not a time shifter. It is time for us to go see Dr. Farley, he is Layton's personal physician and sees to my needs as well."

The ride to Dr. Farley's was a short one and it did not take them long to get there. Rebekka was just as mesmerized this second trip as she was the day before by the tall buildings and speeding transportation going every direction. The building they entered was large and had a strong chemical odor as they entered. They went to another traveling room that took them higher into the building, exited, and found themselves in a lavish well furnished waiting area.

Ellise walked over to a woman seated at a desk and as she approached the woman stood and said, "Right this way Miss Wells, Dr. Farley is expecting you."

Ellise looked over her shoulder and said, "Come on Rebekka, we don't have to wait like other folks for our doctor appointments."

Rebekka just smiled and followed a few steps behind Ellise. As they entered the room where the doctor would meet with Ellise, Rebekka noticed all kinds of mechanical things attached to the walls and standing in corners. The doctor entered, only looked at Rebekka before he turned to Ellise and began to look her over.

"How many years have you been gone on this time shift of yours?" he asked.

"Only a few days," was Ellise's reply.

"That is quite impossible, are you sure, less than a week?" the doctor asked.

"I assure you, Dr. Farley, I have been gone from here less than a week my time."

The doctor just stood and kept looking Ellise over until he commented, "You look at least five maybe seven years older than the last time I saw you." He then referred to some papers he had brought in with him and stated, "The last time you were in for an appointment was the first of last month. I am going to have to give you a complete physical."

When the doctor had finished his complete examination of Ellise he commented very seriously, "You appear to be about twenty years of age, but your charts say you are only fourteen."

With that he walked over to a box on the wall and pushed a button and talked into it saying, "Miss Kinsley will you page Dr. Conrad Jordan and have him come here right away."

When he turned away from the box he saw that Ellise had a distressing look about her and walked over to her and said, "It may be nothing but I want Dr. Jordan's opinion since he works for Layton in the physics department and is the expert in the theory of time travel."

Ellise only nodded and sat there stone quiet until Rebekka could stand it no longer and went over to her.

She put her arm around her shoulder and said, "I am sure everything will be all right." Rebekka tried to say this convincingly, but in her mind she doubted whether everything would be fine.

The doctor looked at Rebekka again and then spoke to Ellise, "Does your friend need some supplemental vitamins for her pregnancy?"

Ellise's eyes went wide as she looked at Rebekka's stomach and then she quickly answered the doctor, "Yes, please."

The doctor went to a drawer and took out a bottle and handed them to Ellise and then said, "I will be back when Dr. Jordan arrives to see you."

He then left the room and Ellise turned to Rebekka and said, "You are with child, I did not know! I saw a bulge in your stomach but did not realize the implications until the doctor said something. It is a good thing you are with me for the doctor surely would have questioned you about this in detail."

"Why?" Rebekka wanted to know. "What is so unusual about a woman with child?"

"Because," Ellise stated as if Rebekka should know, "no one is allowed to conceive unless the state says it is ok. Only about half of married couples are allowed to have a child."

Rebekka was indignant, "How could Layton forbid the God given right of a married couple to have a child if they wanted to? What has Glenfair become under his rule?" Rebekka would have gone on in her anger but at that moment two men entered the room and she wisely went back to being the silent observer in the room. But she could not help but think of what the world had become under Layton's evil rule.

Dr. Farley and Dr. Jordan came over to Ellise and began once again to look at her physical features casually.

Conrad Jordan introduced himself once again to Ellise, "I have seen you with Layton and you helped me with some of my experiments.

"I know who you are," Ellise replied. "You developed the technology to enhance the time shifting ability of time travelers."

Dr. Jordan smiled, "There certainly is nothing wrong with your memory. You say you are 14 in actual years?" Dr. Jordan asked amazed. "We have no case history where this has happened to any time traveler. Are you sure you have not been gone for a few years?"

"Yes, very certain," answered Ellise curtly, "only a few days."

Dr. Jordan got very serious at Ellise's answer and said slowly, "How far in time did you travel with the devices I created for Layton?"

Ellise paused to consider and said, "Over two thousand years she replied."

Very wise of you Ellise, Rebekka thought, in not revealing the exact time of where you traveled to.

Dr. Jordan frowned and then said heatedly, "I told Layton that we needed to run more tests before there was any great leaps in time. But no, he was in to much of a hurry and now we have a crisis because of it. He will probably blame me for this incident when it is really his fault."

Dr. Farley was mortified at Conrad Jordan's statement. People had been executed for saying less things about Layton's judgment, and here no less before Ellise, his chancellor.

Ellise was not the least bit moved by the tone of Dr. Jordan's statement but simply asked, "What do you think has happened to me?"

Dr. Jordan regained his composure and said; "I am not sure, we will have to run some genetic tests before we can know what has happened."

"Then do it now," Ellise replied, "we will wait outside for your diagnosis." Both doctors nodded and began to work immediately with the machines in the room. Ellise motioned to Rebekka and they both went back out to the waiting room and sat down. Ellise did not seem worried, Rebekka noticed for she conversed as if nothing were wrong at all.

Rebekka was a little concerned and said, "You do not seem worried at all Ellise."

"These are the best doctors Layton has, they will find an answer," she replied.

Time passed and Rebekka noticed that Ellise was getting a little impatient when the woman that led them into the examining room came to get them once again. They entered the same room and found Dr. Farley and Dr. Jordan waiting for them.

Dr. Jordan cleared his throat and began, "The best we have determined Ellise," and he paused here, "is that you are aging at an accelerated rate. We do not know the reasons but believe it has something to do with the great distance in time you have traveled. Also, to our best understanding the condition is irreversible."

"What are you saying?" Ellise asked.

"You are aging very quickly and there is nothing we can do about it," Dr. Farley stated.

"How fast will I get old?" Ellise wanted to know, panic in her voice.

"We don't know that either," Dr. Jordan stated. "But the greatest changes you will notice have already taken place in your growth and maturity into womanhood. Now that your body has matured, the aging may slow down a little."

"How long will I live?" Ellise demanded of them both in such a tone they both snapped up strait.

Dr. Farley hesitated but finally spoke, "Our estimate is fifteen to twenty years."

Ellise turned pale and so did the doctors at this revelation, while Rebekka just listened, taking this all in.

Ellise finally gained her composure and a smile grew on her face while she said, "No problem, I will just go back a few days and tell Layton that I cannot travel such a great distance without personal harm to myself."

Rebekka was now alarmed, that could change everything, maybe for the worse, and she knew Layton would not take no for an answer to finding the ancients, even if it killed Ellise.

But before she could say anything Dr. Jordan intervened, "No Ellise you cannot do that!"

"And why not?" she asked defiantly.

"Further time travel may make you worse or even kill you," Conrad Jordan said flatly. "And besides, once Layton knew my time amplifying invention would work, nothing would keep him from trying to use it. He would make you go anyway."

Rebekka could stay still no longer and simply said, "Listen to him Ellise, you must not do anything until we know more."

"Who is this woman?" Conrad asked, seeming to notice Rebekka for the first time.

"She is very important to Layton and is my friend," was all that Ellise needed to say. Nothing more was said about Rebekka's presence or input from the doctors.

"I need to be alone," Ellise said. "Leave both of you."

The doctors glanced at Rebekka and then hastily retreated from the room leaving the two women alone.

When they were gone Ellise had tears in her eyes and shook her head saying, "What am I going to do?" Rebekka came over to her and hugged her close as she cried on her shoulder.

"We need to get you back home and then we will decide what to do," Rebekka said in a comforting, motherly fashion. When Ellise had dried her tears they left the same way they had arrived.

In the outer waiting area, the woman they had first met cleared her throat clearly hesitant about saying anything but finally uttered, "Dr. Farley wishes to see you in a week. Please call at your convenience when you wish to see him." The woman then bowed and left the room quickly.

Ellise did not say anything all on the way back to the place where she lived. Once inside her spacious room she went to a couch and sat down, tears showing in her eyes again. Rebekka had to force herself to remember that Ellise was only fourteen years old, it was easy to forget based on her appearance.

"The first thing we should do," Rebekka said softly, "is to eat a good lunch. We will have something brought here for I am sure you do not feel like eating out."

Rebekka pushed the button Ellise had shown her on the arm of the chair and said, "Now, what is your favorite lunch?"

"Pizza," Ellise mumbled, as the same woman who waited on Ellise the day before entered.

Rebekka turned to her and said, "We would like some pizza for lunch."

"What kind would you like?" the woman asked.

Rebekka looked at Ellise who was now watching her, and with her back to the woman mouthed, "What is a pizza?" with a funny expression that made Ellise laugh.

Ellise then said to the woman, "A large combination, and a large sausage. Do you like mushrooms?" Ellise asked Rebekka.

Rebekka nodded and Ellise added, "With lots of mushrooms, and bring us a variety of drinks."

The woman left quickly and Ellise turned to Rebekka and said now smiling, "You don't know what pizza is do you?"

"No," Rebekka said, "what is it?"

Ellise laughed again and said, "You'll have to wait and see."

It was not long before the pizza as Ellise called it arrived. It smelled wonderful and Rebekka could not wait to taste it. She thought that Ellise's appetite would be large as well and was not wrong on that guess as they both began to eat. First Ellise, for Rebekka did not know how to go about eating this new meal for there were no utensils present. When Ellise grabbed a cut piece and began to eat it by hand Rebekka almost laughed.

"What is it?" Ellise said, amused by Rebekka's stifled chuckle.

"Last night we had such formal dining and today we are eating with our hands," Rebekka stated.

Ellise admitted it was pretty funny but also added that unless Rebekka started eating she wouldn't get any. Rebekka did enjoy the pizza very much and was soon full, with Ellise eating what was left over. Rebekka marveled again how much Ellise had eaten. When they were completely finished and after someone had been summoned to clean things up, Rebekka knew that Ellise's outlook would be much better.

"Are you feeling a little bit better?" Rebekka asked her.

Ellise nodded, and then asked, "Why are you so concerned for me? I have taken you from your home and your husband to this strange time, you should hate me. Yet all you have shown me is kindness."

"Hate," Rebekka began, "should be reserved for evil. You are not evil like Layton Teal nor are you like him at all. In fact I have seen your heart and I believe it is a good one. I am sorry for how Layton has hurt you and used you."

"What do you know of my hurt?" Ellise stated.

"Tell me about your family," Rebekka asked, "what has Layton done to them?" Ellise turned pale all the fight now gone out of her. She was silent for a while and Rebekka thought that perhaps she would say nothing.

But finally she began almost in a whisper, "My parents were granted the privilege of having only one child. My older sister was born two years before I was. When I was born they hid me from the state. Then I learned that I had the ability to shift time when I was twelve. People up until that time had kept their mouths shut about my parents having two children. But someone told the authorities that I was a time shifter and Layton Teal came to our home with a small group of soldiers. I had never seen him before, only heard of him, and his very name brought fear to my heart. He told my parents that they had broken the law by having two children, and they were terrified by his personally

144

seeing to this matter himself. The only solution he told my parents was for one of their children to die. I was so scared, especially when he looked at me and said that since the younger one was not supposed to be born, I must die. Layton grabbed me and my father rose to intercede and Layton yelled that if he did not sit down immediately, they would all die. He left soldiers there in our house with guns pointed at them and took me outside. He then bent down and whispered these words to me that I will never forget:"

"If you do as I say you will have anything you ever want except one thing. You can no longer have your family, I am your family do you understand? If you do not agree I will have them all killed and take you with me anyway, is that clear?"

"With that he took my hand and led me away, I heard a shot fired behind us and I know that my family thinks I am dead, probably to this day. A year later I asked Layton if I could see my family and he grew angry and said;"

"I thought we had decided that I am your family, if you want them to stay alive never mention this to me again".

"This is the first time I have mentioned my family since that day."
Rebekka's heart almost broke listening to the story this young girl had told her.
"I am so sorry," Rebekka said with emotion. She came over to Ellise and wrapped her up in an embrace while the girl cried her heart out. Rebekka realized for the first time in years this poor girl had found in her someone that resembled a mother for emotional support. She was no longer angry with Ellise for her abduction, she like many others were only pawns in the games Layton played with people's lives. She also knew that she could not do what she decided was her last resort, override Ellise's mind to prevent her from going back for Layton which would strand him in her time, keeping him from reaching the ancients. Rebekka had come to realize in recent days her mental capacity was so strong that she could override and control another person's mind. She shuddered at the hideous thought of doing such a thing to another human. It loathed her to even consider it, for her code of ethics went far too deep to seek simple justification for such an act. The only reason she even entertained the thought was for the sake of the kingdom of Glenfair. But now that was no longer an option, seeing how much Ellise had suffered.
"There has to be another way," Rebekka desperately thought.

Ellise's sobs were quieting down and she finally uttered a question to Rebekka, "What should I do? Layton wants me to take you back in four days, but if I go I will grow older and die sooner.

"Do not go," Rebekka said simply.

"What?" Ellise said stunned.

"Do not go," Rebekka repeated.

"Layton will be so angry he will kill me and my family if I do not obey him," Ellise said with panic in her voice.

"How?" Rebekka asked.

"He is a powerful man, he can do anything he wants," Ellise said frantically.

"Yes," said Rebekka, "anything but travel in time without a time shifter."

Ellise's mouth dropped open as the comprehension of what Rebekka had said sank past her fear.

A little smile crossed her lips and she said, "He is stuck there three thousand years in the past without me isn't he?"

Rebekka only nodded, satisfied that Ellise saw the truth.

Now Ellise began to get excited, "We are free of Layton, free of his evil forever, this is so great!" But then she paused and began to descend to a sober mood once more.

She looked at Rebekka sadly and said, "But if we leave Layton there it will be bad for your family won't it?"

"Yes," Rebekka said, "it would be," thinking of Raven and the others against an evil Layton with all the weapons he possessed. He would probably conquer their kingdom and the Wickshield one too. It was a terrible thought to consider.

"We must go back then," Ellise said, "even if I die a few years later. I would not want Layton to hurt anyone else so I can have peace."

Rebekka admired the self sacrifice Ellise was willing to make for others and decided she had judged her fairly.

"We must not go back," Rebekka said firmly to Ellise.

"But why?" Ellise asked. "Your family could suffer." Rebekka sighed and decided at that moment to tell Ellise the whole truth.

"Did Layton ever tell you why he wanted you to take him so far back in time?"

"Not really," Ellise stated. "He just said there was some things in history he wanted to track down. But I guessed he was searching for the traitors that escaped him."

Rebekka nodded and began, "Those traitors were people just like you who wanted to live apart from Layton's iron fist. They fled back in time before Glenfair was settled and began the kingdom of Glenfair a thousand years before my lifetime. I am one of their descendants, and so is my husband King Raven. In fact most of Glenfair in our day is descended from those who fled into the past to hide from Layton. If

Layton Teal finds our ancestors and kills them or brings them back here, we and our kingdom will cease to exist. Thousands of people who enjoyed peace, and loved life for a thousand years will vanish from history."

Ellise was mortified, "If I knew this to be true I would never have taken him back the first time no matter what he would have done to me and my family. He has killed millions here in our time, and if I had the power to keep him from killing more I would."

Now tears were running anew down Ellise's face as she kept saying, she was sorry to Rebekka.

Rebekka held her and whispered in her ear, "It is ok, you had no idea. Now you know why you should not go back for Layton, even if people suffer in my time, the kingdom will survive and live on."

Ellise nodded and now Rebekka felt a weight lift from her shoulders. The fate of so many had been decided, and as much as the realization of never seeing Raven and little Edward again hurt her, she knew it was the only way to guarantee the kingdom's continued existence. She knew as well that Raven would make the same sacrifice if he were in her place. That was one thing she had learned from Raven over the years, to see beyond their own needs to that of others. Giving up a part of yourself for others always had a greater impact on the world than living it for yourself. This rationalization did not take away the pain or sorrow Rebekka felt in her decision and she was almost overcome with grief. The thing that brought her out of that downward spiral was the unfinished business before them.

"Ellise," Rebekka asked, "does anyone here know when and where you took Layton?"

"No," Ellise said, "Layton wanted this mission to be kept secret from everyone. Even I did not know how far back we were going until the day we left. Only Blastion Astmos, his top aid knows Layton is gone, but does not know why. I was there when Blastion pressed him for an explanation for his departure, and Layton grew angry and Blastion dropped the matter quickly. I believe after all these years Layton did not want anyone to know he was after the traitors. The unspoken word around here is that the traitors were the only ones ever to outwit Layton. If this trip turned out to be a dead end, Layton did not want anyone to know he failed once again. Layton did not even tell me, I just guessed that he was after the traitors because Merry Sheldon was a time shifter and disappeared with the rest of them, or so I have heard."

"Is there another time shifter that could go and get Layton?" Rebekka asked.

"Not that I know of," Ellise said thinking. "Layton had any known time shifters killed because he feared they would try and change history to eliminate him. Only Merry Sheldon was left alive because he believed she loved him, and he could control her. I am sure there are other time shifters out there but they do not want anyone to know for fear of their lives."

"It seems for the moment we are safe leaving Layton in the past," stated Rebekka.

"What will we do if they find out that Layton is missing?" Ellise asked.

"We will worry about that tomorrow, right now we have time on our side," Rebekka said cheerfully.

Ellise was playing with her pocket and pulled out the pill bottle. It reminded her of the child Rebekka was carrying.

"You are supposed to take one of these pills every day for your baby's health," Ellise spoke as she handed the bottle to Rebekka.

Ellise stared at Rebekka's stomach and said sadly, "It is almost to much to bear to think your baby will never know its father, to have Layton split apart another family like he did mine."

Rebekka said simply, "The baby will know its father for I will tell it all about the greatest King Glenfair has ever had."

"You do not know if it is a boy or a girl, do you?" Ellise said smiling.

"No, I do not, how can you before they are born?" Rebekka stated.

"The doctor can tell you with the machines they have," Ellise said.

Rebekka smiled, "I would rather not know and be surprised when the time comes."

Ellise just laughed and said, "Some things never change."

Rebekka looked at Ellise seriously and said, "Tomorrow I think you should go see your parents."

Ellise was speechless, shocked by what Rebekka said.

"Layton is no longer here to keep you from them, and no one I can see will question what you do right now."

"Oh, Rebekka, you are such a marvelous person, I am glad it was you I had to kidnap." Then they both started laughing at how odd that sounded.

The next day Ellise and Rebekka went to see Ellise's family. As Rebekka guessed, no one questioned where they were going or what they were doing. Ellise was very nervous because she had written off any chance of ever seeing her family again and this seemed to good to be true. The trip took some time and was quite a ways away from the city that Ellise lived in. In fact the place where her parents lived was north of the kingdom of Glenfair as Rebekka knew it. It would have taken two days to travel by horse to where they were going, but with the kind of transportation they had in Ellise's time it would only take a few hours.

Rebekka kept looking out of the window of the flying machine, realizing that she was traveling beyond the confines of her small kingdom into what she called the Wickshield kingdom in her day. She had never been out of Glenfair in her whole life, so she was intent on every detail of this trip. She remembered the excitement of Ellise planning this trip, and when Ellise told her that they were going far north, Rebekka's excitement grew as well.

At first she was very apprehensive about flying above the ground like a bird, but Ellise assured her is was completely safe. It did not take her long to begin to enjoy the ride very much. It was a clear day and you could see as far as your eyes were capable. The first shock for Rebekka was how small Glenfair really was. As they lifted higher in the machine she could see the whole of the valley receding behind her. They flew north over the mountains and pass that the Crestlaws controlled toward the heart of the Wickshield kingdom.

Once they had cleared the mountain range, Rebekka was speechless for the earth stretched out endlessly before her. There were forests and cities and lakes scattered to the horizon. She would never have guessed that the world they lived on was so big, and that Glenfair was so small. She now realized that Glenfair had been her whole world until this moment. It shook her up to realize that the kingdom she used to live in was only a tiny spot on this immense earth. The innocence that sheltered the people of Glenfair from the rest of the world was now gone for her as the truth became apparent. She wondered when the people of Glenfair would realize that an immense world lay outside of the cliffs of their valley. She had heard stories brought in by travelers of the world outside of their kingdom, but that is all they were to her, stories, things too immense to understand until now. It was not that she was incapable of comprehending the truth, she just chose not to give it much thought. Now that was impossible with the things she was seeing.

She turned to Ellise and asked, "How large is Layton's empire? Does it cover the whole earth?"

"No, not the whole earth," Ellise replied, "just the two largest continents."

"Can we go and see all of them?" Rebekka asked.

Ellise just laughed, "No, that would take us two days just to reach the second continent across the ocean."

"I have heard of the ocean," Rebekka added. "Is it really as large as they say? A lake that you cannot see across?"

Ellise now realized how limited Rebekka's perspective on the earth was because of the time in which she lived.

"When we get back to my place," Ellise stated, "I shall show you a map of the world so you can see for yourself."

Rebekka just nodded and went back to looking at all the surrounding land, absorbing as much as she was able.

Soon they were landing at the town where Ellise used to live. It did not take them long to reach the house where Ellise was born, for it was not far from where they had landed.

Rebekka and Ellise approached and before they knocked on the door Ellise turned to Rebekka and said, "I felt that I would never have this opportunity until Layton died, and even then I may have been denied."

Ellise took courage and knocked. The door opened slowly and a young woman that looked very much like Ellise stood there looking at them.

"Donna?" Ellise asked, and then started crying as they fell into each other's arms.

Donna yelled back over her shoulder as she held Ellise, "Mother, father, come quickly, it is Ellise."

Rebekka heard some commotion within the house and a man and woman came running and joined the circle, tears flowing as well. They were weeping with joy and Rebekka found tears in her own eyes as she watched this family be reunited.

Finally Ellise was able to speak, "You probably thought I was dead all these years."

Her father smiled and said, "We did at first when Layton took you outside and we heard the shot, but a few months later we saw you in a news program with Layton and knew you were alive. We always watched the news after that hoping to get a glimpse of you, knowing that we probably would never see you again in person."

Then her father stepped back and said, "My how you have grown, you look older than Donna."

Ellise's mother and sister released her as well and looked carefully at Ellise.

"You are a young woman," her mother stated, "how is that possible?"

"We will tell you everything," Ellise replied, "after we have lunch." Now for the first time her family took notice of Rebekka.

Her father eyed her warily and asked Ellise, "Who is this you have brought with you?" At the same time he looked outside both ways to see who was around and then motioned them inside.

When they were inside Ellise said, "This is my friend Rebekka, it is because of her that I have been able to see you today." Rebekka was carrying a large basket with her and offered it to Ellise's mother. She took it and gasped as she looked inside, for there were the makings of a very fine and expensive lunch, the finest Ellise had been able to gather on such short notice. As her mother began to set the table, Ellise explained that they could only stay for the day and would have to get back before dark.

As they began to eat Ellise's father asked, "How is it that you look older than your older sister?"

It was quiet while they all waited for the answer as Ellise began; "What I am about to tell you must be kept secret here and never go beyond these walls, is that clear?"

They all nodded as she continued, "I have traveled a great distance back in time, several thousand years. That great a shift in time is aging me at a very fast rate and I will grow old quickly."

Her family was stunned, the good news of seeing Ellise was now clouded with the news of her shortened life.

Ellise seeing the sadness this brought her family countered quickly, "There is good news in all of this, Layton Teal is gone."

"What are you saying?" her father asked.

"Do you think Layton would let me see you if he were here and knew about this, Ellise asked?" They were still quiet so Ellise continued, "I left Layton back in the past and he is not coming back. I am the only one that knows when and where he has been taken and I will let them execute me before I tell them."

Ellise's father smiled and said, "You always were a thinker Ellise and you are very brave to do what you have done. Millions of people will thank you for it."

"That's just it," Ellise responded, "no one must know what I have done. I am chancellor of this realm and have the opportunity to change things for the better now that Layton is gone. If people find out that Layton is gone for good there will be a power struggle between his military generals and we will end up with a tyrant ruling us just like Layton. That is why I must go back and try to do something to make this life better for everyone."

Rebekka had been listening and she now admired Ellise for what she wanted to accomplish. The girl was thinking now about the welfare of others and not just herself. She was shaken out of her thoughts by Ellise referring to her name.

"Rebekka," Ellise said, "is from the past and has had experience in ruling over a whole kingdom. Together maybe we can change things for the better."

Rebekka was stunned, Ellise wanted her help in changing this great and large kingdom Layton had built? She did not know anything about this time and Ellise wanted her to help? Well, if Ellise was brave enough to tackle such an enormous problem she would do all she could to help her. They finished their lunch and talk turned to family matters and so Rebekka just relaxed as the time passed. Before long it was time for them to leave and they were all hugging and saying goodbye. As they were ready to leave, Ellise took an envelope out of her pocket and handed it to her father.

Her father looked into it and gasped, "There is more money in here than I have ever seen he declared."

"It is the least I could do for my family," she stated. "If everything goes well I may be able to see you again, but if not know that I love you all dearly." With that they said goodbye and departed for the place where Ellise lived inside the rock boundaries of the little valley that was once called Glenfair.

Once back in her living quarters, Ellise smiled at Rebekka and went to her room. When she emerged she was carrying a round object in her hands.

She set it down before Rebekka and said, "This is the world we live on."

She then proceeded to show Rebekka the whole earth, continents, oceans, and lastly where they were at the moment. Rebekka stared in wonder at the round map Ellise had brought to her till Ellise laughed.

Rebekka looked up in puzzlement until Ellise explained, "I have never seen anyone get so much pleasure from geography before. I want you to have this as a gift from me."

"Oh Ellise, do you really mean that? It is such a wonderful gift," as she went back to looking at the small scale model of their world.

Rebekka suddenly stopped and pushed the round map aside and looked at Ellise, "We must discuss what we are going to do about Layton's disappearance."

Ellise smiled at Rebekka, "I think I have a plan."

"It had better be a good one," Rebekka replied "For I fear that things may not go well with us if anyone in power finds out the truth."

"That is true," Ellise said thoughtfully, "but I believe this can work if we can gain some support from a few in his cabinet. The first person we should talk to is Blastion Astmos, his top aid. He is the only other person who knows Layton is gone. We have a little time to work on this for Layton often withdrew from public life for weeks, only to appear and take care of some problem in his empire. I think people secretly long for those quiet times when he is absent. So people will wonder where he is, but will not wish for his soon return."

Rebekka nodded as she began to absorb the fear and cruelty people had endured under the rule of Layton.

"Before you tell me your plan," Rebekka remarked, "I want to know about Layton's officials that help him rule this large kingdom. I need an understanding of how things are done here before I can judge weather your plan will work or not."

Ellise nodded thoughtfully and began; "Layton's power base is built in his cabinet, leaders of different branches of government; defense, economics, transportation, education, and agriculture."

"Who in this group is most likely to try and take the power for himself?" Rebekka asked.

"That would be the minister of economics, Max Bane. I can tell he is evil to the core and hungers for wealth and power. If he thought he could get away with it, he would have killed Layton himself and then taken his position."

Rebekka nodded, noting the name and position he held in this cabinet Ellise spoke of. It had not taken Rebekka very long to learn that this world she now was trapped in functioned much different than Glenfair. It seemed that most things functioned on basis of wealth or power and people were caught up in the flow that Layton himself had created.

"Who" Rebekka now asked, "in this cabinet will we be able trust to help us?"

Ellise thought for a moment and then answered, "It may sound funny, but I believe our best help could come from the minister of defense, John Martin. He never openly spoke out against Layton, but I could see that he loathed some of the military operations Layton commanded him to carry out. When he returned from some of those operations that had cost people their lives I could tell he was ready to quit or challenge Layton but he never did. He only developed a deeper sadness after each campaign. I believe him to be a moral man caught in a bad situation, like"...

"Like yourself," Rebekka finished for her.

Ellise looked down sadly, "No, not like me, I liked what Layton gave me, the position of chancellor, the wealth and power. I just believed I would never hurt anyone, but I have. You made me see Rebekka that there should be more to life than thinking only of yourself." Ellise snapped out of her self judgment and continued.

"I believe John Martin will help us, and he has the respect of the rest of the cabinet. Besides he commands the military and without him we would be powerless to make any major changes."

Rebekka now summed up the political arena, "So it comes down to evil Max and the defense minister John Martin. And whoever wins the rest of the cabinet will follow?"

"That is how I have come to understand the political situation," Ellise replied.

"How do you know all of this Ellise?" Rebekka asked.

"Since I was chancellor I was present at all of the cabinet meetings. People respected my position with Layton and gave me a seat in the cabinet, but I never made any policy decisions. Since no other person my age was ever allowed in their meetings I felt a great responsibility to learn as much as I could about what was going on. Most of them act as if I do not exist, but I listened and learned as much as I could during every meeting." With that Ellise was silent, which surprised Rebekka for she expected her to continue.

"After a moment of silence Rebekka asked, "So what is the plan you have devised to save us when Layton's absence is known?"

Ellise smiled at Rebekka and said enthusiastically, "It is easy, you will rule in Layton's place."

Rebekka's mouth dropped open with the shock she felt from Ellise's statement. Never in a thousand years had she expected Ellise to say this. She was expecting some sort of compromise that would allow them to somehow escape execution.

Ellise laughed at Rebekka's expression saying, "I knew you would not be prepared for that."

Rebekka regained her senses and stammered, "That is a crazy idea Ellise. How can I rule this realm, I am from another time and place?

"Exactly," was all Ellise said smiling. "Now shut up and listen."

Rebekka closed her mouth and sat there thinking Ellise was showing more maturity than she had given her credit for. She would listen and see what this young girl had in mind. After Ellise finished outlining her strategy to Rebekka, she had to smile at the young girl's ingenuity. It was so far fetched it just might work.

Rebekka had one question for Ellise, "Why do you want me to rule instead of someone else?"

"Because," Ellise said hopefully, "if there is any chance you can make this realm even a little like the Glenfair you have told me about, it will be better for us all. Glenfair is still here, it is just a part of a much bigger kingdom. Since you cannot go back to the Glenfair of your time will you help us here? You could help millions of people if you say yes."

Rebekka thought about her situation and decided it did not matter when or where you lived. If you had the ability to make life better for others one must make the sacrifice to do so. Rebekka knew that God would hold every person accountable for not only what they did, but what they could do for others.

Rebekka looked at Ellise and said firmly, "Yes I will do my best to make this work."

"Good," Ellise said cheerfully. "We will get some rest and tomorrow we will begin by meeting with Layton's personal aid Blastion Astmos."

That night Rebekka did not sleep well. So far she had been busy enough that she had no time to dwell on missing Raven. But the days events coupled with Ellise being reunited with her family began to take its toll on Rebekka. She lay there for a while trying to keep the aching away from her heart but finally it burst through creating a powerful burst of thought that echoed through the corridors of time;

"I am sorry Raven, goodbye forever my love." After this tremendous emotional release she began to sob and cry uncontrollably until she felt arms around her, holding her and calling her name.

"It's ok, Rebekka, I know you miss your family, I am sorry, so sorry." And then Ellise began to cry too, for if any person at that time understood what it meant to be cut off from her family it was Ellise.

The next day they ate breakfast quietly in anticipation of what would happen when they put their plan into action. When they had finished breakfast and had dressed for the days meeting, Ellise pushed the button that summoned the woman that waited on Ellise.

Ellise simply told the woman; "I want you to contact Layton's personal aid, Blastion Astmos, and inform him I want to speak to him here as soon as possible."

The woman nodded and left immediately to perform the task Ellise had given her to do.

Rebekka watched this exchange with interest, especially the way Ellise dealt with the woman. After she was gone Rebekka asked Ellise why she never said thank you to the woman and treated her like she had no feelings.

"You don't know do you?" Ellise remarked. "Of course you wouldn't. The woman that waits on me is an android, a robot, not a person."

Rebekka's eyes went wide, "You mean that woman is a machine?"

"Yes," Ellise said laughing, "only the most wealthy have androids to wait on them. It was one of Layton's gifts to me some time back."

Rebekka paused and thought for a moment and then said, "I have only known one android and even though he says he has no feelings I believe he really does. We do not treat him as a machine, Andronicus is our friend, and I believe he cares for us as well."

Ellise was shocked beyond speech for a moment. "You - - you know about androids?" Ellise asked with awe in her voice. "How could you?"

"Andronicus came with the ancients from this time to the past. They left him active so their descendants would be able to find him and learn how the kingdom of Glenfair began."

"So that is how you knew about Layton," Ellise said, putting the pieces of the puzzle together.

"What is your androids name?" Rebekka asked.

"I cannot remember, I didn't pay much attention when they brought her to me," Ellise replied, "but I will find out when she returns."

A short while later the woman returned and informed them that Blastion Astmos would be arriving in about thirty minutes.

"Is there anything else miss?" the woman asked.

"Yes," replied Ellise, "what is your name?"

"I am designation 3.141592654," said the woman.

"No," Ellise interrupted, "not your number designation, your name, what is it?"

The woman answered solemnly, "Pi."

"Your name is Pi?" Ellise asked. "Like the formula for determining the mathematical equations of circles?"

"Yes," Pi, answered.

"However did you get that name?" Ellise asked.

"My programmers said I answered irrationally to certain questions they asked of me in my cognitive tests, and so they gave me an irrational number designation and the name Pi."

"What kind of questions did they ask of you that you would give to them an irrational answer? Please give me an example," Ellise asked.

Pi thought a moment and then answered, "Two children are in danger of being killed, I can save only one of them so what should I do?"

"What was your Answer?" Ellise wanted to know.

"To pick the child that could be saved with most certainty and keep it from harm and lament the loss of the other."

"That does not seem irrational," Ellise replied. "Please give me another example."

Pi began the second example; "If the last person on earth were dying and I could not prevent that occurrence, what would I do? I told them it would bring great sadness to be left alone and I would attempt to assemble another such as myself. They were very curious about my last statement so they asked me why I would attempt such a construction. I told them it would be for the purpose of companionship. I stayed there a great length of time before they returned after this session and gave me my name and designation."

Ellise was more curious now than ever and asked, "Why do you think there was a long delay after these questions Pi?"

Pi looked at Ellise and said very plainly, "I believe they considered deactivating me because of the answers I gave to them. I heard them still arguing as they left that an android that showed any emotional response must have something wrong with their programing."

Ellise was shocked and stated, "I was told androids did not have any emotions at all, and were only created to serve us."

"That is true of androids as a rule," Pi related, "but a few of us were made and programed differently than the rest for a short time. I believe my responses caused them to alter their manufacture and programing so that is no longer the case with androids."

"How long ago were you manufactured?" Rebekka asked.

"Fourteen years and 6 months ago," Pi answered.

"When did my ancestors flee from Layton?" Rebekka asked Ellise.

"I was only a year old when that took place," Ellise replied wondering why Rebekka was asking this question.

Rebekka turned once again to Pi and asked, "Were there others that were manufactured and programed the same as you?"

"Yes," Pi replied, "there were eight before me."

"Was Andronicus one of them?" Rebekka asked.

Pi paused for only a moment before answering, "Yes, Andronicus, designation 76754B was the forth in that series."

Rebekka smiled, that explained a lot to her about Andronicus. It seemed that he was always making the excuse when asked about emotions that he was a machine and not prone to emotional response. Now she knew that was not true, he only wanted them to think he did not feel loneliness, sadness, joy or other emotions.

Ellise asked Pi a question, "How long have you been in my service?"

"Eight months four days," Pi answered.

"And what did you do before you became my android?"

Pi answered emotionally, "Before I came here I was left in a vault instead of being deactivated. I was left there with no one to talk to for many years, it was terrible. You are the first human I have served since my manufacture."

"Where do you stay when you are not needed?" Ellise asked.

"In the service closet on this floor," was Pi's only answer.

Then Ellise looked very intently into the face of Pi and asked, "How do you feel since I have never thanked you for anything, nor ever talked to you except to make requests?"

Pi stood up strait but did not answer. When Ellise kept staring and waiting Pi finally answered, "Neglected and unappreciated."

Ellise took this answer in and said with real sincerity, "I am sorry for treating you that way. If you would like you may stay in this room from now on instead of the service closet."

"I would like that very much," Pi answered, showing a hint of a mechanical smile.

"One more thing," Ellise, said, "do you want another name besides Pi?"

"Thank you for the offer but I think I will keep this name, it suits me."

Ellise nodded and stated, "I think it does."

Blastion Astmos arrived at the scheduled time and knocked on Ellise's door. She opened the door and looked to see if there was anyone else with Blastion but he was alone so she invited him in. Blastion smiled at Ellise and began to say something when he noticed Rebekka standing there.

"Who is this Ellise?" Blastion asked, apprehensively. Being Layton's top aid had made him cautious, very cautious of anything unknown.

"She is a friend of mine," Ellise answered, "and very important."

Blastion looked at Ellise more carefully now and remarked, "My how you have grown up since I saw you last."

"Yes, people have a way of doing that," Ellise shot back.

"Yes," Blastion said slowly, "but not that fast. Something is going on that I am not aware of, isn't that true?"

"OK," Ellise began, "I will get right to the point. You know that Layton was taking a little trip with myself and a few others. In fact I know that you were the only one who knew he was to be gone a few days. And I am back and Layton is not so what does that tell you?"

Blastion was getting very nervous by Ellise's pointed questions. He began to glance around the room looking for recording devises or for a spy, all he saw was Ellise's android standing against the wall still and staring forward.

Ellise did not give Blastion a chance to answer as she continued, "Do not worry about recording devises, there are none in this room. After all why would anyone want to listen to a fourteen year old who lives alone with an android? I have my own recording devise for this meeting."

Blastion stuttered, "You do?"

"Yes," Ellise said, pointing to Pi. "Androids remember everything that they hear word for word."

Now Blastion was flustered and exclaimed, "What are you trying to do to me, set me up, get me killed?"

"Relax," Ellise said forcefully.

And then turning to Pi she said, "Do not repeat any of the conversation in this room unless I tell you to, or if I die, do you understand?"

Pi nodded in the affirmative and Ellise swung back around to Blastion. She had seen hardball politics plenty of times setting quietly in the meetings but had never said anything so Blastion was really shocked by her strength and forcefulness. Rebekka was impressed as well even though she had coached Ellise on how to handle herself in adult politics of this magnitude. Actually it did not take much coaching by Rebekka at all, it seemed that Ellise was a natural when she finally came out of her shell and Rebekka was enjoying seeing her in action.

Ellise continued, "You know I am a time traveler and Layton and I took a little trip together to the past. The far past, several thousand years to be precise. I left him there stranded and he is not coming back. Is this sinking in Blastion?"

Blastion turned white as a sheet and almost passed out before he was able to utter, "He will kill you, and he will kill me because I now know what you did to him. He will think I was in on this plan of yours, you have signed my death warrant!"

"Be quiet and listen Blastion," Ellise said as she took charge again. "Layton Teal is not coming back. No one knows when and where I took him and I am not telling anyone. In fact you are the only one who will know the truth." Blastion felt his knees getting weak and sat down immediately.

He tried to grasp the words Ellise had told him and before long he began a nervous laugh, "You, you left Layton stranded in time?"

"That's right," Ellise said, and emphasized, "he will never come back either."

The color began to come back into Blastion's face and he began to regain control of himself.

"Why have you told me these things?" Blastion asked.

Ellise smiled and said, "Now that you are thinking again I will tell you. What do you think will happen here if people find out Layton is not coming back? I will tell you what will happen, there will be a power struggle for control and we all will probably end up as casualties in the process, especially if Max Bane comes to power."

Blastion began to realize what Ellise was saying and knew that whoever came to power would purge the old regime of Layton's power base including himself.

"We are still dead," Blastion said sadly placing his head in his hands.

Ellise now had him where she wanted him, his life seemingly over. Now she was able to offer a way for him out of this certain destruction.

"Not if you help me," Ellise countered.

"What do you want?" Blastion said sadly, not believing anything could help them now.

"I need you to give credibility to our plan when we call a meeting of Layton's cabinet. Layton was getting bored with this realm, he had conquered everything here and wanted a new challenge at the end of his days. So he went to the past seeking new kingdoms to battle and conquer as his last challenge. He has searched the present and the past and has picked this woman (with that Ellise pointed to Rebekka) to rule over everything in his absence."

Blastion looked from Ellise to Rebekka and then realized his mouth was hanging wide open in shock and closed it quickly.

"I knew," Blastion began, "that Layton was bored, but this?"

Ellise laughed, "We all know that Layton was bored, but that is not what happened. What I have told you is the story we are going to tell the cabinet. What really happened is Layton went in search of the traitors and had me take this woman hostage to obtain information. He told me to return with her in four days but we decided not to do that, so he is stranded there forever."

"Let me get this strait," Blastion interjected, "you want me to tell the cabinet the story you related to me that Layton wanted another challenge and appointed this woman to rule in his stead? Why don't you rule Ellise?"

"Don't be silly," Ellise replied. "I have no credibility with the cabinet to be able to rule, but no one knows Rebekka. Because they don't know who she is, nor will be able to find out, it will keep them guessing."

Blastion rubbed his chin in thought and said, "If you can pull this off it will be the greatest coup détat in history."

"It will be more than that," Ellise emphasized. "Rebekka will help us all by undoing some of the damage Layton has done to our world. Think about it Blastion, haven't you ever wanted to do something to help the suffering of our people?"

"I have thought about it and I will help you," Blastion said. "Not because I think you will succeed, but because I have no other choice."

Then Blastion softened and said, "Anything to keep Evil Max from ruling or Layton from coming back."

He then turned to Rebekka, "You are willing to rule Layton's realm?"

Rebekka spoke now for the first time since Ellise invited Blastion in.

"I do not wish to rule," Rebekka said, "but if it will help others and undo some of the evil Layton has done I will do all I can."

"You are a foreigner from the past," Blastion said listening to Rebekka's speech. "This may work," Blastion said almost enthusiastically. "Except for Evil Max. I know he won't allow it."

"Leave Evil Max to me," was all Rebekka said.

Blastion shrugged his shoulders saying, "You outfoxed Layton, I guess you can handle Max Bane. When do you want to call a meeting of the cabinet?"

"Tomorrow afternoon," Ellise replied.

Blastion nodded and said, "I will inform you of the time." With that he left to go schedule the meeting.

"Whew," Ellise said after he was gone, "I didn't know that I could do this."

"You did very well," Rebekka said proudly.

"What did you mean you would handle Evil Max?" Ellise asked.

Rebekka was silent for a moment and then said, "Did Layton ever tell you why he wanted you to take me away?"

"No," Ellise said thinking, "I never understood why Layton wanted me to take you here."

"Because," Rebekka answered, "I am a telepath and Layton did not want me reading his mind."

"No one can read Layton's mind if he did not wish it," Ellise stated matter of factly. "He was one of the most powerful telepaths alive."

"I could," Rebekka answered.

Ellise looked at Rebekka with awe and said, "What else can you do?"

"I can make people do whatever I wish, and I can kill someone with my mind," Rebekka stated.

"Are you going to kill Evil Max tomorrow?" Ellise asked apprehensively.

"No," Rebekka said quickly, "I could not do that except in self defense or I would be no better than Layton."

Ellise was silent for a while and then said softly, "You could have killed me, or made me do what you wanted couldn't you?"

Rebekka nodded, "I thought about it, but then I realized that I could never do that to anyone unless I feared for my life. And making a person do as I wish against their will can only bring permanent harm to them mentally."

"You would have gone back with me to Layton then?" asked Ellise.

"Yes," Rebekka said, "I would have. I could not harm you. That is the past Ellise, let us think about our plans for tomorrow."

"How will you handle Evil Max?" Ellise wanted to know.

"I have a plan," Rebekka said, and began to tell Ellise what she had decided to do about Evil Max Bane!

Chapter 7
The Battle For All Ages

"What thinkest thou of war? Man's wicked heart hath spawned it in ages past and shalt perpetuate it in the ages to come. Be thou ware, O King, that thy warring be not unto self gain. For if thou warrest for any other reason than the defense of thy people or others, thou shalt suffer loss even though thou winnest."

--The Chronicles of the Ancients

The garden lawn of Andronicus' retreat began to take shape as the time travelers began to emerge from their travel to see the ancients. It was only moments before that Master Fields had bid them farewell and he was just beginning to speak with Andronicus when they were back. At first Master Fields thought something had gone wrong with the time travel but then realized that they would probably return close to the same time they left. As the time travelers took in the familiar surroundings, Raven stepped forward to face Andronicus. And before anyone knew what was happening Raven hit him square on jaw, knocking him to the ground.

Everyone was stunned and so shocked that they just stood there as Raven said. "That was for not telling us of the harm it would do to Lorriel when she traveled so far back in time. You knew it would make her age quickly with such a long time shift." Then shaking his hand he added, "That really hurt!"

Andronicus stayed on the grass and only sat up looking perplexed. "King Raven," he said, "striking me thus will only injure yourself or damage me, I would recommend you vent your aggressions differently. I did tell Lorriel of the danger this long shift in time would pose for her, I felt it was her decision to make."

"That is where you were wrong," Raven stated still angry. "As King of this realm I am responsible for the safety and well being of any of its subjects, especially my own sister. By not informing me of this danger you circumvented my authority."

Andronicus nodded solemnly and said, "I apologize for not informing you of the consequence this long time shift had for Lorriel. I did not see things from your perspective and I ask your forgiveness. I sought only to keep the rest of you from any more anxiety than you already had. Would you have prevented her from taking you to see the ancients?"

Raven shook his head, "No he said sadly, I would not, but you should have told me nonetheless." With that he held out his hand to Andronicus to help him up. Andronicus grasped Raven's hand and rose to his feet.

"May I ask," Andronicus said in his normal tone, "were you successful in finding help from the ancients?"

Raven allowed a slight smile to form on his face when he said. "Yes, I believe we found an answer. Let us go inside and lay the plans for tomorrow's confrontation with Layton."

As Andronicus and Raven walked together toward the glass mansion, Master Fields spoke softly to Andrew, "I do not understand any of this. What did King Raven mean when he spoke of Lorriel, did something happen to her?"

Andrew nodded and said plainly, "We will tell you everything that has happened the last few days.

"Days!" Master Fields interjected. "You were only gone a few...." He stopped mid-sentance and looked at Andrew, "Days you say? My understanding of the world and time will never be the same after this."

Andrew only smiled, knowing what changes had taken place in his own understanding since they had found this place.

Once inside the mansion and seated around the table the discussion turned to Lorriel's condition. When it was explained to Sauron and Master Fields that such a long journey ages the time shifter, they could now see the visible signs of aging they had missed before.

Sauron asked, "Is there nothing we or Andronicus can do for Lorriel?"

Raven looked at Andronicus for an answer to which Andronicus shook his head and said. "Samuel Crestlaw worked until Merry's death to find a way to reverse the aging process brought upon her by the long time shift. Though he valiantly tried, nothing was found to help her condition."

He then looked at Lorriel, and Andronicus saw a hint of sadness upon Raven's face. "I am sorry Lorriel, there is nothing that can be done." There was silence for a while as everyone looked at Lorriel.

She in turn looked back defiantly and said. "We should discuss the problem at hand and how to defeat Layton."

Raven nodded and began to outline what they had learned from the ancients concerning the weapons and tactics Layton often used. He also explained that they had learned Lorriel could control time differently than simple time travel within the perimeter of the stones.

"How will that help us?" Master Fields wanted to know. "Will you transport him to some other time or place?"

"We cannot do that without Lorriel going with him as well, and that we will not do. No, the answer lies in her ability to manipulate a single object or person within the circle of the stones. To slow them down or speed them up in relation to the time everyone else is in."

Sauron cleared his throat and said, "Sire, I do not understand what you are trying to tell us Lorriel can do."

Raven started again. "Within the circle of the stones Lorriel can speed me up so I will be able to move faster than the eye can follow, every one else will look as if they are standing still or barely moving to me."

With that Master Fields interjected, "You could disarm Layton's whole force before they knew what was happening."

Raven nodded, "That is the theory and plan we have." Raven looked on the faces of the others and saw that Sauron and Andronicus were disconcerted. "Is something wrong he asked them?"

Sauron responded, "Are you sure this will work? I do not like the word theory. Have you tried and tested it to make sure it can be done? Things can go wrong with the best laid plans."

Andronicus added, "Time manipulation of this difficulty has never been successful before. Are you sure it can be done?"

Andrew now spoke and assured Andronicus of the tests and success of Lorriel when they had practiced with the ancients.

After another moment of silence Raven continued. "It is the best plan we have, and it is the only plan we have. Here is what we will do: We will have the Dukes wear the stones and surround Layton's small group of soldiers. Master Fields will wear my stone as well to make use of all five. The Dukes will stay mounted on their horses in this circle and will only draw their swords to distract Layton. He will think that we mean to attack and will only be amused by the notion. But the Dukes and the rest of you will not advance, only I will step forward a few paces to address Layton."

"How will Lorriel know when to initiate the time control?" Andrew asked.

Raven smiled with that question, and held up the knife with Layton Teal's initials inlaid in the handle. "I will return this to him and that will be the signal for Lorriel to start her time control. I will toss it to him, while it is in the air she will begin."

They all nodded at the plan with Master Fields asking one question. "How will you get the Dukes to cooperate? Surely they will not understand any of this, I barely do."

"Leave that to me," Raven said. "I will address them tomorrow before we ride to meet Layton. Now we must head back to Sauron's castle and prepare for tomorrow."

They rose from the table and began to leave except for Raven, he remained seated with a far away look in his eyes.

When the others were gone, Andronicus asked Raved, "You are still troubled are you not my friend?"

"You still call me friend after I clobbered you?" Raven asked.

"Yes," Andronicus answered, "I know why you hit me, and it was just. You have had much on your shoulders lately and even now something weighs heavily upon you."

Raven looked up and asked, "How long will Layton be a threat to the safety of this kingdom?"

Andronicus with that same blank stare said unemotionally. "As long as he lives."

"You fear disarming him is not enough to keep us safe, do you not?" asked Raven.

Andronicus nodded, "No one is safe from Layton until he is doad." Andronicus could see this truth mirrored in Raven's eyes. "What you intend to do may separate you from Rebekka forever," Andronicus added.

"I know," Raven said sadly. "But if I do not, then even what we had may vanish. I cannot take any chance for the sake of the kingdom." As Raven rose slowly a heavy weight seemed to be upon him, Andronicus joined him and placed his arm about his shoulders. Together they walked in silence following the others down the path to the edge of the falls. The others were already there waiting for them and as Raven parted ways with Andronicus he thought he saw a tear in the old man's eyes.

"That cannot be," thought Raven, "he himself said he is only a machine."

Andronicus watched the group of people leave. A few of his kind had accidentally received emotions through a different manufacturing technique that was quickly abandoned. The only sacrifice he had made in his existence was agreeing to the loneliness that came from his isolation at the top of the falls. For a thousand years he had waited and finally they had come and what wonderful people they were. They had filled his life like he never thought possible, and now to see them in such difficulty pained him greatly. He hated Layton for what he had brought upon them. Lorriel's life shortened, King Raven carrying another burden any human or android would be crushed by. And most of all, beloved Rebekka, the one he talked to with his mind perhaps gone forever. He would kill Layton himself if his programing would have allowed it. All he felt now was an emptiness, an aching that would not go away. Is that what humans called a broken heart? Andronicus shrugged that off, for he told himself he had no heart. He raised his hand to his eyes and the lubricating fluid was leaking out in drops, he would have to check that when he was back in his room. Slowly he turned back toward the glass mansion that was his home to wait for the outcome of tomorrow's events. His steps, slow and defeated.

When Raven and those with him arrived at the Crestlaw's castle, Duke Rollins and his son, Terry were already there waiting for their return. Raven saw the distressed look on his face when they approached him and said.

"Thank you for coming Jasper and you as well Terry."

Duke Rollins asked, "Sire, is there a danger for the kingdom, another war?"

"There is danger," Raven answered. "An evil has come upon us that may destroy us. Tomorrow, when the rest of the Dukes arrive I will tell everyone what we face. But now we need rest, for tomorrow will be an important day." With that Raven pushed past him and headed for his room. The others were silent as well except for Sauron who said to Jasper Rollins, "Come, I will show you your quarters for the night."

That night Raven was laying in bed trying to sleep, but it eluded him. His emotions swirled and twirled about, taunting him like elusive spirits who's cries he could not quiet. Exhausted, he lay there still when above the thoughts that raced through his mind came a cry from Rebekka: "I am sorry Raven, goodbye forever my love."

Raven sat bolt upright in bed, he could not have imagined this could he? It seemed real enough, and even sounded like Rebekka. Was it merely his longing for the love of his life and the inevitable decision he had made that might separate them for the rest of their lives? Amidst all the swirl of emotion he faced, he did not know if it was his imagination. How could Rebekka know about the decision he would make? Raven decided it must have been his own longing or design that enabled him to hear Rebekka in his mind. Raven lay back down tired and weakened by that last burst of emotion. The supposed echo of Rebekka had pushed him past the point of exhaustion and he finally succumbed to sleep.

Early the next morning Raven waited with Master Fields in the large hall of the Crestlaw castle, toying with the breakfast that was set before him. Master Fields watched him with interest, having known Raven too long for his mood to escape his notice. Master Fields knew the king was carrying a great burden, but he also knew that it was one he would keep to himself. Soon the other Dukes arrived and gathered in the hall to be briefed by the King for the reason they were so hastily summoned.

Raven stood and looked at them and spoke. "Years ago when I gave each of you the armor of your ancestors, I mentioned the need for us to stand together against any evil that came to threaten our kingdom. Such a time has come upon our fair land and I need your help to defeat it." Raven looked at them to see how this news would be taken and was satisfied that he had their full attention. "I also told you that there may come a time of crisis that requires us to trust each other fully in order to be victorious. So I now ask all of you to trust me in the matter I am about to reveal to you. Even if you do not understand what I tell you we must do, you must believe it is the only way this evil can be defeated."

As King Raven finished these words Mason Zandel stood and said forcefully, "I know the King has the kingdom's best interest at heart. If he were to tell me I must die in order to save the kingdom, so be it, for I know that he himself would do the same for all of us."

Mason sat down and Sauron Crestlaw rose and said, "Well spoken Duke Zandel." And raising his fist said, "For the kingdom." Every one of the Dukes raised their clenched fists toward Raven in agreement and shouted; "For the kingdom."

That moment would forever be remembered by Raven as he was touched by the loyalty of every Duke. This great kingdom cannot end today, Raven thought, even if it takes great personal sacrifice. Raven was thankful for the strength the dukes gave him for the decision he had to make.

Raising his hand to gain their attention once again Raven continued; "Our ancestors, the ancients fled an enemy long ago and came to this place and began our kingdom. Since that time the enemy has tried to find them and he has come here looking for our ancestors to destroy them."

"That is impossible!" Terry Rollins stated. "The ancients have been dead for over a thousand years. This certainly cannot be the same enemy!"

"You must believe me when I tell you that he is the very same enemy, I have no cause to lie to you," said the King.

"How can that be?" Bandon Prescott asked.

Raven thought for a moment, time did not permit him to explain the whole story to them and answer all their questions. Then suddenly he had the answer.

"This enemy is like an evil sorcerer with great power. He wants to know about the ancients in order to find them and destroy them."

"Then we should not tell him anything," replied Duke Rollins.

"I wish it were that easy," Raven said sadly, "but he has taken the queen hostage in exchange for our information."

Mason Zandel jumped up once again with fire in his eyes. "We must fight to save the queen."

"No," Raven interjected, "that is exactly what we must not do. He has weapons that can burn all of us to ashes in a matter of seconds. He did that to poor Jerddin when he took the queen the first time." Mason sat back down and Raven could see that the rest were bewildered at this news.

Bandon Prescott stated, "We should then tell him what he wants to know, get our queen back and let the ancients worry about him." Raven smiled softly at the logical but wrong answer Bandon had given.

"Bandon, what happens if this enemy kills your ancestor in the past before he has any children?"

Bandon Prescott was not stupid and the impact of Raven's statement settled upon him immediately, as well as the rest who were listening.

"What are we to do then?" Mason asked.

"I have a plan," Raven replied, "that needs the help of every one of you to succeed." Raven took the soft leather bag containing the stones and took one of them out for all to see.

"The ancients made these stones long ago to use against the enemy. They have no power of their own but can be used by someone who has the power to do so." Raven then went from Duke to Duke handing each a stone. The last stone he gave to Master Fields.

When he returned to his place, Terry Rollins asked, "Who among us has the power to use these stones?"

Raven looked over his shoulder to where Lorriel was standing unnoticed until that moment and said, "Lorriel does."

There were audible gasps as all eyes focused on Lorriel and she could not help but blush from their stares.

Raven turned back to the Dukes and said very sternly. "There is a price to Lorriel using the stones, she will grow old faster than any of us because of it." Then Raven hung his head down slightly and said, "Her years will be shortened by more than half." Before anyone could reply or protest his head snapped back up, a fire in his eyes that brought everyone to full attention.

"Be sure you do exactly as I tell you or her sacrifice will be in vain, as well as that of the queen. We must surround this wicked enemy with these stones, only then can we defeat him. You will ride dressed in your armor with the chain and stones about your necks. When we get close to the enemies camp we will split up and form a circle around him. Go no closer than 100 paces from his camp and stop there on your horse. What ever you do, do not advance and do not attack, am I clear?"

They all nodded, understanding what the King had said but not fully knowing the reason why.

Raven softened a little as he continued, "The enemy does not know about the stones. He thinks we are simple, ignorant people who cannot fathom his purpose. He also has no idea that we know who he is and why he is here. So to distract him after we form the circle about his camp, watch Andrew Crestlaw as he draws his sword and do likewise, but do not advance. Am I clear? I, and I alone will speak and deal with the enemy. Is that understood? Now, are there any questions?"

A few were put forth and were answered as simply and quickly as Raven could. Then he sketched out the enemies camp and showed each Duke where they were to position themselves in the circle. When that was finished Raven dismissed the counsel with this token; "May we have victory."

They all began to leave the large hall when Lorriel caught Raven's arm and spoke to him. "Tell me once again how will I know to begin the time control for you?" Raven smiled and drew out the knife with Layton's initials inlaid in its handle.

"I will return this to him. When I toss it into the air to Layton, that is when you begin the time control."

Lorriel had a little panic in her voice when she said, "I do not know how long I can maintain your time acceleration Raven."

He smiled at her and said simply, "It will not take long to do what I have to do, just do your best."

As they headed out to join the others already mounting up for the ride to the Halfstaff Raven said to her, "There is something very unpleasant I must prepare you for."

No one said anything as the company rode quietly south. Time dragged on for all of them as they approached the river. Soon the smoke from Layton's camp could be seen plainly by all so Raven did not have to indicate where they were to circle about the enemy.

"How confident he seems," Raven thought, "not worrying about a surprise attack or anything. But why should he with the weapons he had brought with him."

As they neared the rise that hid Layton's camp from view they stopped and Raven motioned for the Dukes to split and encircle Layton's camp. As the Dukes started out, Raven, Sauron, Andrew, Master Fields and Lorriel rode up over the rise. Again there was a short scramble as Layton's small band of troops took formation with their weapons ready. Raven rode slowly down the rise and soon saw the other Dukes circling around the camp. Layton's group noticed it too, but seeing it was only a few more riders did not get overly excited but merely turned to form a small circle themselves. At the bottom of the knoll Raven and those with him dismounted and began to walk toward Layton's group. When they were the proper distance from him they stopped and waited for the rest of the Dukes to take position. When they were all positioned where Raven wanted them to be he looked at Andrew who drew his sword and held it high for all to see. The Dukes did likewise with their swords in the circle they had formed.

Layton was eager when the third day dawned, eager to be done with this business of waiting. He was disappointed when the king of the land did not immediately appear that morning. He felt sure that they would be there eager to trade information that they surely thought useless to get their queen back. When the dew began to dry off the grass he began to be restless. Why were they not here, were they gathering a large force to attack him? He did not think so after the demonstration of how easily he could kill any of them with their weapons. Layton felt no remorse for killing the man a few days before, but he felt no enjoyment in the task either. It was something that needed to be done to get what he wanted, so he had done the thing that prevented the most bloodshed from occurring. Now they respected and were afraid of him and his power. He liked it that way so no more foolish things would waste his time. He had waited all these years to finally have victory in this intriguing pursuit. Now that the day was finally here he found himself impatient. He chided himself for his impatience, for that was not like him, but he could not help it this day of all days. Mid-morning came and just when he began to wonder if something was wrong with his plans riders showed themselves on the knoll and began to descend toward him. He smiled to himself with the satisfaction that he could always predict human nature so accurately.

As they came down the hill toward him he noticed other riders north and south beginning to form a circle about his camp. He expected these backwoods people to bring more with them the second time and was a little disappointed that there were so few. If they thought to intimidate him by circling about his camp to surround him, they were simpler than he thought they were.

"How odd," Layton thought, the telepathic woman did not seem to fit into this ill prepared group of feudal people. Her mind was well developed, more so than any he had encountered. Maybe she was the power behind the throne and now that she was gone they were ill advised and unprepared. He spoke to his first officer to stand his men down from alert to ready, for there was no real threat. The group stopped their advance and then drew their swords. It was impressive, in a sort of humorous bravado to his band of trained soldiers and not one of them even flinched.

Layton looked at the King of this small band and said, "I hope you are not thinking of attacking us, remember what happened to one of your men last time." And with that he motioned to the mound of stones off to the left of the King.

He saw the King glance at the mound of stones and then spoke again; "You see I am not as uncivilized as you think, we gave him a decent burial. But make no mistake, if you insist on a fight I will not bury your corpses as I did this one. Your special armor will not protect you from my weapons. Instead I will leave your bodies lying in the sun for the fowls to feast upon." He paused here to see how this statement would move these people but shrugged it off when there was no response.

They are a brave people, Layton concluded. I will have to concede that to their credit.

"If you want your queen back," Layton said loudly, "tell me what I want to know." Layton could have read the mind of the King or others who were gathered around him, but felt it a waste of effort. These simple people would tell him what he wanted in exchange for their queen he was certain.

Raven watched unemotionally as his men drew their swords. He did not expect it to have any outward effect on Layton's trained soldiers, but merely wanted it as a distraction to Layton's mind. When Layton made mention of the grave where Jerddin lay he only looked in that direction and then back to Layton. When Layton threatened them Raven did not flinch, nor did the rest of the Dukes to Raven's amusement, for they had seen battle and death before.

When Layton demanded the information in exchange for the queen, Raven smiled and then replied, "I will tell you what you want to know, Layton Teal. But first I have a message for you from Merry Sheldon and Uriah Kallestor, for I am Raven Kallestor their descendant."

Alarm and warning rang in Layton's mind at the mention of his name and that of Merry and Uriah. So powerful a surprise it was that for the first time in many years he was shocked and confused for a moment. Layton's mind was racing, he had underestimated these simple folk. They knew who he was and the names of those he sought. And the information that Merry and Uriah had descendants was shocking. The truth of Merry and Uriah together having descendants settled upon him immediately. It should have been Merry and him having children and not Uriah. His anger burned at that thought, hotter than it had since they had fled his presence. But that soon was replaced by a feeling almost forgotten to Layton, fear. For the first time in his life he felt like he was loosing control of a situation. Somewhere in his mind a little voice was telling him he had wholly underestimated these people and was going to pay for it. Every sense in him was alert and he was trying to figure out what would come next, but his ability to predict human response had been lost in his confusion.

Raven took out Layton Teal's knife that had been given to Merry Sheldon as a gift. It was sheathed in its scabbard and Raven held it up for Layton to see.

Then he said, "Merry wanted me to give this gift back to you, and to tell you *no thanks*." With that Raven tossed the knife underhanded in a nice unthreatening arc toward Layton Teal, and in the same instant he began to draw his sword.

Layton tried to concentrate and read the King's mind to find out what was going on, but there were to many conflicting emotions in his mind to focus his telepathy. Things were happening too fast and the King was speaking again, holding up his knife and telling him Merry wanted the gift he gave her returned to him. Then like the bolt of a locked door opening, the logic of his brilliant mind caught up to the events around him. A time shifter, they had to have a time shifter or they could not have known that many details about him. His eyes swept to the woman behind the King and he knew at once she was the one. He saw the King drawing his sword and then he began to vanish. An almost imperceptible streak raced across the distance that had separated them. As he turned his head to follow it, what he saw caused a lump to begin rising in his throat. It was as if a giant scythe was slicing through his men toward him so quickly he knew he could not move out of the way.

As Raven tossed the knife toward Layton he felt rather than saw time around him slow down. The knife he threw was almost still in the air in its journey back to Layton. Raven did not waste time for he did not know how long Lorriel could maintain the time shift around him. He ran to the farthest of Layton's men and began to swing his sword through them one by one. It bothered him because they were so still and unable to protect themselves from his fast sword. The only thing that kept him from stopping was the knowledge that Layton and his men would kill them all if he failed. Plus the added fact that the lives of the ancients depended on him. Raven had struggled with this moral dilemma the whole evening before and that morning as well. The original plan was for Raven to disarm everyone with Layton and take them prisoner. But if he missed even one hidden weapon, a laser pistol, or an explosive device that the ancients had warned him of, he could doom them all. Raven knew it would take too long to search each individual soldier and discover all their weapons. Lorriel, he knew, could not maintain this time control for a lengthy period of time. So with no other option he could think of, he had decided the only course of action that protected the ancients and the kingdom of Glenfair was the death of Layton and his soldiers. And what kept his emotions in check while he carried out this terrible task was the fact that Layton would kill the ancients just as easily, only he would enjoy it.

Lorriel saw the signal to start the control of time within the stones' perimeter as Raven tossed the knife into the air. Although there were more stones than when she practiced, they were a greater distance apart and she almost faltered. She felt her control slipping and increased her concentration on Raven. She had to watch Raven for he was the main object of her time control. She was glad he had prepared her for what he was going to do, for she surely would have lost control otherwise. She remembered questioning him if this killing were necessary and the look he gave her showed all the turmoil and sadness in Raven's decision. She knew then that the King knew of no other alternative. She recalled the ride to Layton's camp and the thoughts that silently went through her mind. How terrible it must be to make the decisions a king must make at times.

Since Lorriel was the one shifting time, she was not insulated from the sight of what Raven was doing like the others. She winced as Raven killed the first soldier and almost quit concentrating on Raven, but somehow she continued knowing Raven's life was at stake if she failed. She had never seen killing or war personally, only the results of the Wickshield war. Now forced to watch, her revulsion grew as Raven's sword brought death with each blow. As Raven approached the end of the band of soldiers and where Layton was, Lorriel knew that she could not maintain the time shift any longer and felt it slipping from her grasp.

Raven felt the accelerated time began to slow as he approached the last two soldiers. With all of his effort he sprang toward them and cut through them both as they were turning toward him. Layton was a couple of steps away but already he was raising his weapon toward Raven.

Layton watched as the scythe slowed down and the form of a man began to take shape before him. His last two soldiers were already falling as he began to swing his weapon around toward the king of Glenfair. Layton knew he had one shot and he could not miss or all was lost. The laser pistol came to bear on Raven and his finger began to tighten on the trigger when the king's sword came down quickly across his arm. Layton raised his arm but there was no weapon there and then he realized what had happened.

"So this is how it all ends," Layton thought as Raven's second swing came around and into the body of Layton Teal. As Layton fell to the earth dying, the knife with his initials inlaid in the handle landed beside him.

Raven took a step away, dropped his sword and fell to his knees crying in a loud, mournful cry the name of his beloved wife, feeling he had closed the door forever to her return. Almost at that same moment Lorriel collapsed back into Andrew's arms fainting from the sight of death and the exertion it took to shift time in that manner. Everyone else was in confusion and shock, not fully grasping all that had taken place in the blink of their eyes.

Master Fields was the first to realize all that had happened and ran to the king, seeing Lorriel was being ministered to by Andrew and Sauron. When he reached Raven he saw the anguish on Raven's face and hesitated before asking.

"Why, Sire? I thought you were going to take them prisoner and make them return our queen."

Raven looked up at Master Fields with tears in his eyes and replied, "I could not take any chances with Layton. One mistake and all would be lost for everyone, not just Rebekka."

"Sire," Master Fields asked once again, "how will we get her back? Only Layton knew where she was taken to."

Raven shook his head sadly, "I do not know," was all he could say.

The other dukes were riding up at that time and Raven realized he had better deal with the situation. He stood, and setting aside his grief picked up his sword, cleaned it and resheathed it at his side. He then faced the others who were surveying the dead laying on the small battlefield. He saw the questions in their eyes and waited patiently for them to be asked.

Finally Terry Rollins asked, "How, King Raven did you kill them all so quickly?"

"The stones you wore helped Lorriel make me almost faster than the eye."

Now Mason Zandel spoke, "They did not attack, nor move to fight, yet you killed them all. I do not judge you for they took our queen and I heard with my own ears their leader admit to killing Jerddin. I believe they deserved to die, but with the stones they stood no chance at all."

Raven stepped forward and picked up one of the laser rifles, took aim at a nearby rock and fired. The rock exploded and turned to dust before their eyes. Raven then turned the power setting to its highest and aimed at Tor grazing in the distance and fired once more. A bolt of light went streaking to the Tor and it exploded into flaming bits. Raven looked at his Dukes and their mouths were open in wonder at the weapon Raven held.

"If we were to allow them," Raven emphasized, "to use these weapons against us, we would all be smoldering bits on the ground right now just like that Tor. Mason, you were right, what I did to these men was not fair at all. But the evil enemy knew our weapons were no match for his, and he would not hesitate to use them on us if it served his purpose. He would not use swords against us to be fair, he would use these weapons. I will gather the weapons so no one gets hurt, and then we will bury the dead."

Bandon Prescott asked Raven as he started to collect the laser rifles. "What will you do with these weapons once you have collected them?"

Raven stopped and looked at them all. "I will destroy them, for these do not belong in the hands of anyone of our time. Improved swords and armor are one thing, but these should never be used again."

Raven was surprised at the amount of weapons Layton's soldiers had on them as he searched, pistols, knives, and round exploding devices were found on each one. He knew then that he would not have been able to disarm them all in the short time Lorriel maintained the time shift around him. He felt no remorse for having to kill them, but an emptiness at the loss of life still persisted in his soul.

At last all the weapons were stockpiled and the burying of the dead was finished, then the dukes gathered to receive further instruction from their king. Raven stood before them not knowing how to start what he wanted to say to them all, and so began with the stones.

"The stones are a very powerful weapon and will be kept in the vaults behind each of your crests in the weapons room of the king's castle. I hope there never arises a time when we need to make use of them again. But if there is a need, we will meet as one at the king's castle and there to take counsel for battle." One by one they removed the stones and brought them to the King.

When that was done, Mason Zandel asked, "With the evil enemy dead, how will you get the queen back?"

Raven shuddered at the question he knew must be answered. Looking at them all he said truthfully; "I do not know where the enemy has taken Queen Rebekka. I can only hope for her safe return to us. But let it be known that your actions today and the sacrifices made by Lorriel and the queen have saved the kingdom from its destruction. You may return to your dukeships and I will remain here in case the queen arrives."

"Will you need arms to rescue her? asked Mason.

"No," Raven replied, "if she is returned, it will be with only a young woman, there is no need for you to stay." Slowly the dukes began to depart with Bandon hesitating.

"Return home," Raven spoke to Bandon. "I will bring you word in a few days." He saw Bandon sadly turn away and mount his horse and begin to ride south. As he watched him and the others go Raven felt someone at his side grasping his arm. He turned to see his faithful friends all standing behind him, Master Fields, Andrew, Lorriel and Sauron. They all had questioning looks in their eyes that caused Raven to feel the guilt of not confiding in them that he had decided to kill Layton instead of simply disarming him.

"I am sorry my friends for not telling you what I had decided to do. I was afraid that I could easily be talked out of what needed to be done in order to get my beloved Rebekka back safely."

Andrew seemed to be the most emotional about the whole turn of events when he said with tears in his eyes; "Surely we would have dissuaded you from this plan of action, for we love the queen too much to not have guaranteed her safe return. But in defense of the king let me tell you all that the Ancients, our ancestors were terrified of Layton and felt he could not be defeated or killed. With all the weapons that his troops had hidden on them we surely would have missed some and then Layton would have prevailed and the kingdom would have been lost. He then most assuredly would have killed Lorriel for the threat she posed to him as a time shifter. The King has made the right decision in killing Layton to save the kingdom, it is the only way the kingdom will ever be safe."

And then turning to Raven he said with even more emotion; "Raven, my beloved friend, you must have been tormented and torn by this decision. It was a decision no person had the right to make but you, and you have once again been forced to decide what is best for the whole of the kingdom while suffering loss yourself. We will wait here with you to see if the queen returns."

Raven could see the sadness his friends felt for the possibility that Rebekka was not to return.

"No," Raven said suddenly, "I wish to wait here for Rebekka alone. Andrew, you and Master Fields should take these weapons to Andronicus to be disassembled and destroyed. He will know how to safely take care of them. Lorriel, would you return with Sauron and make sure little Edward is fine."

When they saw that Raven really wished to be alone, they gathered the weapons and their belongings and left the king standing alone by the Halfstaff River.

Andronicus watched the small band approach Layton's company from the top of the falls. He was fearful for the outcome of this confrontation with the man his creators thought invincible. A second emotion raged within, vying for superiority of his fears. One made of hope and confidence that Layton Teal had never encountered a group of people more capable of handling his genius. If there was any chance Layton Teal would fall to other than time itself, it would be today.

Andronicus had to smile at the fact that no great stride had been made to greatly lengthen anyone's life more than twenty years. That was one foe Layton Teal could never gain the upper hand on, for all succumbed to old age eventually. Andronicus was glad that humans had not gained victory over the basic aging of the body. To have a Layton

Teal that would live for hundreds of years would be unbearable to the point of causing even an android to take a life.

Andronicus' hopes came to a reality when he saw the outcome of the confrontation. A part of him mourned, as he could not help but do at the loss of any human life. Yet another part triumphed knowing Layton Teal would no longer bring hurt to any others from this day on, forever. It was over for now, though he knew that tyrants could rise in any generation as wicked as Layton had been.

Andronicus watched as the Dukes respectfully buried the dead. He continued watching as the Dukes all left and then the king's friends left as well. As he stood at the top of the falls contemplating the end of the confrontation with Layton, he noticed that Andrew and Master Fields were coming up the river toward him with the weapons he had seen gathered by the King. He could not see their faces but Andronicus had gotten used to other features which enabled him to recognize individuals at a distance. But what he noticed most of all was the solitary figure left alone on the banks of the Halfstaff River.

"King Raven," Andronicus thought, "I never told you I had emotions as well as you. When asked about feelings I always changed the subject or answered in the negative. I can guess what you are feeling, for I miss her too. No one ever touched my mind with greater compassion, enthusiasm, or logic than that of beloved Rebekka."

With those thoughts a feeling he had rarely ever felt came upon him. It was anger welling up from all the injustice life had dealt them all. But mostly anger at how the king had to suffer for doing what was best for others. Of all the humans Andronicus had known in more than a thousand years, none had made greater sacrifice for others than King Raven. And none had suffered more in the process than he. It was a confusing paradox that Andronicus was unable to solve. Was the reward for sacrifice suffering, or was suffering the very foundation of sacrifice? This part of humanities composition would always be an enigma to Andronicus.

He did not realize he had spent so much time contemplating the ethics of human suffering until Master Fields and Andrew Crestlaw arrived with the weapons. He greeted them, but saw that they too felt the sufferings the king and queen must be enduring.

"The king," Andrew spoke, "has requested that we bring these weapons to you for disposal."

Andronicus nodded, "I can take care of these so they will never be used or found again."

Master Fields turned to go, but Andrew did not remove his stare from the face of Andronicus.

Andronicus noticed the intense look of Andrew and asked. "Is there something weighing heavy upon you that you wish to ask me?"

"Do you think the queen will be returned to us?" Andrew said plainly.

Andronicus shook his head sadly not able to hold Andrew's bold stare.

"It is hard enough," Andrew continued, "with Lorriel's life being shortened, and then to lose Rebekka as well will make the rest of our lives less joyous. It will be very hard on Lorriel for they were the best of friends, but the worst will be for our beloved king."

"It will be hard for us all." Andronicus choked out the words tying to keep his emotions in check. Andrew noticed the expression on Andronicus' face as well as his broken reply and said.

"You are not merely a machine, are you?"

Andronicus only reply was: "I must deal with these weapons," and picking some of them up he headed toward his home. Andrew watched for a moment and then turned and left with Master Fields.

Andronicus knew the perfect solution to the destruction of the weapons. Hundreds of years before he had found a cave close to the head waters of the Halfstaff River. It was a small cave but it went deep into the very bedrock of granite that surrounded the Kingdom of Glenfair. There he took the weapons, far back into the cave where a small tunnel made a sharp curving right and ended in a small bulbous room almost large enough for Andronicus to stand in. There he deposited the weapons placing the explosive devices in a circle around the rest. He pressed a green button on all of the explosive devices and took one and opened a small panel. There he keyed in the time and pressed a blue button which linked all of the devices together. When he depressed a red button, all the devices lit up as the count down to the explosion began. He placed the remaining explosive in the circle with the others and headed outside to wait.

In about five minutes an explosion was heard that shook the ground around him. Andronicus waited for the dust to clear in the mouth of the cave before going in once again. Reaching the small tunnel he was surprised to see that it had not collapsed completely. The very hard granite had resisted the small blast. He peered into the small tunnel and saw melted rock glazing the walls in the places that were left intact. He knew then that the explosive devices produced more heat than concussion in their explosion. He smiled to himself knowing that the weapons had been blown apart and then melted and fused to the rock. Anyone finding this place would be hard pressed to know exactly what had happened here in this small chamber.

Raven waited for two full days by the Halfstaff where Layton Teal's camp had been. What he knew in his heart was becoming reality, as any hope for Rebekka's return began to evaporate with the passing of the second day.

When the third day began to dawn, Raven knew all hope of Rebekka's return was gone. Layton would never have waited this long to fulfill his end of the bargain in returning Rebekka. He would have been eager to get the information and hunt down his prey. Now Raven knew that there must have been some way for Layton to signal the young woman to bring back Rebekka after he got the information he desired. By Killing Layton he had prevented any signal from being sent. His only hope had been that the young woman would have gotten curious and wondering why there was no call or signal would return to investigate. But he knew that was wishful thinking. No one who knew Layton Teal would disobey his orders intentionally. If the young woman was told to wait until he summoned her, that is exactly what she would do. As this realization settled into him, his resolve began to disappear. He was weak from not eating and drinking very little the past two days, and now deeply depressed he wished himself to die there. At that moment several people appeared over the same knoll he had before crossed to reach Layton's camp. It was Andrew, Lorriel, Master Fields and Sauron. They came to him leading his horse that he had let wander off the day before. When they reached Raven they dismounted, and bringing some food encouraged him to eat.

"I am not hungry," was all Raven said. They all looked at each other, bewildered at the king's depression.

Master Fields then spoke; "Sire, staying here will not bring her back, you must return home."

"Return home?" Raven asked. "Nothing awaits me there I want to return to."

"You have a kingdom to run, your Majesty," Master Fields tried once again.

"I have given all I can give to the kingdom, I have no more to give," was all Raven could say.

Lorriel came forward then and grasped his hand, he looked into her face and the gray hair he saw brought him grief, not solace.

Lorriel saw this but did not flinch when she said, "There is a reason for you to go on, Raven, a little boy named Edward needs you very much. He needs to see by example how a kingdom should be run if he is to be a good king someday. He will also need you when he finally realizes that his mother is not returning to him. And lastly of all Raven, we need you to be our king once again."

Raven looked at them all and for the first time in days he felt something else besides grief, the love that his friends had for him. At that moment he could not contain the sadness that he had held in check for two days. He pulled Lorriel close and cried loudly upon her shoulder. The rest all wept as well, not even stern Sauron was able to keep the tears at bay. When finally after some time their grief was assuaged, they persuaded Raven to eat some food. He then thanked them for coming and told them what needed to be done.

"Lorriel, you and mother bring little Edward home the first of the week and we will tell him together about his mother. Master Fields and I will head back to the King's castle and then I will go to the Prescott dukeship. I promised Bandon I would let him know about his daughter personally. There is also some other business I need to attend to while I am there. And thank you all for coming, you have revived my soul."

The next day as Raven approached the Prescott dukeship, he wondered how he would break the news to Rebekka's family. He did not have long to debate the issue, for as soon as he was seen to approach the castle the Prescotts came out to meet him at the front gate. Raven stopped his horse and dismounted looking at their anxious faces.

No one said a word for a few moments until Bandon asked. "Has my daughter returned?"

Raven shook his head sadly and said, "No, the queen has not returned to us. I am sorry."

Lilly Prescott threw her hands over her mouth to stifle a cry that came with the news. Bandon said nothing but turned and stormed off back into the castle.

Lilly came forward then and put her arms around Raven and said, "Please excuse Bandon's behavior. Although he and Rebekka sometimes argued, he loved her very much." And then she said more pointedly, "I know you loved her most of all and miss her just as much." Raven could only nod at the statement, fearing to speak for all the emotion that he felt.

Finally Lilly said, "Come, you must eat with us."

The meal was well prepared and the food excellent, but Raven had little appetite. No one talked unless it was necessary through the whole meal. When the meal was almost finished, Rebekka's younger brother Gregory spoke to Raven.

"Do you think there is a chance that Rebekka will come back someday?"

"I do not know," Raven said truthfully. "But the chances are highly unlikely now."

Bandon Prescott could hold his peace no longer, with anger in his voice he said, "Why have you not formed a search to look for Rebekka?"

Raven could see the pain showing in his face as he answered back. "If Rebekka were somewhere on this earth where she could be found I would never cease until I had found her. But she has been taken somewhere into the far future where we cannot find her."

"Bah," Bandon said in mock disgust and disbelief.

Lilly at that moment said, Bandon! "I am ashamed of you. You of all people should know how much the king loved Rebekka. You yourself have said to me many times that their love was to wonderful to hide from anyone."

Raven rose from the table and said, "Come with me Bandon, I must speak with you and show you something in your castle." Bandon rose reluctantly, only because he knew Raven meant the secret room he had shown him not to long ago.

When they had entered the secret room, Raven told Bandon that he now knew how to open the vault in the floor.

"How do you now know how to open the vault when you could not earlier?" Bandon asked.

"Uriah and Amnon showed me when we were with them," Raven said.

Bandon looked blankly at Raven and then said, "The stress and everything has mixed your mind up King Raven."

"No," Raven said smiling. "We did go back in time to see the ancients. Lorriel took us there before we met with you to confront the enemy. Lorriel has the power to travol in time using the same stones that were worn in the battle. The stones made it possible for Lorriel to take us with her."

"I would not believe you at all save for the impossible slaughter of the men I saw in the battle, if you would call it that," Bandon said.

"What I tell you is the truth," Raven said. "Lorriel will grow old before her time and die in about fifteen years as a result of taking us back in time. Using her power that way did something to her. How do you think Layton Teal, the enemy of the ancients came to be here in our time?"

Bandon thought about that and said, "If what you say is true, he had to have a time traveler with him."

Raven nodded, "That time traveler took Rebekka into the far future, and that is where she is right now."

"I thought our ancestors were from the past," Bandon said.

"Not originally," Raven answered. "They fled from the future into our past to hide from Layton Teal. The enemy just had the bad luck of coming here to look for them."

"If that is true," Bandon said, "then our ancestors had to have a time traveler with them as well." Raven smiled for Bandon was finally getting the picture. He had a much greater cognitive imagination than Raven had given him credit for.

"There was a time traveler with them, her name was Merry Sheldon. She became Uriah Kallestor's wife and my ancestor. That is where Lorriel gets her ability from."

While Bandon was rubbing his chin, absorbing the things he had heard, Raven looked down at the mosaic in the floor of the room. A farming scene with sheaves of grain stacked in a field by a red barn, with a family sitting down to lunch, taking a break from their work. It was a wondrous scene that captured the essence of a family content with their life on a farm. Two sheaves of grain stood alone and two heads of grain were higher touching each other in the same way that Uriah and Amnon did in their secret handshake. Raven reached down and pushed on both heads of grain at the same time and they depressed. Raven stepped back and Bandon jumped as the vault began to open.

When the vault had opened, you could clearly see inside a small stash of weapons. Raven reached in and picked out a laser rifle, similar to the one Layton's men had brought with them. Raven held it up for Bandon to see and then asked him a question.

"Did you ever wonder how I knew about the weapons the day I killed Layton?"

Raven could see the thoughts racing in his head as Bandon said, "Yes how did you know how to use them?"

"I learned from the ancients, Uriah and Amnon." Bandon now softened, his anger dissipating in the truth that Rebekka was lost somewhere in the future, beyond their reach.

Bandon asked Raven, "If you knew about these weapons, why did you not use them against Layton?"

"We did not have the time to come and retrieve them," Raven said. "Plus I was afraid they would malfunction after so many years." Raven turned on the laser sight and a red dot appeared on the wall. He took off the safety and squeezed the trigger, and the laser sight dimmed and went out. One by one he tried the weapons and all the power cells had been drained with time.

Raven turned to Bandon saying, "None of these works, it has been too much time since they were used. But I still need to take these weapons and destroy them."

Bandon nodded as Raven began gathering the weapons. There were quite a few of the round exploding devices, and Raven was sure they still worked. Uriah had told him they operated on a different power source than the laser rifles. After Raven had finished gathering the weapons, he showed Bandon how to open and close the vault. When that was finished and he was preparing to leave, Bandon caught his arm.

"King Raven," he said, and then paused, "no, I mean Raven my son-in-law. I am sorry for the way I have acted toward you."

"I miss her too," was all Raven said.

Bandon continued, "Is there anyway she can be found? Maybe Lorriel could..."

Raven shook his head. "No, we do not know where to look, or when. If we had any idea of where Rebekka was I could not keep Lorriel from reaching her, even if it shortened her life further."

Then Raven grabbed Bandon's shoulders and said. "There is something we can do for her though, never let the people of this land forget that the queen sacrificed herself for the safety of the whole kingdom." When Raven said this he saw that there were tears in Bandon's eyes.

Bandon reached out and hugged Raven and said. "It shall be done!"

Raven waited at the king's castle impatiently for the return of Lorriel, his mother, and little Edward. He knew there was only one way to deal with Rebekka's disappearance, and that was to tell Edward the truth. It tore Raven's soul to know how much that would hurt his little son. But he could not have him believing his mother would return any day and be disappointed over and over again. Raven tried to occupy his mind with a way for the kingdom to remember the queen's sacrifice for them all. An Idea stuck him as he thought about it. An inscription, no a casting with a tribute to her where everyone who came to the King's castle could see and remember. For the first time in days Raven had something to occupy his mind.

When little Edward arrived, Lorriel, Joanna and Andrew brought him into the great hall where Raven was seated. When Edward saw Raven he dashed into his arms. Raven had to try hard to keep from crying. He set little Edward down and the others gathered around. Raven was glad that Andrew decided to come along as well. They all waited quietly for Raven to begin.

He looked at Edward and started to speak but little Edward interrupted him saying, "Its about mother is it not?"

Raven nodded and began, "Edward your mother was taken away by an evil man to a place we cannot find her. The evil man is dead, but your mother can never come back to us." Edward looked around on the faces of those who encircled him and saw that what his father said was true.

He began to cry, and through his sobs he said, "I wished I could have said goodbye." Tears fell from Raven's eyes and he saw through the haze that the others were crying too. Lorriel gathered Edward up into her arms and held him until his sobs subsided. Raven stood and saw Master Fields watching the whole scene from the opposite end of the great hall. Raven motioned to Andrew and they walked over toward Master Fields.

When they reached him Raven said, "I have decided to commission a casting with an inscription honoring Rebekka so the kingdom will always remember her sacrifice." Master Fields and Andrew both nodded and agreed it was a wonderful idea.

"Andrew," Raven asked, "what would be the most durable metal we could cast? Can we duplicate the ancients metal?"

Andrew shook his head, "We do not have the tools to create the durable metal of the ancients, but searching through the hall of wisdom's metallurgic files I saw something durable that we can duplicate. It is a gold, nickel and tin alloy that would last a very long time. Gold by itself is too soft and could be defaced or vandalized. This alloy is very hard."

"Lets go find Smithy then," Raven said, "and get him working on Rebekka's tribute."

Three weeks later, the kingdom was called to the King's castle. When the courtyard was full and people were outside the gate of the castle, Raven began the ceremony.

He stood on the balcony that overlooked the courtyard and said. "Most of you know by now that the queen has been taken from our kingdom. But what many of you may not know is without her sacrifice we all surely would have perished. We must all remember her sacrifice from generation to generation. So I present to you the inscription to Glenfair's greatest queen." With that a canvas was pulled away to reveal a plaque of hardened gold alloy embedded in the largest stone of the courtyard fountain. It read:

To the queen who willingly sacrificed herself to save the kingdom. We will always remember you in our hearts as the greatest of Glenfair's queens. May you prosper wherever you have gone.

Love Raven

The people one by one filed by and read the inscription and enjoyed the refreshments provided by the king. As the day stretched into afternoon, the people began to leave. A quiet reverence settled over the whole of the castle, and when the guests had gone Raven went down to the courtyard himself. He stood there awhile in front of the inscription, thinking of his beloved wife. He kneeled down and thanked God for the days they had with each other. And Raven knew, like his father he could never love anyone like that again. He rose from his knees and placed a single white rose beside the inscription and went back into the castle.

A month after the dedication of the inscription, King Raven was in his counsel chambers working on the business of the kingdom. He was going over the statistics of each Dukeship when a powerful voice echoed in his mind.

"We have a baby girl Raven!" Raven dropped the paper he was holding with the shock and recognition of Rebekka's voice. He knew at that moment it was not his imagination, for he was not thinking of her at all right then. His heart also welled up because of the news of him having a daughter. He was comforted as well because this had been a cry of joy, not of despair or anguish.

He closed his eyes to hold back the tears and thought, "May you and our daughter be blessed and prosper wherever you are." He decided at that moment he would go see Andronicus. Besides, he needed to take the weapons he had found at the Prescotts to be destroyed.

Just then there was a knock at the door and Raven said, "Come in." Master Fields entered and seeing Raven's red eyes started to leave but Raven bid him stay.

"What can I do for you Master Fields?"

"Sire," he began, "I am not getting any younger and I have not chosen an apprentice to be weapons master in my place when I am gone. If I am to train one I must begin now." Raven nodded seeing the truth of what Master Fields was saying.

"Do you have someone in mind?"

"Yes," Master Fields said, "Robert, Terry Rollins younger brother wants to be a weapons master." Raven smiled remembering the little boy he had saved from the charging Tor years ago.

"It seems," Master Fields continued, "after the time you saved him from the Tor he has devoted himself to the art and study of weaponry. He has become quite good. I need to go to the Rollins Dukeship and live there to train him. He has the skill but needs the knowledge to be able to instruct others, especially the royal house. You will be able to train your own son quite adequately, for I have taught you all I know."

Raven shook his head saying, "I doubt that is the truth Master Fields. But yes, I release you from your duties here to instruct young Robert. When are you planning on leaving?"

Master Fields cast his eyes down and said slowly, "Today if it would be the king's pleasure."

Raven smiled and said, "Good, I will ride with you to the falls, for I wish to see Andronicus myself today." A smile came back on Master Fields' face as he realized he would ride with the king today as friend and not in any official office.

As Master Fields and Raven stopped below Brickens Falls, where they would part. Raven told him of Rebekka's message she had somehow sent to him.

Master Fields smiled, "A girl eh?" Raven nodded smiling back.

"Tell Andronicus hello for me," Master Fields said as he crossed the Halfstaff River. Raven continued on toward the falls and soon he was in the garden heading down the path toward the Hall of Wisdom carrying a large sack full of the weapons he had gathered.

Andronicus met him on the path and Raven handed him the sack and said, "The weapons from Amnon's stash." Andronicus nodded and took them into the glass mansion. After talking awhile and enjoying some refreshment, Raven told Andronicus about Rebekka's message she had sent him.

"I know now," Raven recounted, "that all those messages I heard were from Rebekka and not my imagination."

Andronicus was amazed, "It defies all logic," he said in response to what Raven told him. But Raven could tell that Andronicus did not doubt the truth of it either.

"There is something," Raven said changing the subject, "that I wish to ask you. And I ask that you be honest with me. You have always told us you are only a machine, as if you had no feelings. That is not the whole truth is it?"

"No, I am one of the few machines ever created to have emotions."

"Somehow," Raven said thoughtfully, "I always knew you did."

Andronicus smiled and said, "You always treated me like anyone else, a true friend." There was silence for a long time and finally Andronicus said, "I miss her too, Raven."

Chapter 8
Undoing The Evil

"If thou canst undo another's evil, thou must. But be thou ware, evil canst only be overcome with good. Evil canst not triumph over evil, it only addeth thereto."

--Chronicles of the Ancients

The next day came all to quickly for Rebekka. She had wanted more time to prepare but time would not wait for them. There was a knock at Ellise's door and Pi opened it to allow Blastion Astmos to enter.

He looked at Rebekka and Ellise and said apprehensively, "The cabinet meeting is scheduled for one, just after lunch. I do not have to tell you how curious everyone was to the purpose of this meeting."

"What did you tell them?" asked Ellise.

"I did not tell them anything except that Layton wanted it convened," Blastion said with irritation. Both Ellise and Rebekka could see that Blastion had not slept well because of all that was at stake. His life was in the hands of a couple of women and he did not like it at all. Never mind that it was not his choice, for Ellise had made it clear he did not have a say in this whole scheme.

"Are you sure you want to go through with this?" Blastion asked.

Now Rebekka took over and replied, "We are sure, and you had better make sure that you do your part."

"Oh, don't worry about me," Blastion shot back, "its only my life that is hanging in the balance. I still don't know how you plan to pull this off but I guess I will know at one this afternoon." With that he walked to the door, looked over his shoulder and then left.

Ellise looked at Rebekka and said, "We had better get back to our plans for the cabinet meeting."

Rebekka nodded and then spoke to Ellise's mind, "You will make sure that all my wishes are carried out." Ellise nodded in response to Rebekka's statement.

"How did that sound?" Rebekka asked Ellise.

"I think you have that part under control," Ellise said smiling. "Now we had better make sure the rest of our plans go as well."

Rebekka nodded and then added, "I do not like the deception we have to bring about for this to work. If there were any other way to deal with this I would take it besides lying."

Ellise nodded, "I know that this whole plan bothers you but we don't have very many options. Let me tell the story and then you can take it from there."

Ellise and Rebekka walked into the room where the cabinet was to meet. Blastion was there and escorted them to their places and called the meeting to order. He then turned to the cabinet and said, "Layton Teal has sent Chancellor Ellise with a message for the whole cabinet, so I will turn this meeting over to her." Ellise stood and thanked Blastion for the introduction and began.

"I think most of you know by now that Layton is not here and has asked me to chair this meeting."

Almost instantly Max Bane stood and said with a stern voice, "We all know your title of chancellor is only a token position that Layton gave you to make you feel important. I can't believe that Layton would put you, a young girl in charge of any official meeting. I know something is going on because you do not look at all like the little girl you were the last time I saw you. And who is this woman with you?"

Ellise was not shaken by Max Bane's outburst for she expected this from the cabinet. "Sit down Max," and I will explain all of this to you."

Max Bane still stood until John Martin said angrily, "Sit down Max so we can find out what is going on." The rest of the cabinet was starring at Max so he reluctantly sat, scowling and grumbling as he did.

"Thank you," Ellise said as she began again. "Layton confided in me a little over a week ago that he wished to take a trip into the past to escape the boredom he was experiencing here. I took him a long ways into the past and he has decided to stay there as an early retirement." Rebekka could see the shock this statement had on everyone in the cabinet.

John Martin asked Ellise, "Why would Layton want to retire from the empire he has built?"

Ellise smiled and said, "You all know how Layton liked a challenge, something to conquer. Well, there is not anything left for him to conquer here anymore and he was getting bored with all the politics of his empire. So he wanted a new frontier to challenge him and he found it in the past. The reason I look older to you is an unexpected side affect of traveling so far in time. As a result I will age rapidly and die in less than twenty years."

Charlotte Frank, the minister of agriculture now spoke, "Why didn't Layton inform us of this plan of his to disappear?"

Ellise just laughed, "You know how Layton was, he did not trust his plans to be known openly, but only to those who had to know. I myself didn't know until the day we were to leave."

"Who is this woman with you?" asked Chan Quon, minister of transportation.

"She is the main reason for this meeting," Ellise replied. "She has been chosen by Layton Teal to rule in his place." There was a moment of confusion and then everyone was talking at once until Blastion Astmos raised his hand and motioned for everyone to be quiet.

"What you have heard from Chancellor Ellise is true. I knew Layton was going to travel to the past and retire. I also knew that he would choose someone to take his place but I did not know who until yesterday. This woman has been sent here by Layton Teal from the past to rule and her name is Queen Rebekka Kallestor. Long live Queen Rebekka" And with that Blastion bowed low in a respectful bow to Rebekka's authority and position.

Rebekka glanced at Ellise and spoke to her mind, "Did you tell him I was a queen?" Ellise shook her head no, very slightly in response to Rebekka's question.

So convincing was this statement and introduction by Blastion that the cabinet was once again stunned into silence until John Martin spoke.

"What do you have to say for yourself?" Queen Rebekka he asked, not hiding the amusement in his voice. Rebekka stood and looked everyone in the eye before answering.

"Layton Teal did send me here from the past, and I will rule in his place."

At the end of that statement Max Bane stood up and shouted, "This is insane, a woman we have never seen before comes in here and claims Layton's empire for her own. How do we know that Ellise and this woman have not conspired to get rid of Layton and take his empire for themselves."

As soon as this statement was finished a laugh started low and then got louder. Everyone froze, especially Max for they all knew this laugh, it was the laugh of Layton teal echoing in their minds.

"Max, Max," the voice said. "Do you think that a fourteen year old girl and this woman could conspire against me and come up with this idea to take my place? Come, come, you must think I am slipping or incompetent, don't you?"

"No Layton, I don't," Max said shaking.

"I have looked into all of your minds, and you, Max would love to rule in my place. You would have killed me long ago if you thought it could have been done. That is why I want none of you to have the control of my empire and I have chosen Queen Rebekka for that position. I think we should take a recess for all of you to think this over and decide I made a good decision. Be back here in half an hour."

When the voice of Layton Teal stopped, everyone was shaken except John Martin who had an amused look on his face. Max Bane on the other hand looked weak and pale by comparison.

Blastion Astmos was the most surprised of all and kept glancing around the room until Rebekka came up to him and asked; "Where shall we retire for the recess?"   Blastion quickly regathered his wits and said, "Why Layton's private chambers, of course. Please, follow me."

Once inside Layton's private chambers and the door was shut, Blastion in an agitated voice said:

"All right, what is going on? Where is Layton, I know he set this whole thing up now. What I want to know is, why?"

Rebekka just smiled and spoke to Blastion's mind in Layton's voice saying, "Layton is gone, we told you that." Then in her regular voice said, "What we did not tell you is I am a telepath and know how to sound like Layton." Blastion's mouth dropped open and a frown came across his face.

"You should have told me what you were going to do."

"You had to be surprised like the rest for this scheme to be believable," Rebekka remarked. "How do you think it went?" Blastion started to answer when there was a knock at the door. Blastion was waving his hands in a motion to Rebekka and Ellise not to answer.

But Rebekka just smiled and said, "Come in." The door opened and John Martin entered and closed the door behind him. He looked at Ellise and Blastion and then walked over to Rebekka and said.

"I don't know who you are but I do know this was not Layton's plan."

Blastion interrupted and said, "You heard his voice, we all did, this is what he wants."

John Martin continued, ignoring Blastion, "I don't know how you did that with Layton's voice but I know he would never have said those words. So, are you going to tell me what is going on or not?"

Rebekka looked at John Martin with a serious stare and said, "Layton sent me here with Ellise, not to rule but as a prisoner. Layton went in search of the traitors who disappeared about fourteen years ago. I was taken hostage to elicit information about the traitors from the people of my kingdom. Once we were here I convinced Ellise not to return for Layton and thus stranding him in my time until he dies. He cannot travel anywhere in time without Ellise."

"That still does not explain Layton's voice we all heard in our minds," John Martin stated.

"I am a telepath, even more powerful than Layton. I have listened to Layton's mind and I know what he sounds like."

John Martin shook his head disbelievingly, "Layton Teal outwitted by a couple of women. This was a brilliant plan you came up with."

"Actually," Rebekka stated, "it was Ellise's idea."

John Martin looked at Ellise admiringly and said, "I see we have underestimated you Ellise." Rebekka looked over at Blastion and he was pale and looked very faint.

"Are you all right she asked?"

"No," he replied. "You pull this off and you go telling him what you have done? You have a death wish for the three of us don't you?"

Rebekka ignored Blastion and said, "Well minister Martin, what are you going to do now that you know the truth?"

"Answer me one question," he said. "Why do you want to rule?"

"I do not," Rebekka answered truthfully.

"Then why go to this great risk to do so?" he asked a little confused.

"What would happen," asked Rebekka, "if you knew Layton was gone for good?"

"I would declare martial law and act as the ruling head of the government," John Martin stated quickly.

"And do you think the rest of the cabinet would let you do so, especially Max Bane without a fight?"

"No," John Martin agreed. "There would be anarchy and perhaps a war or revolution if that happened. No cabinet person would ever accept another ruling in Layton's place without a struggle," John Martin added, seeing the point Rebekka was trying to make.

Now Rebekka took charge, "Ellise has told me that you are a good and decent man, John Martin, but it is better someone else rule for the time being instead of a cabinet member, especially Evil Max."

John Martin rubbed his chin in thought and then asked. "What are you planning to do with Layton's empire and what qualifications do you have for running it?"

Rebekka said in a saddened tone, "I want the empire to be a place free from oppression and tyranny where people can live in peace without fear. I was also queen of a kingdom back in the time where I lived. I have Blastion and Ellise to help me and the cabinet can advise me in matters of state."

Ellise came forward, facing John Martin and said. "Minister Martin, don't you want to help make this empire a better place for people to live, for once in your life to make a difference for good now that you can?"

John Martin's face calmed and a small smile formed, "Yes I do Ellise, and you have my support Queen Rebekka." Blastion let out an audible sigh of relief as John Martin headed for the door.

He stopped and looked back over his shoulder and said, "I guess you like it here more than where you used to live if you are so set on staying." Rebekka and Ellise looked at each other and minister Martin said, "What, did I say something wrong?"

You could feel more than hear the sadness in Rebekka's voice as she said. "It is for the love of my kingdom I dare not return even though I love my husband more than life itself and even now I carry my husbands child. I cannot return because Layton must remain there. Someday John Martin I will tell you the whole story."

He looked at Rebekka and was sure for the first time since he had met her that she was not lusting after power or position, but had instead lived a life of sacrifice. Now more than ever He was convinced she would be good for the empire.

When the cabinet convened after the half hour recess and everyone was seated, the voice of Layton Teal came once again into their minds.

"So, now that you have thought it over, let us take a vote. Not that I care mind you, but we will vote just the same. How do you vote minister of defense?"

"In favor," John Martin answered. The vote came one by one in favor until at last it came to the minister of economics, Max Bane.

Layton Teal's voice asked once again, "Max Bane, how do you vote?"

"In favor, imperial ruler," Max said.

"Good," the voice of Layton said, "I like unanimous votes on my motions. I will be watching and listening to all of you, so don't make me come back personally and set things right. You will follow Queen Rebekka as you followed me with one exception; she isn't me, so don't expect her to see or do things the brilliant way I did. Remember, I will be watching."

With that the voice ended and in the ensuing silence no one moved or said a thing hoping that Layton was really through.

Rebekka took control by saying, "My first order of business as head of this empire is to order an execution." Everyone looked shocked as they followed her gaze to Max Bane who had once again turned very white.

"You have caused the most trouble, and have voiced the most opposition to my rule." Max tried to find words but no audible sounds came out of his mouth as Rebekka continued, "How do I know that you will not give me trouble or hardship as minister of economics?" There still was no sound from Max as he squirmed and choked trying to say something.

"As I thought," Rebekka said mockingly, "you will be of no use to me alive."

At last Max found his voice and cried out in panic, "I will be of use to you, I will serve you, please give me a chance."

Rebekka sighed as if she was bored, and said, "Ok, but cross me once and you are as good as dead." John Martin watched this exchange with amusement thinking how brilliant Rebekka was by having Max Bane already in her debt for sparing his life. He was snapped out of his thoughts by Rebekka speaking again.

"I want to make something very clear about how my cabinet is to function. When I ask for input and your opinions I want just that, even if you think it is not what I want to hear. No one will be punished for sharing their opinions during our cabinet meetings. But when I have all the information I need and I make a decision, that is not the time to question me. If everyone understands these rules we will get along just fine.

We will convene a cabinet press conference tomorrow at eight in the morning to announce to the people of this empire my new position. Following the press conference we will have our first working cabinet meeting to take care of business. Thank you all for your support, you are dismissed." Rebokka said this with a curt flat tone and a wave of her hand that showed her indifference to their opinion of her.

As everyone rose to leave she caught the fleeting thoughts of her cabinet which told her at this moment she was successful in her plan to guide the empire. How long that would last she did not know. She especially feared that Max would regain his boldness and challenge her tomorrow before the press conference.

The press conference was Blastion Astmos' idea. After all as Layton's personal aid he handled all of Layton's press. He had explained to Rebekka how powerful the media was and what it could do for a person if they controlled its presentation to the public. Rebekka had doubts right away that Blastion knew what he was talking about until Ellise also said it was true. Rebekka had a hard time accepting this because of the way things ran in the small kingdom of Glenfair. In Glenfair the public formed its own opinion of people and what was good or bad from what they did. She felt it was backwards to try and influence people to accept or reject a person or policies before they could prove themselves. Their insistence however outlined for Rebekka how little she knew about the politics of Layton's empire. She agreed to the press conference but still believed that people knew what was right or wrong for the empire.

"You can hold on to that little fairy tale if you want," declared Blastion, "but it is not reality. People cannot make the right decision if they are not told the truth or all the facts. People have been told only what their leaders wanted them to know or only what their leaders wanted them to believe. It has been that way long before even Layton came to power."

Rebekka was appalled and disgusted with this truth and stated plainly. "From now on it will not be so, we will tell the people what really goes on in the empire and we will keep our promises or we will not make them at all!"

Blastion only blinked when Rebekka said this and only after a long pause did he say; "You are serious about this aren't you?

"Very serious," was all Rebekka said.

"Our political life will be very interesting," Blastion said, "even though it may be short lived." Rebekka smiled at that statement realizing how much things were going to change. She knew the changes would be too fast for most of her cabinet, but too slow for her own liking. She tempered this with the truth she needed patience and slow planning for anything to be accomplished. The first major change came right away by Blastion insisting Rebekka move into Layton's palace immediately. If she was to act like the empire was hers she had to play the part. Rebekka agreed only on the condition that Ellise could come with her and any thing else Ellise wanted from her home. Blastion saw no problem with that request and immediately had Queen Rebekka and Chancellor Ellise transported to the palace.

John Martin was also a great help in this matter for as minister of defense he commanded some control over the palace guard. He informed them of Queen Rebekka's appointment as head of state in place of Layton Teal and commanded them to guard her as they had their former emperor. The palace guard had no problem with this new assignment for they could not conceive such an order as this coming from the minister of defense if it were not the wish of Layton himself. Once he had established Rebekka firmly in the palace he gave orders to the head of the palace guard not to allow anyone into the palace without Queen Rebekka's or Chancellor Ellise's permission, including himself. The head of the palace guard took this admonition very seriously as if his life depended on its fulfillment, which indeed it had under the past rule of Layton Teal.

So thanks to Blastion Astmos and John Martin, Queen Rebekka was established in the palace and protected by the palace guard before the sun descended that evening.

It was a good thing such quick action took place for as soon as Max Bane had left the cabinet meeting he began to realize that this was the best opportunity he would ever have to make a bid for power. Gathering his power base around him, he quickly plotted Rebekka's assassination and how he would use that moment to make a grab for it all. But before his plans were finalized word came to him through his spies that the new emperor, Queen Rebekka was already entrenched in the palace with the palace guard faithfully protecting her. Max Bane's plans were dashed with that news and he was shocked that this had taken place so quickly. How had this happened? This all smelled of Layton Teal, he had to be behind so quick a move knowing it would be the weak link in executing this change of leadership. He had to give

Layton credit, he seemed to always be one step ahead of him all the time. Nevertheless he would keep plotting and somehow kill this woman and take her place as ruler of this empire. He felt it would be so, it was his destiny.

Rebekka Kallestor could not believe how quickly events had unfolded. One moment she was the prisoner of Layton Teal, the next, ruler of his empire and living in his palace. She had to laugh at the absurdity of the whole situation. If Layton Teal had known what was going to happen to his empire in his absence he surely never would have left. This was the only consolation Rebekka had for being trapped the rest of her life in the future away from the people she loved most. She would try her best to undo all Layton had worked for. His evil hold and repression of the people would be broken somehow, she determined. She was tired from the stress of the day's events and knew she must rest for the next day would be just as taxing.

The next day came early for Rebekka as she had to prepare for the press conference Blastion Astmos insisted take place with all the cabinet members present Blastion informed her that the press was quite eager for a conference since there had not been one in quite awhile. Ellise was very nervous about the press conference and Rebekka had a hard time understanding why. Ellise had been at press conferences before standing beside Layton Teal, but she was never required to speak. She had stood up so well under the pressure of Layton's cabinet and the criticism of Max Bane that for her to be nervous about this little press conference puzzled Rebekka.

Pi, Ellise's android was amused by both Rebekka's and Ellise's response to the press conference and tried to encourage Ellise to eat some breakfast. Pi had no trouble getting Rebekka to eat since she had an increased appetite because of her pregnancy. But Pi was concerned for Ellise because the girl had developed an enormous appetite since the long time shift and her accelerated aging.

While Pi argued with Ellise about breakfast a voice came from somewhere over their heads that said:

"Queen Rebekka, Blastion Astmos is here to see you, shall I allow him to enter the palace." Rebekka looked around to see where the voice was coming from and Ellise got up and depressed a button on the wall and responded.

"This is Chancellor Ellise, send him up right away."

There was a hesitation and the voice spoke again, "I am sorry Chancellor, my orders were to allow no one on the palace grounds without Queen Rebekka's permission." Rebekka thought she now understood the source of the voice having been exposed to much of the technology of Layton's time.

She spoke loud as she responded, "This is Queen Rebekka, do send Blastion Astmos in right away." Then Rebekka added, "Who are you and what is your name and position?" She could hear the man's voice being cleared as she waited for his response.

"I am Sargent of the palace guard and my name is Sherman Templas."

"Sherman," the queen replied, "after the press conference and cabinet meeting today, I would like to meet with all of the palace guards, can that be arranged?"

"It shall be done," was all Sherman answered.

Rebekka then turned to Pi and said, "Would you be so kind as to receive Blastion and bring him into our presence?" Pi smiled and left to meet Blastion. She liked Queen Rebekka because she treated her as she would any other person. She was also grateful for the change Rebekka had brought about in Ellise's attitude toward her. She was still Ellise's property, but now she was viewed as more than a simple machine to produce things for Ellise's comfort on command. She even hoped that with time she would be accepted as a trusted servant and friend.

When Blastion appeared with Pi, Rebekka warmly greeted him.

"Are you ready for the press conference," asked Blastion. And then he added, "My spies have informed me that Max Bane is already plotting to get rid of you."

Rebekka nodded knowingly, "It is to be expected. An evil man like Layton Teal spawns others of similar ambition and morals." Rebekka then looked at Blastion and said, "How do you know so much of what is going on?"

Blastion blushed, "Intelligence was my main job for Layton, not just being his aid. Being his aid was just a front for the real job of spying for him."

"I appreciate what you have done for me Blastion, but you do not need to spy for me. Max Bane's actions will be known soon enough."

Blastion was appalled, "You mean you don't want to know what others are saying about you behind your back?"

Rebekka smiled, "That is the last thing I want to know. If I wanted I could read people's minds, but that would be unethical without a compelling reason to do so." Blastion looked at Rebekka with awe, it had been a long time since he had met someone with such character.

You will do the empire good if you survive, he thought.

"We had better get to work for there are some necessary preparations we must make before the press conference," Blastion said.

John Martin was waiting at the front of the palace to escort Queen Rebekka and Ellise to the press conference. It seemed he too was worried about Rebekka's safety. They arrived at the government complex where they had the cabinet meeting the day before and entered, escorted by John Martin's soldiers. The other cabinet members were there waiting except Max Bane who was no where to be seen.

Chan Quon was the first to speak to Queen Rebekka, "What kind of press conference are we going to have today?"

Blastion took this as his cue and spoke up; "The press conference will be seen by everyone, and its purpose is for this cabinet to tell the empire of Queen Rebekka's appointment as head of state."

No one countered this after the previous day's meeting and the dramatic conclusion so Rebekka said, "We will have a short cabinet meeting before the press conference." When everyone was seated Rebekka began the meeting with the news that there would be some difficult changes under her rule.

"But first, I want everyone to know that you will be asked to make some sacrifices for the good of the empire." Rebekka eyed everyone to see how this would be received and seeing no response continued. "I myself have made sacrifices in coming here by Layton's choice. I have left a husband, son, and another kingdom to be here. And even now I am carrying..." at that moment Max Bane entered the room to join the cabinet meeting.

Rebekka stopped in mid sentence and looked at him scornfully, "It is nice of you to join us Max," was all she said as she began again. Everyone looked at each other to see what Rebekka would do, for Layton would never have tolerated such insubordination and indifference that Max was showing Queen Rebekka.

"As I was saying," Rebekka continued, "we will have to make sacrifices for the empire. I am carrying my husband's child, and it will be born in another time and place than he would like, but that cannot be helped. Now, I require certain information before the press conference is to take place today, mainly concerning economics," and with that she glanced again scornfully at Max Bane.

John Martin was getting worried, for if this is as tough as she was going to get with Max's insubordination, they all were in trouble. The first question I have is about the state held funds of the empire.

Max smiled and said, "That is my category, due to the thrifty fleecing of the people we are now several trillion dollars in the black and that can probably be increased more this coming year since we have no immediate war campaign to pay for," he said this last bit glancing at John Martin.

Rebekka nodded and asked the rest of the cabinet, "Do you agree, we have an ample surplus in revenue at present?" They all nodded in agreement to her question.

"How much in tribute or tax would we need to support the empire at the present level of expense?" There was discussion and after some debate they estimated probably half the taxes the people were paying at present would be sufficient.

Rebekka then asked, "How much wealth have each of you acquired since you have become part of this cabinet?" Everyone's mouth dropped open and they looked at each other until Rebekka asked pointedly, "Chan Quon, what is your net worth in wealth?" He stuttered and made some noises until Rebekka stated forcefully, "I asked you a question Chan, so do answer."

"Three billion," was his answer. Rebekka had discussed the monetary system and values extensively with Ellise until she was sure she understood the value and currency of the Empire.

"How about you, John Martin?" Rebekka asked.

"One billion," he answered flatly.

"Esther?" Rebekka continued.

"Seven hundred million," she answered.

"Charlotte?"

Charlotte Frank frowned in thought and then stated, "Almost a billion I believe."

Then Rebekka turned a serious stare toward Max Bane, "Well Max, your turn."

Max turned red faced and exclaimed, "I do not see what any of this has to do with a press conference. Our net worth is not important to the functioning of this cabinet."

"Max!" Rebekka said in an icy tone, "I am sure Layton Teal knew all about this but I do not, so answer my question."

Max paused for a moment and then said, "Six billion."

"And what is my net worth occupying Layton's place in the empire?" Rebekka asked everyone.

Max scoffed, "The empire is yours, all the money collected from the taxes is at your disposal, it comes from whatever you want to squeeze from the people." Rebekka nodded, already realizing this, but having it stated vocally was part of her plan.

"It seems we have all gotten quite wealthy off of the people."

"What about Chancellor Ellise?" Esther Smith asked.

Rebekka looked puzzled and said, "You all should know that Ellise has no real net worth at all, she has an expense account with the empire, that is all."

"We did not know," John Martin stated, "Layton never revealed his arrangement with Ellise to us."

"I do not think anyone will object to the arrangement staying as it was under Layton," Rebekka said without waiting for an answer.

"Now to get to the heart of the matter before the press conference. What do you think would make the people most happy in the realm?" Everyone looked at each other and not one put forth an answer to her question. Rebekka could see that the welfare of the people really had never been an agenda before in the cabinet meetings.

"Come, come now, someone in this cabinet must know of something that would make the people happy."

Charlotte Frank cleared her throat nervously and said, "Reducing the peoples tax burden would make everyone happy." As she said this she began to laugh as if it were a joke. The rest of the cabinet joined in laughing except John Martin who just smiled.

"That is exactly what I propose we do." Everyone quit laughing when Rebekka said this.

Max Bane then stood and said, "You must be crazy, Layton would never stand for this!"

"Sit down Max," Rebekka said with such steel in her voice that Max obeyed immediately without thought. "Just yesterday Max you said that you would cause me no problems, and now you show up late for our meeting and oppose my decision. I could have you killed but that would be too easy. Instead I will fine you one billion dollars payable to the empire's treasury by tomorrow at this time."

Everyone's mouth dropped open except for John Martin who had an amused look on his face. And once again Max Bane had turned very pale at Rebekka's words.

"You, you can't do that," he stuttered.

"Oh, Max," Rebekka said smiling, "I can too. If that money is not deposited by tomorrow morning it will be two billion, and if that is not paid I will come knocking at your door and strip you bare and then kill you, Is that clear?" All Max could do was nod.

"Good," Rebekka stated. "Now do not be late for another meeting." John Martin watched this whole drama unfold with amusement. His confidence in Rebekka had been restored with the punishment she had inflicted on Max. The rest of the cabinet now had much to consider when their own fortunes might be at stake.

"A cut of tribute, I mean taxes will not affect your wealth at all, only mine," Rebekka continued, "and it will be good for the people."

Chan Quon nodded knowingly, "It will make you very popular with the people as well, he stated." Rebekka just smiled in response to his statement.

"Well now, we have a press conference to host," Rebekka said, "so Blastion should invite them in."

Blastion took this as his cue and left hastily and soon returned with the press and cameras following. Once the equipment was set up the conference began with Blastion calling the conference to order and explaining that a matter of great importance was to be announced to the empire.

And with that introduction he turned and said, "Chancellor Ellise will explain the situation and the changes that have come for us all." With that Blastion bowed respectfully, "Chancellor Ellise," he said as he backed away from the spotlight.

Ellise stood and began: "Layton Teal has decided to take a long leave of absence from the rigors of his empire. Do not make the assumption that he is dead just because he is absent, for he is very much alive. In his absence he has chosen someone to rule his empire in his place. Someone who is not from our time, she is from our far past. She was queen of a kingdom in that other place and time and has made a great sacrifice to come to ours and rule. She has left her family, her home, and even now carries the unborn child of her husband within her womb. I know that she will rule us well, and she has my support and that of the cabinet to do so."

John Martin then stood and said, "We have all been convinced that Rebekka should rule in Layton's place. For public record, all of the cabinet will give their support publicly to Queen Rebekka. Chan Quon, do you give your support and loyalty to Queen Rebekka as ruler of this empire?"

Chan stood and said, "I pledge my loyalty and support to Queen Rebekka our ruler." One by one the cabinet stood and pledged loyalty to Rebekka until at last it came down to Max Bane. Having been caught off guard by the previous meeting, he could think of no alternative but to stand and pledge with the rest of the cabinet.

After that was finished, John Martin said, "May I present to the empire, its temporary ruler, Queen Rebekka." Rebekka then stood and thanked John Martin and the rest of the cabinet for their support. She then began to speak to the empire in the accent of their forefathers.

"As you now know, Layton Teal is no longer ruler of this empire. There will be some changes under my rule, hopefully for the benefit of all the citizens of this great empire. The first thing I propose as the new ruler of this empire is a fifty percent cut in the taxes that businesses and individuals are paying." There was stunned silence in the room as Rebekka let this announcement sink in.

"I would also like to see individuals have more freedom without the fear of state reprisal. In order for you to believe that this is true I lift the ban imposed by the state to control the number of children any married couple desires to have." After another short pause Rebekka said. "Do not mistake this generosity as a tolerance of evil. Any crimes that are committed in this empire will be punished swiftly and justly. The penalty for murder, kidnapping, and rape will be public burning at the stake. For lesser offenses that result from intentional injury to another, grand larceny, and extortion will be punishable by hanging. Petty theft will require the thief to labor until he has restored four-fold back to those he has stolen from. Do not test me in these matters for I will be unwavering in their enforcement. Thank you, and may the empire prosper."

Max Bane left quickly after the press conference was over, he did not want to stay a moment longer than he had to in that woman's presence. Layton Teal had been hard enough to tolerate, but at least Layton never dipped into his personal fortune as a form of punishment. He could be slowly drained of his wealth by this woman, and that he could not allow. There is only one way for this to end, the woman must die. He continued home at a frantic pace in order to begin planning Queen Rebekka's death.

John Martin stayed after the press conference to speak with Queen Rebekka. As he watched he saw how fast Max Bane left and knew the reason why. That is what he wanted to speak to Rebekka about. After the others had left and Rebekka, Ellise and Blastion Astmos were the only ones there he said flatly to Rebekka.

"You will have to kill Max Bane." Rebekka did not flinch from this statement and only waited for John Martin to finish. John Martin went on, "I admire your bravery in punishing Max in a way that Layton never did, his pocketbook. His fortune is more important to him than his own life so he will now try and kill you for what you are doing to him. I suggest you kill him before he finds a way to assassinate you." Rebekka waited for a moment to see if the others would say anything before she spoke.

When no one said anything more she said. "I know that past habits die hard. Layton cured any problems by executions. If I start down this road I will be no better than him. No, the people need to see that I am different if we are to bring the power back into the people's hands. If we can hang on a little while we shall be rid of Max Bane. I want to hold a public election and let the people choose their cabinet members. Evil Max will then be voted out of office and loose his power base, since the power will be transferred back to the people."

"And what of the assassination attempts that surely will come from him before this election can take place?" John Martin asked.

"Attempted assassination," Rebekka remarked, "is a hanging offense. But we cannot hang Max without convincing proof before the public or they will think it is politically motivated. To be successful, we must convince the public that we are different politically than Layton Teal. We cannot go killing off the opposition as Layton did and think the people will see any difference."

John Martin nodded at Rebekka's wisdom and only said. "I hope you live long enough to accomplish your goals. By the way, how long do you plan to remain as ruler of the empire?"

Rebekka smiled, "To give the people back their empire is all I want, and after that I will resign."

As John Martin left he thought, she is a queen that cares for the people, I will gladly be her subject.

The people of the empire watched the press conference with great interest. Nothing this interesting had happened for a long time. At first, most thought this a ploy or joke by Layton Teal pretending to be gone. But as the press conference progressed they began to hope that perhaps it really was true. No one was willing to bet that the tax cuts would really take place, but it was a good thing just to hear it even proposed.

The next day at the palace, Blastion Astmos brought word to Rebekka of the empire's condition. The fine against Max Bane had been paid into the treasury as Rebekka had demanded. But to her dismay, public executions of criminals, both burning and hanging were taking place all over the empire. In all of her years in Glenfair she had never witnessed a public execution, so the amount of crime the empire had, greatly disturbed her.

Her only comment was, "Evil leadership spawns evil practices by the people it rules." This went on for almost a week before the people who were inclined to commit these crimes were convinced the practice would continue. After this crime began to drop sharply in the empire. Quick painless execution was one thing, but no one wanted to suffer the terrible, painful death of burning. Rebekka was glad that executions for crime had dropped to less than a fifth of what they were and were projected to drop much lower than that in another week.

Blastion was discussing the coming tax collection in two months time with Rebekka when there was a call from the palace security.

"This is Sherman Templas Queen Rebekka, there is an android here to deliver a gift to you."

Rebekka looked at Ellise, Pi, and Blastion before she spoke, "Has the android been thoroughly checked as a security risk?"

She heard a chuckle from Sherman as he said. "Everyone knows that an android cannot intentionally harm a human, but yes we checked him for bugs and weapons nonetheless."

"Then send him in," Rebekka stated.

Pi rose from her place to meet the guest and to escort the android into their presence. When Pi returned she was followed by a well groomed young man carrying a package.

The android stepped forward and said. "This present is for you, Queen Rebekka." Rebekka took the package out of his hand and began to open it, but then paused.

"Who sent this package?" she asked the android.

"I do not know," the android stated, "I have never seen the man before. I asked my master and he suggested I bring the package to you."

"Who is your master?" Blastion asked.

"George Trundle," the android answered.

Blastion left immediately to find a computer terminal to research George Trundle. Meanwhile Rebekka opened the package to reveal ornately decorated crab cakes with a note inside which read: "I hope you enjoy this delicacy as much as we are enjoying your reign." Rebekka smiled, for she had received little gratitude so far for what she was trying to do for the people of this realm. She began to reach inside for one of the cakes when Pi snatched the whole box from Rebekka and placed it on the table.

"What are you doing?" Rebekka asked Pi.

"Just a minute," she said as she took a crab cake out of the box and placed it on a small plate.

She placed it on the floor and called out, "Simon, Simon, here kitty." There was a winsome meow from the palace cat and soon it came rushing into the kitchen and over to the crab cake that had been set on the floor. The cat sniffed only once before digging into the delicacy.

"See," Rebekka said to Pi, "there is nothing wrong with the food, Simon loves it." At that moment Simon growled, his fur and tail stood strait up and he fell over dead.

Everyone was shocked for a moment until Pi said unemotionally, "We will need another palace cat."

Ellise swung quickly around to face the android and said, "That food was poisoned, you could have killed Queen Rebekka or us."

Pi yelled "No Ellise," at her words but it was too late to undo the damage. The android made some garbled noises coupled with contorted facial expressions and fell over and was still. Ellise tried to rouse him but he remained still.

At that moment Blastion came barging into the room and yelled, "Don't eat any of that food!" Then seeing the dead cat and still android asked with a bewildered expression, "What happened?" Pi took charge since it seemed Queen Rebekka and Ellise were still perplexed about the events that had unfolded before their eyes.

"I tested the food on Simon and it was poisoned. Before I could stop Chancellor Ellise she accused the android of trying to poison the queen and overloaded his circuit imperative causing him to shut down."

"Oh great," Blastion said, "now we will never get to the bottom of this assassination attempt." Ellise gathered her senses back together and asked Pi what had happened to the android.

"You really don't know much about androids, do you Ellise?"

"No, I guess I don't," Ellise said.

Pi uttered what seemed like a sigh and continued, "They are programed with an imperative not to intentionally harm any human. Even a supposed accusation of harm such as this causes the imperative to short circuit and shut down any android. He must be sent back to the makers to be repaired and reprogrammed. His former life and memories are now gone."

"You mean he died?" Ellise asked fearfully.

"In a sense, yes," Pi answered. Pi, seeing Ellise's distress over the incident added, "But unlike humans, this android had no emotions and felt no pain or sorrow in his positronic destruction. He will be repaired, reprogramed, and will live again in the service of another."

Ellise looked at the still android feeling remorse, and then at Pi and said, "Can that happen to you?"

"I am programed with a similar imperative, but with broader parameters for interpreting harm. That was the goal of my original programmers, my emotions were an unexpected byproduct of that programing. Your statement would not have had the same affect on me if I were in the same situation. There was no real harm done to any human so your accusation would have little effect on me."

Blastion moaned as he realized the only lead they had to the attempted assassination was lying on the floor with its memory erased.

"Whoever did this knew the android would shut down erasing any evidence."

Rebekka frowned, "I thought androids could not harm humans?"

"They can't intentionally harm," Blastion corrected. "This android did not know the food was poisoned. This smells of the kind of deed that Evil Max would do. I ran a security check and found out George Trundle is a fictitious name a person used to buy this android just yesterday. It has all been very well covered and would take a great deal of money and effort to hide identities this well in the purchase of an android. There is a very limited supply of them in the empire." After he said this Blastion went over to communication device and called up Sherman Templas.

"Sherman, get up here right away, someone's been poisoned by that food you sent up." In a very short time a shaken Sherman appeared in the kitchen and beheld the still android and the lifeless cat on the floor.

"Sherman," Blastion said, "it is your responsibility to protect Queen Rebekka from this sort of thing. You assumed an android could not harm the queen, you were wrong." Sherman was speechless and pale. Layton surely would have him executed for such a lapse as this. Rebekka saw the look on his face and felt the fear Sherman exuded.

"Calm down, Sherman," Rebekka said gently. "We called you here to learn from this, not to punish you." Blastion started to object but Rebekka raised her hand to silence him and continued: "You are a good man Sherman, may this lesson make you better at palace security in the future. You may go, but take the body of Simon and find us another palace cat. We will deal with the android ourselves." Sherman Templas quickly scooped up the poisoned crab cakes and the limp cat and headed for the door.

When he was gone, Ellise put her had to her mouth to stifle a laugh. Even Blastion was smiling at the morbid humor of the whole situation. For none of them liked Simon the cat much, he had an evil temperament like his former owner Layton and would often act like he wanted to be petted and then bite and scratch you out of malice. He had done that once to Rebekka and she had turned her mind on him and he never bothered her again. But the rest were still victims of his sneaky deceptive evil. They had already discussed replacing him before this incident occurred.

Rebekka broke the silence by stating; "Pi, could you use some help around the palace? I think we could use a butler don't you?" Motioning to the still form of the android on the floor.

Pi smiled, "Yes that would be a lovely idea."

"Who," Rebekka asked, "were the ones who made and programed you?"

"Castor and Johnson Robotics," Pi answered. Rebekka asked Blastion to get them on the communication devise. As the screen came on, the face of a woman appeared, and Rebekka said.

"This is Queen Rebekka, I wish to speak to the one in charge of your company." The woman's eyes went wide and quickly another face was transmitted onto the screen.

"I am David Castor, may I help you Queen Rebekka?" Rebekka was glad the media had done their job and she did not have to explain who she was.

"Yes," she replied. "We have an androld that has shut down and needs repair and reprogramming."

"No problem," the man said, "I will send someone over right away. Are you at the palace?"

"Yes," Rebekka said, "but I wish something else from you."

The man turned back to the screen and said, "Yes anything you need."

"About fifteen years ago you programed some androids with a program that resulted in them developing emotions."

Now the face of David Castor narrowed, "How do you know about that?"

"Lets just say I know a couple of the androids." The surprise on the man's face was obvious.

"That is highly unusual since there were only a few and some of those are now out of service, and even Layton Teal did not know about our experiment," the man stated.

Rebekka got right to the point, "Do you still have the same programing available?"

"Yes, we have saved it and studied it over the years and we are no closer now to understanding why it caused Androids to have emotions than we did fifteen years ago."

"I want this android programed the same way as that small group years ago," Rebekka said. The man looked as if he were in a vise that was quickly closing in on him when he finally said.

"I would highly recommend against such programing."

"Why," Rebekka asked, "has any of those androids caused harm?"

"No, none of them has ever had a logic malfunction, but it is frightening to give androids emotions. We do not know the long term effects of such a program. This is the only reason we allowed those few to enter service, to see if they would cause harm or have some kind of logic collapse."

"I know for a fact the long term effects are stable and safe," replied Rebekka. "And I want this one programed exactly the same way you did the others fifteen years ago, is that clear?"

The man nodded and said, "It will be done as you request."

"Thank you," Rebekka said smiling, "you will be amply rewarded." When Rebekka turned her attention back to the others Pi was the first one to speak.

"Why do you want an android programed with emotions like me?"

Rebekka smiled and looking at Ellise said, "An android with emotions is much more interesting to be around, don't you agree Ellise?" Ellise nodded with a smile causing Pi to smile as well.

Blastion cleared his throat to get their attention. "What are you going to do about Max?" he asked.

"I think it is time we had another cabinet meeting," Rebekka replied. "Only invite Max fifteen minutes early so I can speak to him alone." Blastion looked alarmed by Rebekka's statement so she added, "Not fully alone, you and Ellise will be there, but without the other cabinet members present." This seemed to relax Blastion and he nodded and left.

The next day at the cabinet meeting Max showed up right at the time he had been told by Blastion. He entered and saw Ellise and Blastion seated at the conference table with Rebekka. He cautiously approached and sat down.

"Where are the other cabinet members he asked?"

"They will be along shortly," Rebekka said, "but first I wanted to discuss some business with you. It seems that someone tried to poison me with a gift of food at the palace."

Max just shrugged, "Anyone at the top is a target by the extreme fringes of our society."

Blastion then said, "Very few would have the resources to hide the trail of the assassin like it was."

"What are you getting at?" Max asked, still relaxed and amused.

Rebekka said simply; "I know this whole attempt at poisoning was set up by you Max."

"You cannot prove a thing," he said still relaxed.

"That is true," Rebekka said. "For if I could I would hang you like any other criminal. But I know you had something to do with it so I am going to fine you another billion dollars."

Max jumped to his feet, "You cannot do that he said as his face reddened."

"Yes I can," Rebekka shot back, "and the same conditions as the last fine apply."

Max looked sick, "You have reduced my net worth from six billion to four billion in less than two weeks."

Rebekka just smiled and said, "It will be reduced even more if there are any more attempts on my life, or else you had better pray they succeed."

At that moment John Martin arrived followed by the rest of the cabinet. They could all see that Max Bane was really flustered so John Martin asked.

"What is going on?"

"Oh nothing important," Rebekka stated. "Max and I were discussing finances, that is all."

When everyone was seated the meeting began. Rebekka turned to Chan Quon, minister of transportation first and asked.

"Are there any restrictions on the people of the empire to travel where they want?"

"Of course there are," Chan Quon stated. "People are allowed to travel to their work and home again with only one trip to a purchasing center a week. Layton saw this as an important tool to controlling the people."

Rebekka nodded and then said; "I want all restrictions on travel lifted. If they have the money to travel they should be able to go anywhere they wish." The cabinet was stunned, but no one argued. Next Rebekka turned to the minister of agriculture, Charlotte Frank and asked.

"Does the empire impose restrictions on those who provide our food?"

"Yes," Charlotte stated, "we do this to make sure everything that the people need is provided."

Rebekka nodded once again and stated, "Do you not think that the people will know what they want and need she asked? I want you to lift any restrictions on agriculture. I want it to be a free market. In fact I want all business to be based on a free market." Max Bane interjected in a polite way, refraining from jumping into the argument as he did before.

"Queen Rebekka, you must understand that by doing what you suppose will ruin the stable economy we have worked so hard to maintain."

"The fifty percent tax cut will help to stabilize the changes we are proposing in the economy. Any change of this magnitude will be difficult and the empire will falter at first, but it will recover. Now is the best time to make those changes with the tax break as a cushion."

The cabinet nodded at Rebekka's statement, so she continued. Next, Rebekka handed Esther Smith a small notebook outlining her desired changes in education. The minister of education waited patiently for Rebekka to summarize what was contained in the notes.

"I want education to stop its indoctrination of blind obedience to the state. Instead I want the basic tools taught that will enable people to think on their own without a state agenda. Facts without fabrication, is that clear?" Esther Smith nodded while clutching the notebook Rebekka had given her. It was clear that she did not like Rebekka's approach but would not argue the point either. At last she turned to John Martin, minister of defense and said.

"John Martin, you will make it clear that any service in the military is voluntary, not by conscription. Anyone wishing to leave military service can do so with two months severance pay." John Martin nodded smiling, for he had always hated the forced military service demanded by Layton Teal.

"Good," Rebekka stated, "I want all of these changes in force by the time taxes are due in two months time. This cabinet meeting is adjourned."

The cabinet all left except for John Martin who stayed behind to ask what the earlier discussion was about with Max Bane. Rebekka told him there had been an attempt on her life by very subtle poisoning. And if it were not for the deceased palace cat, Simon she would be dead. Nothing could be proven, but she knew it was Max Bane's doing so she had fined him another billion dollars. When

John Martin heard that, he exclaimed, "Do you have a death wish or what? Max will not set back while you siphon his personal wealth away."

"I know that," Rebekka replied, "but it will slow him down and make him plan the next attempt very carefully with the threat of losing more wealth." John Martin simply shook his head at Rebekka. "Time is what we need, John, if we are to change things," Rebekka said anxiously.

"Yes, but you are going too fast as it is."

"If I were to take it slow, I would be killed before I get anything accomplished. If I can hold out until the tax cut and freedoms are instituted we will have a chance to do some good."

John Martin nodded, "Be careful Rebekka, I don't want to lose a good friend."

She smiled at him and said, "I will."

Max Bane reached his headquarters and stormed in, "That woman has got to go!" His staff, corrupt and evil as he, reacted immediately.

"You want us to try and kill her boss?" one asked.

"No!" Max yelled. "I want you to protect her, understand?" He saw by their stunned silence they didn't so he began again. "She fined me one billion dollars for that poisoning attempt."

"No way could she have traced that to you boss," said a pudgy little man who was in charge of that attempt.

"She didn't have to, she just decided it was me," Max stated. "Now every attempt on her life even by some lousy stupid punk will cost me a billion dollars. We got to make sure there are no more attempts, understand? I can't afford to lose any more money. So I want you all to work overtime protecting this queen of ours from any attempts on her life."

Then you don't want to kill her?" asked a tall thin man.

"Of course I do," Max stated. "I just have to plan it very carefully to make sure we don't fail, is that clear? Now get out there and start watching our queen." They all began to scamper from the room as Max called to the pudgy little man.

"Arden, do you know of a great sharp shooter?"

"Yeah," the little man said, "we have used his services in the past, he's the best the military has got."

"Good," Max said, "I need him for my plans."

The time for the collection of taxes came, and to the peoples amazement Rebekka kept her word of a fifty percent tax cut. That, coupled with the new freedoms the people were given caused a great joy to echo throughout the empire. The press was singing her praises without any political prodding on her part. For the first time in many years people had hope of a better life instead of just existing. Her popularity was growing leaps and bounds with the people. Something else was growing as well, her pregnancy was almost to full term and the baby could come at any time now.

In the next week she met three times with the press and answered their questions as candidly as possible. The people did not think it strange that Rebekka was from the past, for time travel was a well known fact at that time. One straightforward question was: "Did the child she carry belong to Layton Teal?" Rebekka did not flinch at the question although it repulsed her.

"No," she said plainly. "You all know of my past. This week I have explained my strange speech to you, telling you I am from the past. The child I carry is my husband's, King Raven Kallestor."

"Do you miss your husband?" someone asked.

"Yes, very much so," Rebekka stated.

209

"Will you be going back to him soon?" Rebekka was sure the reporter had no idea how much that question pained her, but she answered anyway.

"I have much to do for the good of the people of this realm. When that is finished and the time is right I may return. Please, no more questions. I must retire for the day." The reporters respected her enough not to hound her, and if any reporter tried the rest headed him off.

The news business had boomed since the empire had relinquished it to the people. Ellise and Blastion escorted Rebekka back to the palace. Their new butler Simon (named after the departed cat, though no one told him that), waited for them at the door with a message for Rebekka from her doctor. It requested her presence every three days now that she was close to delivery.

Rebekka marveled at the change in people after the reforms were instituted. Her doctor who at first did his job for fear of his life, now seemed to be genuinely interested in her and the child's wellbeing. Send word if you will, Simon, that I will see him in three days. Simon left to contact the doctor and Rebekka sat in a comfortable chair to relax while the others gathered round to discuss what to do next in the empire. Pi was now a very real part of their discussions, giving her own input and treated like anyone else. She had become very fond of Rebekka, but was fiercely attached to Ellise, constantly worrying about her aging and health.

Ellise's aging had seemingly slowed down because she had reached maturity and didn't show the aging as much. But she still aged at an accelerated rate limiting her life span.

"What's our next plan for the empire?" Pi asked joyfully.

"The next step is to institute free elections of the empire's leaders by the people. When that is done, the empire will be back in the people's hands and I will resign."

"When do you want that to take place?" Blastion asked.

"A couple of months after the baby is born would be a good time," Rebekka said.

Blastion nodded and said, "I will begin the necessary press releases to accomplish that purpose." And then he said, "I never would have believed you could have accomplished this much in such a short time."

"I believe it is God's will that people be free," Rebekka said seriously. "If I am a tool for that to be done, then maybe it was God's purpose that I was taken to this place. His ways are far beyond our understanding and his plans transcend time." The room was once more silent as everyone contemplated her statements.

A tall thin man named Lance stood before Max Bane. "My spies have informed me that the queen will be seeing her doctor every three days now that she is close to delivery."

"Good," smiled Max Bane, "a dependable route will make it much easier." Max called the pudgy little man to his side and said.

"Arden, you and Lance get together with that sharp shooter and go over the route she will use to go to her doctor and take the queen out in three days, understand?" They did, for they had been planning this attempt for the last couple of months. They were certain as well that this time the attempt would not fail.

The time came for Rebekka to have her three day check up from her doctor. Blastion and Ellise always went with Rebekka to the doctor. Though Ellise was going because she would assist in the delivery, Blastion's attachment did not make sense to Rebekka. As she thought on Blastion's presence she began to realize that the only time he was not by her side was when she was safe inside the palace. Everywhere she went outside of the palace, Blastion was there with her.

As she was trying to sort this out in her mind for the reason why, their transportation stopped and they began to get out. Blastion exited first followed by Rebekka. He held out his hand to help her up for which she was grateful. As she stood and turned facing the street Blastion saw a small red dot, almost imperceptible to the eye in the middle of Rebekka's chest. In the instant he pushed her a bolt of light caught Rebekka in the shoulder. Faster than the eye could see a laser pistol appeared in Blastion's hand and with reflexes that come only with genetic engineering he swung around and took out the sniper before he could get off another shot. For any normal human it would have been an impossible shot, an incredible distance with a pistol. But Blastion had trained his whole life for situations just like this, plus the added fact that his pistol was not a normal laser pistol saved Rebekka's life.

As Rebekka was falling to the ground, the darkness closing in on her from the shock of being shot, a funny thought hit her about Blastion, his impossible reflexes and quick action reminded her of someone. As the darkness closed over her she realized Blastion reminded her of Raven.

As the light began to come back into Rebekka's eyes, a hospital room began to take shape around her. She recognized it by the ceiling and all the machines round about her. Her hands instinctively went to massage her stomach and she felt that it was flat.

"No," she screamed, "no."

Ellise was at her side immediately saying, "Its all right, Rebekka, everything is all right."

"My Baby," Rebekka wailed, "it was the only thing I had of Raven's with me."

"Your baby is fine," Ellise said quickly. "She is in the next room." Rebekka was still groggy from the anesthesia and it took a little time for Ellise's words to sink in.

"My baby is alive?" Rebekka asked again.

"Yes," Ellise said smiling, "she is doing just fine."

"She?" Rebekka asked. "Raven and I have a baby girl?"

"Yes," Ellise said again squeezing Rebekka's hand, "you have a healthy baby girl."

Rebekka closed her eyes and concentrating all of her mental powers shouted, "We have a baby girl Raven." She opened her eyes and said, "I want to see her." At that moment the her doctor came in.

"It is good to see you awake Rebekka." he said smiling. "We decided to take the baby fearing you would go into labor from the trauma of being shot in the shoulder. The lasers have knit your shoulder back together and in a few days you can go home. You are very lucky to be alive."

Rebekka started to remember what had happened, Blastion shoving her aside and feeling a bolt of lightning hit her shoulder, then darkness. She searched the room and found Blastion standing in the corner watching her. At that moment Ellise came into the room holding Rebekka's baby. She placed her gently in Rebekka's arms and stepped back. Blastion came closer to see the child as well, a smile on his face.

"What are you going to call her?" Ellise wanted to know. "We never did discuss names before for your child."

Rebekka smiled down at her daughter and said. "Her name is Adriell Kallestor."

"What a pretty name," Ellise said. "I have never heard anything like it before." Rebekka smiled for she had named her daughter after the dearest friends of her past, Andrew and Lorriel Crestlaw.

After holding the baby for a while Ellise took her back and said. "You must rest Rebekka and get well so you can care for your baby." Rebekka only nodded for she was very tired and soon fell into a restful deep sleep.

When Rebekka awoke the next day she felt much better and sat up as soon as she was awake. She moved her shoulder that had been shot and realized the doctors of this time could heal a person much faster than in her days. She looked around the room and there stood Blastion in the same place he was the day before.

She looked at him a moment and said, "You were not merely a personal aid to Layton Teal were you?" He smiled and shook his head no. "I have only seen one person who had reflexes like you have and that was my husband, Raven Kallestor. He inherited those reflexes from his ancestor Uriah Kallestor." At the mention of the name Uriah, Blastion's mouth fell open in such a way that Rebekka had to laugh.

"You know of Uriah," Blastion said amazed.

Rebekka nodded, "That little girl is a direct descendant of Uriah, and I am Amnon's descendant." Blastion could not believe it, his eyes filled with tears from the wonder of it all sinking in.

"Little Adriell is a long removed relative of mine," he said shaking his head in wonder.

Now Rebekka's mouth dropped open, "What are you saying Blastion?"

He smiled now having the upper hand once again as he explained. "Uriah and I are brothers." Rebekka was shocked, but it was all making sense now, the reflexes that the family possessed. "We were both genetically engineered by Layton Teal to be his body guards. Everyone knew that Uriah was Layton's body guard, but no one knew of me, I was to be his backup in case Uriah failed somehow. He gave us different names so no one would know we were related. I always envied Uriah for finding a way to leave Layton and find love. I never had the courage to do that. But now I see the fruit of his labor in a way down the line niece."

Rebekka smiled at him and said; "Your are not the fearful little aid people think you are." Rebekka said that as a statement, not a question. "I always knew there was something special about you Blastion, despite your act."

He laughed, "It was part of the cover, but I have been doing it so long that it is quite easy for me now."

"Well," Rebekka said, "you don't have to act like that any longer, Layton's gone."

Blastion just smiled and said, "I better bring you that great niece of mine." As Blastion was returning with little Adriell, Ellise and Pi entered the room.

"What are you doing with the baby?" Ellise said with a puzzled expression on her face. That was the last thing she expected Blastion to do, hold a baby.

"I'm an uncle," was all he said as he took the baby to Rebekka.

Ellise looked at Rebekka and mouthed the words, "What?"

"I'll tell you later," Rebekka said. Right now it brought her comfort to know that an ancestor of her daughter was there to look out for them both. "That reminds me," Rebekka said, "Blastion, thanks for saving my life."

He smiled and said, "If I knew what I know now I would have given my life for you and little Adriell."

Pi looked at Blastion and said with a laugh, "What is this little Adriell stuff, have you gone soft on us or what?"

"I guess I have," Blastion said smiling.

At that moment the doctor entered the room and asked how Rebekka was feeling.

"Better," Rebekka said. "Can I go home now?"

"You are not scheduled for release until tomorrow," the doctor stated. "Maybe it would be best to wait until then." Now Blastion was once again all business.

"If you have scheduled her for release tomorrow others might know. Can she leave right now?"

"Yes, I believe she can," the doctor said, "but I want to follow up on her."

"Fine," Blastion said, "come to the palace, she will be safe there." The doctor nodded, now understanding that someone had know of her scheduled appointment a couple of days ago.

"I will come to see you tomorrow," he said smiling. Rebekka dressed and Ellise gathered up Adriell and they headed for the entrance to the hospital. The hallways were filled with the palace guard, watching her and keeping her safe.

"Did you ask all of them to come?" Rebekka whispered to Blastion.

"No, they came on their own. Seems you have had a great influence on them, much different than Layton ever had." They were smiling and wishing her well as she passed. They were now forming ranks in front of her as well as behind. She then realized it would take a great effort to get through to her with all the guards around. Transportation was waiting outside and she was ushered into it and soon they were heading to the palace.

Blastion spoke to Rebekka, "The empire is outraged by the attempt on your life. If we were to even drop the name of Max Bane casually, they would burn him at the stake immediately."

"You and I know who did this," Rebekka stated. "But the best way for him to be defeated is in the election."

"As you wish," Blastion said, "but it still would be great to see him burn."

Rebekka glanced sideways at Blastion and thought: "He really does mean that. I sure am glad he is on our side, knowing now just how deadly he really is."

Max Bane was livid, "How could you have failed you little weasel, Arden?"

"I don't know," Arden said trembling. "Someone took out the sniper before he could finish off the queen. None of us knows how it was done."

Max just growled again, "I guess I will have to do this myself." As he was leaving he spoke to the tall man. "Lance, take care of the little weasel, make him pay." Lance just nodded as he turned back toward the pudgy little man trembling in the center of the room.

Rebekka stayed within the palace for the next two months, having plenty of time for affairs of state since Ellise and Pi both enjoyed taking care of Adriell. John Martin came by to see how she was doing several times, and she appreciated his visits. He was a kind man and always cheered her with his warmth. On his fourth visit, Rebekka told him it was time for the people to choose their own leaders. John Martin nodded, knowing it was the goal of Rebekka for the people of the empire.
"I will call a cabinet meeting," John said as he left.

When the cabinet was assembled with Rebekka in her seat once more, John Martin this time began the meeting.
"I have called this meeting at the request of Queen Rebekka to inform you that in a short time she will be leaving her position." John Martin could see genuine concern from Chan Quon and Charlotte Frank at this news, but Max Bane and Esther Smith just sat passively still. Rebekka stared at Max with hard eyes, both knowing who had tried to kill her and her child. But even then she could not get a response from him. She felt like pulling a dirty trick on him and yelling at him in Layton's voice, but that was over. She no longer needed Layton's support to rule this empire, she had the support of the people. When John Martin finished Rebekka rose and spoke.
"Minister Martin is correct that I will soon be resigning my position as head of the empire. Before I do though, there is one more item of business that needs to be taken care of." At that statement, Rebekka saw Max Bane raise his eyebrows a little but that was all. "All along my goal has been to give the empire back to its people. Too long it has been run by tyranny and oppression. In order to do that, our leadership must be voted upon by the people of this empire."
"You mean," Chan Quon said, "you are going to hold an election for our positions?"
"Yes," Rebekka said smiling, "and those of you who are worthy will retain your positions I am sure."
"Are you going to run?" asked Charlotte Frank.
"No," Rebekka said, "my time will be over once the elections are over. Someone else will have my position, but only by the will of the people." At this statement Max Bane began to laugh. Everyone turned to see what was so funny, but he was not looking at anyone in particular.
He then turned to Rebekka and said, "Layton Teal never chose you to be ruler in his place did he?"
Rebekka smiled, "No he did not. In fact I was Layton's prisoner, sent to this time with Ellise. We were to return in four days but I convinced Ellise not to go and we stranded Layton in the past. For

without Ellise, he cannot return. It is too late for Layton Teal, he is history."

"We all heard him speak to us," Esther Smith stated. "I know that was Layton."

Rebekka smiled again and said, "I am a telepath and I spoke with Layton's voice to your minds." Everyone was silent except for the slight laugh of Max Bane.

"We cannot allow a public vote," he said. "Why in the world would you want to give the people that kind of power?"

"So another tyrant like Layton Teal or you will not come to power, or take it by force."

"Well," Max Bane said, "it is time this charade ends." With that he stood up with a gun in his hand pointing it at Rebekka. John Martin clenched his teeth, he should have seen this coming. Max Bane smiled as his finger began to tighten on the trigger.

No one saw when Blastion drew his pistol or even aimed it. All they saw was a flash of light that caught Max Bane in the chest sending him flying backwards to the floor in smoldering death. Blastion could have shot Max in the arm, or even his gun, but he decided he had seen more than his share of evil, power hungry men in his lifetime. It took everyone a few seconds to realize what had happened. John Martin looked at the former meek and mild Blastion, now realizing just how deadly he really was. Blastion caught his eye and John Martin just nodded his approval for what he had done.

Rebekka stood calmly and said, "We will take a short recess and reconvene the cabinet in half an hour."

After the cabinet came together again, everyone decided it was in the best interest of the empire to have free elections.

"What are we going to do about Max Bane's death?" Esther Smith asked.

"Tell the people the truth," Rebekka said. "The truth is always the best for everyone."

"They may believe the story is fabricated, though with such public opinion on your side I doubt that it will matter," spoke Chan.

Blastion now spoke, "They will see the truth, pointing to the cameras in the corners of the room, our meetings are always recorded." He then produced the document that all the cabinet signed to bind the ruling body of the empire to elections every four years. They then adjourned the meeting and Rebekka held a press conference to inform the people of the coming elections.

The people were saddened by the announcement that Rebekka was resigning as the head of state, but also rejoiced that they now had such freedom to choose their leaders. As the press conference was ending Rebekka admonished the people of the empire with these words:

"Be careful never to take the freedoms you have gained for granted. As they have been given to you they can also be taken away. Choose your leaders wisely and choose those who believe in freedom and personal responsibility. For if you trade your freedom for the promise of security, you will end up with tyranny again. Do not let fear rule your decisions for freedom is more important than life. Remember, this kind of freedom only comes through sacrifice. Do not depend upon the state to provide for you, it is your own responsibility. If you begin to choose leaders that promise to give you provisions and reward, you will find that free things from the state are not as free as you think and they always come with a price. That price will come with the erosion of the freedoms you now have been given and will lead to your enslavement once again. The enslavement of a populace always takes place by the apathy and permission of its people. Choose leaders who will guard this freedom more than their political careers and you may keep this freedom for a very long time. But be warned, I and others may not be here to guard these freedoms for you, it is your responsibility, so be vigilant. May the empire prosper in its new found freedom."

For weeks after Rebekka's speech, the press published and promoted her words to the populace. So powerful were her words that many believed it should become part of the state's oaths of office for the future leaders who would be elected. In any case the press did all it could to make sure her words would be remembered by the people.

The elections took place three months later. John Martin was named as the new head of state. Sherman Templas was named the new minister of defense. Chan Quon and Charlotte Frank both retained their seats, but Esther Smith was replaced by Calvin Hart who had championed education reform away from indoctrination. Ellise retained her position as Chancellor and moved back to her old apartment with Rebekka, Adriell and Pi. Simon stayed on to help in the palace where John Martin would now stay. He had tried to persuade Rebekka to stay as well, for their was ample room at the palace. When she still insisted on leaving, John Martin took her aside and in his most humble tone said.

"Since you are stuck here in our time, would you consider being my wife?" Rebekka saw how he really meant this, so her reply was very gentle.

"John, there is no other man I would rather be with in this time than you. But even though in our time here King Raven is dead, in my time he is still alive. I could never devote myself to another man while in my heart my husband is still alive. You deserve someone who will devote themselves to you, and you alone. As for me I have but one love to give, and that will forever be given to Raven."

"I understand," John Martin said. And somehow he really did. That is what made Rebekka special, her devotion to principal and determined conviction to stand by her decisions. He had known heroes in his day, but none would ever rank as high in his eyes as the woman he would always call Queen Rebekka.

Chapter 9
Reunion

"Nothing is sweeter than the reunion of heats separated by circumstances or time"

> --The Wisdom of Fathers

FIFTEEN YEARS LATER......

"You are getting old and slow," the young man said as two swords clashed in practiced battle. Raven chuckled at his son Edward's statement. If he pulled out all the stops he could disarm Edward easily, and that would not be as beneficial for him as learning to defend against such an unorthodox attack. Back and forth they went, thrusting and parrying, move countered with move. Raven had followed the exact training formula that Master Fields had used so successfully on him.

"After all, one does not improve on the master," Raven thought. He did miss Master Fields, but knew that his whole energy was now being poured into another trainee, young Robert Rollins who would take Master Field's place as the royal weapons master after Master Fields passed on. When Master Fields thought Robert was ready, he would bring him to the royal court and present him to the King. From that day forward Robert Rollins would be known as Master Rollins to everyone in the kingdom.

His lack of attention and thought almost caused him to be disarmed by Edward. Just as Raven was loosing his balance and was about to lose his sword he leaped into the air spinning backwards and landed on the top rim of the courtyard fountain.

How does he do that? Edward thought. As Raven spun back down into the courtyard with sword ready, Edward smiled. He thought he had his father that time, backed up against the fountain and nowhere to go and then he pulls those impossible stunts. Edward knew his father was special, no one in the kingdom could do the things the King could. And yet he was gaining every day in his great goal of being like his father.

Raven watched his son's bewildered face with amusement. Years ago Raven had feared his son would not inherit his reflexes. His training responses seemed clumsy and unorganized. It took great patience on his part not to force too much on his son in those early years of training. When he had almost given up hope that Edward would be blessed as he was, the hidden genetics bounded forth. Edward's abilities did not come to him as fast as Raven's had, but they were growing nonetheless. If he kept improving, Raven had hopes he would equal him someday. Edward was already older than Raven had been when he had fought in the great Wickshield war.

"Enough!" Raven said as he stepped in and disarmed his son handily. "You are gaining more and more every day. Soon you will catch up to me in the art of battle."

Edward smiled, "I think you will best me until the day you enter the grave."

Raven put his hand on the strong shoulders of his son and thought; "I wish you were here Rebekka, to see the great man our son has become."

"Let us go to the balcony and talk of the kingdom," Raven said. Edward nodded, he liked the times of instruction about the governing of the kingdom.

Raven was always perplexed at his son's willingness to listen and be instructed in the proper way a king should govern his people. When he and been growing up, he thought all the kingdom stuff boring until he was thrust into the middle of it all by circumstances. Not so with Edward, he eagerly waited each instruction and lesson about the kingdom. Raven did not know that his mother Joanna had a great part in Edward's interest. For she often took Edward on walks when he was young and told him he should listen and observe his father who had become the greatest king Glenfair had ever had. To see if he could understand what made the king great in the eyes of the people. She kept prodding his curiosity, and guiding his questions until it became the desire of his life to be admired like his father by his subjects.

Edward had come to realize in these last few years that the people of this fair land loved their king. And finally he was coming to understand why by hearing all the stories others told of his father. If Edward were to describe his father's reign in a short statement, it could be summed up in this way; the King sacrificed himself for others. He had been told many times by Duke Andrew Crestlaw and Duke Mason Zandel of the sacrifices his father had made for the kingdom. He wanted to be like that, to live his life for the people's good.

Raven knew his son's desire, and was proud that the land would get another good king after his departure. When they reached the balcony he said to Edward as they looked at the courtyard below.

"You are living up to your uncle's namesake, Edward. You will be a great king as he would have been."

Edward looked at his father before asking, "If your brother would not have died, he would be King instead of you. Would that bother you if he were?"

Raven smiled, "No, not at all. Edward would have been a great king and I would still have married your mother and had you."

Edward smiled for he could see that his father could mention his mother Rebekka, without the severe pain and guilt he used to have. Time had eased some of the pain out of the mention of her, so his father could enjoy the memories he had of her. For Edward though, her memory seemed to be far away and out of reach. He could see her face sometimes, but it grew dimmer with the passing years.

All of a sudden they were shaken out of their thoughts by a rider that came galloping into the courtyard, screeching to a halt and then dismounting. Raven drew his sword and threw it toward the rider. The sword spun and stuck into the ground at the rider's feet causing him to jump and look up to see where it had come from. When he saw the King on the balcony he grabbed the sword and headed up to speak to him.

Edward just shook his head, what son could not enjoy having a father who pulled such outrageous stunts. The man came onto the balcony, handed the King back his sword and bowed.

When he rose he said puffing, "I bring news from the Crestlaw Dukeship. Duke Crestlaw begs your presence quickly for your sister Lorriel's health is fading." Raven and Edward looked at each other for a moment and then quickly headed for the stables.

An old woman came into the room where Adriell and Rebekka were dressing.

"Hurry up," the old voice rasped, "or you will be late for the ceremony."

Rebekka turned and smiled, "You know Ellise that I really do not want to go. I feel strange about this whole thing. Everyone had a part in the changes that took place in Layton's empire. You, John Martin, Blastion and Pi...." But before she could finish Ellise interrupted her.

"But none more than you, dear Rebekka."

Adriell laughed and said, "Come on mother, this will be fun."

At that moment Pi entered the room and said, "It is time for us to go."

Adriell spoke to her mother's mind, "Don't be a spoil sport mother, in school all the teachers talk about the freedoms you helped to give us."

"Ok," Rebekka spoke to Adriell's mind, "lets get this over with."

They could have walked to the civic center of the city for it was not far. But Ellise was an old woman now because of the accelerated aging acting upon her so they took the transportation that waited for them downstairs.

At the civic center a dignitary dressed in medals of distinguished service approached their vehicle and opened the door for them, it was John Martin. He escorted them to their places of honor and the ceremony began.

The new head of state elected by the people after John Martin refused to run for a fourth term stood to address the assembly.

"Today," he said, "we honor a great person who through bravery and self sacrifice has changed our empire forever. Her only goal was to give the empire back to its people so they could live free from oppression and tyranny. With that goal accomplished, she relinquished her position as head of state to the elected officials by the will of the people. Never have I met someone who served others as graciously as her. To me she will always be a queen, may I present to you Queen Rebekka!"

The crowd stood and roared with deafening applause as a canvas was pulled down to reveal a statue in the center of the civic center of Queen Rebekka. She walked to podium and immediately the crowd quieted for her.

"Citizens of the empire, I am greatly honored by your generous tribute to me this day. Only I alone am not responsible for the freedoms you now have today. Others have made sacrifices and have supported this as well. John Martin who we all love as the first elected head of state. Chancellor Ellise who is suffering her own consequences of sacrifice for the empire and our current head of state, Blastion Astmos." The crowd applauded loudly once again, and when they were quiet Rebekka continued.

"Never take your freedom for granted. As it has been given back to you it can be taken away. True freedom is always maintained through personal sacrifice, if not your own then someone else's. May God grant you the power to preserve this freedom for years to come, thank you." The people applauded with a standing ovation as Rebekka headed back toward John Martin and Ellise. She could see her daughter was beaming with pride at the recognition her mother deserved.

Adriell looked at her mother, she was a Queen, everyone could see that. From the time she was little her mother had told her stories about her past life and her father. They seemed to her as fairy tales, a king with his dukes fighting evil for the safety of their kingdom. It was hard for her to grasp the other life her mother had experienced in that long ago kingdom she called Glenfair. The thing that made it so romantic was her father was a great king in this land, the greatest king they ever had her mother told her. That's what made this day so exciting. Blastion and the others had told her of the secret outing they had planned as part of this celebration. She watched as her friends circled around her congratulating her. Then everyone was silent with funny smiles on their faces and Rebekka knew immediately that something was up.

"All right," she said, "what is going on?"

Blastion smiled and said, "We have a surprise for you but you must come with us."

Rebekka shook her head and said. "No, I have had enough for one day."

John Martin laughed when he said. "This you will appreciate believe me."

"Lead the way then," Rebekka said to the excited group. They led her to a vehicle and getting inside they headed for the middle of the valley.

"Where are we going?" Rebekka asked Blastion who only smiled back in answer. It did not take long for them to reach their destination and the vehicle stopped. When they all got out Rebekka realized now where they were.

"The king's castle," Rebekka said excitedly. "I did not know that there would be so much of it left after three thousand years."

"There wasn't," Blastion said to Rebekka. "A couple of years ago I commissioned some archeologists to restore this old castle and they have been working on it ever since. I apologize, that they have only gotten it half finished." Rebekka stood frozen, looking at the partially restored castle that had once been her home when she whirled on her friends exclaiming.

"This is wonderful, thank you."

Adriell came up to her mother and asked. "Mother why did you never bring me here in all these years?"

"I was afraid, that it would bring me pain to see the ruins of my former home, but now all I have is joy."

"Come," Rebekka said to Adriell, "and I will give you a tour of where I used to live." As they started into the courtyard, an archeologist came to Blastion and talked with him excitedly. John Martin, Blastion, Pi and Ellise all went with him to view their latest find in the center of the courtyard. Rebekka did not notice their absence because she was deep in nostalgia telling her daughter all that had taken place within the walls of the castle. She was looking up and pointing to the partially restored balcony when she heard her name being called. She turned to look and her friends were motioning for her to come over to where they were gathered about the ruins of the old fountain. As she approached she heard the archeologist telling Blastion that this very day they had begun to restore the old fountain.

"We dug this stone out and began to set it back in place when we realized there was a metal casting in its front. We cleaned it off and were excited to see how well it has weathered the centuries." Rebekka pushed forward through her friends and saw a gold colored casting embedded in the rock. She peered closer and began to read:

To the Queen who willingly sacrificed herself to save the kingdom. We will always remember you in our hearts as the greatest of Glenfair's Queens. May you prosper wherever you have gone.
Love Raven

Rebekka fell to her knees in shock, after three thousand years a message from Raven had survived to speak to her.

Adriell came up and asked. "What's wrong mother?"

"This message," Rebekka said pointing to the gold casting, "was written by your father." Adriell bent forward and read the writing, then she looked at her mother and saw that she was visibly shaken.

The archeologist was confused until John Martin explained to him that the queen mentioned in the inscription was the one kneeling on the ground in front of the casting.

Adriell took her mother's hand and kneeling down beside her said.

"I wish we could go back and see father." Ellise was listening to the conversation and tears came to her eyes to see the old wounds opened again for Rebekka. She stepped back and whispered to John Martin, he nodded for Blastion and Pi to join them a ways off in conversation. Blastion nodded and left quickly while the others waited for Rebekka and Adriell to finish their thoughts of the past. Finally Rebekka rose and faced the others.

"How can I thank you for bringing me here? she said. "It means more than you will ever know." A visible relief could be seen in the group who had mixed emotions about Rebekka's response to the inscription. She began to tell them of all the wonderful gatherings they used to have in this courtyard. She talked of the games and competitions, the feasts and then looking at the partially restored balcony she paused. Looking at Adriell she saw wonder in her daughter's eyes and asked what was wrong?

"Nothing," Adriell said, "you make this all sound so real, so alive. It must have been the best of times from the way you tell it."

"It was," Rebekka said, remembering the double wedding that took place on that balcony. Rebekka looked around and noticed that Blastion was missing. "Where is Blastion?" Rebekka asked.

"He will be back in a short time," John Martin said. Rebekka took them around the castle explaining what took place in this room and that, the archeologists following along taking notes furiously. The secret passages were no longer secret as their hallways and entrances were now exposed by the ravages of time.

They finally worked their way back out to the courtyard where Blastion was waiting for them. When they approached he spoke only to Ellise.

"Are you sure?"

Ellise took the bag from him and opened it. Inside were the amplifiers that allowed Ellise to take long trips in time. She took one out and handed it to Rebekka who looked at it and said.

"We cannot go back Ellise, it may harm you more."

Ellise shook her head, "My life is almost over," she said, "please let me do this for you."

"What about Layton?" Rebekka asked.

"What about him?" Ellise said sarcastically. "What can he do to an old woman anyway? Please Rebekka, in another month I will not have the strength to take you anywhere in time. Let me return to you some of what you have given us. We all know your heart has always been there, it never left." Rebekka looked at the rest and they were smiling and then she heard crying. Adriell was making small sobs and it smote Rebekka's heart.

"Oh Adriell," Rebekka said with compassion. "This is the only home you have known. I will not force you to go and I will not leave you."

"No Mother," Adriell said, "I have wanted to go see father and Edward my whole life, I just can't believe it is really possible."

Rebekka hugged her and said to Ellise, "Are you sure?"

"Yes," Ellise said, "I want to do this."

"Hold it," Pi said, "you are not going anywhere without me Ellise. Besides, I have become very attached to Rebekka and Adriell, I helped raise her."

Ellise nodded and reached into the bag and handed Pi an amplifier, and gave one to Adriell as well. Then taking one for herself she showed them how to turn them on. Blastion came forward and hugged Rebekka, and then embraced Adriell with a strong compassionate hug.

"I will miss you my niece," he said.

"I will miss you too uncle Blastion."

John Martin looked at Rebekka and smiling said, "Thank you for changing our world, Queen Rebekka."

Ellise then spoke: "Do you want me to take you to the same time and place you left?"

"Heaven's no," Rebekka said laughing. "I left there pregnant and cannot return with a fifteen year old. No take us fifteen years into the future from that point and to the south of the front of this castle."

"Why there? Ellise asked.

"There is a graveyard there and I want to make sure Raven is not dead before I go marching into the castle looking for him."

Ellise nodded, took a deep breath and began to concentrate. Their surroundings began to fade away as the journey back in time began.

Raven and Edward got to the Crestlaw Dukeship as fast as they could. They had taken an extra horse a piece to make the trip as quickly as possible. When they galloped into the courtyard of the castle, there were already men there waiting to take their horses and others awaited to usher them into the castle. They hurried into the room where Lorriel was lying on a bed with Andrew kneeling at her side. When Andrew saw Raven enter he said.

"Thank you for coming my dear friend, Lorriel has been asking for you." Raven came beside Lorriel, her accelerated aging made her look like an old woman, and Raven could tell she was failing.

He bent close and said, "Lorriel, it is Raven, I am here."

Lorriel smiled and said, "Oh Raven, I am so glad you have come. I wanted to tell you before my passing that I regret but one thing."

Raven had tears in his eyes when he asked, "What do you regret dear sister?"

"I regret that I could not bring Rebekka back for you." And before anyone could say anything she continued; "Thank you for making it possible for me to marry Andrew, the light of my life. I have two beautiful children, what more could I ask for? My son, Jason, come near please." Jason came near to his mother and waited.

"Is little Edward here?" (she always called him that)

"I am here aunt Lorriel," Edward stated.

"Then come, each of you and take each other's hands and swear that you will each sacrifice your life for the other as good friends will do, like the friendship of your two fathers."

They looked at each other and said: "We swear." They were waiting in the silence for Lorriel to say something more, but those were the last words she uttered.

When everyone realized that Lorriel was gone, Raven looked at Andrew. Their eyes met, and for a moment they searched the depths of each other's souls, sharing grief that only the closest of friends could share. Finally Andrew closed his eyes in an effort to hold back the tears. Raven came to him then and embraced him and said.

"Why do you forbear my friend?" Andrew still kept his eyes closed in an effort to control his emotion while saying.

"It is not fitting to show grief in your presence. Even though her life was shortened, I had her much longer than you had Rebekka."

This tore at Raven's heart and all he could say was, "It is fitting my friend," before he himself began to weep. A dam burst within Andrew and he could not hold back the grief that he had guarded so closely.

When it came he realized he no longer wanted to hold back. He needed this, and he needed his closest earthly friend for comfort.

The next morning Raven, Edward, and the Crestlaws journeyed toward the King's castle with the body of Lorriel. Raven had requested that she be buried in the King's cemetery with the rest of his family. Andrew consented with one condition, that he too could be laid to rest along side of Lorriel when his time came.

To that request Raven assented saying, "You are as much family as any of us, it shall be done." During the trip to the king's castle Raven and Andrew took the opportunity to explain to their sons why they were such good friends. They thought that if they both understood the magnitude of what they had went through together their sons could honor Lorriel's last request better. The boys listened intently, constrained to do so by their promise. Much was shared and the two young men marveled at what their fathers had gone through together. Some of the stories were old ones they knew, but others were new and perplexing, especially those of the ancients. For both Raven and Andrew had decided to wait until this agreed time to tell their sons the secrets very few knew about.

Raven Kallestor stood by a fresh grave on this crisp fall day. The funeral had just finished. Everyone else had left. Only five remained at the grave: two young men, a young lady, and two older men weathered by time and the trials they endured. One had been blond but now was mostly white, and the other once had black hair but now it was peppered with gray, accenting the gray beard the King wore.

Raven turned to Andrew and said, "I am sorry. I know how you feel to lose someone so close."

"Do not be," replied Andrew, "you gave me the best years of my life, making it possible for me to marry your sister."

The two young men were Raven and Andrew's sons and they were the best of friends. The young lady was Lorriel's daughter, who, like her mother possessed an extraordinary gift. Raven had just finished telling them how it all started, the Crestlaw and Kallestor friendship, and why they should be friends forever, like their parents. Soon they would give their sons the rings they each wore. For now, they waited patiently with tears in their eyes for this chapter in their lives to close.

The king knelt down and placed a single white rose on the grave and thought, "When my time comes, will anyone place a single white rose on my grave? I hope it will be so..."

As Raven stood and looked at the graves of his father and mother, brother and sister a feeling he had not experienced in a long while crept into his soul. It was soothing and loving, a soft presence in his mind. Raven stiffened, frozen in place as a million emotions raced through him at once.

Then a soft voice came into his mind saying, "Raven, I have returned." He whirled around and saw four women standing at the gate of the cemetery. The others followed Raven's gaze to where the four women stood. He shouted her name and ran to her as she in turn stepped forward from the others to meet his embrace. Nothing was said, only tears streamed down their faces as they held each other. When Andrew and the others joined them, Rebekka pulled away to look into Andrew's face. What she saw there made her heart sink and she knew the grave was Lorriel's.

She came forward and hugged Andrew saying, "I am sorry, I am too late." Andrew withdrew from her embrace so she could see him smile as he said.

"You bring us joy in our sorrow by your return, do not be sorry." Rebekka looked at Raven with pleading eyes and he nodded for her to go to the grave. As she went, Edward started after her but Raven held his arm.

"Give her a few minutes alone at the grave, Edward, they were the best of friends and loved each other dearly." Raven then turned back to the others standing there and spoke first to the old woman.

"You were the young girl who took Rebekka away years ago, were you not?"

The old woman said with shock, "How did you know?"

"I knew the time travel would make you old as it did to my sister, Lorriel. Let me thank you for bringing her back to us."

"You are not angry with me?" Ellise said.

"No," Raven said calmly, "you were young and those were terrible circumstances for anyone to be in." Before Ellise could answer, Raven turned to the young lady standing beside Ellise and said.

"You must be my daughter."

"How do you know that?" Adriell asked. At that moment Rebekka joined them wiping the tears from her eyes. Raven smiled at his daughter and said.

"Well, first of all your mother left here pregnant. And secondly she told me she had a daughter."

Now Rebekka was shocked, "How could I have told you?"

"Three times our minds touched briefly in the first months of your absence."

"How," Rebekka asked, "is that possible separated by such time?"

"I do not know," answered Raven, "but I know it was you." Rebekka looked over her shoulder nervously and asked.

"Where is Layton Teal?"

"I killed him three days after you disappeared. I am sorry I prevented you from coming back for all these years," Raven said sadly. "I did it for the safety of us, and for all of the kingdom. I hope you can forgive me."

"I could have come back," was all Rebekka said.

"What do you mean?" asked Raven.

Rebekka looked at him sadly, "I convinced Ellise not to return in four days as Layton had commanded her. I felt the ancients would be safe if he could not travel in time. By not returning we effectively stranded Layton here in our time. I always felt guilty for what I felt Layton might do to everyone when he found out he was stuck here. I am so sorry Raven, if I had known he was dead I would have returned in four days." Neither of them spoke after that, and Andrew finally broke the silence.

"It seems the both of you made very hard decisions in the best interest of the whole kingdom."

Rebekka asked Raven then, "How did you kill Layton Teal?"

"That is a long story I will tell you some other time," Raven said. "Let me just say we could not have done it without the help of the ancients, our ancestors." Rebekka's eyes went wide at the mention of the ancestors helping them, so Raven explained.

"Lorriel took us back in time to meet them and learn how we could defeat Layton. Because of that she aged very quickly..." Rebekka held up her hand for Raven to stop for she saw how much this pained Andrew to remember. Raven paused and then said one more thing; "Lorriel saved us all by her sacrifice, it was she who really defeated Layton. But enough of this, you have a son that is a man now." Edward held out his arms and Rebekka embraced him.

"Oh Edward," she said, "you have really grown up. I want you to meet your sister, Adriell." Edward started to shake Adriell's hand but Adriell rushed forward and wrapped her arms around him in a big hug.

"It is the answer to my prayers to finally meet my brother," Adriell said. And then looking at Raven said, "And my father." She came to Raven and hugged him as well. While Raven held her he started crying again, he could not believe that his arms were finally holding the daughter he thought he would never see.

"We have a lot of catching up to do," Raven said. "In the castle are refreshments and others that will rejoice to know of your return." They headed for the castle and as they walked holding hands, Raven asked Rebekka.

"Adriell is a wonderful name, how ever did you choose it?"

Rebekka laughed, "Think Raven, what does the name sound like."

Raven thought for a moment and then a smile came upon his face.

"Like Andrew and Lorriel combined. What a marvelous wit you have about you," Raven laughed.

When they entered the great hall Raven made the announcement right away. In our grief this day, God has sent someone to cheer our hearts. The Queen and her daughter have returned. There were audible gasps from the crowd, for many had come to the funeral and were having refreshments in the great hall while the close family said their last farewell.

Rebekka caught the eye of a man she knew right away to be her younger brother Gregory. Beside him was an old man that leaned on a staff. She ran up to them and hugged Gregory, then kneeled in front of her father. She could see his eyes were dim and there were tears streaming down his cheeks as he asked in almost a whisper.

"Is it you my daughter, is it really you?"

"Yes it is, father," Rebekka answered. "And you have a granddaughter named Adriell." Rebekka motioned for Adriell to get closer to her grandfather as he held out his hands.

"Come here child," he said. Bandon let his hands move over Adriell's hair, and then to her hands that he held lovingly.

"Even though I cannot see well," Bandon replied, "I can tell you are very beautiful."

Adriell blushed, "Oh grandfather, you are such a tease!"

Bandon smiled, "She is like you, Rebekka."

Rebekka took his hands and said, "I have a very special gift for you father since your eyes are not what they used to be. Calm your mind and let me speak to your mind and I will show you." Rebekka closed her eyes and not only spoke to Bandon's mind, she shared her visual memories of Adriell growing up. Her birth, first birthday, and childhood flashed before Bandon's mind in vivid color and sound, and when Rebekka was finished she had shown Bandon most of Adriell's life. Tears once again streaked down Bandon's face as he spoke.

"How did you do that my daughter?"

"I really do not know," Rebekka said. "It was something I thought of just now to do for you."

Bandon smiled and said, "Now I can enter the grave in peace since I have seen that which I have missed." With the help of his staff he stood with effort and said to Gregory, "Come we must be heading home."

Gregory looked at Rebekka and said, "Come see us soon."

Rebekka nodded, "We will."

Rebekka took Adriell's hand and said, "Come out onto the balcony with me, there is someone special you must meet." When they were outside Adriell was puzzled because there was not one soul on the balcony. Rebekka saw her puzzling look and said.

"Join my mind."

Adriell did speaking to her mind, "I am here mother."

"Stay with me as I take you to meet someone," Rebekka's thoughts echoed in Adriell's mind.

"Andronicus?" Rebekka questioned, and almost immediately came the answer.

"Welcome home," Andronicus said. "When I detected the time shift I hoped it was you. I had a hard time refraining from contacting you, but I knew you needed time to properly greet Raven and Edward. I have missed the touch of your mind immensely these past years."

"I have yours as well," Rebekka echoed. "There is someone here I want you to meet."

A new voice came to Andronicus' mind, "Hello Mr. Andronicus, my name is Adriell and I am Rebekka's daughter."

"How wonderful to meet you," Andronicus said.

"He is an android," Rebekka told Adriell.

"Are you sure she can...of course she can understand," laughed Andronicus. "She is from the future and knows all about androids. Do come and see me when you can."

"We will," Rebekka said. "But until we come I will speak to you every day."

"Me too," the soft, little voice chimed in "Now that I know what your mind sounds like I can talk to you whenever I want."

"Are you telepathic as well?" Andronicus asked.

"Yes I am," Adriell said laughing.

"How wonderful," was all Andronicus could say.

"Good night, Andronicus," Rebekka and Adriell said.

"Good night," he echoed.

Raven saw Rebekka and Adriell go to her father and brother. He smiled as he watched them go and then turned to the new acquaintances of Ellise and Pi.

Ellise," Raven said as they sat at one of the tables in the great hall, "how can I ever thank you for bringing Rebekka back to me?"

"Seeing this joyous occasion is all the thanks I need," she replied.

Raven could see in that one answer how close a friend Ellise had become to Rebekka.

"Strange," he thought, how circumstances and twists of fate turn enemies into friends.

"There is one thing," Ellise said, interrupting Raven's thoughts.

"Yes, anything you want," Raven stated.

"Rebekka has always told me how good barbecued Tor is. In the future there are not many of them so we do not eat them. It surely would be a treat for this old woman to taste something new."

Raven laughed and motioning toward Edward said, "Tomorrow Edward and I will hunt Tor and have it prepared for you." Still smiling,

Raven turned to the other woman. "You have not said much since arriving here."

Pi looked at Raven and smiled, "I have been observing and watching everything," Pi stated. "But I believe there is something you need to know about Queen Rebekka and what she did all those years she was away."

Raven stiffened, he was not sure he wanted to hear what this woman Pi would tell him. His mind flashed to the possibility that Rebekka had fallen in love with someone else, but then he pushed that aside. He always believed Rebekka's love for him was as pure as his was for her, he would not doubt her now. Pi watched the conflicting emotions move over the King's face and then settle into peace.

When he did not say anything she continued; "Queen Rebekka put herself in danger for the sake of all the people of Layton's empire. She took Layton's place as head of state and in less than a year she undid most of the damage Layton Teal had done to enslave the people. She gave the people back their empire. On the day we left to come here, the people of the empire unveiled a statue of her, to honor the sacrifices she made for the empire and its people. She was almost poisoned, shot once, and almost was shot again until an evil man named Max came to his end. But after it was all over, the people became free once more. I wanted to tell you this because of the heartache you both feel for the time you have lost. Please understand that the time you were apart was not wasted or lost. Many people will live life much happier now for what she accomplished."

Raven nodded, "It was good then that she helped a few people in your time."

Pi laughed, "King Raven, it was not a few. Layton's empire is thousands of times larger than this small kingdom. She helped millions of people." Raven was shocked! He had no idea that Rebekka had done so much for the people of another place and time. Then he smiled and said.

"Rebekka is a Queen in any time or place."

Ellise smiled at that statement saying, "You are more right than you know, she will always be known to those people as Queen Rebekka." At that moment Raven had an overwhelming desire to be with the Queen he had missed so much. He said a polite "thank you" to Ellise and Pi and went to find her.

Raven found Rebekka and Adriell alone on the balcony and went to where they were standing. He hugged Adriell again and asked.

"What are you two doing out here all alone?" Rebekka smiled and said.

"Touching an old friends mind that I have not touched in many years."

Raven smiled too, "He has missed you much over the years my dear. Did you know that Andronicus is not just a machine like he wanted us to believe, but has feelings like unto us?"

Rebekka nodded, "I know he does," was all she said. Raven put his arm around his wife and just stood beside her.

In the silence Adriell cleared her throat, "I think I will go find Edward and get acquainted with my older brother." With that Adriell left the two alone on the balcony. When she was gone Raven said.

"Let us go to the garden and walk."

"I thought you would never ask," Rebekka said laughing. They went down to the courtyard and as they passed the fountain Rebekka stopped and looked at the casting with the inscription remembering her. Raven watched her read it and said.

"I guess we do not need to keep that there any longer since you have returned."

"You must leave it!" Rebekka stated in an almost panicked voice.

"Why?" Raven asked.

"Because, in the future, more than three thousand years from now I will read this message from you. It is that message that prompts us to return here to you."

Raven was amazed, "I cannot believe it survived so long into the future."

"Nothing is coincidence," Rebekka replied, "there are reasons for everything." They were silent for a time as they walked into the garden, then Raven stated.

"I know there are reasons beyond our own limited understanding that God doth employ. Pi told me how you helped to change an empire while you were there." Raven held her as he said this next statement: "I would that you were here all these past years, but since that was not possible I am glad that you were able to help a great number of people in another place and time."

She looked into his eyes and said, "I learned that from you my King."

Raven shook his head, "No Rebekka, you always had that gift within you." She smiled and changed the subject saying.

"I have to tell you something about Pi."

"What about her?" Raven asked.

"She is like Andronicus, an android," Rebekka said plainly. Raven thought for a while before answering.

"We should not tell Andronicus about her yet. He feels he is the only one of his kind in the world right now."

Rebekka nodded, "Yes, but we should tell him sometime."

"We will," Raven said, "but just not now. Why did you bring Pi with you?" he wanted to know.

"Ellise, Adriell and I are like family to her, she wanted to come."

"Then she shall be like family to us," Raven replied.

As they entered the garden off of the castle courtyard, Raven once again held Rebekka in his arms.

As he held her she whispered in his ear, "I have something special to show you, quiet your mind." Raven closed his eyes and as he did Rebekka let the memories of the past years flow into his mind as she had done for her father. It seemed like years before Raven came back to their present time, although it had only been moments. Tears once again filled his eyes as he now possessed the memories of when Rebekka and Adriell were away.

When he gained his composure he asked Rebekka, "Join minds with me once more please." She did and Raven now knowing what to do shared the memories of Edward growing up. He also shared the missing years of Lorriel and her final regret of not being able to bring Rebekka back to Raven. Rebekka was the one who now had tears in her eyes as she held onto Raven. After they calmed down their emotions, Raven and Rebekka headed back into the great hall where the others were. The knowledge that they had a completed and expanded family warmed all their souls on that fall day.

A great joy filled the kingdom as the news spread of Queen Rebekka's return. Adriell adjusted faster to living in Glenfair than Rebekka expected her too, and became close friends with Jason and Lucinda, her cousins. All of us came to love the woman who took our Queen from us. Chancellor Ellise died a year later and Pi greatly mourned her passing. I feel never in history has there been a greater kingdom, nor a greater King and Queen than Raven and Rebekka. It is to my joy that they shall outlive me being united once again. When I think of all the events of the past, I cannot help but believe that God gifted four young people to change the world greatly in the past, present and future. Our kingdom, though small must have drawn the favor of the Almighty, for he was not willing to let it vanish from history. When I think of God's designs and plans, my senses grow dull. His ways are far above any mortal's understanding for our good.

I, Master Fields thought it fitting to tell you this story that you may know what makes a king great. Andronicus summed up the matter quite well:

"A great king sacrifices himself for others, and great sacrifice is always accompanied by great suffering."

Why these two seem to be inseparable is a question I will ask the Almighty when we meet face to face. Until then, may you enjoy peace in your own kingdom. Farewell my friends,

Master Fields

Epilogue

It was a warm spring day with a light breeze blowing as two women and two men gathered around the grave of the King. They were all silent until Edward spoke:

"Today the kingdom loses the greatest King it has ever had. He saved our land in the Wickshield war and he fought for our very existence against a powerful and evil enemy. Because of his sacrifice for the kingdom he was greatly loved by all. Father, believe me when I say that you have taught me the how to be a great king. I promise I will sacrifice myself for our people, and I pray that I will be half the King you were."

After Edward finished, the four came forward and each placed a single white rose on the grave of the King. Adriell was last, and as she placed the rose on the grave she knelt down and said quiotly, "I love you father. When my time comes, will anyone place a single white rose on my grave? I hope it will be so..."

The King's Descendants

From Book 3 of the Kingdom of Glenfair

Coming Soon.....

Lucinda stood appalled at the burned castle. Its doors were charred and shattered, hanging at odd angles. she stepped through the ruined doors and called out. There was no answer, only the silence of the empty courtyard. Tentatively she took a few steps into the courtyard of the king's castle and listened. She could tell the destruction of the castle had been very recent, for she could still smell the smoke from its burning. She had no idea what had happened, or where everyone had gone. An eerie coldness swept over her as she realized she was alone. Lucinda had never felt this way in her whole life and she started to turn and flee when movement at the burned gates caught her eye. A figure clothed in rags, hiding its features approached her.

"So, you are searching for the inhabitants of this castle. They are gone, dead, destroyed. The whole kingdom is destroyed." Then he began to laugh wickedly. He came closer and paused. Lucinda could tell whomever he might be was observing her with interest. Then he spoke again: "I thought I had killed you. No matter, this time I shall make sure you are thoroughly dead!"

Lucinda almost panicked at that moment, but was able to concentrate on the past she knew so well. She could see the stranger reaching out for her as the surroundings began to shimmer and change, and heard him scream with rage as she vanished from his grasp. At that moment the courtyard of the king's castle began to take shape, only this courtyard was full of life and noise. She saw the astonished face of Master Rollins, and she tried to take a step toward him, but every thing went black.

Lucinda faintly heard someone calling her name. As her head began to clear she could make out the face of Master Rollins staring down at her. Then she saw Edward and Adriell were there too. She sat up quickly and saw the great hall of the king's castle and she began to cry. Master Rollins knelt down beside her and hugged her close.

"You will be fine. You have become a time shifter like your mother, has the time shift frightened you?" Somehow Master Rollins' words settled and comforted Lucinda.

"How do you know that?" Lucinda asked.

Edward smiled, "Master Rollins watched you appear out of thin air in the courtyard. I think it has frightened him much more than it has you. You could only do that if you had shifted time." Actually, Master Rollins was not as shaken as Edward expected him to be at such an unexpected event. He had explained the time shift in such a calm and rational matter it surprised Edward. The way he had comforted Lucinda was unusual as well. There seemed to be more than Edward could see under the surface. He would have to ask Master Rollins about this sometime.

Lucinda exclaimed, "The time shift did not frighten me at all, it was what I saw there that did. When I felt the change come upon me I could not resist traveling in time. Father warned me this would happen, and I should have consulted Jason and the rest of you. Instead I decided to travel alone, two years into the future. The Prescott castle and this castle were empty and burned. There was no sign of any one in the king's castle except the stranger I met." Lucinda shuddered as she remembered that evil laugh. "He said that the whole kingdom was destroyed and that you were all dead. He said he would make sure I was really dead this time. As he started toward me I concentrated on the courtyard in this time, it was all I could think of."

"What did this stranger look like?" Edward asked.

"I did not see his face, for it was covered. But the voice sounded like that of Andronicus. I know beyond any doubt it was not Andronicus, because, whomever it was, he was completely evil."

Edward now felt the pressures of being King and having to decide what was best for the whole kingdom. He had learned this from his father, Raven, the greatest King Glenfair had ever had. Why did he feel so helpless, inadequate for the task that lay before him. Had his father ever felt this way when faced with a terrible crisis? It seemed the whole world was upon his shoulders, a dark cloud of evil on the horizon that he could feel, yet neither see nor touch. If what Lucinda said was true, the whole kingdom was in danger of being destroyed, pillaged and burned. Adriell, Lucinda, and Master Rollins waited anxiously for Edward to decide on a course of action. Finally he turned to them and said; "We must go to Andronicus and ask his advice on what we should do to stop Glenfair from being destroyed. Adriell, contact Andronicus and inform him we will be coming."

Adriell, concentrated her mental powers and spoke out for Andronicus to hear but there was no answer. She tried again and still there was no answer. With her face turning pale she said to the rest: "Andronicus does not answer, neither can I feel his presence at all, it is as if he has vanished."

55958874R00143

Made in the USA
Columbia, SC
20 April 2019